NOTHING IS FORGOTTEN

NOTHING IS FORGOTTEN

A Novel

PETER GOLDEN

ATRIA BOOKS

NEW YORK   LONDON   TORONTO   SYDNEY   NEW DELHI

ATRIA
BOOKS

An Imprint of Simon & Schuster, Inc.
1230 Avenue of the Americas
New York, NY 10020

First Atria Books hardcover edition April 2018

ATRIA B O O K S and colophon are trademarks of Simon & Schuster, Inc.

For information about special discounts for bulk purchases, please contact Simon & Schuster Special Sales at 1-866-506-1949 or business@simonandschuster.com.

The Simon & Schuster Speakers Bureau can bring authors to your live event. For more information, or to book an event, contact the Simon & Schuster Speakers Bureau at 1-866-248-3049 or visit our website at www.simonspeakers.com.

Interior design by Laura Levatino

Manufactured in the United States of America

10 9 8 7 6 5 4 3 2 1

Library of Congress Cataloging-in-Publication Data has been applied for.

ISBN 978-1-5011-4680-0
ISBN 978-1-5011-4682-4 (ebook)

For Bruce Davis, who was there at the beginning

And for my late uncle, Leonard Golden, an American hero

And for the memory of Martin Lewis and Arthur Weiss

And for Annis and Ben, who gave me the courage to remember

To be ignorant of what occurred before you were born is to remain always a child. For what is the worth of human life, unless it is woven into the life of our ancestors by the records of history?

—CICERO

Part I

1

South Orange, New Jersey

I was never too interested in my family's history. My indifference wasn't just the apathy of a kid bored by school and obsessed with rock 'n' roll; it was because my father and his mother, Emma Dainov, preferred not to talk about it.

"Misha, *ne sprashivay,*" my grandmother would reply in Russian on those rare occasions I prodded her with a question. *Don't ask.*

Still, some of the history was unavoidable because we seemed different from the other families in South Orange and Maplewood, a pair of suburban Edens with houses in every style from redbrick Federals to flat-roofed split-levels that resembled spaceships. Our neighbors were hardworking Jews, Italians, and Irish, along with some black families to prove no bigots breathed among us, and at the top of the food chain, a papery-skinned layer of Wasps whose chief purpose, as they perused the financial pages in the gin-soaked ambience of their restricted country club, was to provide some incentive for their social-climbing inferiors.

As a boy, I learned that Daniels wasn't our original name while I was digging through a trunk in the basement and found my father's passport from the Soviet Union, with its faded green cover and strange lettering. I was holding the passport when my father, a wan, asthmatic beanpole with a Brylcreem-resistant cowlick, came down with a laundry basket, a chore he had handled ever since my mother refused to separate his lights and darks.

"You the detective now?" he asked in his slightly accented English, peering at me through his pince-nez.

I shook my head, and he smiled a little sadly—the Russian smile, my grandmother called it, like a weak sun in a winter-gray sky. Then he said that in 1934, at the age of eleven, he had landed at Ellis Island with his father, whose imagination was aflame with Yankee-Doodle dreams of striking it rich, which was why he Americanized their surname from Dainov to Daniels, and my father's first name from Lev to Lawrence. My grandfather died before I was born, leaving Larry Daniels to run his empire—Sweets, a candy store on Irvington Avenue, a five-minute walk from our modest Colonial in South Orange.

The name change was odd enough, but what perplexed me was why he had emigrated to the United States without his mother. My father squeezed the rubber bulb of his nebulizer and cleared his airways by drawing on the mouthpiece before he wheezed, "My parents had a divorce, and my father, he took me away."

Divorce wasn't fashionable in those days, so my grandparents splitting up was further evidence of our family's difference, but it—and the mutation of Dainov into Daniels—might have remained a minor puzzle had I not been the baffled owner of four first names. On my birth certificate, I was Michael, and that was the name my mother and teachers used. My father called me Mikhail, and to my grandmother I was Misha, short for Mikhail, or Mishka, an affectionate form of Misha. This left me with a touch of multiple personality disorder and was a point of contention between my parents.

My father's English was excellent, though out of some nostalgia for his boyhood, perhaps, and undoubtedly to irritate my mother, he often spoke to me in his native language. I didn't mind. It was cool using words none of my friends understood, and I needed Russian to understand my grandmother. She insisted that I answer her in English, because my father was completing his degree in accounting at Seton Hall University—a few blocks up Ward Place from Sweets—and he wanted his mother to take over the business after he passed his CPA exam and opened an office.

My mother, a violet-eyed beauty with a pug nose and poodle-cut hair she dyed a shimmery copper, hated that my father spoke to me in Russian. She was born in New Jersey and lorded it over her husband, as though hailing from the Jewish ghetto of Paterson, with parents who worked themselves to death in that city's silk mills, qualified her to be next in line for the British crown, a view of herself fortified by the fact that after high school she had masqueraded as an Episcopalian to work as a secretary at a law firm in Manhattan that didn't hire Jews.

My father, needling his wife about her pretensions, frequently referred to her as "Queen Shirley the First." Nor did he stop conversing with me in Russian even after the blowup at Clinton School with my fourth-grade teacher. Miss Smethers was an elderly taskmaster whose dark dresses gave off a whiff of mothballs and who would order you to stand by her desk and face the class if she caught you smiling. On this morning, she was writing multiplication problems on the blackboard while in my head Big Mama Thornton was singing "Hound Dog," a bluesy wail that I—and the deejay Jocko Henderson, the self-proclaimed Ace from Outer Space—couldn't get enough of. I was sketching Big Mama's face on my math homework—the big grinning face with the devilish eyes I remembered from an album cover in Village Records—when suddenly students were turning to gawk at me, and Miss Smethers said, "Michael, we're waiting for your answer."

You couldn't admit that you weren't paying attention, not if you wanted to avoid standing in the place of shame. Without thinking, I replied, "*Ya ne znayu.*"

The class broke up as if I'd cut the world's loudest fart instead of saying that I didn't know. Miss Smethers, believing I'd cursed her out, marched me to Principal Furrie's office and, before returning to the classroom, suggested he wash out my mouth with soap. The principal was a jolly rotund fellow who combed his hair east and west to hide his baldness. I explained that I'd spoken Russian by accident. He nodded sympathetically, then phoned my mother. For the last week she'd been going on about a sale at Bamberger's—arguing with my father about her spending limit—and I hoped she wasn't home. No such luck—she stormed into the principal's office, eyes blazing. Mr. Furrie told her what happened and asked if

I'd ever been dropped on my head as a baby, which could account for my confusing two languages.

"My husband's a schmuck," my mother said. "That's why he's confused."

Grabbing my shirt collar, she dragged me through the school yard to her Country Squire and drove to Sweets, where my father was arranging packs of cigarettes in the honeycomb behind the cash register.

After telling him why I wasn't in school, my mother said, "I told you to stop with the Russian. Everyone'll think Michael's a commie spy."

This was the 1950s. Ethel and Julius Rosenberg had been sentenced to die in the electric chair for selling atomic secrets to the Soviets; Senator Joseph McCarthy had accused everyone except President Eisenhower's parakeet of spying for Moscow; and Hollywood was blacklisting directors, actors, and screenwriters if they'd ever taken a sip of vodka.

"Calm down, Shirley. You'll have stroke."

Her voice rose. "They'll blacklist our son."

I piped up. "Will I get to miss school?"

My mother whipped off her shoe and, with the spiked heel, swatted my backside. A geyser of pain shot up my spine. She wasn't shy about hitting me, but I refused to cry; she might enjoy it. The enraged stoic—that was me.

Glaring at my father, she said, "This is your fault," and then she was off to Bamberger's.

I looked at my father. He shrugged helplessly. "Mikhail, you shouldn't use Russian with your teacher."

And you, I recall thinking, shouldn't let your wife smack your son with a spiked heel.

2

Other than sitting in my room and drawing in my sketchbook, or lying in bed at night listening to the patter of deejays between bursts of Howlin' Wolf, B.B. King, and Fats Domino—both foolproof methods for escaping my parents' bickering—my childhood refuge was wherever my grandmother happened to be. And before Emma learned English and was still reluctant to leave the house, that was the kitchen with its eggshell-white cabinets, mustard-colored linoleum, and aquamarine, chrome-legged dinette set.

My mother's pursuit of haute couture and her mah-jongg habit limited her cooking to throwing a steak on the broiler and serving it with Birds Eye french fries and mixed vegetables or heating up Swanson TV dinners. So it was my grandmother, after she arrived at her house from Europe in 1948, who enlisted me as her sous-chef and taught me the glories of sweet-and-sour brisket, potato pancakes, and baked apples stuffed with raisins and brown sugar.

Once my grandmother decided to concentrate on her English, Emma and I spent hours in the den, where we read the dictionary and watched the Philco television in its burled-wood cabinet, and I translated for her and corrected her pronunciation. Learning another language wasn't too difficult for my grandmother. She also spoke Ukrainian, Yiddish, some German, and French, and by the time I was in fifth grade, she was running

7

the candy store, and my father was a certified public accountant with an office across from the train station in the commercial heart of South Orange Village.

Back then, it wasn't uncommon for families to reside with a grandparent or two, but Emma wasn't like my friends' grandmothers. There was no calling her Nana or Bubbe or Nonnina, the affectionate term my Italian pals used. She insisted that every kid, including me, call her Emma, a revolutionary casualness in that more formal era. Nor was Emma stubby or hunched over from lumbago. She was tall and slender, and instead of shapeless dresses, she wore long colorful blouses cinched at the waist with a leather belt, wide black trousers, and brown boots or, in warmer weather, black Converse high-tops. Her dark gold hair, with its threading of silver, fell past her shoulders, and she had a pale round face with a perpetual expression of amusement and an intriguing slant to her sea-green eyes, which didn't appear to believe a thing they saw.

My grandmother was happiest when kids filled the candy store on weekday afternoons before catechism or Hebrew school, and on Saturdays after football games or Little League. They gathered at the wall rack, pulling out the latest *Archie* and *Superman* and *MAD*, and bought packs of Topps baseball cards, stuffing bubble gum into their mouths as if the pink wads were plugs of tobacco as they worked out trades for Mickey Mantle and Willie Mays, their dickering blending into the whirring Hamilton Beach spindles. Emma made milkshakes in the steel beakers and ordered everyone to wait their turn at the shelves across from the marble-topped soda fountain, where the rows of glass jars were brightened by red and black licorice strings, fireballs, Mary Janes, Tootsie Rolls, jawbreakers, root beer barrels, sugary pills on paper strips, candy necklaces, wax lips, and wax bottles of syrup.

I was so proud that the kids adored her. She let them reach over from the stools to work the handles and spritz soda into their cherry Cokes, placing a carton of Ring Dings on the counter so they could help themselves. And she was nonchalant about money: no child ever walked out empty-handed. "Pay what you got," Emma told them; and if they had nothing but lint in their pockets, she said, "I'll put in for you." I remember her smiling at the joy on the children's faces as they filed out, saying, "Thanks, Emma," and my grandmother, demonstrating that learning English from TV had a comic upside, would raise her right hand like the Lone Ranger and reply, "Hi-yo, Silver! Awaaay!"

Her finest moment, the moment that boys will still recall when they have become old men sharing a fifth of Scotch, was the afternoon she took a broom to Miss Doyle.

The schools had been closed by a snowstorm, and after me and my two best friends, Rollie Raduzza and Birdman Cohen, had shoveled sidewalks and driveways and earned a fortune, thirty-eight bucks apiece, we went to Sweets for hot cocoa and discovered, to our delight, that the February *Playboy* had been delivered. In those days, because *Playboy* featured photos of naked women, it wasn't sold on the magazine rack out front where kids could see it, but was displayed in an acrylic holder on the wall behind the register with a brown paper wrapper blocking out everything on the cover except the title. The men who bought *Playboy* seemed embarrassed asking Emma for a copy, mumbling the request and, after she put the magazine in a bag, taking off as if a vice cop was chasing them.

For all Emma appeared to care, she could've been selling them a Dutch Masters cigar, and clearly she thought the fuss about kids looking at the magazine was preposterous because whenever my friends and I were at the store and the new *Playboy* came in, she deposited one on the soda fountain, and we would stand there gazing at the centerfold like archaeologists who had just unearthed the Dead Sea Scrolls.

That was what Rollie, Birdman, and I were doing when Miss Doyle showed up, her white hair twisted in curlers and partially covered by a black kerchief. Rollie, whose mom was Miss Doyle's second cousin, had told me she'd quit being a nun to marry an ex-monsignor, but he ditched her for a manicurist he met in the pool at Palisades Amusement Park. Typically, Miss Doyle ignored Rollie if he was in the store during her weekly stop for a carton of Pall Malls. However, on that snowy afternoon, Miss Doyle stepped past the counter until she was a foot away from Rollie, who was standing between Birdman and me, and holding open the *Playboy*.

"Rolando Raduzza," she said, her eyes pinpoints in her long, witchy face, "put that filth down."

Rollie was a tough, stubborn kid who would become an all-state full-back in high school, but Miss Doyle was glowering at him as if he were Jack the Ripper, and she had Rollie rattled enough that he froze.

Emma, who was removing a carton of smokes from the cabinet behind the register, called out, "Candy's worse for their teeth than those pictures are for their eyes."

"That's filth, Rolando," Miss Doyle said. "Put it down."

Birdman, as gangly as a pelican, which was how he got his nickname, was the voice of reason among our trio. He said to Rollie, "Do like she says."

Rollie replied, "No way," and Miss Doyle punched him in the chest so hard that he went back over a cardboard display case of Fritos, dropping the *Playboy* and winding up spread-eagled on the floor.

Miss Doyle, satisfied that she had done her part for public morality, turned to get her Pall Malls, but my grandmother blocked her path, clutching a broom in her hands as though it were a rifle with a bayonet.

"You don't hit the children," Emma said, jabbing the broom handle at Miss Doyle, who backed up against the greeting-card wall pockets opposite the soda fountain.

"And you shouldn't give them that magazine."

"*Poshol ti nahoo.*"

My father often said this to my mother; it meant *Go fuck yourself.* And though Miss Doyle didn't speak Russian, her reply indicated that she'd caught the gist of Emma's suggestion. "I'll get the police, you greenhorn—"

My grandmother ended Miss Doyle's half of the conversation by pressing the tip of the broom handle into her throat. I'd never seen Emma angry before. Her face was flushed, and her body seemed to vibrate.

"Don't hit the children," she hissed. "And don't come here no more. You understand?"

Miss Doyle took off. Emma lowered the broom, and as she returned behind the register, it dawned on me that my mother had never hit me when Emma was around, and that maybe she knew something about my grandmother I didn't know. But being more interested in today than yesterday, I never bothered to ask her.

3

Despite the goodies that Emma gave away, she was making more money than my father ever had. Her success was due to the two additional telephones in the back storage room, which she had installed at the urging of Eddie O'Rourke, a graying dapper leprechaun with eyes the color of an iced-up lake, a fedora tilted at a rakish angle, and a paisley flame of silk in the breast pocket of his sport coat. Eddie and his wife, Fiona, lived halfway up the slope of Radel Terrace, fifty yards from our house. It was an open secret that Eddie O had once worked for the mobster Longy Zwillman, who hung himself my last year at South Orange Junior High, and then for Siano Abruzzi, the silver-haired patriarch of a large happy clan involved in numerous ventures throughout New Jersey, at least 50 percent of them legitimate.

The O'Rourkes had no children, and they were revered among the local kids for giving out candy apples on Halloween. Every morning Fiona and Eddie came down to Montague Place, the corner where we lived, and Fiona turned left to go to Our Lady of Sorrows for mass, and Eddie went straight toward Sweets. The first time I became aware of the extra phones was during my spring vacation when I was helping my grandmother by putting out chocolate Easter bunnies. Emma was behind the soda fountain with a glass of tea, while Eddie O sat on a stool paging through Emma's dog-eared copy of Merriam-Webster's *Pocket Dictionary* and saying to her: "You're lookin' lugubrious today."

"I know this word."

"You didn't figure I knew it?"

Emma laughed. "Not till you read my dictionary, you didn't."

"Fiona makes me play Scrabble with her, and she's kickin' the tar outta me. I gotta learn words with *q* and *z*. Them's the ten-point letters."

Emma and Eddie were Sinatra fans, and my grandmother had a radio tuned to WNEW next to the Hamilton Beach blender. Above Frank singing "Fools Rush In," I could hear the phones ringing in the storage room until a beer barrel of a guy in an electric-blue shirt and an orange necktie shiny enough that he likely needed sunglasses to knot it gave Eddie a slip of paper and went outside. I must've looked surprised because Eddie said to me, "That's Gerald. He's my financial adviser."

I doubted that was true, but Eddie O wasn't a guy you'd question. "Quiz," I said.

"Quiz?" Eddie asked.

"It's got a *q* and a *z*."

"I owe ya one, boyo," he said, getting up off the stool. "See ya tomorrow, Emma."

When he was gone, I looked at my grandmother.

"Don't ask, Misha."

Two days later, my father stopped in and heard the new phones and saw Eddie O perched on a stool, and that evening he came into the den while Emma and I were watching *Dragnet*.

"What're you doing, Ma? Eddie O'Rourke collects money for Abruzzi loan sharks. And he's using those phone to do what? Talk to gangsters? Threaten the schnooks behind on their payments?"

"I don't know his business. Why you making such a big deal?"

"Because it's against law."

"In the war, my life was against the law, but I'm still alive."

"Ma!" my father said, glancing at me.

They switched to Yiddish, their customary tactic when they didn't want me to understand, but I was decent at languages. French had been my one good subject in school, and I'd picked up enough Yiddish to follow their exchange. My father kept referring to Eddie and the Abruzzis as *nishtgutnicks*—no-good people—and Emma countered with "*deigeh nisht*"—don't worry—and when my father observed that Emma would have plenty to worry about if the police raided the store, she said, "*Az me schmiert, fort men*," which roughly translates to "Grease your wheels, you'll ride," and meant that some under-the-table cash would help the cops lose interest.

They carried on for weeks, and it was Eddie O, probably at Emma's urging, who settled their dispute by taking my father to lunch at the Famous in South Orange Village with Julian Rose, Eddie's closest friend. Mr. Rose had been Longy Zwillman's protégé, but got out of the rackets young and became one of the richest real estate developers in the state. His picture was frequently in the papers: posing with the archbishop of Newark outside a new surgical wing he helped to pay for at St. Michael's or attending a fund raiser to renovate the sanctuary at Congregation Beth El, where I was bar-mitzvahed. Over pastrami on seeded rye, Mr. Rose, whose company headquarters was across from the village library and a short walk from my father's office, retained Lawrence Daniels & Associates to do his accounting.

As the news spread that my father was working for Julian Rose, he was besieged by clients, and after expanding his office by renting the floor above him and hiring a gaggle of CPAs, bookkeepers, and secretaries, he was too busy to bug Emma about Eddie O. My mother was tickled pink by my father's exploding income, and she was an admirer of Julian Rose, commenting whenever she spotted his photo in the newspapers that he could be a double for Cary Grant, to which my father inevitably replied: "You'd think I'd look like Cary Grant if I was worth the hundred million bucks."

"Tell me when you get there," my mother said, "and I'll let you know."

On a Sunday during my sophomore year at Columbia High School, my parents and I were in the village eating eggplant Parmesan at Victor's when my father announced: "Shirley, if the stock market doesn't collapse, I only got ninety-nine million more to go."

That milestone pleased my mother until the waiter cleared our plates. "We need a bigger house," she said.

I assumed my mother wanted one of the humongous Moderns in Newstead, a ritzy enclave at the northernmost top of South Orange that was home to people like Julian Rose. I didn't want to leave our neighborhood, but as long as I didn't have to switch high schools, I didn't care. Yet Newstead wasn't tony enough for my mother. She wanted to move farther up South Orange Avenue to the gold-plated countryside of Short Hills. Founded a century earlier by a nature lover who got rich inventing the window-shade roller, the town was beginning to welcome Jews along Old Short Hills Road, a spot the Protestant natives now referred to as "Bagel Hill."

Moving to Short Hills meant that I'd have to change schools and leave my friends, plus Beryl Wilner, whom I'd had my eye on since seventh grade. I stewed about it for a week until the night Birdman's dad picked us up from the Isley Brothers concert at the Mosque in Newark and dropped me off at home. My parents were sitting at the kitchen table, my father sipping a cup of Sanka with the steam of the instant coffee fogging his pince-nez; and my mother adding to the chain of cigarette butts in the black plastic ashtray she'd swiped after seeing Dean Martin and Jerry Lewis at the Copacabana.

"I don't want to move," I said.

My mother puffed on her Kent. "We're not taking a vote."

My father said, "Those Jew-hating snobs in Short Hills won't want us there."

I suspected that all his talk about prejudice and snobbery wasn't the real reason for his reluctance. He had grown up poor, putting in forty hours a week at the candy store with his father while he was in school, which he'd been pointing out to me ever since I begged him to buy me a Schwinn three-speed for my tenth birthday. The bike wasn't that expensive, but he refused to buy it until Emma gave him a tongue-lashing in Yiddish.

"What's the goddamn money for?" my mother asked him.

"You mean, if not to make you happy?" he replied.

"Something wrong with making me happy?"

"And me and Mikhail," he asked. "We do not count?"

My mother didn't respond, perhaps thinking the answer should have been apparent to him. In the den, which was out through the kitchen and the dining room, I could hear my grandmother watching Lawrence Welk and his orchestra play a polka.

I said, "If you move, I can stay here with Emma."

"What will people think, us leaving our son? And your father's selling this house. If your grandmother chooses not to join us, she can buy her own."

I should've kept my mouth shut, but her willingness to abandon Emma infuriated me, and my father wasn't talking. "That's stupid. Emma doesn't drive and likes walking to the store."

My mother, jabbing another Kent into her Copa souvenir, stood and stepped toward me, glaring. Her dye job had darkened at the roots, and sometimes I wondered if she hated me because due to some genetic quirk, I looked more like Emma than her—tall, with sandy hair, a fair complexion, and the same green eyes.

"Nobody asked your opinion," she said.

"That's why I'm offering it."

Two years had gone by since my mother had smacked me, but when she drew back her arm, I was a boy again, a frightened little boy routinely hit for leaving his socks on the floor or failing to put his plate in the sink, a list of transgressions so long I couldn't remember them. I could see the anger in her eyes, but she also looked puzzled, unable to comprehend why her husband and son were conspiring to deny her the palace where she belonged. My fear turned into something else, and the boy was replaced by a teenager with eight inches and forty pounds on his mother. As her arm began to swing forward, I balled up my right fist, horrified because I knew that if she touched me, I was going to hit her back.

"Don't," I said, and saw a sobering flicker of recognition in her eyes.

Her arm froze. My father was staring into his coffee cup. Behind me, I heard Emma say, "Mishka, come watch *Gunsmoke*."

"Go," my mother said, reaching for her pack of Kents on the table.

And so I went.

—————

My father promised that the only way my mother would get him to Short Hills was if he dropped dead and they started burying Jews on Bagel Hill. In response, she listed our house with a Realtor, and he unlisted it. To placate her, my father bought her a canary-yellow Fleetwood Cadillac, but she threw the keys at him and stuck to her station wagon. Their conflict escalated into a competition to see who would get the last word, a question that was answered on a Sunday afternoon on the Garden State Parkway. According to an eyewitness, a toll collector who spoke to the troopers, my father was driving the Caddie with my mother screaming at him when he apparently suffered an asthma attack and slammed into a bridge abutment.

I'd been playing basketball at the Community House, and on the way home I went to Sweets, where Emma, her eyes glistening, hugged me and said that my parents were dead.

For years, the news left me in a slight state of shock, and the worst of it was that I couldn't cry—not as I helped Emma make the arrangements; stood in the receiving line at Apter's thanking our neighbors, the candy-store regulars, my father's clients, and my mother's mah-jongg partners for coming to the funeral. Not as I listened to Rabbi Adelberg's eulogy about a husband and wife now joined forever in love; rode in the limousine with Emma behind two hearses on the Parkway to the Mount Lebanon Cemetery; and stood over my parents' graves reading the Mourner's Kaddish and summoning my best memories of them.

I recalled the Saturday morning I sat in the den watching *Crusader Rabbit* on TV and my father knelt beside me mimicking the voices of the cartoon characters and translating their dialogue into Russian, and how I laughed until he got up to go to work. And the day, in grammar school, when I was home with a fever, and my mother bought me a Strathmore sketch pad and a box of Venus drawing pencils. *Mom, I can't draw,* I told her. *Here, Michael, it's not hard.* And she drew a portrait of our faces side by side. *It looks just like us, Mom,* and she said, *When I was your age, I wanted to be an artist. It was silly. My mother took in sewing to make ends meet, and I had to help her at night.*

Now their caskets were being lowered into the ground, and I was ashamed of my inability to grieve. Emma noticed my discomfort as visitors paraded through our house during the week of shiva, the majority of them stopping in the den where the trial of Adolf Eichmann was on TV. Videotapes of the proceedings were airmailed around the world from Jerusalem, and now, on-screen, Eichmann, the balding, turkey-necked former SS officer in charge of deporting Jews to death camps, was seated in a bulletproof glass cube peering at the witness stand through black-frame glasses and wearing headphones to hear the translation of the testimony.

The witness, a woman dabbing at her eyes with a handkerchief and speaking in heavily accented English, was recalling the sight of her daughter being herded with other children into a gas chamber at Treblinka. Eichmann was gazing at the ceiling. Nor was anyone in the den paying attention to the witness. They were debating whether Israel had the right to kidnap Eichmann from Buenos Aires and put him on trial until Eddie brought the argument to a close by saying, "And everybody says Jews are shrewd. Why they pissin' away dough on this bullshit? They should shoot the fucker."

I chuckled, earning a scowl from Rabbi Adelberg, who readjusted the tartan plaid yarmulke on his head, a gesture that signaled he was on the verge of launching into one of his moralistic snoozeathons, delivered with the lockjaw phrasing that he'd imported from Oxford, which he'd attended, as he often reminded his congregants, on a Rhodes scholarship. I was curious about how Eddie O would react, but Emma prevented the showdown by shooing Eddie toward the liquor bottles in the kitchen and giving the rabbi a plate with smoked sturgeon on a salt bagel.

"You eat, Mishka?" she asked me.

"I'm not hungry."

She glanced at the television screen, where Eichmann was testifying, and her face tightened in concentration. Then she looked at me and said in Russian that grief is never what you imagine it will be.

"*Otkuda ty znaesh*?" I asked—How do you know?

She stroked my cheek. "Trust your grandmother."

I did, which also partially explained my lack of grief. My parents might be gone, but I still had the most important person in my life. I still had Emma.

4

By March of my senior year in high school, I had no plans for the future, telling myself that the car wreck had destroyed my faith in tomorrow, a perception heightened by reading Camus's *The Stranger* in French class. My existential self-dramatization, I suppose, had less to do with the accident than teenage angst and the resulting wish that nothing would ever change. Nonetheless, change was coming. Rollie had a football scholarship to Miami; Birdman had been accepted at Yale; and Beryl Wilner, who had visited me every evening during the shiva and shortly thereafter had become my girlfriend, would be off to the University of Chicago.

Emma had asked me if I was going to apply to college, offering to handle the cost, and when I responded with a shrug, she said nothing. That didn't mean she wasn't cooking up something for me to do. Between my father's life insurance and his savings, my grandmother could've sold the store and retired, but Emma had no patience for laziness. She was at Sweets before six in the morning and didn't get home before seven at night, except on Sundays, when she closed up at three. Other than working, all Emma did was watch TV, go to sisterhood meetings at the synagogue, look through the art books that she borrowed from the library—Picasso, Chagall, and Matisse appeared to be her favorites—and take summer trips to Europe by herself.

Neither I nor my parents knew exactly what Emma did on her travels, but she always brought us gifts—Gucci wallets, bottles of 4711 cologne, Lacoste polo shirts, and the summer before my parents died, Rolex watches. I'd never heard of them—this was before Sean Connery made the brand famous in the James Bond movies. The Rolexes were beautiful, and obviously pricey. My father, opening his box and seeing a yellow-gold watch on a matching small-link bracelet and a cyclops crystal magnifying the date, said Emma shouldn't be spending this kind of money. My mother, who received the same watch in a smaller size, retorted, "Why shouldn't she? No one's starving here," and Emma, surprisingly, backed up my mother, saying, "It don't hurt listening to your wife once in a while."

My Rolex was a stainless steel Explorer with a black dial. Emma said the salesman had informed her that Sir Edmund Hillary had worn the same kind when he became the first man to reach the summit of Mount Everest.

Smiling, I kissed her cheek. "I don't like heights."

"You could learn," she said.

Emma rarely splurged on herself, but she'd bought her own steel Rolex, and it was the oddest watch I'd ever seen. The black face had a magnified date and was circled by a red and blue bezel with a dot at the top and the numbers 2 through 22 around it. The watch, she explained, made it easy for the wearer to tell time in twenty-four-hour segments, and an extra red arrow on the face kept track of another time zone.

I calculated that if I kept helping Emma out at Sweets, I could avoid a discussion with her about my plans, and it seemed to work. One thing she did say: "Mishka, whatever you do, remember this your whole life. You fix the past in the present, not in the past."

I was too young to understand it then, and too distracted by Beryl, with her blond ponytail and dimples. Emma, thrilled that I had a steady, pronounced us as beautiful as the Barbie and Ken dolls advertised on TV, but Beryl, who had volunteered with the Essex County chapter of JFK for President, was no hollow-headed Barbie. She constantly spoke about politics and the Peace Corps, which she wanted to join after college. We knew that by Labor Day we'd be on separate paths, a reality that paled beside going to the movies and parties and Don's Drive-In for pizza burgers, milkshakes, and fries. One of our favorite weekend stops was in South Mountain Reservation, where we steamed up the Country Squire with our kissing and touching, and once, during a pause, discussed whether Beryl would prefer to lose her virginity in South Orange or Chicago.

"Let's see," she said, and smiled so that her dimples seemed an inch deep. "Where'd you lose yours?"

Feeling myself blush, I admitted that I'd be losing mine, too. Naturally, I voted for South Orange and proposed that she practice losing her virginity with me so that after she got to Chicago and lost it again, she'd know what to do.

Beryl laughed. "You're funny."

"So what do you think?"

"I think I'll think about it," she said, and kissed me on the nose.

On Saturday, as I walked to work at the store, the sun was melting the crust of dirty snow on the lawns. Eddie O was at the soda fountain, improving a vanilla milkshake with a pour from his silver whiskey flask.

"Hey," he said. "I been meaning to ask: you play an instrument?"

"Just the radio."

"He listens to that cockamamie music half the night," Emma said, and went to wait on the customers at the register.

Eddie O sampled his shake. "You ever hear of payola?"

"Sure. WABC fired their biggest deejay, Alan Freed, for it. It was in all the papers. Freed and hundreds of other radio jocks admitted to taking bribes from record companies to play certain songs."

"There ya go. And even if paying the disc jockeys wasn't illegal now, the deejays couldn't play the songs they took money for. The music's old, and the station managers won't let them."

"Radio's about today, not five years ago."

"That might be true, but listen. Some of the record companies had partners, and these guys paid the deejays, and they care about money, not music."

That was an understatement. I'd read in the *Star-Ledger* that the Abruzzis, along with some New York mobsters, were involved in payola.

Eddie said, "And these guys, they're insisting on hearing the songs they paid for. Siano himself had an idea. He's got teenagers, and they're crazy about the old songs, so Siano says we should do an experiment. Set up a little station to see if the kids listening will go for it, and then we talk the big stations into doing it. Personally, I think he's doing it for his own kids, but Siano had a studio set up, and you could be the disc jockey."

"I don't know how. And don't you need a radio operator's license?"

"Not for this station. We'll go over Monday at five. The job doesn't pay, but you could learn, and something might come of it."

"Did Emma put you up to this?"

"You don't wanna make a liar outta me, do ya?"

"No, sir."

"That's the spirit."

———————

WSOV-FM was in South Orange Village, on the second floor above Town Hall Deli, in a windowless room that had eggshell cartons glued to the walls—a futile attempt, I'd discover, at soundproofing. Against the back wall were the door for a bathroom and a beige couch, the torn leather cushions doctored with duct tape. The rest of the studio was taken up by four apple crates filled with stacks of 45s in their sleeves and a metal desk with a turntable cabinet on either side of it. On the desk was an RCA audio-control board, a microphone, a pair of headphones, an alarm clock, and a telephone.

"Where do I start?" I asked.

"The six big buttons in the middle of the board are the faders. They're preset and got punch labels telling you what they control. Don't touch the one on the far right. It's the master volume for the board."

"You were a deejay?"

Eddie O removed a pack of index cards from a pocket of his sport coat. "Nah, I had a guy write out directions, and I did my homework. Go on, sit."

I sat in the wooden swivel chair. "If I get stuck, could I ask him some questions?"

"He's not talking much. His jaw's broken."

I didn't want to hear that story, but Eddie O took a 45 from a crate and said, "Don't sweat. The guy was a greedy SOB and owes a thousand plays.

But he knows his onions, and it's on these cards." He handed me the record: "See You Later, Alligator," by Bill Haley and His Comets.

"Deejays had to be bribed to play Bill Haley?"

"Can't say. The crates of records are from a station that went bust. Now get those cans on your head, and I'll read ya how to put on a song."

"Cans?"

He held up an index card. "Headphones. It says here they're called cans."

I clamped on the cans, and Eddie O read out the instructions. One of the switches above the faders was marked AUDITION, and after pressing it, I had to push a button labeled TT 1, which controlled the turntable on my left. I twisted the fader to the right, placed the 45 on the felt-covered turntable, and cued up the record. When I heard the music begin, I backed up the 45 and reset the fader to zero. Still holding on to the record, I hit the button labeled PROGRAM, which sent the music to the air, then fired up the turntable, cranked up the volume, let go of the 45, and heard Bill Haley singing, with the drums and sax going at it.

I hollered, "How can you tell if the music's coming through?"

Eddie O shuffled through the index cards, then disappeared in the bathroom and closed the door. He came out as the song ended, and I took off the cans.

"There's a radio on the back of the toilet," he said. "Music was coming in fine."

"Who can hear the station?"

"Some of Essex County. The antenna's somewhere up in the Watchung Mountains. Listen, we should practice more. I ordered us a Sloppy Joe."

The Sloppy Joe, Jersey style, was Town Hall Deli's contribution to Western civilization: a triple-decker sandwich on thinly sliced rye, cut into eight sections, with roast beef, pastrami, Swiss cheese, coleslaw, and Russian dressing.

"Take a gander at those 45s, and I'll get the eats."

"Mr. O'Rourke?"

"Eddie, I'm Eddie."

"Thank you."

"My pleasure. You're a nice kid. And your grandma's a helluva gal. Don't be sore about her interfering. Nothing wrong with knowing there's better than working in a candy store."

During the week, I practiced alone in the studio with the smell of sour pickles rising up from the deli. I loved watching the records spin, monitoring the volume-unit meter on the board, and ratcheting down the fader if the needle flicked into the red. I left the bathroom door open when I spoke into the mike, and it was magical hearing my voice filtering out from the radio and imagining its trip through the ionosphere. I decided to do a three-hour show Sunday through Thursday beginning at ten P.M., so I could go out with Beryl on weekends. The hardest decision was who would I be? My favorites, Jocko Henderson and Dr. Jive, were black, and the white guys I'd listened to—Alan Freed, Murray the K, and Cousin Brucie—either talked as if they wanted to be black or blabbered like frat boys zooming on dexis.

By Sunday afternoon, I hadn't come up with anything original and sat in the studio doodling on a pad, drawing two pictures of myself, one in a cowboy hat and the other in a beret. Before going home for dinner, I sifted through the crates of 45s again and found a recording by Kenny Ball and His Jazzmen that I'd read about in *Billboard*. It was a redo of a Russian love song, which, according to the article, featured such a plaintive accordion that the writer was tempted to commit suicide in a snow fort. I stared at the 45 and knew who I was going to be.

At ten on the dot, I put on the 45, and after thirty seconds of the swinging, brassy song, I lowered the volume and spoke over the music, keeping my voice soft and deep: "That's Kenny Ball and His Jazzmen . . . 'Midnight in Moscow,' and you're in lovely downtown South Orange with me, Mikhail Dainov, the Mad Russian, on WSOV-FM, 100.7 on your dial. *Dóbryy vecher* . . . Good evening."

The records in the crate were mainly doo-wop and early rock 'n' roll, so I played oldies for three hours and jabbered away in English and Russian, throwing in sayings that I'd heard Emma use, everything from *yaytsa kuritsu ne uchat*—eggs don't teach a hen—to *nichto ne zabyto*—nothing is forgotten. I ended the show with a toast to love—*Za lyubov*—and whispered into the mike, "*Spasibo, schastlivaya puti.* . . . Thank you, have a nice trip."

23

For the next month, I enjoyed my shows yet felt like one of those drunks in a Bowery doorway talking to himself. Rollie, Birdman, and Beryl were tuning in, and a handful of students at school said that they'd heard me, but I estimated my audience to be in the single digits. That is until the night a Mrs. Hurling phoned the studio in tears. I asked her to hold on, put down the phone, and pressed a button on the board to transfer the call to the air.

"Go ahead, ma'am. We're listening."

"Our dog, a wirehaired pointer, ran away in Maplecrest Park. He's wearing a navy sweater with snowflakes on it. My daughter knitted it for him for Christmas."

"What's his name?"

"Einstein."

"Real smart, is he?"

"Yes, yes, he is."

"Hear that, everyone? The bow-wow's smart and his name's Einstein, he's got his Christmas sweater on, so let's hit the streets, and if you see him, get the Mad Russian on the line at 555-WSOV."

I couldn't believe it—inside a half hour, there were seventeen calls, and the pooch was located looking in the window of Schulte's Pipe Shop. The next night a reporter from the *News-Record* showed up at the studio with a camera, and my picture, accompanied by a story, made the front page under the headline "The Disc Jockey Who Saved Einstein."

Emma framed the page and hung it behind the soda fountain, which I figured was the extent of my fame. Except the *News-Record* also covered local sports and political squabbles; ran obituaries, wedding and birth announcements, classifieds, and real estate listings; and named everyone the cops busted for assorted stupidities. Thus, most of the thirty thousand people in South Orange and Maplewood glanced at the paper every week, and I didn't appreciate the impact of my publicity until I brought Nikita Khrushchev to WSOV.

A couple of years back, the Soviet leader, a pissed-off bowling ball of a man with a habit of flinging his arms up when he spoke as if he were drowning, had made a fool of himself at the United Nations. When a delegate proclaimed that the Soviet Union had no respect for freedom, Khrushchev countered the accusation by pounding on his desk with his shoe. I'd thought it was funny then, and on this evening, as "Midnight in Moscow" played, I was leafing through *Time* magazine and saw an article on the spy-plane pilot Francis Gary Powers, who had been captured by the Soviets and had just been swapped for a Soviet spy. That gave me the idea, and as the record ended, I said, "Mr. Khrushchev, what's your opinion of WSOV?"

I waited a beat. Then: "Oh, right, you don't speak English." I asked again in Russian and answered for him by taking off one of my Jack Purcell sneakers and hitting the mike with the sole.

"Really? You want Mrs. Kennedy to lend you her pillbox hat?"

I smacked the audio console three times with my sneaker.

On and on I went in English and Russian, banging on the mike, and after I asked if any listeners had a question for the Soviet premier, the phone didn't stop ringing until I signed off. I was so jazzed by the response that when someone inquired as to how Mr. Khrushchev disposed of his vodka bottles, I smashed an empty Coke bottle on the floor.

5

My Khrushchev routine became a fixture of my broadcast. Sometimes I had him accompanying songs with my sneaker and a kazoo, and I began getting callers from West Orange, Livingston, Short Hills, Millburn, Montclair, Glen Ridge, and Bloomfield. One of them said he'd heard about WSOV from a carhop at Don's, which was centrally located way up on South Orange Avenue, past the wooded hills of the reservation. That my show was being talked up by carhops was a kick, but what happened next was unreal.

One afternoon I was sharing a malted with Beryl at Gruning's, a junior high and high school hangout in the village. A bunch of eighth-grade girls stopped by to ask for my autograph, and as I drew a quick squiggly self-portrait in their binders and wrote *The Mad Russian* underneath it, Mr. Gruning came over and asked how much it cost to advertise on my show.

Stunned, I finally replied, "If I mention you once a night, twenty bucks a week."

He peeled four twenties from a wad. "I'll take a month."

First thing I did was check with Eddie to find out if I could hang on to the dough.

"It's yours," he said. "All you gotta do is play them records. You're makin' people happy, and there's lots of guys without broken legs 'cause of you."

Before I knew it, businesses around South Orange were advertising: Village Records; Bellin's Boys Town; and Ruth Satsky Jewelers. Town Hall Deli had me talking about their special after-school snack, buttered rye-bread ends for a dime; and Romoser's Bakery was offering students a discount on glazed doughnuts, a nickel for a sugary taste of heaven.

By May, when Emma went on her annual vacation to Europe, I was averaging four hundred bucks a month, incredible money for a kid. Birdman, Rollie, and Beryl were glad to help me run Sweets, because who cared about classes by spring of your senior year? I traded in the station wagon and bought a used Plymouth Fury convertible in fire-engine red. During the glittering summer that follows high school graduation, I was at the Shore every weekend. Birdman's family had a huge house in Deal, Rollie's had a bungalow in Seaside Heights, and we were allowed to stay at both places with our girlfriends if they slept in different rooms.

On a rainy Saturday, Beryl and I had gone for lunch by ourselves at the Howard Johnson's on the boardwalk, a glass-walled flying saucer of a building with a view of the deserted beach. We had finished our barbecued beef and were deciding which of the twenty-eight flavors of ice cream to choose when Beryl whispered, "Suppose I want to practice losing my virginity in Asbury Park?"

She hadn't noticed the gum-cracking waitress in the orange HoJo uniform standing beside our booth.

"It's as good a town as any," the waitress said. "You want ice cream first?"

Beryl and I got the giggles and forgot about dessert. In the warm, salty drizzle, we walked down Ocean Avenue to the Berkeley-Carteret Hotel, a redbrick relic of the 1920s with a doorman decked out like the Emperor of Candy Land.

Upstairs, the bedding was mildewed, which I quit noticing as we undressed. Figuring it couldn't hurt to be optimistic, I'd been storing two Trojans in my wallet since June, though I was having trouble moving past our usual kissing and touching, a hesitancy rooted more in ignorance than in fear. At last, with Beryl's studying me as if I were conducting a science experiment, I rolled on the condom and then we were together, moving sort of in unison, and I tried to control myself by thinking about John Glenn

27

blasting off into space back in February and silently ticking off the count-down: *Six, five, four, three, two, one, zero, ignition, lift-off. . . .*

And then it was over.

Beryl suggested we get ice cream. The rain had stopped, and we were more inventive at HoJo's than we'd been at the Berkeley-Carteret. Beryl ordered a double-dip macaroon, and I had pecan brittle. We wanted to spend the night at the hotel, but we had tickets to see Ray Charles and officially we were sleeping at Birdman's. His folks were strict about taking attendance, so we strolled down the boardwalk holding hands and met up with Rollie, Birdman, and their girlfriends at Convention Hall.

That year the summer didn't linger. On Labor Day, the cold swept down from Canada, clearing the beaches along the Shore. Around Maplewood and South Orange, the leaves flamed up and fell, and on weekends fathers and sons raked them into yellowish-brown mounds and lit bonfires at the curb, and the smoke blew through the bare trees. In October, after President Kennedy announced that Soviet ballistic missiles had been uncovered in Cuba, I had to put my Khrushchev number on ice, and took phone calls for most of my shows during the crisis, my favorite being the one from Louie, a fourth grader at South Mountain Elementary, who asked me why he had to have a bedtime if America was going to get blown up. Earning the gratitude of his mother, who got in touch at midnight to thank me, I told him that Khrushchev was plotting to trade the missiles for Mrs. Kennedy's Oleg Cassini inaugural gown, so Louie should get some shut-eye, all the while thinking that if warheads hit New Jersey, a huge payoff for me was that I'd stop missing Beryl.

I had been in a daze since she'd gone to Chicago. We wrote each other twice a week, letters full of trivia and signed with love and "I can't wait to see you." Then one afternoon in November, Beryl buzzed me at the store. I was refilling the syrup dispensers, and Emma answered the wall phone behind the register and held up the receiver. I set down a can of chocolate syrup, and after I said hello, Beryl told me that she was going to Arizona for Thanksgiving.

"I met someone," she said.

"A cowboy?"

With a forced sunniness, she replied, "He does have a hat. Like the Cisco Kid."

I pictured a four-eyed bookworm in a sombrero. It was comforting. Momentarily.

"Michael, I didn't want to tell you in a letter."

"Oh, it's a lot nicer on the phone." Beryl didn't deserve the sarcasm, but a queasy mix of anger and sadness was rolling through me.

"I'll be home for Christmas break. Maybe we can see each other."

"Sure."

When I hung up, Emma said, "You're a good-looking boy. And there's plenty of girls in the sea."

Normally, I was tickled by Emma's fracturing clichés, but I wasn't in the mood for it now. "Fish. There are plenty of fish in the sea."

"I'm not requesting the English lesson. I'm telling you: Next time, be smart. Don't put your balls in one basket."

"Eggs. Eggs in one basket."

"In Yiddish, *beitzim* is the eggs. And the balls." Emma smiled at me. "Life goes on, Mishka. Finish the syrup."

Beryl cruised the Caribbean with her family over Christmas vacation, so I didn't see her, and life went on. I visited Rollie in Miami and drove to Yale to hang out with Birdman, who turned me on to my first joint. The girls I met around town were in high school, and on occasion I asked one out, though after a couple of dates they seemed too young. I earned some extra cash that summer at Tony Mart's down the Shore, introducing acts and even meeting Del Shannon, who had a conga line of suntanned drunks dancing on the bar.

One of the dancers was a divorcée from Indiana, a shapely, doe-eyed brunette in her thirties who was renting a house in Long Branch and decided I was a splendid candidate for a crash course in the erotic arts. She was a savvy judge of potential. It was an hour drive from her rental to South Orange, and I began sleeping over several nights a week. I never got specific with Emma about the arrangement, but now and again, with a sly smile, my grandmother observed that it was unusual to spend a summer at the beach and not get a tan.

The divorcée returned to Bloomington in September, leaving me with a wealth of information and an indelible memory of peeling off her damp leopard-print bikini. The following Memorial Day she came back to Long Branch, called me at WSOV, and offered me a similar tutorial. I accepted, and after that summer I saw only her when I dreamed of curvy girls in skimpy bathing suits. For the rest of those two years, I was bored and sleepy. What with working at the store until dinner, then eating and taking a nap until my alarm rang, and transforming myself into the Mad Russian for three hours, some nights I was so beat after my show that I sacked out on the couch in the studio until I had to help Emma with the morning papers.

The Friday afternoon that JFK was assassinated, Emma had me bring a portable TV from home and set it up behind the soda fountain. Eddie O was at the store almost round the clock, drinking straight from his flask and telling everyone, in a tone that discouraged disagreement, that the country never wanted a mick in the White House. I saw Jack Ruby shoot Lee Harvey Oswald, and the president's funeral, and I was as numb as the day my parents died. I'd recently bought a cassette recorder, and on Thursday morning I walked across the street from my house to Underhill Field and interviewed fans during the Thanksgiving Day football game between Columbia and West Orange High, planning to run them that night. The flag was at half-mast, but even though people were less focused on the news than the score, I had the feeling that the game was a temporary distraction and reality as I understood it had had its ass kicked to the curb.

That July, Emma flew off to Paris, and one day, as I served Eddie O a vanilla Coke, he said, "Kid, you act like you're a hundred years old. You're ready to blow this burg."

"Where am I gonna go?"

"You done good at WSOV. Get yourself a radio operator's license. I'll help you. I got ins at some of the big stations in New York."

I figured Emma was the impetus for this latest career push and felt rotten about worrying my grandmother. Yet I sensed that hiding behind her humor and stoicism was a mournfulness that she shared with no one, and I was reluctant to leave her alone.

"Ain't no law against being happy, boyo. You think about it."

I was still thinking about it on September 9, 1964, the day my family's history caught up with me.

I had slept at the studio, and early that morning, after I crossed the avenue and went through the alley to the parking lot behind Village Drugs, the Fury wouldn't start. I got under the hood, wiped off the battery connectors and checked the gaps on the spark plugs, but I couldn't get the engine to turn over. I didn't want Emma to deal with the newspapers by herself, and it was only half a mile to Sweets. I walked through the village, with the spiky green burrs falling from the chestnut trees and rolling on the sidewalk. The twine-wrapped bundles of papers were still stacked in the doorway. Emma must have overslept, which had been happening more frequently, another reason I was reluctant to move to New York. I took out my key, but when I tried the door it was unlocked, and the lights were on over the soda fountain.

"Emma?"

No answer. Figuring she'd forgotten to switch off the lights last evening, I brought in the papers. The scissors to cut the twine were in a drawer under the cash register. Pushing through the low swinging gate that led behind the counter, I saw Emma sprawled on the floor by the soda fountain. She was on her back, with three penny-sized holes in her chest and blackish-red blood splashed across her white blouse. I'd seen gunshot wounds in the movies, and I felt as though I was looking at a screen through the popcorn-scented dark. It didn't occur to me that Emma could be dead as I dashed to the wall phone, dialed the operator, and shouted, "My grand-mother's been shot! Send the rescue squad! Three-ten Irvington Avenue."

"Did you shoot her?" she asked.

"Fuck you!" I screamed, and slammed down the receiver.

Kneeling over Emma, I took her hand, telling her that she'd be fine. Her eyes, a dull jade, stared up at me. I recalled her singing a melancholy tune: *Shlof, mayn kind . . . shlofzhe, zunenyu.* It was my first memory of her voice, and I'd thought it was Russian until fourth grade when I was at the soda fountain and Emma was mixing me an egg cream, and Paul Robeson was singing it on the radio and I learned that it was a Yiddish lullaby. *Mishka*, Emma had said, staring out toward something only she could see. *I used to sing that to you: Sleep, my child . . . sleep, my darling one.* I was humming the lullaby now and leaning over my grandmother, crying while the phrase "Nothing is forgotten" repeated itself in my head in Russian until a man said, "Michael? Michael, it's Officer Nelligan."

I looked up. A moonfaced South Orange cop was holding a revolver.

"My grandmother's dead."

Part II

6

That evening, as Yulianna Kosoy drove through town, loneliness seemed to be everywhere. In the doorways of the dark shops along Adaskina Boulevard, and the deserted stalls of the market square. In the glimmer of the bell-shaped streetlights, each lamppost crowned by a wrought-iron Communist star framed with a laurel wreath. Even in the chimney smoke, redolent with cabbage soup and roasted chicken, that rose from the tin-roofed bungalows on the side streets, an announcement that families were at supper.

Yuli had no family, just the man who had found a scrawny, terrified child hiding in the woods on an August morning twenty years ago, the husky, dark-eyed man with a salt-and-pepper beard, the man the locals referred to as Der Schmuggler—Yiddish, she'd discover, for his vocation: smuggling. All Yuli owned on that day was her tattered coat and dress and a book of fairy tales swathed in a piece of sheepskin, with her name written on the front flyleaf. Picking her up, Der Schmuggler carried her to his home. He had no wife or children and treated Yuli as a daughter. She began calling him Papka, and after completing high school, she went to work for him.

Yuli was working for Der Schmuggler now and stopped to fill up his car at the petrol station. The town of Otvali was in Southern Russia, wedged between the port cities of Rostov-on-Don and Taganrog, a handy location for the buying and selling of *kontrabanda*, and Yuli did business in both places. Tomorrow, though, she had to be in Dnipropetrovsk, a seven-or-eight-hour ride west into the Ukraine, and Yuli wanted to make a stop before going there.

A couple of hours later, she was asleep in a rooming house owned by an associate of Der Schmuggler in Donetsk, and by morning, Yuli was staring up at the great stone edifice of a theater with a heaviness in her chest that made her gasp for breath. The inside of the theater was one of her rare childhood memories. The city had been called Stalino then, and Yuli had a dim memory of watching her mother float across the stage to Tchaikovsky's *Swan Lake*. Yuli could picture herself sitting on the edge of her seat in the front row and the orchestra below the stage, but most of the seats were empty, and Yuli surmised that her mother had been rehearsing for a performance. Her other memories were of panic-stricken grown-ups talking about the Nazis and of leaving Stalino crammed into the back of the truck, her face pressed against the legs of a woman in a musty wool dress. Yuli recalled a sudden *crack-crack-crack*, and someone crying out that the Germans were shooting and mothers and fathers shouting for their children to run. An older boy had taken her hand and dragged her with him as he ran. Yuli had come to Donetsk before in an effort to fill in the blank spaces of her past, hoping to reclaim another sacred detail of her mother or to conjure up a misty image of her father. She never did.

Yuli breathed easier once she was back in the car, driving past grain-fields and Cossack huts with hipped roofs and churches with gilded onion domes glinting in the sun. Half the trip was on rutted dirt roads, and she arrived in the city of Dnipropetrovsk in the late afternoon and met Pyotr Ananko on the embankment of the Dnieper River. Pyotr had attended the Mark Twain English-language school with her in Otvali, gone off to Dni-propetrovsk State University, and now wrote for *Dneprovskaya Pravda*, the regional mouthpiece of the Soviet Communist Party. He was still the same shy, baby-faced boy with lank whitish-blond hair who proclaimed his esteem for American beatniks by dressing in black—from his turtleneck to his brogues. Yuli had grown close to him when they'd translated Allen Ginsberg's "Howl" into Russian, then enlisted the other rebellious *bitniki* at school to create copies of the poem by typing it up with carbon paper, and sold the officially forbidden literature—known as samizdat—to teen-agers in Rostov-on-Don for two rubles a copy. His job at the newspaper demanded that Pyotr become a less overt rebel, but he had some leeway. His skill at translating news from the United States astounded his supe-riors, and he reviewed the films—*The Defiant Ones*, *West Side Story*, *To Kill a Mockingbird*, *Some Like It Hot*—beloved by the younger genera-tion of Soviets, who otherwise would have ignored the political dribble in *Dneprovskaya Pravda*.

"You brought everything?" he asked as they joined the couples walk-ing along the Dnieper, the river glassy in the cool autumn light.

"*Da*." Concealed in a compartment under the rear seat, Yuli had a suit-case packed with ten copies of the record album *Meet the Beatles!* and three new Blaupunkt Sultans, a splendid German shortwave radio. Pyotr would sell them to the hipsters on Karl Marx Avenue and keep the money as payment for providing Yuli with information.

"You had no trouble?"

"*Nyet*, Petya. I used Papka's Volga."

The black sedan was favored by the Komitet Gosudarstvennoy Bezo-pasnosti, particularly the KGB officers who were visiting from their head-quarters in Moscow, and the local police were too intimidated by state security agents to stop such a car and try to extract a bribe from the driver.

At a stand, Pyotr bought them eskimos—vanilla ice cream with a choc-olate coating on a stick. When they had been in school, Pyotr, like most of the boys in their class, had had a crush on Yuli. She possessed an unset-tling beauty—strange, discordant. She was small and delicate boned. Her ash-brown hair was cut in an unruly pageboy, and she had an angelic face, impossibly high cheekbones, a snub nose, and full, bowed lips, but her dark blue eyes appeared even darker against her cream-white complexion, and it was the darkness of those eyes that seemed out of place in such an ethereal young woman.

They finished their eskimos, retrieved the suitcase from the car, and walked to a cluster of Khrushchyovkas, the five-story concrete apartment buildings that the Soviet leader had ordered built to alleviate the housing shortage.

"Excuse us," Pyotr said to a short, squat man in a *telnyashka*—the light-green-striped shirt worn by border guards—who was blocking the entrance, facing away from them and weaving drunkenly. Yuli heard the splash of his piss against the door, and when he turned, his eyes were blurry.

"Where the hell you going?" he said, leering at Yuli.

As she dipped her right hand into the leather document bag on her shoulder—acquired from a Red Army lieutenant on leave in Taganrog for a pair of Levi's—Yuli replied with the tone of a cheerful schoolgirl: "To fuck your mother."

Anger sparking in his eyes, the drunk stepped toward Yuli, who pressed the button on the horn handle of a switchblade and held up the four-inch stiletto, a gift from Der Schmuggler, who had brought it back from a trip to Italy.

"You syphilitic bitch, you have plans for that knife?"

"Stay and we will both find out."

Watching her, the drunk backed up into the courtyard, then spun around and staggered off between the buildings.

Pyotr, his pride nicked, said, "I could have scared him off."

"I know, Petya, but you have the suitcase," and to smooth his ruffled male feathers, added, "And I was in a hurry to go upstairs with you."

Pyotr occupied a one-room apartment that seemed hardly bigger than a coffin. It had two windows, exposed pipes on the water-stained walls, and a concrete floor painted the vivid red of the Soviet flag. Before Yuli could remove her boots, Pyotr kissed her. She broke off the kiss and undressed, Pyotr watching her as if she might fly away. Their first time together had been after completing the translation of "Howl." Yuli hadn't been physically attracted to Pyotr, but she had admired his mastery of American slang. Had she not been a practical girl eager to be rid of her virginity, Yuli would have been disappointed that Pyotr proved more adept as a translator than as a lover. Still, Yuli slept with him on occasion, and with other boys too, while Pyotr was in Otvali and after he had left for the university, though she saw no need to share this news with him. Pyotr was kind, easily hurt, and a generous source of information.

In the morning, they strolled across the bridge to Monastyrsky Island, Yuli removing an old FED camera from her bag and taking pictures of the wide blue river. It appeared innocent enough, but they had to be careful.

True, Nikita Khrushchev had denounced his predecessor, Joseph Stalin, for his egotism, ineptitude, and brutality, and had enacted the Ottepel—the Thaw—which thinned out the population of political prisoners in the Gulag, reduced the government's hostility toward free expression, and encouraged engagement with the outside world. So it wasn't unusual to spot foreign-camera-toting tourists in Moscow or Leningrad or Odessa. But never in Dnipropetrovsk, a city closed to outsiders because it was home to the Yuzhmash plant, where the Kremlin designed and built its intercontinental ballistic missiles.

Yuli put away her FED and sat on a bench with Pyotr.

"You sure?" she asked impatiently, tapping her foot on the ground.

Pyotr glanced at his watch. "Soon."

When Pyotr had called her in Otvali, all he'd said was that she should visit him and bring her camera, a cautious choice of words because even though he was using a public telephone booth, you never knew which lines the KGB were monitoring. Last night, Pyotr had explained why he'd phoned, and Yuli was pleased that she'd come. The information would be valuable in some way. Exactly how valuable would be determined by Der Schmuggler.

When no one appeared on the shaded path that Yuli was observing, she began to think that Pyotr had simply wanted her company, and she grew irritated at him.

"Petya, did you invite me here to see something that doesn't exist?"

He smiled. Yuli was referring to a remark that she'd made when they were at school. The students were assigned to read *Sputnik Ateista—The Atheist's Companion*, a standard Soviet text—and Yuli commented that it was a ridiculous exercise, because it was impossible to study nonexistence. The class had been amused; the teacher less so.

Pyotr jabbed his head in the direction of three men striding down the path, saying, "There," and Yuli was ashamed for doubting his motives.

Yuli recognized the two older men; she had photographed them months ago. On the left was the general director of the Yuzhmash plant; on the right was the chief of engineering. It was the one in the middle that had brought her here—a chubby, freckle-faced young man with bushy red hair, terrible posture, and a purple houndstooth suit that fit like a sausage casing.

His name, according to Pyotr, was Kazimir Zolnerowich. He was nineteen and had already earned a PhD from the Moscow Institute of Physics and Technology, a school that Khrushchev liked to brag in interviews was more rigorous than the great U.S. technological colleges in California and Massachusetts.

Yuli said, "You heard Zolnerowich designs missiles?"

"What else would a Soviet physicist design? Nothing to help the people."

Yuli watched the trio disappear down the path.

"They will be back soon," Pyotr said.

"You better go."

"I could wait for you by the bridge."

"No, Petya." If the KGB caught her, she would be interrogated by their sadists in the Lubyanka prison, and there was no reason he should suffer the same fate. And Yuli was trying to discourage Pyotr, who wanted more from her than she could give him.

His hurt expression didn't go away after she kissed him, and he said, "*Paka*, Yuli. Be careful."

She waited until he was gone, then crossed to the other side of the path, glancing around to make certain no one was watching her. Kneeling behind a row of poplars thick with leaves, Yuli attached a Jupiter lens to her camera, and when the trio returned, she zoomed in so closely on the young physicist's face that she could've counted his freckles.

7

That evening, in Otvali, her legs cramped after the long drive from Dnipro-petrovsk, Yuli parked the Volga behind the high concrete walls of the compound where she lived and walked down the graveled road to town. The first whispers of winter were in the breeze, and Yuli stopped on Adaskina Boulevard and undid the cardigan tied around her waist. Slipping into the sweater, she glanced up at the bronze statue of the girl in a plain frock who had given the boulevard its name. Maria Adaskina was eighteen in 1941 when the Nazis invaded the Soviet Union. The Fascist scum thought Russian girls were theirs for the taking, and when a captain tried to force himself on Maria, she grabbed his Walther and shot him dead. Maria was hung from a telegraph pole and left to rot.

Velikaya Otechestvennaya Voyna—the Great Patriotic War. *No escaping it,* Yuli thought, cutting through an alley to the rear of the wood-frame synagogue and entering the bathhouse. Beyond the vestibule was a washroom lit by a bulb in the ceiling, then an archway that led to the *banya*—a sauna—and finally the stone stairs down to the mikvah, the ritual pool observant Jewish wives used to purify themselves when their periods ended. The bathhouse was closed now, the attendants gone, the only person in the steamy washroom a naked, wide-hipped woman with closely cropped grayish-brown hair.

"Y'all late," she said to Yuli in English, dunking a besom of green birch leaves into a wooden bucket of water.

"Next time I go to Dnipropetrovsk, I'll bring my wings and fly home."

Every other month for the last year, Yuli had come to the bathhouse to meet this woman. She knew her as Bashe, though Yuli was unsure whether that was her real name. Her voice was full of Eastern Europe yet possessed an odd drawl, like the characters she'd seen in *Gone with the Wind*. At different times, Yuli had greeted Bashe in Russian, Ukrainian, Polish, and Yiddish, but Bashe, in all likelihood to obscure her identity, had replied in English. Yuli guessed that she was a Hasid living in the southern United States. Her long-sleeved dress and sheitel—the wig devout Jewish women donned out of modesty—were hanging on a peg; her hair had been clipped down to fuzz; and Yuli was aware that Der Schmuggler, either at the request of the CIA or Mossad or both, had recruited operatives from the Lubavitcher sect because the insular Hasidim were impenetrable by the KGB.

"There is something y'all have for me?" Bashe asked, her plump breasts bobbing up and down as she massaged her back with the wet leaves.

It was always the same with Bashe. Yuli didn't mind her being brusque or naked. What disturbed her was the hunger in Bashe's eyes while she stared at Yuli. Bashe had a wedding band on her finger and the faded stretch marks of pregnancy on her belly. Wasn't a Hasidic wife and mother forbidden to lust after women? Maybe it wasn't lust. Maybe Bashe enjoyed needling her. An amusement to pass the time.

Yuli held out a film canister with adhesive tape wound around it. "A new physicist. I wrote his name on the tape, and I take his pictures."

Bashe looked at the canister. "And where should I be putting this?"

Yuli, deciding to pay back Bashe for making her uncomfortable, lowered her gaze to the ferny tangle between her legs.

Dropping the besom in the bucket, Bashe scowled. "You wicked girl."

Yuli answered her with a beatific smile.

"Put it there yourself."

Yuli kept smiling.

"A girl like you should swim for a week in the mikvah."

"I have no one to be pure for. Not that this is your business."

Bashe chuckled, a sound like she was gargling pebbles. "Towns talk and Bashe listens. And let Bashe tell you what she knows. Boys don't want wicked girls for marriage."

Yuli knew she was the subject of gossip, which bothered her more than she let on, but her body was her own and she would do with it as she pleased. Still, Yuli suspected that Bashe was correct. Nobody in or around Otvali—not a Jew or a Communist or a Cossack—had ever proposed to her, nor had the witch of a shadchan, who would mate a dog with a cat to earn her fee, tried to arrange a match for her. So what? She already cooked for Der Schmuggler and nursed him when he was sick. That was enough. Why did she need a husband and the inevitable children? Yuli was fine without them.

Bashe gazed at Yuli. "Take off your clothes, we'll sit a spell in the *banya*. We can steam ourselves."

Yuli was lonely enough to be tempted. Would it make a difference, being loved by a woman instead of a man? Yuli didn't know. And she was curious about so many things. Not tonight, though. Tonight she had other plans.

Yuli put the canister with the film of the physicist on a bench and headed home.

8

The road up from Otvali ran for a kilometer past the compound, tapering to a dirt path as it curved through fields of wheat and sunflowers before disappearing into a birch forest and ending at the shore of Lake Bereza. Yuli had been hiding in those woods when Der Schmuggler discovered her, and as she approached the compound gate, the moon was turning the trees a ghostly white. She had come to the forest with the other children who had been pushed out of the trucks when the Nazis began shooting at the convoy from Stalino, and by the time Der Schmuggler found her, the other children had been killed by the Germans. Yuli preferred not to recall their dying, so over the years the images dissolved like when you woke up from a nightmare and all that remained was the fear.

Now, after locking the gate, Yuli saw a light in the kitchen window of the main house and Der Schmuggler sitting at the table by the white-stone wood-burning *Russkaya pech*, the same sort of Russian oven that had been warming peasant huts and shtetl houses for centuries. Every evening, when he finished reviewing the inventory lists, Der Schmuggler would put together the jigsaw puzzles that he brought back from his trips to U.S. military bases in Germany, Italy, and Spain. When Yuli was young, she used to help fit the pieces into place until the pictures appeared: an American cowboy lassoing wild horses; Sleeping Beauty lying on a bed about to be kissed by the handsome prince; and her favorites, those paintings by Norman Rockwell—a young woman holding up her white prom dress in front of a mirror, and a boy sitting with his arm around a girl while they gaze at the moon.

Lately, Der Schmuggler worked on puzzles that were so complex Yuli became dizzy looking at them—bizarre splotches of color, as though a drunken artist had sprayed paint onto a canvas with a hose. These puzzles were difficult, and Der Schmuggler worked on them late into the night, pausing only to replenish his tea glass from the brass samovar and eat spoonfuls of the black currant jam that Yuli prepared for him. Most mornings Yuli fired up the samovar by lighting a pinecone and dropping it in the chimney of the urn. An electric samovar would've been more convenient, but Der Schmuggler wouldn't use one, saying that the piney fragrance reminded him of his boyhood in Rostov-on-Don.

He seldom spoke about his past. Yuli knew that his father had been a grain merchant and owned a gristmill, and Der Schmuggler had worked with him before the war. When he had brought Yuli out of the woods, the town of Otvali hadn't existed. All around, the land was cratered from shelling and bombing. Hundreds of elderly couples and widows with their young sons and daughters, and veterans, many of them missing limbs, had lost their homes and wives and children. There was a young priest whose church had been burned, and a dozen Hasidic families who had hidden in an underground shelter from the Einsatzgruppen—the SS killing squads—were living in lean-tos around a sagging barn and chicken coop.

Because Premier Stalin believed that he and his lackeys could control the economy from the Kremlin, the Soviet Union was bound from head to toe in official red tape. A foolproof method for escaping these restrictions was *blat*, a Russian term that encompassed the panoply of corruption by which the nation functioned, trading on connections with the Communist Party big shots who ruled the localities, and the *nomenklatura*—the administrators who oversaw everything from access to telephones to production in the pencil factories. As a child, Yuli learned that Der Schmuggler had mastered the art of *blat* by accompanying him to Rostov and Taganrog and watching him drink vodka with the dockworkers, who knew him from the grain business. These sticky-fingered men enabled Der Schmuggler to carve out his own substantial niche of the black market, and he used these goods to bribe anyone who could help him.

The director of a concrete plant was the first official he bribed; then someone with access to trucks, excavators, and tractors. Soon loads of copper wire, tin, cast-iron pipes, glass, and gravel were delivered. Within a year, the lean-tos were gone; houses had sprouted on the new streets; wells had been dug, septic tanks buried; and stalls were operating in the market square. People displaced by the war, and POWs returning from their Nazi captors, whom Stalin wanted executed for surrendering instead of dying in battle for the motherland, were still wandering the countryside, and Der Schmuggler welcomed them. Within four years, electric lights had replaced kerosene lamps; a synagogue, church, and school were built; and the walled compound was complete—barns for cows and horses, a garage, outbuildings for the handful of men who resided on the property and for storing *kontrabanda*, and a concrete fortress of a house painted the rich shade of borscht with a gabled roof and tall factory windows.

Around then, Yuli started to hear gossip. An old man at a fish stall, who was smoking beech leaves rolled in strips of newsprint, told Yuli that he'd heard it was Der Schmuggler who had persuaded Comrade Stalin to grow his mustache when they were young, and Stalin still consulted him on the weightiest matters. Yuli overheard the men who came to Otvali from the countryside to sell their grain, produce, meat, and poultry at the market proudly claim, when they were sober, that Der Schmuggler was the last of the Jewish Cossacks and as skilled a swordsman as had ever ridden a horse across the steppes. Their opinion of him began to change as they drank their *samogon*—home-brewed alcohol that could pickle a wild boar—and when the bottles were empty, they declared that Der Schmuggler was plotting with other Jewish Elders of Zion to control the world.

"Is any of the gossip true?" Yuli asked Der Schmuggler one day while they were driving to Moscow.

"Why waste time with these crazy tales? Our town has five thousand people and no name, and you are supposed to help me think of one."

Yuli was perhaps nine years old—she didn't know her birthday—and even at that age she detected the fear behind his dismissiveness and concluded that the stories contained clues to his past, a history so dreadful that he decided it was off-limits to her.

Eleven hundred kilometers later, they reached Moscow without naming the town, and checked into the Hotel Metropol. Yuli was in awe of the arches and crystal chandeliers in the lobby. After unpacking, they walked to Red Square, Der Schmuggler carrying a khaki haversack fastened at the top with a cord. While they waited at the northern gate, Yuli looked at the colorful domes of St. Basil's and thought the cathedral resembled a fairy-tale castle. A soldier in a wedge cap approached and waved for them to follow him to the street, where a pasty-faced older man in a smoke-gray hat and suit was leaning against a long black four-door ZIL.

"Tovarich," he said to Der Schmuggler. *Comrade.*

Der Schmuggler bent forward in a slight bow that Yuli had never seen him perform, and gave the haversack to the man. He undid the cord and peered inside. Yuli stood on her tiptoes to look and saw tin cans of Nesquik, a chocolate powder that she liked to mix into her milk.

"My grandchildren will be pleased," the man said. "And Comrade Beria sends you greetings. We must come visit your operation, no?"

Der Schmuggler performed that bow again, grasped Yuli's hand, and began ambling toward the hotel.

"Who was that?" she asked.

"A deputy minister of state security."

"But Nesquik is from America. From the capitalists."

"To be successful here, you must become a connoisseur of irony."

Yuli didn't understand the words *connoisseur* or *irony*, but she had a more pressing question. "When he asked to visit, why did you say nothing?"

"Because he would not like what I wanted to say."

"Which was?"

"*Otvali.*"

Yuli giggled. *Otvali* meant "Go away," or if spoken in a harsh tone, "Go to hell."

"*Otvali,*" Yuli said. "That should be the name of our town."

Der Schmuggler put his huge hand on her head and smiled down at her. "Yes, yes, it should."

47

Yuli had her own suite in the main house—a bedroom, bath, and an office where she maintained the accounting ledgers for Der Schmuggler.
Although she was exhausted from her trip to Dnipropetrovsk, Yuli didn't
go in to sleep. In fact, on her ride home through the Ukraine, she'd kept
alert by imagining this part of her evening. The compound was lit by spot-
lights bolted beneath the roof line of the house, and Yuli went past a barn
to a concrete box that was forty square meters, which Der Schmuggler still
referred to, with the annoyance common to the parents of teenagers, as
Solod Magazin—the Malt Shop.

He'd had it built years ago, when Yuli was in school and complained
that she and her friends had nowhere to go on Saturday nights, but Der
Schmuggler had been reluctant to do so. The Kremlin was serious about
the indoctrination of Soviet youth, and he was careful not to cross a line
that officials couldn't ignore. He did, however, permit Hasidic youngsters
to attend an illegal yeshiva: So many Hasids had been slaughtered by the
Nazis, Der Schmuggler didn't have the heart to let their remnants die out,
and the presence of four or five hundred of them in Otvali would provide
cover for messengers like Bashe. Yet the English-language school was op-
erated by the numbers: Named for Mark Twain, whose loathing of Tsarist
Russia endeared him to the party, the students spent half the day immersed
in the government-blessed curriculum in Russian and the other half taking
courses in English, all while a portrait of Vladimir Lenin, the founder of
the Soviet state, stood guard on a wall of every classroom, glaring at the
students as if accusing them of harboring the forbidden desire to own private property. Der Schmuggler also decreed that children participate in the
groups the Kremlin believed would indoctrinate them with an allegiance to
the state and its leadership akin to religious devotion. Teenagers had to join
the Komsomol, the Young Communist League. To refuse could cost them a
spot at a university or alienate a member of the party committee in Rostov,
who would prevent them from securing a decent job or apartment.

Der Schmuggler had explained this to Yuli when she told him about her
dull Saturday nights, and she responded by saying, "Papka, I do everything
you want and seek nothing in return."

He attempted to explain again, but she interrupted him, screaming, "Fascist!" and stalked off, and for the first time in their life together he was tempted to strike her.

Yuli gave him the silent treatment for two weeks, and he relented and ordered his men to build her the Solod Magazin, even adding some modern touches to the design that he had seen in an American architectural journal, a white roof like the raised wings of a swan and steel-rimmed porthole windows.

Yuli apologized for her name-calling and did make a concession in the event one of the party faithful came to inspect the Malt Shop. She and a couple of girlfriends painted a mural on a wall of five Red Army soldiers doing a jumping, heel-clicking dance in front of a scorched Nazi tank. Their one other argument was when Yuli pasted cork over the wall across from the mural and tacked up movie posters of Elvis, James Dean, Paul Newman, and Marilyn Monroe; and postcards of the Hollywood sign glowing at night, and the Empire State Building. Der Schmuggler said the posters could stay; the postcards had to go.

Yuli kissed him on the cheek. "It will be fine. Just tell anyone they bother that I am identifying targets for our missiles."

Since Yuli had received her diploma, most of her classmates had relocated to the cities, and she no longer socialized in the Malt Shop. It had become a refuge where she could be alone, which, strangely, eased her loneliness, as though with no one to witness her pain, the pain itself didn't exist. Now Yuli kicked off her boots and switched on the pole lamp next to the white-and-red soda machine that dispensed carbonated water plain or with pear or lemon syrup. On the wall opposite the machine was steel shelving, and from the shelf below the Blaupunkt shortwave radio, Yuli grabbed a Bass Weejuns box. The shoes had been procured for her by Der Schmuggler through an arrangement he had with a sergeant at the American army post exchange in Munich, and as Yuli slid on the burgundy loafers, she wondered if her mother had felt the same pleasure when she'd stepped into her ballet slippers.

Yuli tuned in the radio. The reception was excellent. The Americans must have put up new towers far enough from the Soviet transmitters that the ministry of communications couldn't jam the frequency. A month back,

Yuli had dialed in the program when she was cycling through the stations, and she hated to miss it. Petya was also a fan. Last night, while they listened together, Petya said that the young people left the streets of Dnipropetrovsk whenever the jammers couldn't drown out the broadcast with noise like a revving truck engine.

"*Dobryy vecher*," the disc jockey said. "Good evening. We're in lovely downtown South Orange, and I'm Mikhail Dainov, the Mad Russian. . . ."

Yuli stood still, her arms folded across her chest, her eyes closed. From the first time she'd heard Mikhail's voice, Yuli had been enchanted by its texture, a hypnotic blend of honey and sand, an American voice straight from the home of rock 'n' roll—that wondrous kingdom, the air clear as glass and full of music, with people gliding over the sidewalks, going in and out of the bright stores, their arms loaded with packages while children rode bicycles on freshly tarred streets and waved to each other. Perhaps this America was nothing more than propaganda foisted on the world by the West, but this was the America, new and clean, that Yuli saw in her dreams, where the only party that counted was one with ice cream and cake, and sour, colorless men didn't jam radio stations. Oh, what a country this America was, a land without memory, so unlike the Soviet Union, the land that forgot nothing.

Yuli started to dance. Mikhail was playing Little Richard's "Tutti Frutti," and the relentless beat of his piano and the saxophones sent her across the beechwood floor, kicking up her feet, extending her arms, spinning so that her hair whipped against her face and her skirt whirled upward, her movements both controlled and exuberant—the synchronicity of soldiers marching, the grace of the Siberian cats leaping between rafters in the barn. Every thought was driven from her head, a comforting blackness, infinite, warm, like a summer night on a blanket with one of her boys, after drinking vodka and lemon soda from a canteen, Yuli on her back, brimming with a sweet tension until the boy collapsed, exhausted, at peace, while her tension persisted, weighting her to the blanket like a stone.

Loneliness surged through Yuli as Mikhail whispered, "*Vot moyo serdtse, ono polno lyubvi*—here is my heart, it is full of love," and played another record, the Paris Sisters singing "I Love How You Love Me," a slow song of gratitude and wonder. Yuli imagined she was dancing with

Mikhail, raising her arms, his hands cool and strong in hers. She couldn't see his face because her cheek was on his shoulder, and she pressed against him, fighting off her loneliness the best she could.

Outside, Der Schmuggler stood looking in through the window and watched Yuli dance in the glimmer of the pole lamp. He could hear the faint music on the radio and figured that this was the show she had told him about, with the boy Mikhail Dainov who spoke English and Russian, and talked about his grandmother Emma.

Emma Dainov.

Der Schmuggler could still see Emma that icy day on the outskirts of Rostov. He was searching for his girlfriend, Maria Adaskina, but a Nazi soldier spotted him, and as the soldier raised his rifle, Der Schmuggler heard a gunshot and was surprised to find himself alive. The soldier fell forward and behind him Der Schmuggler saw Emma, whom he'd known since childhood, standing there with her dark gold hair spilling over her shoulders and holding a pistol in her hand, smoke rising from the barrel.

Turning from the window, Der Schmuggler glanced up at the moon, thinking about God and His intermittent desire to author a story with a plot, a final chapter that revealed the fates of all the characters involved.

Der Schmuggler walked to the veranda, sat in a rocking chair, and put his head in his hands, waiting for the present to banish the past.

Part III

9

Rain was falling on the Friday morning we buried my grandmother, a cold autumn rain that slashed through the open sides of the lawn tent and sent streams of muddy water into her grave. Rabbi Adelberg, in a tan bucket hat with a red-and-blue ribbon, recited the Kaddish. As the pine box, resting on straps, disappeared into the ground next to my father, I began to cry again, feeling as if I were alone despite the two hundred people standing behind me.

Grief, Emma had observed after my parents died, is never what you imagine it will be. Beneath my sadness I was aware of a pure terror, an unshakable belief that I couldn't go on without my grandmother—my one loving, reliable constant for as long as I could remember.

The shiva was an effective distraction even though Rollie and Birdman couldn't make it, though they had come for the funeral. Rollie was in the middle of football season, and Birdman was organizing a conference at Yale to protest President Johnson's bombing of North Vietnam. The house was packed with Emma's friends and acquaintances from the synagogue and the store—apparently handing out free candy to kids forges an eternal bond—and teenagers who listened to my show. Eddie's wife, Fiona, was in charge of the refreshments and booked the caterer. It was all done how Emma had wanted it. She had made the arrangements for her funeral, writ-

55

ten out instructions for the days of mourning, and because I wouldn't be twenty-one until January, appointed Eddie the executor of her will. He had told me about it, but I was in no mood to discuss it with him.

"Something on your mind, boyo?" He gave me the once-over like I was a welsher who owed him money.

"Nothing." His look should've unnerved me, but I was too angry at him to be scared. Neither the South Orange police nor the detectives from the Essex County Prosecutor's Office had any leads in Emma's murder. The cash register hadn't been touched, and no one along our commercial strip of Irvington Avenue had spotted anybody going in or out of Sweets. During my interviews with Officer Nelligan and the Essex County detective, I was afraid to mention the Abruzzis and the phones in the storage room, and I wasn't asked about them. Once robbery was ruled out, the sole explanation for the shooting had to be connected to those phones, and I decided that after the shiva I'd talk to Eddie, and if he refused to tell the cops about his operation, then I would.

For the rest of the week—except for Yom Kippur when no one came by—I felt like a hostage in a noisy delicatessen. That last evening, after the house emptied out, I went for a walk to escape the odor of sour pickles and whitefish. At the corner, right before I turned toward the candy store, I glanced through a living room window and saw two children, a man, and a woman watching *Rawhide* on TV. Emma hated to miss that show, and I used to tease her that she had a crush on Clint Eastwood. A sob caught in my throat, and I went down Irvington Avenue past Beth El, the triangular-shaped wall of the sanctuary lit up for Friday-night services.

The only thing the cops knew about Emma's final evening was that she had a ticket to a dinner at the synagogue, where a social worker who assisted concentration camp survivors was scheduled to speak. Emma, however, didn't make it to Beth El, and getting shot didn't account for her absence. The coroner said that my grandmother hadn't been murdered until five or six in the morning.

I was cold, and cut over on Prospect Street back to Montague Place. I had to reopen Sweets, but I couldn't picture working there without Emma, and then I remembered a conversation we had a couple of weeks after Beryl dumped me.

I was restocking the candy jars, and Emma was behind the soda fountain watching me.

"It doesn't matter," she said.

I knew she was referring to Beryl, but I wasn't in the mood for any homespun wisdom, so I pretended not to hear her.

She said it again, louder. "It doesn't matter."

I was annoyed enough to answer. "Yeah, it does."

"No, it don't."

"Fine. Then what matters?"

"That you're alive, Mishka."

"That's it? That I'm alive?"

"That's it. Dead people don't have no fun."

"You got a point," I replied, wanting our discussion to end.

Emma flashed a triumphant smile. "I usually do."

10

On Monday, I brought the bundles of newspapers into the candy store at five forty-five, and by eight, after the first wave of customers, I felt as if I'd put in a twelve-hour shift. Some of it was being at Sweets without my grandmother, but mainly I was anxious waiting for Eddie to show up so I could let him know that one of us was going to tell the cops about those phones.

"Morning," Eddie said, taking a seat at the soda fountain. "Can I get a vanilla Coke?"

I was fuming and afraid as I stirred his drink, and he said, "Emma used to keep the radio on."

The radio was by the blender, and I spun the dial to WABC as the Beatles broke into the chorus of "She Loves You."

"No Sinatra?"

"I'm modernizing."

Mr. Beer Barrel rolled in and went to the storage room, then came to the counter and said to Eddie, "Door's locked."

I said, "It's closed. Till further notice."

Beer Barrel gaped at me as if I was speaking Babylonian. He had the face of a boxer, and not an especially skillful one. Scar tissue had erased most of his eyebrows, and his ears looked like a puppy had used them for chew toys.

"Eddie, this kid get stupid gradual or has it come on recent?"

"Michael's been working on it for a while. Why don't you wait in the car, Gerald?"

"I got to stay here and make some calls."

I inched my hand over to the scissors I'd positioned below the syrup dispensers. "Go grow some eyebrows."

Gerald, displeased by my suggestion, stepped toward the counter. Eddie stuck out his arm like a crossing guard, moving him backward, and when he was gone, said, "What's with you?"

"Some piece of shit murdered Emma."

"And you figure Gerald was involved?"

"The phones—"

Eddie sipped his vanilla Coke. "Those are Abruzzi phones, and anyone knowing that wouldn't have the balls to shoot your grandmother here. That's why I'm concerned. About you."

"Me? Why me?"

"Somebody aces Emma, nothing gets taken, and no other stores get hit. It don't add up. Maybe the shooter does an encore, ya understand?"

My mouth was dry. "Why would anyone want to kill Emma?"

"I'm trying to find out—me and some other guys. For now, I got Gerald and a pal of his watching your house at night."

"Really? I didn't see them."

"You ain't supposed to. But they can't watch you forever. You need to go on a vacation till this gets taken care of."

"What about the store? My house?"

"I'll handle that. And you inherited plenty of dough. We'll go over that later."

A woman was standing at the register. Eddie glanced at her and, lowering his voice, said, "I got something cooking. You be at my place at four thirty. And unlock the storage room. Gerald's coming in. With his pal. They'll close up for you. Got it?"

Before I could answer, Eddie said, "Go wait on your customer."

Walking to Radel Terrace on a brilliant September afternoon, it seemed inconceivable that I could be in danger until I recalled Emma in her blood-soaked blouse. A maroon Thunderbird I didn't recognize was in the O'Rourkes' driveway. I rang the bell and Eddie came to the door and led me up a carpeted stairway, through a den, and out onto a roof deck with a view of Underhill Field. Julian Rose, tall, broad-shouldered, and wearing a muddy-patterned tweed sport coat, was leaning on the railing, watching the Columbia football team doing jumping jacks on the grass.

Julian turned. "Hi, Michael. It's terrible about Emma. What a lady. I apologize for not getting to see you before now."

"I understand, Mr. Rose." He'd been sitting shiva for his wife and daughter, who were killed by a drunk driver on Labor Day. I'd gone to the funeral with Emma. She'd known Julian ever since my father had been his accountant. He used to pop into Sweets to chew the fat with Eddie and Emma. The stories of Julian Rose and Longy Zwillman during Prohibition were part of New Jersey folklore, and Julian was Eddie's closest friend, so I didn't question whether he'd been a tough guy. It wasn't obvious, though, since he looked like Cary Grant, as my mother liked to point out to my father, and was as soft-spoken as a librarian.

I was wondering why Julian was there when the doorbell chimed, and Eddie went down and returned with a guy who reminded me of my high-school chemistry teacher—lanky, with a buzz cut the color of a tarnished nickel and the bland expression of someone who studied the periodic table for fun.

"Taft," Julian said and, after they exchanged a fast, back-slapping hug, the man extended his hand to me. His arms were too long for his charcoal suit coat.

"I'm Taft Mifflin. And you must be Mikhail Dainov, the Mad Russian."

We shook. He didn't strike me as a regular listener. "My real name—"

"Michael Daniels, I know. I work for the Four Freedoms Radio Committee. I've been friends with Julian since we served together in the war. We were talking a while back, and he told me that the kids around here are huge fans of your show."

According to a profile I'd read of Julian in the *Newark Evening News*, he'd fought in Europe during World War II as a member of the Office of Strategic Services, and the OSS was a forerunner of the Central Intelligence Agency. I was attempting to think up a shrewd way to ask Taft if he was a spy when he said, "Four Freedoms Radio broadcasts programs into the Soviet Union, and I help manage the station."

"Like Voice of America? I've heard about Willis Conover and his jazz show."

"VOA operates under the U.S. Information Agency. We're a private company. Several months ago, we decided we needed a rock and roll program, and our New York office heard about you speaking Russian on the air and started taping you off the towers, then flew the tapes to our headquarters in Munich, and we've been broadcasting them in Russia."

"That's legal?"

He raised his hands, palms up. "Don't complain. You're a big hit there."

"How do you know?"

"Teenagers write letters to Munich, we interview Russian tourists in Europe, and we analyze that information and estimate your market penetration. So last week I was talking to Julian—he told me about your grandmother, I'm sorry about that, Michael—and he said you needed to get out of town."

"That's Eddie's opinion," I said.

"Because it's the truth, boyo. Listen to what the man has to say."

Taft continued, "I'm offering you a deejay spot in Munich. You'll have a producer to handle the technical stuff. All you'll have to do is write out the playlist and talk. And Munich's terrific. Plenty of eager fräuleins. We'll put you up in a hotel, and you'll make five hundred a month. You'll have a blast on that kind of money in Germany. What do you say?"

Eddie said, "He says he'll take it."

"I do?"

Eddie gave me one of his colder glares.

Taft placed a reassuring hand on my shoulder. "I'm sure this is difficult for you, Michael. I've been trying to find out what I can."

"Why?"

"Julian told me he was friends with your grandmother, and I wanted to see if I could come up with a lead for the police. In my line of work, you get to know people who know people, and it helps that we're required to do a background check on potential employees, so during your check, some things came up about your grandmother. You feel like answering a few questions?"

I nodded.

"Any idea why your grandmother applied for a tourist visa in August to the Soviet Union?"

"She was born in Russia."

"In a town in the western Ukraine, according to what she wrote on her visa application. But that town no longer exists. Stalin worked it over, and the Nazis finished the job. Did you ever meet a relative with the last name Adaskina?"

"I never met any relatives. Why?"

"That was your grandmother's maiden name. Why'd she go to Europe every year?"

I replied, "I don't know. Because she liked to vacation there?"

Taft smiled. "That makes sense. Did she ever say anything about being in a concentration camp?"

"Never. Why would she? Was my grandmother in a camp?"

Taft shrugged. "No record of it, but I saw a note somewhere, maybe on some old immigration paperwork. Forget it. The immigration guys processed a lot of people after the war who didn't speak English, and they made plenty of mistakes. Tell me. Between the stamps on her passport and the record of the purchases she paid duty on, we can tell that your grandmother spent time in Geneva, Munich, and Paris. Do you know why?"

"All I know is she bought me and my parents presents from her trips."

Taft was looking at the Rolex on my wrist, the one with the red and blue bezel marked with white numerals 2 through 22.

"Is that one of her presents?"

"It was hers." I'd had the bracelet resized and wore it now instead of the Explorer model that Emma had bought me—a way to keep her close, I suppose.

Eddie said, "And she was still wearing the Rolex when Michael found her. And no money was missing from the register."

"Interesting," Taft said. "May I see the watch?"

I held out my left arm.

Taft stared at my wrist. "This big red hand, not the one for minutes or hours, the arrow that shows another time zone. Did you reset it so it's six hours ahead of us?"

"No. Emma must have."

"Any reason she'd be keeping track of the time in Europe?"

I shrugged and considered telling him that Emma was always glancing at the watch even though there were two clocks in the store, but I was scared, and I wondered, for one crazy moment, if Emma could have been a spy.

"On her trips, your grandmother always stopped in Nice."

"Where's Nice?"

"In the South of France."

"She didn't talk about her travels."

"Sorry about the questions, Michael. I'll keep asking around and let you know if I come up with anything that'll help the investigation. I noticed from your background check that you have a passport."

"I do." Last summer, after Emma was done with her vacation, Rollie, Birdman, and I had planned to fly to Italy and visit Rollie's cousins in Siracusa. Rollie got mono instead.

"Good. It'll take me forty-eight hours to get the arrangements squared away. Our New York office will call you."

I thanked him, because I'd been taught to be polite, but if Taft Mifflin was the manager of a radio station, I was the king of Siam.

As Julian and Taft went downstairs, Eddie turned to me and said, "Don't look so glum. You'll have some fun over there, we'll find out what happened here, and in a couple months, this'll all be behind you. C'mon, Fiona's got bingo at the church. Let's go to Alex Eng, and I'll tell you about the will."

At dinner, Eddie said that my father had been optimistic when he told my mother that he'd hit the million-dollar mark. Most of his net worth was the result of a temporary jump in the stock market. He had left about 70 percent of that amount with his life insurance, and Emma had invested most of it in bonds and blue-chip stocks that paid a nice dividend.

Somewhere between Eddie's mentioning that my approximate annual income would be twenty-six grand, more than enough for me to get by, and that I'd inherit all the money when I was thirty, my attention wandered and, not for the first time, I wondered if Eddie had been more to Emma than a casual friend. Thinking about my grandmother in that way didn't improve my appetite, and I put down my spare rib.

"Not hungry?" Eddie asked.

Unsure how to ask him such a personal question, I poured tea into my cup.

"Spit it out, boyo."

I avoided his eyes by staring at the dish of duck sauce. "Why did Emma put you in charge of her estate? You and her, you were friends, but why would she—"

"Jesus, I don't know whether to laugh or crack you one."

"Do I get a choice?"

Eddie laughed. "Yeah, you could get yourself a girlfriend like I keep saying so you'd have other things to think about. But listen, Michael."

Extending his hand across the booth, Eddie tapped me under the chin. I looked up.

"You figure your grandmother had an easy life? Losing her son, working at the candy store, taking care of you?"

"I guess not."

"You're damn right not. And did you ever hear her complain?"

"No."

"Me either. And I admired her. So when she asked me to be her executor, I was flattered. And even if she didn't ask, I would've looked after you. You're a good boy—when you're not dreaming up stupid questions. So I promised Emma, and I ain't breaking that promise. Which is why you're going to Munich until I know you'll be safe here."

I had been on the fence about going to Germany. Maybe if Beryl was still around, I would've argued with Eddie, but there was nothing to keep me at home. Whatever Eddie's relationship with my grandmother—and I mostly believed him—he was too fond of her to lie about my needing to get out of South Orange. Besides, the idea of something new was exciting. If my radio gig in Munich dragged on past New Year's, maybe Rollie and Birdman could visit, and we could travel around Europe. Meanwhile, Eddie would take care of the bastard who shot Emma, and then I could come home.

The next two days passed in a blur. I did a final show at WSOV, telling the audience that I was off on an adventure and promising to speak to them again soon.

It was not a promise that I'd keep.

Part IV

11

Munich, West Germany
October 5, 1964

Four Freedoms Radio had booked me into the Henrik Ibsen. According to
an engraved brass sign in German and English above the key boxes, the
hotel had been renamed thirty years earlier to honor the Norwegian play-
wright who had written *Hedda Gabler* there in 1890. The elevator was out
of order, and the doorman, who doubled as a bellhop, offered to assist me.
He was an elderly, shrunken man in a top hat, cutaway coat, and striped
trousers, and I didn't have the heart to let him carry my luggage. After
giving him ten dollars in deutsche marks, I grabbed my bags and followed
him up three flights of stairs. The walls of my room were covered with saffron wallpaper blotched with water stains, and there was a window above
a courtyard hemmed in by piles of rubble—the handiwork, I assumed, of
American and British bombers.

I was exhausted from my trip, but it was the middle of the afternoon, too
early for sleep, so I explored the neighborhood, and when it began to rain,
I ducked into a café for a hamburger and a Coke. On the barstools, young
men and women—students from the University of Munich, I guessed—
were staring up at the radio on a shelf behind the bar. The broadcast was
in German, and although I'd memorized a batch of phrases from a Ber-
litz book, I couldn't understand it. So when my waiter, bald and heavyset,
brought the bill, I pointed at the radio. *"Was ist das?"*

"*Der Prozess in Frankfurt am Main.*"

"I don't understand. *Ich verstehe nicht. Sprechen Sie Englisch?*"

"The trial. Guards from *das Todeslager.*"

"*Todeslager?*"

He sighed deeply. "Camps for death. Guards from Auschwitz. *Verstehen Sie* Auschwitz?"

"*Ja.*" That word I knew. At Beth El, I had a Hebrew-school teacher, Mrs. Tarski, a spindly Polish immigrant with long white hair and a heavy accent. It was common knowledge that she'd survived Auschwitz, but her eight-year-old students would sooner have asked Mrs. Tarski about her bra size than her internment. Nor would Mrs. Tarski want to scare us by bringing up such horrific business, though whenever she raised her left hand to write on the blackboard, I felt frightened by the numbers tattooed on her veiny forearm. I didn't ask my parents or Emma about the tattoo. They never discussed the war, and the only exposure I had to it was via Birdman Cohen's father. He had fought in Europe, and his Silver Star was hanging in a frame on the wall behind the Ping-Pong table in the basement rec room. One Rosh Hashanah, when Birdman and I were in seventh grade, we were talking baseball with his dad outside Beth El before services while Mr. Cohen smoked a Camel. A young guy I didn't recognize drove into the parking lot in a black Mercedes-Benz two-seater with the top down. Mr. Cohen started shouting that the ignorant prick should go park his Kraut-mobile somewhere else. The driver ignored the shouts until Mr. Cohen was halfway to the Benz, flinging his lit cigarette into the beige leather interior, and the guy peeled out of the lot.

"The trial is for the bad apples," the waiter said, his accent thick and grating. "So the *Juden* stop accusing all *Deutschen.*"

My indignation at hearing him say *Juden* blindsided me, because I hadn't even reacted that way when kids told Jew jokes in school. By now, three years after the testimony of Adolf Eichmann's accusers had been televised around the world, I'd assumed that Germans would be embarrassed to blame Jews publicly for anything. Maybe the waiter thought that hanging Eichmann had absolved the rest of Germany.

At my hotel, I bought a copy of the European edition of the *New York Herald Tribune*. Buried in the back of the paper, across from a Red Smith column lamenting that the Mets had lost over a hundred games for the third straight season, was an article about the twenty-two former members of the SS—out of the estimated six to eight thousand assigned to Auschwitz—who were being tried for murder. A survey revealed that more than half of the German population detested the trials and opposed further prosecutions. A member of the Bundestag, the West German parliament, was quoted as saying that the hour had arrived for West Germans, and their brothers and sisters trapped in the Soviet-controlled prison of East Germany, to understand that "we were all victims of Hitler." This was why, he said, the Bundestag should vote against extending the statute of limitations for Nazi crimes, which would prevent any trials after 1965.

We were all victims of Hitler. . . .

I read that sentence over and over again, and I was still thinking about it much later, when I put down the paper and dozed off.

In the packet that the Four Freedoms Committee had mailed to me, I was instructed to be outside the hotel at nine thirty A.M. I'd be picked up and driven to the station, where I was to meet Taft Mifflin in his office on the second floor. I dressed in my deejay outfit—a Levi's Trucker Jacket, white shirt, black knit tie, and Jack Purcell sneakers with that nice blue smile on the toe cap. I picked up the rust-colored V-neck sweater Emma had bought me. She'd been gone less than a month, so the tears filling my eyes were to be expected, but rubbing the wool between my fingers I felt guilty, because we'd had one of our rare fights over the sweater. It was a December evening, and I was leaving to do my radio show when Emma came out of the kitchen with the sweater in her hand. "I bought this for you. Put it on."

I was suddenly furious. "I'm old enough to dress myself."

"Who says?"

That was Emma making a joke, and I stood there with no explanation for my fury beyond my struggle to feel like a grown-up.

"You youngsters want to be stupid—by me that's A-okay. But, Mishka, isn't it better to be stupid and warm than stupid and cold?"

"Not necessarily," I replied, and left without the sweater.

Now, I was ashamed of the teenage stubbornness that had prevented me from accepting the gift. If I'd known more about Emma, it might have occurred to me that for my grandmother, born in the Russian empire soon after the century turned, dressing for winter was a matter of life or death.

I took off my jean jacket and slipped on the sweater.

"Sorry, Emma," I said.

12

Four Freedoms Radio was located in a muddy field outside Munich, and I was driven there in a Volkswagen bus with a guard in the passenger seat: a man with a shaved head, aviator sunglasses, and a submachine gun across his lap. The station was housed in an elongated four-story building that had all the charm of a dog-food factory. The one bright spot was a large head-and-shoulders portrait of President Franklin Delano Roosevelt on a wall with raised brass words below it:

We look forward to a world founded upon four essential
   human freedoms.
The first is freedom of speech and expression.
The second is freedom of every person to worship God in
   his own way.
The third is freedom from want.
The fourth is freedom from fear.

   FDR, State of the Union Address, January 6, 1941

"Come in, come in," Taft Mifflin said as I knocked on the frosted glass of his open door.

He was sitting behind a wooden desk in a short-sleeve white shirt and skinny black tie. We shook hands, and after I sat across from him in a folding chair and he inquired about my flight and the hotel, I told him everything was swell and blurted out, "Have you heard anything about my grandmother's murder?"

"I've made more calls, and I'm waiting to hear back."

"Who was the guy in the VW with the Grease Gun?"

Taft grinned as if I were inquiring about a sideshow at a county fair. "When the war ended, Munich was occupied by us and attracted refugees from Eastern Europe who hated living under the Communists. Three million East Germans ran away to West Berlin. That's why Khrushchev put up the Wall. But he couldn't do a thing about Munich, so the Soviet propaganda machine denounces the city as the Center of Subversion."

"Because refugees came here?"

"No, because we broadcast the Western take on the news and commentary and music behind the Iron Curtain—anything to undermine those bastards—and some of the émigrés get on the radio to say the Kremlin and its Communist bloc puppets are no better than Nazis."

Taft removed his charcoal-gray suit coat from the back of his chair and put it on. "Ten years ago, before I got here, the Kremlin sent KGB agents to strangle a Four Freedoms employee and dump another one in the Isar River. Security guards were hired, and the KGB backed off. But a few years later, a KGB agent—with Khrushchev's approval—assassinated a couple of the Soviet's Ukrainian critics in Munich. He used a cyanide-gas gun."

"Sounds like a Rube Goldberg contraption."

Taft opened a drawer and placed a 5x7 black-and-white photo on the desk. "It's too simple for Rube, and the KGB is proud as hell of it. Take a look."

I leaned forward. The gas gun appeared to be a six-inch metal tube with a lever on top.

Taft said, "Point it at the target's face, press the trigger and gunpowder ignites a cyanide capsule. The vapor works fast, and whoever finds the body figures it was a heart attack. We learned about it because the assassin got so disgusted with his KGB handlers he defected to West Berlin. The émigrés trumpeted the defection on the radio. The Kremlin hated the negative publicity, so they called off their dogs and concentrated on using their transmitters to fill the air with signals that jam our programming. But our employees still feel safer with the guards, even though there's nothing to worry about."

Ever since I was a kid, when somebody—usually my father—told me not to worry, I worried even more. That the person reassuring me at the moment probably worked for the CIA didn't lessen my anxiety, nor did the sheet of paper that Taft slid across the desk. "Put your John Hancock on this, and I'll give you the ten-cent tour."

There was one sentence on the paper: *I, (the undersigned) pledge that I will not reveal any involvement of the United States government in the operation of Four Freedoms Radio.*

I said, "At Eddie's, you told me Four Freedoms is a private company."

"It is. But the funding is from different sources and—" Taft gave me a ballpoint pen. "Don't worry."

I signed on the dotted line. And I worried.

Taft introduced me to program executives, secretaries, and announcers. He was fluent in Russian, but spoke with a hesitant formality and apologized for it, saying that he'd learned the language after returning from the war and enrolling at the Russian Institute in Manhattan. I was fretting about KGB assassins and beginning to think that coming to Munich was a mistake when Taft mentioned the German custom of *zweites Frühstück*, the second breakfast, and led me to the cafeteria. The Formica tables were crowded, and my outlook was improved by white sausages, soft pretzels dipped in sweet mustard, and a bottle of Franziskaner Weissbier, a locally brewed wheat beer with a pleasant bittersweet taste and enough alcohol to calm my nerves.

I asked Taft: "Is Four Freedoms reporting on the Auschwitz trial?"

He asked me how I heard about it, and I told him about the article in the *Herald Tribune*, and my waiter's anger about the Jews slandering his country. The West Germans, Taft said, were having trouble overcoming their past, and the trials embarrassed them. They didn't like the big fish being tried at Nuremberg or the guards from Auschwitz and Bergen-Belsen that were tried and hanged in Lower Saxony or the American military court trying the leaders of the Einsatzgruppen—the SS death squads—sick bastards who liked murdering old men, women, children.

Even having seen Emma with blood staining her blouse, I couldn't conjure up a vision of the millions of innocent victims, and it was disconcerting, knowing that Taft was telling the truth about the death squads yet feeling incapable of comprehending it.

"Is America still chasing war criminals?" I asked.

Taft removed a pack of Lucky Strikes and a Zippo lighter from a pocket of his suit coat and offered me one. I shook my head.

"Smart. Surgeon General swears these'll kill you." He lit the Lucky, then pocketed the lighter. "The United States no longer has any jurisdiction. We can extradite them, but—"

"But?"

"Germany surrendered, and we planned to denazify it. No dice. Too damn many of them. Over forty million. Half the country, if you count groups like the Hitler Youth and League of German Girls. And that doesn't include the businessmen who didn't join but got rich on slave labor or by stealing from Jews. The East German press still goes on about West Germany being lousy with Nazis, and they're not wrong. Right here in Bavaria, over eighty percent of the state judges and prosecutors belonged to the party."

Taft flicked the ash of his cigarette into the glass ashtray. "We knew Stalin was going to be a pain in the ass, so we hired ex-Nazis to help us fight the SOB. East Germany was better about rounding them up. The Kremlin insisted. Understandable. The Soviets lost over twenty million, and they won't be done counting their dead till the next century."

"Will the Bundestag really let the statute of limitations expire?"

"Most of their constituents want the trials to stop, so they might. And some in our government support ending the trials. Their view: If we go to war with the Russians, we'll need the West Germans, and they'll be stronger, more confident, with Hitler a faint memory." Taft gazed down at the blackened cigarette butts in the ashtray. "I don't know if that's true, but Four Freedoms is a guest in West Germany and we avoid that particular debate."

He puffed on his Lucky, the smoke wreathing his narrow face and pointy chin. Taft seemed to be there and not be there, a man you wouldn't pick out of a crowd or remember except perhaps for his eyes, which were the somber shade of steel shavings.

"Here's what I do know," he said. "The price for West Germany's support was to leave mass murderers alone, free to collect their pensions and die in their sleep. But there are people who don't want anyone forgetting the Nazis' crimes. Ever."

A frog-eyed man was clomping toward us. He had almost no hair on top and a grizzled mass of curls growing like wings from the sides of his head. When he reached our table, he said with a Russian accent, "Zis your American deejay?"

"Yes, indeed," Taft replied, his tone jovial. "Mikhail Dainov, meet Konstantin Stasevich. He's your program director."

I stood and extended my hand. Konstantin, who evidently was unacquainted with deodorant, eyed me as if I were pointing a pistol at him, and said to Taft, "You vill destroy the Kremlin vith nigger and Jew music? Sure—and maybe my asshole will grow ears."

Konstantin went back out the way he came in.

"One of your free thinkers?" I asked.

"We're working on him."

13

"Heeet eeet!" That was how my producer, Dmitry Lukin, a twenty-year-old émigré from Moscow, pronounced, "Hit it!" Through the soundproof glass that separated the studio from the control room, I could see him, a hot-blooded Beatles freak with a mop top and black collarless suit, bouncing around in his chair.

Through my headphones I heard Dmitry lower the volume on "Midnight in Moscow," which was my cue to start talking: "You're listening to 'Polnoch v Moskve' on Four Freedoms Radio. *A vot i ya*—Here I am, Mikhail Dainov, Bezumnyy Russkiy—the Mad Russian. Spinning sides for the coolest cats in Sovietville."

Deejaying in Munich was easier than in South Orange. Dmitry cued up the records and handled the audio board, and my show was taped instead of live. Every weekday, after scouring teletype reports from the Associated Press, United Press International, and Reuters for humorous tidbits, I sifted through an extensive collection of old and new 45s and albums, then wrote out a playlist and began recording programs—two hours for Sunday through Friday, and three hours for Saturday evening. At WSOV, the best of my patter had been in English, since wordplay in Russian was beyond me. Nevertheless, Taft informed me, research indicated that upward of 80 percent of my potential audience had either studied English in school or picked up some through the movies, radio, or records smuggled into the Soviet Union.

"Stick to fifty-fifty Russian/English and use short sentences so listeners can catch them through the jamming," Taft said, and instructed me to spice up my show with slang to give it a "Made in America" pizzazz—like Levi's and Pepsi-Cola—that appealed to young Russians.

No sweat, I told him. I threw some into the opening and signed off with "This is the Mad Russian, saying, 'Later, gators.'"

Taft was pleased; Konstantin Stasevich, my official boss, was not. On my second day, Dmitry and I were talking in the studio when Konstantin flung open the door. "Dainov, you must read stories from the TASS teletype and tell the children that the news agency of the Soviet government publishes lies."

"I can't read Russian." Neither my father nor Emma had offered to teach me, and I saw no reason to learn. So much for my career as a fortune-teller.

Konstantin snapped, "*Ty durak!*" meaning that I was a moron. Then he demanded that I open my show with a song that he himself had written and that served as the station's standard lead-in, "March of the Four Freedoms," which sounded like an unhappy marriage between a military anthem and a dirge.

"Fifteen hours of that monkey noise," he said, "you can for one minute have real music."

"Not if we don't want our audience to fall asleep," Dmitry said in Russian, because his English mostly consisted of "Hit it," Beatles lyrics, and my on-air slang.

Konstantin started arguing with him, but when Dmitry called him a *kastrat*—a man with no balls—Konstantin spit at him and stormed out.

Taft told me to ignore the program director, which was fortunate because Dmitry and I were locked in a battle over my playlists. The station had the albums *Please Please Me*, *With the Beatles*, and *A Hard Day's Night*. I was a huge Beatles fan, but when Dmitry pushed me to play all three albums on every show, I said, "*Nyet*."

"Besides your bad taste, why not?"

Because, I replied, my listeners were accustomed to doo-wop and early rockers, and I wanted to stick with that, shoehorning in some new tunes I liked: the Beatles, of course, but also Roy Orbison's "Oh, Pretty Woman" and "She's Not There" by the Zombies, to name just two.

"*Govnyuk!*" he said.

Emma had used that word; it meant shithead. According to my grandmother, it was rumored that Vladimir Lenin used the same word to describe anyone who disagreed with him.

Dmitry was relentless and even pulled a switcheroo on me, spinning "If I Fell" when I'd written "Silhouettes" by the Rays on the playlist. I let it go. Dmitry did bear more than a passing resemblance to Ringo—small and thin with a prominent nose and a hangdog expression that was oddly paired with a perpetual zany smile—but I doubted this explained his obsession. Taft had mentioned that Dmitry had been in West Germany for only three months, and I wondered how a Soviet kid had become so fixated on a British group. Curious, and hoping to end the playlist war, I invited him to have dinner with me.

The desk clerk at my hotel recommended the Hofbräuhaus, and when Dmitry and I arrived, an oompah band was going at it—a tuba, trombone, and clarinet slugging it out with an accordion while patrons swayed drunkenly on the benches and drank from their *Masskrüge*, the dimpled glass steins that held over a quart of beer.

"Too loud," I said.

Dodging three waitresses in colorful bodices and skirts, all of them miraculously carrying ten steins of lager, we went out to a walled garden. It was so quiet in the garden, I could hear water gurgling in the fountain with a granite lion crouched on top. A stringy waitress, her silver-blue hair in tiny pigtails, brought us menus. She was older than the ones inside—old enough to remember the war—because when Dmitry ordered roast chicken in Russian, she looked at me as if she'd fallen in a pool and couldn't swim. I repeated Dmitry's request in my phrase-book German and said that I'd have the same.

"You enjoy scaring people?" I asked after the waitress had gone.

"I only speak Russian, and the language scares Germans. Not that I care. My father lost his legs fighting Fritzes."

I recalled my father saying that the Russians referred to the war as Velikaya Otechestvennaya Voyna—the Great Patriotic War. But I didn't hear about it in school until eleventh grade, when my world history teacher mentioned that the Red Army had lost over eight million soldiers, and that Stalin had been indifferent to the suffering of his people. I asked Emma about it, and she replied, "Stalin was no sweetheart. Now go study for your test." But we had no tests about Stalin or his army. Movies like *The Young Lions* and *The Longest Day*, along with the TV show *Combat!* and *Sgt. Rock* comic books, taught me everything I was expected to know about World War II—America had done civilization a favor and kicked Hitler's ass. With the Cold War in full poisonous flower, I understood why nobody wanted to trumpet Soviet achievements or bring up our former alliance. Yet after seeing the waitress's response to Dmitry, I started thinking about those omissions and the Germans who wanted the war-crimes trials to stop, and it struck me that everyone gets to write their own past—winners and losers and liars alike.

Dmitry asked, "Was your father in the army?"

"He tried to enlist, but his eyesight was terrible."

Dmitry chuckled, but it was off-key, as if he were holding his outrage at bay. "My father jokes that Comrade Stalin and General Zhukov lost so many soldiers they sent the blind to fight."

"Is your father still alive?"

"Oh, yes. He has much to live for. Every May he puts on his uniform and medals and goes to Red Square with his old comrades to celebrate Victory Day—the anniversary of our triumph over Germany. He is a real magician, my father."

"A magician? Like he pulls rabbits out of hats?"

"Like he makes vodka disappear."

Without glancing at either of us, the waitress brought our beers and took off.

Dmitry raised his glass. "To your health."

I returned his toast and sipped my beer. Dmitry was also an accomplished magician, and he made over a pint of lager disappear before setting his stein on the table.

"So how did you learn about the Beatles in Russia?"

"In my business. *Rok na kostyakh*."

"Rock on bones?"

Dmitry reached into a pocket of his suit coat, then gave me a disk the size and shape of a 45 record, only thinner and with a much smaller hole in the center. The disk had a shadowy picture of a rib cage on it.

"Is this an X-ray?"

"Was. Now it is the Beatles' 'I Saw Her Standing There.' Rock on bones, understand?"

I nodded. "What I don't understand is how you copied the songs."

"My friends built machines. A gramophone with an extra stylus connected to another gramophone to cut a groove. You cannot get vinyl in Russia, so we use X-rays. My mother is a doctor at Kremlin Hospital; I was an orderly there and removed X-rays from trash cans. Then I cut them into circles and burned in holes with cigarettes. One of my friends had a brother who was a sailor and could get albums from England. We copied the songs, and I sold them to university students. I earned six times my salary as an orderly."

I handed him the disk, and Dmitry, his face glum, slid it into his pocket. "I carry it to remember home and my mother."

"Why did you leave?"

A logical question, but by asking it, I got a peek at the paranoia that was the hallmark of the Soviet image—from Khrushchev grousing to American reporters about the nefarious forces that prevented him from visiting Disneyland to the antics of Boris and Natasha, the kooky spies on *Rocky and His Friends*.

Glancing over his shoulder, as if the couple getting up from the table behind us were eavesdropping, Dmitry didn't speak until they had gone. "The police started arresting people for making and selling rock on bones."

"Counterfeiting records is also illegal in America."

There was a mix of exasperation and contempt on his face. "It is the music that is illegal," he said, and explained that Soviet leaders considered rock 'n' roll, and the dances that went with it, a threat to society and ordered the police to crack down on the peddlers by using informers from the Komsomol—the Young Communist League. As he spoke, I recalled the Saturday nights at Don's Drive-In, every parking slot filled, the charbroiled burgers on the car-window trays scenting the breeze, and radios tuned to WABC with Cousin Brucie spinning Dion, the Shirelles, and the Four Seasons, when my biggest concern was getting Beryl home by curfew.

"I sold a song to one of those Komsomol farts. I would have been arrested except Kremlin Hospital is for Communist Party *nomenklatura*, and my mother is a surgeon for these big shots. She removed the police chief's gallbladder, and one day he tells her my name is on a list and it would be wise for me to leave Moscow. My mother has an aunt working in the Soviet embassy in Warsaw and she got me a visa for Poland."

Dmitry drank, then wiped his lips with his coat sleeve. "On my short-wave at home I used to listen to your broadcasts from WSOV. And I wanted to put rock in the air instead of on bones. I told my great-aunt I wished to tour East Germany, and she made arrangements. In Moscow, we knew about a farmer north of Berlin who would drive you across the border for two hundred U.S. dollars. I hitchhiked to Neubrandenburg and walked nine kilometers to his farm. I was happy that he spoke a little Russian. Then he doubles the price—once, he says, because I look desperate and twice because the Red Army had set fire to Neubrandenburg."

Dmitry clammed up as our waitress delivered our chicken with sides of potato salad. He watched her walk away. "What could I do? I had four hundred eighty U.S. I had bought on the street in Moscow. I paid him. He had a truck with an open cargo area covered with a tarp. I crawled under the tarp, and he shoveled dried cow shit over me. There were holes in the floor so I could breathe, but do you know how heavy that much cow shit is?"

I couldn't help it: I started laughing, and Dmitry joined in. "I was glad my Moscow friends were not there to make fun of me. But then the truck stopped, and I heard the driver and another man yelling in German. Horns were honking. I was sure we were at the border, and I was scared. If they caught me, it was prison for three years."

"You risked three years for rock 'n' roll?"

"For Beatles in particular. You would not risk it?"

"I didn't have to choose." I stared at the last of the foam dissolving in my stein, and Dmitry asked if I'd lost my appetite. I shook my head, amazed at what he'd done, and after deciding that I would've given up deejaying and listening to music to avoid jail, I felt disappointed in myself.

Dmitry studied my face. "Cheer up, Misha. My story has a happy ending. The farmer got me through to a village. I hitched a ride to Munich and spoke to Taft Mifflin. I was hired, he got me the necessary documents for West Germany, and now you are my friend."

"I am. And I was thinking we should play more Beatles."

"*Da*," Dmitry said, smiling. "A very good idea."

14

By my second week, I started doing a Khrushchev send-up.

One morning, I pulled out a 45 of Sam Cooke's "Twistin' the Night Away" from a rack on the studio wall, and Dmitry said, "Khrushchev hates the Twist. He says it causes drunkenness, sexual perversion, murder, and farting on trains."

"Farting?"

Dmitry flashed one of his grins. "I added that. But he hates dancing. My mother told me she heard stories about how Stalin used to humiliate Khrushchev by forcing him to squat and do the gopak, the Cossack dance, for their comrades."

"Cool. Then I'll teach him some new moves."

I dug out the original recording of "The Twist" by Hank Ballard and the Midnighters, and Chubby Checker's cover of it, and Joey Dee and the Starliters' "Peppermint Twist" and "Twist and Shout" by the Beatles. Dmitry spun the records while I instructed Khrushchev on how to swing his arms and rotate his hips. "Very good, Comrade. But you have to move your feet."

Dmitry suggested that Khrushchev's wife, Nina, should join in, and recruited Konstantin's secretary, a giggly brunette who supplied Nina's voice. "Shake it, Nika," she said. "Come now! You dance like a duck with rheumatism."

We taped seven variations of the Twist lesson. Twice I invited Wilma and Fred Flintstone to the dance, informing my audience that they were twisting on a table with the Khrushchevs, and I had the Soviet premier let loose with a maniacal yowl, followed by Fred Flintstone hollering, "Yabba dabba doo!"

They were mildly amusing bits, and I didn't give them another thought until Friday when Dmitry and I arrived at the studio. Konstantin, holding a teletype page in his hand, threw his arms around me, nearly asphyxiating me with his BO, and exclaimed, "That son-of-a-whore Khrushchev is out! You are the straw that broke his back!"

Releasing me, Konstantin went down the hall, waving the page as if it were a winning ticket in the Irish Sweepstakes.

Dmitry was laughing. "Do you think our boss believes this?"

"Everyone needs reasons," I said.

––––––––––

I received some compliments on the parody, though nothing to rival the praise from our program director. Taft had been out of town, so I didn't hear from him until the next week, when he buzzed the studio and requested that I come to his office.

"Spoke to Julian Rose and your pal Eddie last night," Taft said. "South Orange cops arrested somebody for a stickup at"—he glanced at a yellow legal pad—"Bruce's Pharmacy."

"That's down the block from our candy store. They're nice people at Bruce's. Anyone hurt?"

"No, a detective was filling a prescription and got the drop on the guy. Some crackpot in a Lone Ranger costume: white hat, black mask, pearl-handle pistols. They'll check if the slugs match." Taft looked away, retrieving a pack of Luckies from under the manila folders fanned out across the desktop. "Eddie will be in touch about the ballistics. And he had a couple messages for you. One, don't be scared to use your American Express card, there's plenty of dough in your account. And you should get yourself a girlfriend."

I wasn't opposed to dating, but in my off-hours I wandered the city with my sketch pad and pencils, stopping to draw the elaborate Gothic door carvings or the manicured beauty of the Englischer Garten. I'd never thought about being an artist, though I'd been drawing for as long as I'd been listening to music. In Munich, drawing helped to distract me from wondering why anyone would murder Emma, which often kept me up at night. Before flying to Germany, I'd gone through her filing cabinet in the basement—envelopes of canceled checks, phone bills, electric bills, tax bills, and bills from Sweets—and I hadn't seen one slip of paper that remotely resembled a clue. I doubted the Lone Ranger nut had shot Emma: robbers steal things and nothing had been taken from Sweets. My best guess was still that the shooting was connected to the bookie operation in the back room, but Eddie had dismissed that theory, and he was the one person in the world that I trusted.

Tapping one end of a Lucky Strike on his desk, Taft said, "Konstantin tells me you and Dmitry are going to the ceremony at Dachau."

At noon, a convent for Carmelite nuns was being dedicated on the grounds of the concentration camp by the archbishop of Munich. "Konstantin insisted we go. I didn't peg him as a Catholic."

"He's not. But Konstantin likes us to play up Dachau. The East Germans can't go to the camp, and any ceremony means a lot to some folks in the Soviet Union. The SS executed six thousand prisoners from the Red Army there. Took the POWs straight from the train to the rifle range and used them for target practice."

It was hard for me to picture six thousand people. I recalled my high school graduation, all of us in the middle of the football field, and that was only six hundred.

Taft lit the Lucky. "You wouldn't believe how many people show up for these things. Dignitaries and representatives from international survivor associations, but also former camp inmates from all around the world."

"You've been to the camps?"

"I have." He dragged on the cigarette, deepening the creases around his eyes and mouth, which made him appear less like a chem teacher and more like a soldier with bad memories. "And I need you and Dmitry to do me a favor today—take it easy on Konstantin."

"Konstantin and I are buddies now."

Taft smiled or, more accurately, exhibited his rendition of a smile—a grimace with a tenuous upturn of his lips. "So I hear, but if he gets on you two, cut him some slack. His brother was one of the POWs the SS used for a target."

15

The school bus that ferried the radio-station employees to Dachau passed through a forest straight out of "Hansel and Gretel" and stopped in a parking lot. I hadn't seen so many cars and buses since the sellout at Shea when Koufax was pitching for the Dodgers. A crowd was inching out of the lot to the dedication site, and people were carrying signs on poles with the names of their cities on them: *Brooklyn, Cleveland, Sydney, London, Jerusalem.* Konstantin, who had tried and failed to tame the frizzy wings of his hair with pomade, gave Dmitry a pole sign with *Four Freedoms Radio* printed on it and said, "Follow us!"

Spotting an arrow-shaped ground marker pointing toward a museum, I ambled off in a different direction. Other than a gray-haired woman dozing in a chair, I was alone in the building and inspected the displays of photographs: prisoners in striped pajamas lined up on roll-call square, their heads shaved; SS officers posing at attention, the Nazi emblems of an eagle clutching a swastika in its talons and the spooky skull and crossbones visible above the visors of their hats; American soldiers from the 42nd Infantry (Rainbow) Division filing past a gate bearing the slogan *Arbeit Macht Frei*; and row upon row of naked emaciated corpses stacked on the ground like towers in the skyline of hell.

Moving on, I passed through an actual gas chamber, with pipes along the ceiling and stone walls with phony showerheads; then two other rooms, one for undressing, the other for warehousing the dead; and the crematorium with low redbrick ovens that looked like they belonged in an old-fashioned bakery except for the stretchers sticking out of them. How could a human being sit at a drafting table designing an assembly line to turn innocents to ash and not drown in revulsion? When he completed his drawings, did he run to show them to his colleagues, accepting their congratulations and adjourning to a beer hall where they would toast him while an oompah band provided a celebratory soundtrack?

Queasy, dazed, I left the museum, heading for an open space bordered by a chain-link fence topped with rusty barbwire. A few yards before the fence was a trench with a grass floor and sides of concrete, and beyond the trench you could see the woods through the fence, spruces, firs, and birches as white as bone against the steel-blue sky—and the leaves were nearly gone from the chestnuts, a yellow fire dying in the wind.

Emma was a student of trees. Sometimes on Sundays when I was young, we'd walk to South Mountain Reservation, and after I fed the deer behind the wire enclosure, she'd tell me the names of the trees in Russian: Sosna *is the pine, Mishka.* Dub *is the oak.* I felt better, recalling those afternoons with my grandmother, and I became aware of a murmuring—the echo of my own memory, I thought, because it was the Mourner's Kaddish, which frequently came to mind when Emma popped into my head.

Yisgadal v'yiskadash sh'mei rabbaw. . .

Twenty yards away, I noticed an old man in a chesterfield overcoat and black fedora, with one hand on the crook of a cane, rocking back and forth on the edge of the trench, chanting the prayer. By the third line, he was weeping, and by the fourth he had dropped his cane and began to wobble. Afraid that he'd topple into the trench, I hustled over to him. His hat had fallen off, his wisps of white hair wild in the wind, and he was on one knee, sobbing.

I put a hand under his left arm. "Let me help you."

"Genickschuss!" he yelled, pulling away from my grip and glowering up at me, his watery eyes red-rimmed, his face pasty and crinkled, like wet paper dried in the sun.

Not recognizing the word, I asked, *"Was ist Genickschuss?"*

He answered in English, but I heard Germany in his voice. "You don't understand *Genickschuss*? Let me explain to you *Genickschuss*."

Forming a pistol with a thumb and forefinger, he pressed it against his neck. "Boom! Right here. I seen it. *Mein Sohn*. He a goot boy. I'm starving and he steals for me some bread. Then the guards make me stand here and watch. Boom! Now you know *Genickschuss*."

A feeling of unreality spread through me. "Please let me help you. Are you here with someone?"

The man gazed into the trench, and I imagined that he was seeing his son sprawled out across other bodies and wishing he were in the trench with them. Dead. Free from pain. "My niece. She waits for me in the museum."

I got him to his feet and put the fedora on his head, and as we crossed the roll-call square, he mumbled, "Vhy did dey make me vatch? Vasn't it enough fun for dem to kill my boy?"

Softly I said, "I don't know," and held the man's hand and listened to the gravel crunching under my sneakers.

"Where did you go?" Dmitry asked.

The dedication was over. Most of the attendees were fanning out across the grounds, though a fair number had remained behind for a press conference. In no mood to give Dmitry a recap, I said, "For a walk," as an immaculately dressed man, sporting a bowler and a handlebar mustache, stepped up to a podium and introduced himself, in German and English, as Gerhard Drux, the mayor of Dachau.

The first question was in German. While reporters wrote in their pads, photographers snapped pictures, and TV cameramen filmed, I stared at the roof lines of the houses beyond the camp and imagined a married couple inviting their new friends to dinner and the wife on the phone giving directions: *Go to the crematorium, bear left at the trench where prisoners were shot in the neck, and you're here. Oh, and do you prefer red or white wine?*

"I am aware that many of you participated in fund-raising to re-create the concentration camp as a memorial," Mayor Drux said in the flawless English of a British lord. "I do not object to honoring those who died.

Nevertheless, I am concerned that by re-creating the camp and attracting tourists to it, in the future whenever people hear *Dachau*, they will not think of our town—the medieval jewel of Bavaria—but of a Nazi prison."

Was this guy for real? Didn't he get how monstrously unique the crimes were? No, he didn't, I decided, and started snickering, a mistake since I was directly in front of the podium.

"And you are?" Mayor Drux inquired with exaggerated politeness.

Konstantin snapped, "He is Mikhail Dainov. From Four Freedoms Radio."

The anger was plain in his voice. Konstantin was well off to my left, and the mayor didn't even bother glancing at him, but stared down at me and said, "Mr. Dainov, I must say I am perplexed. You reacted as though I am telling jokes."

His civility had fermented into the patronizing chumminess of a typical politician, the type who takes a leak on your shoes and expects your vote for making it rain. And I was angered by it—and the camp and the Nazis and a guard executing a son with his father as a witness.

"It sounded like a joke. Were you saying that if they built a brewery instead of a memorial, everyone would think of Dachau as the name of a beer?"

"I did not say that. Are there any other questions?"

A woman diagonally across from me, standing with a large semicircle of people under pole signs from San Francisco, Sacramento, Los Angeles, and San Diego, piped up: "Herr Mayor Drux, you didn't fully answer Mr. Dainov."

The woman, who spoke with a faint European accent I didn't recognize, could've been a French movie actress in radiant middle age. Tall and lean, she wore a royal-blue mohair suit with a shell-pink collar. The arrogant beauty of her face had been softened by time and her short, tousled hair was as lustrous as burnished mahogany.

Mayor Drux glared at her until a beefy blond man to her right returned the mayor's glare, and then he looked at me. "You, I can hear, are an American, and Americans set our cities on fire. Innocent women and children died. But we Germans understand that it was a war and we are not persecuting you."

My anger ratcheted up a notch. "Persecuting? We're persecuting—"

The mayor, done feigning calm, raised his arms as if spurring on an orchestra toward a crescendo. "All Germans must pay for the crimes of these madmen? Would you have risked your life to save people you didn't know? Risked your children's lives? Why do you Americans expect Germans to demonstrate a fortitude that you do not have? Your country could have accepted our Jews. You chose not to and then condemn our treatment of them. Is that fair? I think not. Perhaps the Bundestag will come to its senses regarding the statute of limitations, and we can stop the recriminations and forget about trials and memorials. We can leave the past where it belongs. Then it will be a new day in Germany."

Panting from his tirade, the mayor departed without even saying *Auf Wiedersehen*. I looked across at the woman. She shrugged and smiled at me and walked away with the delegation from California following her.

16

"Are you serious?" I asked Dmitry, and set my spoon, entwined with tagliatelle in Bolognese sauce, on my plate.

"Konstantin told me."

"You believe him? He thinks our Twist routine helped Brezhnev get rid of Khrushchev."

Dmitry chuckled. "So ask our waiter. He speaks English."

We were in the side room of Osteria Italiana, where I ate dinner two or three times a week, and had brought Dmitry to repay him for all his help after work with my Russian.

When our waiter, a triple-chinned Italian who had recited the specials with the gusto of an opera singer belting out an aria, stopped by to refill our glasses with Chianti, I said, "My boss says this was Hitler's favorite restaurant in Munich."

"*Sì, signore*. In this room. Over by that window. It was Osteria Bavaria then. My wife, the one that dies. She a waitress for Hitler, Himmler, the gang a them, at the start. She say Hitler order trout in butter sauce and didn't pay his bill and never leave her nothing for service."

Mumbling about cheap sumabitches, he disappeared into the main dining area. I translated his answer for Dmitry and looked at a family with three towheaded children at Hitler's table, all of them dipping bread into plates of olive oil, and in the corner a couple as elegant as Fred and Ginger drinking martinis. At Dachau, I'd felt the horrific weight of its history pressing on me as if the force of gravity had doubled. But here, surrounded by the lively hum of conversation and the soft clink of silverware on china, I might as well have been eating eggplant Parmesan at Victor's in South Orange Village, and it was hard to conjure up a vision of Adolf Hitler dabbing a greasy flake of fish from his mustache with a napkin and assuring his acolytes that a reborn German Reich would conquer Europe.

Sitting there, I realized that history doesn't announce its approach with fireworks and marching bands. It lurks behind events as ordinary as dining out with friends in the bohemian Schwabing district of Munich. Then one day while you're minding your own humdrum business, it lands on your doorstep, an uninvited and unwanted guest, and for years afterward you wonder how it got there.

Winter was nipping at the heels of autumn, and along Schellingstrasse the cafés and beer halls were full of a delightful Friday-night noise that seeped into the street.

"*Spasibo*, Misha. I never ate Italian food. It is delicious. Do you want me to teach you some new curses?"

"Between you and Konstantin, I have plenty."

The Henrik Ibsen was five minutes away, and Dmitry's boardinghouse was ten minutes farther south. On Türkenstrasse, the shop windows were dark and lamps shone like pale stars in the windows of the apartment houses. The sidewalk was under repair and blocked by sawhorses, so Dmitry and I walked single file on the curb. Below the sign outside my hotel, the elderly doorman in his top hat was standing in a pool of neon-blue light. When I was a few steps from him, with Dmitry right behind me, he said, "*Guten Abend.*" Before I could say good evening to him, the high beams of a car parked across the street came on, blinding me. Then there was a drawn-out tinny sound. Like a jackhammer, but not as loud or deep. The doorman's hat flew off and blood spattered the revolving glass door. By reflex, I dove to the ground and heard metal chipping away at the stucco facade of the hotel, the high-pitched complaint of glass shattering, the rev-ving of an engine, the screech of tires as the car peeled away.

Then . . . silence. I was aware that someone had been firing in my di-rection yet, even though I was shaking with fear, part of me resisted that information. I glanced back to check on Dmitry, who was sitting cross-legged and unbuttoning his suit jacket. He looked up from the widening blackish-red stain on his shirt. "Mi-Mi-Misha. Am I hurt?"

The shooting had felt as if it had taken place in a frozen stretch of eternity, but now time leapt forward. With the piercing *ooh-aah ooh-ahh* of police sirens in the distance, I dashed over to Dmitry, got my hands under his arms, yanked him to his feet, hoisted him over my shoulder and, with a spurt of vomit rising in my throat, bolted past what was left of the doorman and into the lobby, where I put Dmitry on a couch and shouted at the desk clerk to call an ambulance.

"Am I—am I hurt, Misha?"

In the movies, they compressed wounds to stanch the bleeding, so lightly I pressed my palms on his stomach, feeling his blood, warm and slippery, oozing through my fingers.

"You are going to be fine," I said, another aspect of first aid I'd learned from Hollywood.

Dmitry gasped for air. "Yeah, yeah, yeah."

Without another word, Dmitry had died before the police or the ambulance arrived. On my first day of work, Taft Mifflin had given me an emergency number, and I phoned him and he instructed me to go upstairs, lock the door, pack my stuff, and wait for him.

Now, two hours later, I was sitting next to Taft in the back of a Mer-cedes with a chauffeur and an armed guard in the passenger seat, and we were going to Taft's hotel, the Regina Palast.

"Why'd someone shoot at Dmitry and me? Because he defected? Be-cause I made fun of Khrushchev?"

"The KGB's usually more subtle. Poison. Strangling. All the police told me was they picked up some shell casings from an MP 40, a German submachine gun from World War II."

"Ex-Nazis? You're joking, right?"

"The Germans manufactured over a million MP 40s, and the Russians grabbed a lot of them."

I kept picturing Dmitry on that couch in the lobby, white cloth upholstery with faded violet cornflowers, and if I hadn't been so furious at Taft and myself, I would've started crying or screaming. Dmitry had risked prison for rock 'n' roll and now he was dead, perhaps because of my stupid Khrushchev routine.

Taft said, "Julian left me a message. Your grandmother was shot with a .25-caliber pistol, and the slugs from the revolvers of that Lone Ranger nut didn't match."

"What a shock. That nut was a robber and Sweets didn't get robbed."

"Could be the shooting here is connected to the shooting there."

"This has to do with Emma?"

"I said *could be*."

"I'm going home."

"Bad idea, Michael, until we know what's going on."

"You can figure it out while I'm in South Orange."

"You think you're bulletproof in New Jersey?"

I'd scrubbed my hands in my room, but they were still sticky with blood.

Taft lit a Lucky. "You're not. We'll tell the press you were wounded and are recovering at University Hospital. We'll work it out with hospital security and the police and station some people there. If anyone shows to finish the job, we'll find out why."

"And where am I going to be?"

"At my hotel for a week. With a guard. Then you'll be with a friend of mine for a while. You'll be safe with him."

"Eddie told me I'd be safe with you."

"Sometimes things don't work out, do they?"

"There's an insight. Why'd you bring me to Munich? To star in my own spy movie?"

"Calm down, Michael."

"Who's this friend?"

"Der Schmuggler."

"The Smuggler? Where am I going with a guy named the Smuggler?"

"Russia."

"Are you kidding?"

Taft lowered his window to let out the smoke. "I never kid about Russia."

Part V

17

Otvali, Union of Soviet Socialist Republics
November 13, 1964

If you could die from paperwork, Yuli thought, eyeing the open ledgers on her U-shaped desk, I would have been dead long ago.

All morning Yuli had been cooped up in the office next to her bedroom, and her temples throbbed from the *clickety-click* of the adding machine. A truck from the port of Taganrog had been scheduled to be at the compound by 0700. But autumn brought rain, and the rain brought the *rasputitsa*, a season of mud that made the roads difficult to navigate. Russians old enough to recall the Great Patriotic War regarded the mud with some fondness, for it had impeded the calamitous progress of three million German invaders. Even so, with the truck four hours late, Yuli was thinking that the *rasputitsa* was a deluxe pain in the ass. Then her phone rang.

"*Allo*," Der Schmuggler said. "We are in Moscow and will be home tomorrow at three. Send Pavel to pick us up at the station."

The "we" included Mikhail Dainov. That American radio man, Mr. Taft Mifflin, had requested that Der Schmuggler bring Mikhail to Otvali because Munich was no longer safe for him. His cover story was that he was a distant American cousin of Der Schmuggler who planned to study Russian at Rostov State University. He would use his real name, Michael Daniels, and Der Schmuggler told Yuli that Michael was fluent in Russian, but he had warned her to speak only English to him in public. On Monday,

99

Yuli had gone to the university and, after eating lunch with Sofia and Vik-toriya, her best girlfriends from school who were currently finishing their medical training, she submitted the forms for registering a foreign student. Der Schmuggler had taken care of getting Michael a visa, then had met him in Munich, and they had traveled by train through Austria, Czechoslovakia, and Poland, crossing into the Soviet Union at Brest and riding on to Mos-cow, where they would board another train for Rostov-on-Don.

"Pavel will be there," Yuli said.

As a rule, their phone conversations were brief. Der Schmuggler's in-fluence extended from the small-time regional Communist Party officials to the almighty puppeteers behind the Kremlin walls in Moscow, an influence maintained by a system of payoffs in American dollars and *kontrabanda* designed to prevent the KGB from raiding the warehouses in the com-pound or monitoring their telephone lines. The KGB did tap pay phones in train stations and airports, and because you never knew when your allies in the party would become enemies, whenever Yuli or Der Schmuggler called home from inside the Soviet Union, they refrained from discussing any compromising information.

"You are taking your insulin?" Yuli asked.

She heard a drawn-out sigh, as if he were both puzzled and annoyed. "No less than two injections every day for the last ten years. You know that. Why do you ask?"

Yuli was stalling until she could gin up the courage to ask him about Michael, this boy who soothed her loneliness by dancing with her in the softly lit corners of her imagination. She assumed that his face radiated strength and kindness, but she couldn't draw a detailed portrait of him in her mind.

"Papka, I always check on you." To disguise her eagerness to hear a description of Michael, Yuli added as if it were an afterthought, "What does your cousin look like? I mean, I want to be able to recognize him."

"He will be with me. Do you remember what I look like?"

"You are very handsome, Papka. What about your cousin?"

Der Schmuggler chuckled. "Ah, I understand. What can I say, dear girl? He is tall and resembles the boys on your bedroom wall—the boys from the beach."

"The Beach Boys."

"Yes, the long, light hair, the nice smile. Green eyes, a poet's eyes. But also rugged-looking. A Marlboro Man, maybe a little, but no mustache or cowboy hat."

Yuli liked what she was hearing until Der Schmuggler asked her to wait a moment, and then he must have turned away from the mouthpiece because his voice was harder for her to hear when he said in English, "In a minute, Michael, I am speaking to Yuli. She wants to know if you are handsome."

"Papka!" she shouted, feeling herself blush.

Der Schmuggler spoke into the mouthpiece. "I am here."

Irritated at him for embarrassing her, Yuli replied, "Please ask Michael why your brains are in your socks," and hung up. Yuli was replacing the tape on the adding machine when the phone rang again. She considered ignoring the call, but decided that it would be more satisfying to have another chance to chastise Papka for his idiocy.

"*Allo,*" she said, and the curtness of her tone unsettled her. Der Schmuggler had a habit of teasing Yuli about boys, and it didn't really bother her, because he loved her, and she understood that it was difficult for a man who had lost his parents, seven brothers and sisters, and his fiancée during the war to watch all those boys chasing her and to speculate on when she might marry and leave Otvali. Nor was Yuli embarrassed that she was curious about Michael the deejay. She was enchanted by rock 'n' roll and the shinier aspects of American culture scorned and outlawed by the Kremlin. But her curiosity about Michael accentuated her loneliness, and the depth of it terrified Yuli. As a young girl hiding from the Nazi soldiers, Yuli was forced to accept that her parents couldn't rescue her and to renounce her feelings of desolation. Otherwise, she wouldn't have survived. And yet here she was, lonely beyond words, perplexed and vulnerable, as if she were a tortoise who had misplaced her shell.

"Yuli, it's Pyotr. You sound upset. Is this a bad time?"

"No, Petya. How are you?" She hadn't seen Pyotr since going to Dnipropetrovsk to photograph the teenage physicist who, according to Der Schmuggler, was designing the next generation of intercontinental ballistic missiles.

"I have a new job. A wonderful new job."

"Tell me."

"I will. I am coming to Otvali tomorrow to see my parents before I leave. Let me take you to dinner, and I will tell you then."

Even if Michael weren't arriving, Yuli would've been hesitant to go out with Pyotr on Saturday evening. The meal and conversation would be fine, but what he would want after dinner didn't appeal to her. Pyotr was a sweet, smart boy who had been so good to her ever since they were at Mark Twain together. Still, although Yuli had been to bed with him, she felt nothing romantic toward Pyotr, no swaying in the dark to daydream music. All the same, he was her friend, and she disliked hurting him.

"We will have a party," Yuli said. "In the Malt Shop. At eight. Like we used to. I will call Sofia and Viktoriya and tell them to bring some people, and you invite anyone you want. Papka's American cousin will be visiting. You can meet him. And I will make you a bird's milk cake. Is that still your favorite?"

"It is," Pyotr said, and she felt guilty hearing his disappointment about dinner.

Through the window, Yuli saw an olive-drab ZIL crossing the compound, a military truck that scared off the policemen who pulled over truckers on some pretext and detained them until they were given a sample of the cargo.

Yuli said, "I have work to do. See you tomorrow?"

"At eight."

"Good-bye, Petya."

"*Do svidaniya*, Yuli."

Yuli tugged on her tomato-red rubber boots, which were made in Finland and part of a shipment that came from a family of Russian smugglers living in Helsinki. The rain had stopped, and she walked through the mud past the cow and horse barns to the other side of the compound, where a few of the men employed by Der Schmuggler were unloading the ZIL and carrying boxes into one of the concrete-block warehouses.

Consulting her inventory list, Yuli checked to make sure the goods were in the boxes—cartons of Marlboro cigarettes, bottles of Canoe Eau de Cologne, and stacks of Levi's jeans. Der Schmuggler had arranged for these items through Taft Mifflin. Yuli was ignorant of the specifics. Papka thought it was safer for her not to know in the unlikely event that the authorities, in a fit of self-righteousness or an effort to increase their payoffs, summoned them for questioning. Smuggling American cigarettes and French cologne was forbidden, though the most serious offense would be the Levi's *dzhins*, which sold for as high as two hundred rubles apiece, the average monthly pay for a worker. The price was less outrageous when you factored in that you could be imprisoned or executed for smuggling Levi's. The Kremlin judged the *dzhins* to be a by-product of the moral rot foisted on civilization by the West, like their cacophonous jungle music and slithery pornographic dances, which threatened the younger generation's dedication to the sacred principles of communism.

When the driver had been paid and the shipment inventoried, Yuli went to her bedroom with bottles of Canoe for herself, Sofia, and Viktoriya. Young Soviet women preferred it to Red Moscow perfume, which had been around since the waning days of Tsarist Russia and had a cloying musky scent that, Sofia said, made her smell like her grandmother. For the next hour, in anticipation of meeting Michael, Yuli tried on clothes in front of a brass-edged floor mirror—Levi's that she had tapered herself until the denim seemed inseparable from her skin and a Breton-striped shirt, a replica of the shirt Audrey Hepburn wore in *Funny Face*, that Yuli had bought at GUM in Moscow, waiting for hours in a line that extended from the department store all the way across Red Square; then a tight dove-gray skirt, also purchased at GUM, and a short, peach-colored cardigan that Yuli had knitted; and white pedal pushers with a black turtleneck, which she had seen on Marilyn Monroe in one of the magazines that Der Schmuggler brought her from a U.S. Army base in Munich.

Unable to decide on an outfit, Yuli took the comb and brush off her dresser. Her pageboy had grown out so it spilled past her shoulders, and she parted it in the center, on the left, then on the right. None of the styles satisfied her, so she gave up and sat on her narrow steel-frame bed, looking at the collage that covered her walls: a copy of the famous painting of Lenin talking to Stalin on a veranda hanging next to a movie still of Abbott and Costello doing a gabby comedy routine, which Yuli had bought on the street in Kiev; record-album covers, ticket stubs from movies; photos of

Anton Chekhov, Allen Ginsberg, and the American actress Shirley Mac-Laine rubbing Khrushchev's bald head when the Soviet premier visited Hollywood; a Soviet poster celebrating the launch of Sputnik; and a tribute to her mother, a framed print of *The Star* by Edgar Degas, a lone ballerina in a white tutu dotted with red flowers, her arms out and left leg raised, standing center stage and on pointe in a splash of celestial light.

Yuli had been covering her bedroom walls with images since she was a child, and gazing at this visual diary was a form of relaxation for her or, to be more precise, a method for blunting her anxiety. The years prior to Der Schmuggler's finding her were like a fitful sleep broken by foggy memories of shivering with other children in a coal mine, hiking through woods and across the steppes of the Ukraine, the whine of German Stukas diving to drop their bombs, hiding in a root cellar in a dacha on the lake-shore, children crying, the yelling of German soldiers searching for them, machine-gun fire, the awful silence.

Now Yuli went to study the Beach Boys album cover of *Surfer Girl* tacked above her dresser. The boys stand in a row on the sand and hold a yellow surfboard with blue and red stripes. They wear plaid shirts and khaki pants, and the foamy ripples of the Pacific touch their bare feet. They grin for the camera, appear so joyously robust and free from the tragic tides of history, five euphoric pagans existing only in the sun-laced purity of this California moment.

Yuli wondered which boy Michael most resembled. Any of them would do, but she preferred the one on the far left, with a thick forelock falling in his eyes and a touch of irony in his grin.

After a while she picked up her comb and brush again and went to work on her hair.

18

Der Schmuggler had a great burly man's laugh, like a Jewish Santa Claus, though his beard was shorter, with more pepper in it than salt. During our train trip he laughed more than he spoke, preferring to bury his head in a book. The first night, in our private compartment, I did ask him his name, and he replied that around Otvali he was known by his Yiddish sobriquet, Der Schmuggler. Away from home, and especially on trains with border guards coming aboard to check papers and passports, he was simply referred to as Der.

At the train station in Rostov-on-Don, one of his employees picked us up in a Soviet clunker painted a shade of yellowish-green that almost persuaded me a car could contract malaria. Forty miles of potholed roads later, we went through a double, iron-spike gate set into a high redbrick wall. The house looked like a two-tier concrete wedding cake with dark strawberry frosting, and my overall impression, as I carried my bags inside, was that the place could have withstood a nuclear warhead.

We walked up a short flight of steps from the entryway to the kitchen, which was as fragrant as a bakery due to the tin sheets of rugelach a young woman with golden-brown hair was removing from the oven of a porcelain stove. The four-burner, with steel pots on top, was wedged against a white-stone wood-burning oven that took up half a wall, and adjacent to each other, they were a portrait of past and present. The woman set the braided pastries on the wooden counter next to the sink and moved gracefully across the plank floor to hug Der.

For the first time since I'd met him in Munich, he smiled and, after letting her go, said, "Michael Daniels, this is Yulianna Kosoy—Yuli."

When Der Schmuggler had mentioned her on the train, I'd envisioned a Russian peasant girl from the pages of *National Geographic*, stocky and thick-legged in a headscarf and caftan holding a milk pail in one hand and a balalaika in the other. That wasn't even close to what I saw. Her clothing could have come from the closet of an American college coed—a black cashmere sweater, tapered Levi's with rolled cuffs, and penny loafers. But at the same time there was something gloriously unusual about Yuli, her beauty both fragile and ferocious. She was small and lithe, so the generous swells and sharp curves of her body under the clingy cashmere and skintight denim appeared to belong to a different woman—earthier, far less ethereal. Her almond-shaped eyes were the same dark blue as the sky at winter dusk, and her mouth curved upward in the start of an impish grin.

I couldn't manage to spit out even the most perfunctory of greetings, because I'd never seen anyone that beautiful in person.

Yuli said, "Does the Mad Russian only talk on the radio?"

It was a moment before I realized she was speaking to me. "No."

"How very nice." She stood up on her toes and gave me a triple kiss—left cheek, right cheek, and the left again. "There will be a party tonight. Perhaps you want rest. There will be food. You can eat then."

Her English was formal and sounded faintly British, but like my grandmother she rolled her *r*'s and fought against the Russian habit of transforming *w*'s into *v*'s, *th*'s into *z*'s, and elongating *a*'s and *e*'s.

As if Der were teasing her, but with an unmistakable note of hurt, he said, "And me? Must I go to this party to eat?"

Yuli patted his shoulder as though consoling a toddler. "I will heat you some of my *zharkoe*." Yuli shifted her body toward me. "You know *zharkoe*?"

The brusqueness of her tone made it sound like an exam question. "Beef stew. I used to help my grandmother make it."

Yuli was studying me, and I was studying the brass samovar on the counter because it was a challenge not to stare at her, and I didn't want to be rude.

"Papka, have a glass of tea, and I will show Michael where he sleeps."

Yuli led me out the other side of the kitchen, up a stairway and down a dim hall to a room lit by lamps with triangular mint-green glass shades. One lamp was on a night table next to a steel-frame bed no bigger than a cot, the other on a dresser lacquered a mintier green than the lampshades. I put my suitcases on the bed and opened a door to what I thought was a closet, but it was a closet-size bathroom—white ceramic tub, sink, and a toilet with the tank up on the wall behind the commode and a pull chain dangling from it.

I was looking up at the chain when Yuli asked, "You know how to use?"

That was the first time I smiled at her. "I've been toilet-trained since I was three."

And she smiled back. "I like when you make jokes. You are the Mad Russian again."

"I'll remember that."

She hesitated, as if weighing her words. "Do—do you like my English?"

I was tempted to reply that I especially liked it when she was speaking to me, but I didn't want to scare her off. "I do."

"You will help me improve it?"

"I'll start now. American use contractions. Say, 'You'll help me.'"

"You'll help me?"

"Yes, I'll help you."

She let her eyes linger on me, and I felt as if she were having a discussion with herself and wished I could hear it.

"Enjoy your rest," Yuli said, and closed the door.

19

Frost sparkled on the paved road that ran through the compound as I walked past the manure-ripened barnyard and saw cars parked beside a building with light filling the circular windows.

I had no idea what to wear to a Soviet party, and I'd been embarrassed to ask Yuli, who had gone to set up the Malt Shop while I was shaving, so I opted for semiformal: a blue button-down, a black knit tie, chinos, an olive corduroy sport coat, and Weejuns. Not that anyone noticed me when I got there. Cigarette smoke shrouded the fifty or sixty men and women, most of them decked out like American college students or bohemians in crazy patterns and loud colors that appeared crazier and louder under the glittering teardrop bulbs embedded in the black ceiling. A reel-to-reel tape recorder sat on a stool in a corner with wall speakers on either side of it, and some couples were dancing to Connie Francis's "Where the Boys Are." Along the wall were tables with bottles of red and white wine and Russkiy Standart vodka, platters of cookies and cake, and one stacked with plates and steaming steel pots, the aroma of the beef stew triumphing over the tobacco smoke.

On the opposite side of the room, Yuli was standing in front of a mural of Red Army soldiers doing a frenzied Cossack dance by the blackened shell of a Nazi tank. She was talking to a redhead and a blonde in tight

Levi's and sweaters, and as I headed toward them, Yuli said something; they all began to laugh; and I wondered what it was about young women standing together laughing that could stop your heart.

I said hello to Yuli, and she replied, "These are my friends, Viktoriya and Sofia."

Viktoriya was the blonde, Sofia the redhead. Neither one was as beautiful as Yuli, but that was no criticism. Both had porcelain skin, big eyes that were shades of gray and green and blue, like the ocean changing color depending on the angle of the sun.

"A pleasure to meet you," I said.

The two women answered in English, saying it was a pleasure to meet me. I looked at the mural of the Russian soldiers and the ruined German tank on the wall, and Sofia said, "The three of us painted it from a photograph."

Turning to Yuli, Viktoriya said in Russian, "You were right. Your papka's cousin is a handsome boy. If he would take off his jacket and shirt, it would be fun to paint a mural of him."

Viktoriya let out a devious chuckle, and Sofia joined her. They would have been less amused if, like Yuli, they knew that I'd understood every word. I welcomed the news that Yuli thought me good-looking, but she didn't seem pleased that I was privy to that information. Her whipped-cream complexion reddened, and she attempted to explain her friends' interest in physiology by saying, "Viktoriya and Sofi are going to be doctors."

I weighed a selection of banal responses, none of which I used, because just then a round-shouldered guy in a belted trench coat and black-frame sunglasses showed up, his platinum-blond hair combed in the more restrained style of Elvis in *Viva Las Vegas*. When Viktoriya and Sofia saw him, their faces lit up, like old pals meeting at a high school reunion, and he shoved his glasses in a coat pocket and exchanged cheek kisses with them. With Yuli, he took the proprietary approach of a boyfriend, putting his hands on the sides of her arms and bending to kiss her mouth. She glanced at me—uncomfortably, I thought—before shifting to the side so his kiss landed on her ear.

Pulling away, Yuli introduced me as Michael Daniels, Papka's American cousin, who was preparing to take classes in Russian at the university.

"Pyotr Ananko," he said, extending his hand to me.

"Good to meet you."

We shook, with Pyotr studying me as though we had met before and he couldn't recall my name.

Yuli asked, "Petya, what is your new job?"

He stood up straighter, obviously proud. "I am a foreign correspondent for *Novosti*."

Viktoriya, Sofia, and Yuli broke out in a burst of congratulations. For the majority of Soviet citizens, travel to the West was neither economically feasible nor permitted by the government. Der traveled to Germany and had been to Italy and Spain, but that was because officials either wanted the goods he brought back or were paid to overlook his smuggling. From the music and dancing and Levi's and packs of Marlboros on display at the party, it was clear that younger Soviets—not just eccentrics like Dmitry— were enthralled by what was happening in the West.

Viktoriya asked, "Where will you go?"

"I will be writing about jazz, so Switzerland and Scandinavia, and perhaps the Netherlands and France. I will also review plays in London and New York. And I am going to travel through the United States to write about the Negro situation."

Pyotr glowered at me as if I'd founded the Ku Klux Klan. Like Yuli, Viktoriya, and Sofia, he was a few years older than I was, but he had one of those pale smooth faces that never seemed to age, so that if he lived to be a hundred he could still pass for a schoolboy.

He said, "Americans want Communist countries to become free and democratic, but that is not a condition they extend to all their own people."

Maybe Pyotr blamed me for Yuli sidestepping his lip lock or maybe he was a true Red commie, but with the three women looking at us, I wasn't going to let him poke me without returning the favor. "We do that so Russians like you don't feel bad about putting up the Berlin Wall or outlawing the Beatles."

Pyotr grimaced. "Are you joking or debating?"

"Both."

He raised a forefinger, and I had the feeling that I was in for a lecture on the failings of America, but before it went any further, Yuli said, "Petya, you did not taste the bird's milk cake I made for you. I am insulted. Go try a piece."

He hesitated, and more forcefully Yuli said, "Go," and as he headed for the tables, Yuli grabbed the sleeve of my sport coat.

"He's your boyfriend?" I asked.

She tugged me by the sleeve. "No need to speak of Petya. You and I will dance."

Yuli's beauty was intimidating, but dancing was one of my strong suits. For a year before my bar mitzvah, my mother insisted that we take private weekly dance lessons so as a family we could impress the guests at the fancy shindig that followed the religious service. Our instructor, the ancient Mrs. Gallagher, was an erstwhile flapper in love with the sequined dresses of the Roaring Twenties, but she put me through my paces with all the disciplined good cheer of a Marine drill instructor with gas pains. Thus when Yuli and I faced each other and clasped hands and the tape rolled into Little Richard's "Rip It Up," I planned to impress her with my jitterbug.

Except I had never danced with anyone like Yuli. She anticipated every turn, whirling in the right direction before I fully realized which way I was going. It was as though her feet weren't on the wood floor, but somehow, in defiance of gravity, I was dragging her through the air. Then Little Richard really started hammering the keys and the drummer went along for the ride until the saxophone took over, the brassy wail quickening the beat. Trying to keep up, I danced faster, but my body was out of synch while Yuli kept floating through the music, dipping, spinning, and not letting go of my hand. People had stopped dancing to watch, and if I wouldn't have looked ridiculous, I would've done the same. Under the tiny ceiling bulbs, Yuli had become a cashmere and denim blur, and as the song built to a climax, she stepped to the side, put a hand on my shoulder, hopped up, and in one dreamlike movement, rolled over my back and landed on her feet, still dancing.

"Bravo!" several couples called out when we were done.

Yuli was grinning at me. I wasn't sure why.

"Thank you," I said, and started to walk away as another song came on, the slow, romantic "Tears on My Pillow," and Yuli put her arms around my neck.

We danced, Yuli pressing herself against me, and I inhaled the clean sweet smell of Canoe, an inexpensive men's cologne that had become popular with young women. Beryl wore it in high school, and I began thinking about her, and then Yuli held me tighter, and Beryl went away, and it took every ounce of my restraint not to bend Yuli backward and kiss her. Instead, I retreated to safer ground and became a deejay.

"This is Little Anthony and the Imperials," I said.

"Interesting."

"Their first hit."

"Very interesting."

"Nineteen fifty-eight."

"Do American men talk this much when they dance?"

"Usually we sing."

I felt her chuckling against me, and after the Little Anthony falsetto faded to silence, we held on to each other. Then: "On the radio I used to like it when you said, 'Here is my heart, it is full of love.'"

"*Vot moyo serdtse, ono polno lyubvi.*"

She put an index finger to her lips. "You are not supposed to speak Russian."

"And you're supposed to use contractions."

Yuli smiled, neither happy nor sad, but something else entirely—a woman intrigued by a game that she wasn't quite sure she wanted to keep playing. "I'll do that."

We stood still, holding each other.

"We're not dancing," Yuli said with that same smile. "What will people think?"

I grinned. "That you want to paint a mural of me."

"I might, but you must let me go."

I dropped my arms, and her eyes briefly held mine before she walked off.

I was standing by the refreshment tables and downing my second *stopka* of vodka when Pyotr came over, his unbelted trench coat and half-scowl fitting accouterments for a cynical globe-trotting reporter.

"Michael Daniels, Mikhail Dainov, this makes sense," he said, taking a cigarette and matchbook from the pocket of his coat. "From what I hear on Four Freedoms, you're in the hospital."

I put the empty ridged glass on the table and wondered if Yuli had told him. No, she wouldn't say anything, but now I understood why he'd looked at me as if we'd already met.

The cigarette had a cardboard tube instead of a filter, and Pyotr put the tube in his mouth and lit it. "I recognize your voice. I've been a fan since your recorded shows from—from South—"

"South Orange Village. You want an autograph?"

He glanced toward the mural, where Yuli was standing. I'd seen partyers stop by to talk to her and noticed that some of the men pulled her toward them and aimed their kisses at her mouth. Pyotr was noticing it now, and you could see the heartache behind his scowl. I was glad not to share his pain. Yuli made me feel happy, but I figured that I wouldn't be around long enough for us to fall in love.

Pyotr let the smoke curl out of his mouth. "Yuli has a lot of dance partners."

"She likes to dance."

He grunted, a sound full of resentment and irony. "Yes, she likes to dance." Pyotr looked away from the mural. "Your secret is safe with me."

"*Spasibo.*"

"You are welcome," he said, and put on his sunglasses and walked through the party and out the door.

20

The next three weeks flew by. Yuli and I spent almost every evening together, eating dinner with Der, then adjourning to the book-lined parlor with its black-and-gold-tiled fireplace. Der had collected a vast library on his travels, and he and Yuli were compulsive readers, Der in Russian, Yiddish, German, and English, and Yuli in Russian and English. I tackled *The Rise and Fall of the Third Reich*, thinking that it would explain how hellholes like Dachau could exist. The camps were no secret in 1960 when *The Rise* was published, yet in over eleven hundred pages they were seldom mentioned, and I asked Der why he thought the author didn't include more.

He said, "In the Soviet Union, I have noticed that people resist accepting bitter truths," and then, with an ironic edge in his voice, asked, "Tell me, is it different in America?"

Good point, and I chose to explore the darker regions of the soul by switching to a translation of Dostoyevsky's *Crime and Punishment*.

Sometimes I'd put down my book and draw Der and Yuli, and when I was done, Yuli would sit on the arm of my chair and page through the pad, complimenting my sketches. I liked her being so close, her thigh brushing my shoulder, and I hoped to be alone with her after Der had gone to sleep. However, Der was as vigilant as the spinsters who chaperoned our junior high dances. Once I suggested to Yuli that we listen to music in the Malt

Shop. Her eyes widened in alarm, and Der replied without glancing up from his book, "It's too cold in there." Nor did waiting for him to go to sleep pan out. He didn't retire to his bedroom off the kitchen until we were in our rooms, and then I frequently heard him, at all hours, come down the hallway to knock on Yuli's door and ask her a question about work—an excuse, I always suspected, for him to check up on us.

———————

Yuli did finally make it into my bedroom. She had left the compound that morning and wasn't home when I went to sleep. Then something woke me up. The light in the hall was shining into my room, and I saw Yuli outlined in the doorway.

"You are awake?" she said softly.

"I think so."

She walked toward the bed.

"I missed you," she said.

"Same here."

"I didn't like it."

"Missing me?"

"Missing you."

I held up the blanket, an invitation for her to climb in.

Yuli saw the gesture, but all she was did was say "I wanted to tell you. Before I forgot."

"Forgot to tell me or forgot that you missed me?"

She giggled. "Both. Good night, Misha."

So it wasn't only Der who was in the way of our romance. Yuli herself was hesitant. That was puzzling. At the party, Pyotr Ananko, plainly one of her ex-boyfriends, had made it clear that she was no prude, and her reluctance left me wondering what was wrong with me. I had no answer, not out of modesty, but because not only did Yuli stay close to me in the evenings, on the days when she had completed her work, she asked me to have lunch with her in Otvali, a short walk down the hill from the compound.

The hustle and bustle of the town made me homesick for South Orange Village. At the north end of the main thoroughfare was a gas station, a stable, a market square with open stalls that were empty in winter, and a modest circle of a park with a statue. Farther down the street were the shops; a sandstone synagogue attached to a yeshiva and study house; a Russian Orthodox church, St. Sergius, with gold onion domes; and the redbrick Mark Twain English-language school. Food shortages, Yuli explained, were rife across the Soviet Union, but the local collective farms and state farms supplied a thriving black market, and because Der Schmuggler always had goods to trade, he made certain that the shortages were not so severe in Otvali. Women in babushkas went in and out of the shops, their netted string bags bulging with fruit, vegetables, bread, and cheese, and a few shopkeepers stood outside, munching on a pickle and waiting for anybody in the mood to chat. Young men in sheepskin hats rode their horses to the stable, then gathered in the park and drank *samogon*—Russian moonshine. Father Nikolai, the old white-bearded priest, made the sign of the cross whenever he passed anyone, including the Hasidim in their beaver hats and frock coats. Yuli said the priest, who was nearly blind, didn't want to miss any of his flock, and he believed that even Jews and Communists could use a blessing.

The nerve center of Otvali was Café Pobedy: in English, Café Victory. Every town has one—in South Orange it was Gruning's Ice Cream Parlor—a place to exchange gossip, debate the headlines, go on a date, and celebrate with friends. The café was much noisier than Gruning's, a rip-roaring opera of Russian, Yiddish, and Ukrainian rising from the plain wood tables and chairs. Of course ice cream parlors don't serve alcohol, yet there was another difference, too. Ever since meeting Konstantin and Dmitry in Munich, I'd been aware that World War II was a heavier weight to bear for Russians than for Americans. Part of it was the scope of Soviet losses—over twenty million dead and the destruction of so many cities and towns—but it was also a facet of the Russian character, the conviction that history was a chilling, inescapable shadow that fell across the present.

Café Victory had been named to honor those who fought in the Great Patriotic War, and the white plaster walls were crammed with black-and-white photographs of their triumphs and sacrifices: the Red Army marching past the charred huts of liberated villages; a Soviet medic carrying a skeletal man through the main gate of Auschwitz; children, tears on their faces, kneeling at a hilltop memorial; and a photo, blown up to twice the size of a poster and hung over the doorway, that the regulars frequently gazed at as if paying respects at a shrine—a Russian soldier on the roof of the Reichstag with the ruins of Berlin below him as he raises the Soviet flag with its five-pointed star and crossed hammer and sickle.

"Yevgeny Anan'evich Khaldei took that picture while he was working for TASS," Yuli said the first time I saw it. "Like me, he was from the Ukraine. His mother was murdered in a pogrom, and the Nazis killed his father and sisters. That has been the most famous picture in the country since it appeared in the newspaper, and Yevgeny was fired after the war."

"Why?"

"Stalin never liked Ukrainians, and he got mad at the Jews. They would not stop speaking Yiddish and there were rumors that thousands wanted to go live in a Jewish state."

While we ate, Yuli encouraged me to talk, never taking her eyes off me as I spoke, and when I recounted my parents' car accident and Emma's murder, she put a hand on mine. And she had plenty of questions. Did I see Elvis and the Beatles on *Ed Sullivan*? (Yes.) Is there really such a thing as a pizza burger? (Absolutely!) Would I rather watch a movie in a theater or at the drive-in? (Depends on the weather.) Did I have a girlfriend?

"Ex-girlfriend," I answered, and when she pressed me for details, I told her about Beryl and skipped those summers with the divorcée, who, from my perspective, defied classification.

For someone so interested in my life, Yuli was reluctant to share much about herself beyond that she was an orphan who had been taken in by Der. In fact, when I asked how old she was, Yuli arched her eyebrows in comic pique. "What? I'm a chicken, and you want to know if I'm too old to cook?"

I laughed, but her message was clear: *Ne sprashivay*, as Emma was fond of saying—Don't ask.

Our usual spot at the café was in the quiet back room where the old men played chess, and on this afternoon, as we were digging into beef stroganoff, a young guy with a patchy beard came staggering drunkenly toward our table. He was only an inch or two over five feet and wore a red-and-yellow plaid jacket and a tall hat, like a woolly version of Abraham Lincoln's stovepipe without a brim.

Draping himself around Yuli, he said in Russian, "We never see each other."

As adroitly as a wrestler escaping a clinch, she squirmed free. "I am busy, Stenka."

He stood up. "With an American, I hear."

Stenka glanced at me with disdain and then, reeking of moonshine and self-pity, said, "You and I, Yulianna, we are done?"

Yuli's romance with Pyotr Ananko was in the ballpark, a school friend and a journalist. But this jerk? I didn't get it. And when Yuli looked at me and just as quickly looked away, I figured she was thinking along those lines, and having me there as a witness explained the mortified expression on her face.

"AshitAmerican," Stenka said, slurring his words together. "Ashit-American*Zhid*."

While not a direct translation, *Zhid* was equivalent to kike. That Stenka used it with Yuli, who I assumed was Jewish, and who was brought up by Der, whom everyone in Otvali knew was Jewish, demonstrated that *samogon* and stupidity were a regrettable combination. Growing up, I'd heard people joke about Jews being cheap crooks, and Rollie had a cousin who wouldn't stop insisting to Birdman and me that "Dirty Jew bastards killed Christ," until Rollie punched him, saying, "And an Italian gave you a fat lip." I didn't get overheated about the jokes or Rollie's cousin, who was so dumb he flunked eighth grade. In Munich, I'd been indignant when that waiter had implied Nazi war criminals wouldn't be on trial if not for the Jews, but hearing *Zhid*, I had a new reaction. I imagined smashing the wine bottle over Stenka's head. Visiting Dachau, I concluded, could make a Jew touchy.

"Do not speak like that," Yuli said, her eyes shining as if she were about to cry, though I couldn't say whether it was from anger or sadness.

Stenka shot me a drunken smirk, which I made disappear by standing. I was a foot taller and towered over him. He backed up, and I offered him my hand. "Michael Daniels. *Ochen' priyatno,*" meaning that I was pleased to make his acquaintance.

We shook, and I twisted his arm, a trick that Rollie had taught me, flipping up his hand and putting him in a wristlock. With a yelp, Stenka went down on a knee.

"*Ischezni*," I said—Get lost.

Stenka broke into a goofy smile, as if we were kids fooling around after school. "You speak Russian. This is excellent."

I shoved his arm forward so his head hit the floor and his hat fell off. "*Ischezni*."

Without a glance at Yuli or me, Stenka grabbed his hat and wobbled away, bumping into two waiters before he made it out the door.

I sat. Yuli's eyes were wet. "I don't know my exact age. In my twenties, that's all."

"I was curious. It's not important."

"Not to you. To me it is. When Papka tried to find my records in Stalino—the city is Donetsk today, because Khrushchev wants to erase Stalin and changes name—there were no records. Germans murder hundreds of thousands in the city. And burn records. Death is not—how do you say—sufficient? For Germans, it had to be they did not ever exist."

I wished that I hadn't asked Yuli her age and characterized the answer as unimportant. When would I smarten up? Not every childhood was centered around a candy store, cartoons, Little League, and double features for seventy-five cents with the soda and popcorn.

We finished our lunch without talking, nor did we speak on the way to the compound. Snow had started to fall, but at the gate Yuli waved to the two men sitting on barrels with shotguns across their laps and kept walking.

"Where we going?"

"Another kilometer."

Yuli stopped where the graveled road narrowed to a path that went uphill through a field with yellowish-green wheat beneath the snow. At the top of the hill a birch forest stood out against the dull gray sky.

Yuli stared at the white trees. "I remember my mother, a ballerina, dancing on a stage. And running with her to the trucks when the Germans came. After that . . . Did you ever wake up and know you dreamt but can remember nothing of the dream?"

"Sure."

"This is my life before Papka. Except up there. I remember what happened up there."

I watched her breath steaming in the snowy air.

"Will you walk there with me, Michael?"

"*Da.*"

The snow was deeper and the air colder the higher we climbed, so even with the fur cap, quilted jacket, and felt boots Yuli had given me, I was shivering as we entered the woods. Icicles hung from the spidery branches of the birches, and after a few minutes we came out the other side to a frozen lake. Across the ice were summer dachas, small A-frames painted emerald and sapphire and vermilion. Some stood close to the shoreline, and I could see the pointy-tipped snow-covered roofs of other dachas behind them in the woods.

"Lake Bereza," Yuli said. *Bereza* was Russian for birch tree. "Eleven of us made it here from the Ukraine. After walking and hiding and walking some more."

"Us?"

"Children. In Stalino, right before the Germans came, my mother took me to a synagogue. We never went to pray, but now I see a line of trucks outside. Young men and women, the drivers, were shouting for us to hurry and get in. I believe they were Zionists. Stalino, I'm told, was known for its Zionists. I estimate seventy or eighty children board those trucks with their parents. We drove away, but the Germans followed us, and by that evening they weren't far behind. The trucks stopped near a village. I could smell smoke from the chimneys. Mothers and fathers told their children to run, and helped us out of the trucks. That is all I remember. I cannot even remember if Mama kissed me good-bye."

Yuli was gazing at the dachas, and I was thinking that when I was a child, we considered it an adventure to ride a bus by ourselves to South Orange Village.

"Children ran everywhere. We had no idea where to go. So many died in the Ukraine before we got to Lake Bereza. Thirst. Starvation. Typhus. And the Ukrainian Auxiliary Police—evil as Nazis—caught some crossing the steppes and shot them."

Behind us, tree branches cracked and fell, and Yuli flinched.

"The oldest one of us at the lake was fourteen. His name was Dovid. I could never forget his hair—it shines like a copper kettle. And his freckles—I had not seen that many freckles. His sister Faiga, she had them, too. I was very young, but Faiga was younger and follows me like my shadow. So Dovid, he cares for us both. He has a German machine pistol and a Soviet submachine gun. Picked up in a field we had gone through where there were dead Russian and German soldiers. And we think we are safe here. Dovid told us that peasants believed birch trees could protect Russians from misfortune. And we never went hungry. Dovid hunts deer and rabbit, and the girls fish in the lake. And those dachas, some of them, have root cellars with potatoes. Then Faiga is sick. I do everything, Michael, everything. I sing to her and bathe her in cold water because Faiga is burning, and I hold her in my lap. I was holding her in my lap when she died."

Her voice broke, and she leaned against me, saying, "Two mornings after Faiga dies, we hear tanks and trucks far away. Dovid goes to see and comes back and says a German patrol is walking up the hill. The children hide in the root cellars. Not Dovid. He hides in the woods behind the dachas, because he is the—the looker?"

"Lookout."

"Lookout. Dovid is the lookout. And I go with him. We see the Germans circle the lake and go into the dachas. Dovid and I can hear the shooting. And the screaming. The children scream. I thought their screaming would never stop. I prayed for it to stop. Then it was silent and we wait until the Germans go and leave our hiding place. But not every German is gone. And one shoots Dovid."

I moved my hand up to her elbow, turned her toward me, feeling as if I wanted to cry. Yuli was composed and dry-eyed, so what right did I have to my tears?

"How did you ever survive that?"

"I disagreed with the Nazis. I didn't believe the world would be improved if I wasn't in it."

"I meant Dovid was right there, the soldier shot him. How—"

"I hid."

It occurred to me that there was more to the story, but I looked at her, thinking what I often thought—no face could be so perfectly heart-shaped, no skin that milky, no eyes the exact shimmering blue of twilight—and I put my right hand on her back and kissed her. I was prepared for Yuli to retreat. Instead her lips, cold and pliant, moved sweetly against mine, her arms going up, her fingers massaging the back of my neck while I lost my hands in her hair, which, incredibly, was even silkier to the touch than to the eye. The snow fell like a curtain of silvery-white lace, and the flakes melted on our faces as our lips grew more insistent, her mouth opened, and our tongues played, and I wished that we weren't bundled up in our quilted jackets so I could feel her body against mine. She was holding me tighter now, her arms surprisingly strong, and pulling me down toward her and whispering, "I had enough of missing people. I can't miss any more people."

We stepped back then, looking at each other as if to appraise the changes brought on by what we had just done.

Yuli said, "We should go. I have a trip to prepare for. A month, Papka says."

"A month? Why a month?" Yuli had often taken day trips, and sometimes she was away overnight. I was curious about what she did, but when I asked Der for permission to accompany her, he replied that Taft Mifflin would not want me to get arrested, a distinct possibility if I bumped into an official who hated capitalists or who hoped to be paid to release me.

"I don't know yet. Why do you sound angry?"

"I don't."

"You do," she said.

I wasn't angry, I was hurt, because if Taft gave Der the all clear while she was away, then I wouldn't be in Otvali when she returned, and while that didn't appear to bother Yuli, it certainly bothered me.

"Say something, Michael."

"What do you expect me to say?"

Yuli laughed. "You say, 'Later, gator'?"

"I do?"

"On the radio you did."

Yuli took my hand, and as we walked the compound, I realized that deejaying felt as if it had become a piece of my distant past, a souvenir you toss in a drawer and don't see again until you're packing to leave home.

21

By mid-January, sunlight poured through the high windows in the kitchen, and I heard ice breaking up on the roof. Der wasn't in the house. He'd said that Yuli would be back the evening before, and I'd stayed up waiting for her. When she didn't show by midnight, I went to sleep, and the disappointment was still with me in the morning as I filled a glass of tea from the samovar and headed to the parlor to choose a new book, a British paperback of stories by Gogol.

Reading "Diary of a Madman," I felt a kinship with the narrator. His tedious government job and hopeless crush on his boss's daughter led him to conclude that he was the king of Spain, and by the last page I was frantic to get on with my life before I reached an equally insane conclusion. I'd ushered in 1965 alone with a bottle of Sovetskoye Shampanskoye. The wine merchant in Otvali had told me that Stalin had declared the champagne crucial to *la belle vie*, but all it did was give me a hangover. Yuli had been away for weeks and I was miserable without her, even though now, despite our kissing by the lake, a romance between us seemed about as realistic as the one I momentarily imagined with Ann-Margret after seeing *Bye Bye Birdie*. I felt as if I were under house arrest and wanted to go home. The shooting in Munich and Emma's murder were scary, yet I didn't buy Taft Mifflin's assurance that I was safer in the Soviet Union than South Orange. The only logical theory that I'd come up with was that I'd pissed off somebody by lampooning Khrushchev. And if Oswald could assassinate JFK, in spite of his Secret Service protection, then it shouldn't be all that challenging to shoot me, and I preferred getting shot in the comfort of my own neighborhood.

At noon, after finishing the stories, I felt glum and threw my clothes into my suitcases, thinking that once I returned to New Jersey, I'd never see Yuli again. Unable to shake the hollow feeling, I walked to Otvali, the sun so bright I put on my Ray-Bans. The townspeople, spotting a chance to cure their cabin fever, had come out in droves. Women were shopping; a group of children too young for school were standing in a circle on the steps of St. Sergius holding hands and looking upward to feel the sun on their faces; and men, who had left their heavy overcoats at home, were drinking and talking on the terrace of Café Victory.

My mood noticeably improved when I spotted Yuli sitting on a bench underneath the statue in the park. She was talking to Der Schmuggler, and they were facing each other, so they didn't see me as I approached. Yuli was wearing a white fisherman's sweater with corduroy slacks tucked into high leather boots. Nothing strange about that, but her face was tanned, and her long hair had been streaked a lighter gold by the sun. Where, I wondered, did she get a winter suntan in the Soviet Union? The USSR did cover eight and a half million square miles across eleven time zones—15 percent of the planet—so there had to be some area ruled by the Kremlin where Yuli could go sunbathing. Yet as I got closer to the bench, Yuli glanced toward me, and I realized, with a pang of jealousy, that I was less interested in geography than whether she'd gone off with another of her boyfriends.

Standing and smiling, Yuli asked, "How's life?"

"*Normalno.*" Things didn't feel normal, but I planned to let her know about my decision to leave in private—hoping, I suppose, that she'd try to talk me out of it.

Placing her hands on my shoulders and going up on her tiptoes, we exchanged the triple kiss, and I thought about how much I loved her fingers, not because they were long and slender and graceful and moved to a music all their own, but because sometimes she used them to touch me.

Looking at Der, Yuli said, "You should tell Michael."

"Tell me what?"

Der was staring up at the bronze statue. I'd noticed the statue before without really seeing it, nor could I read the Russian on the granite base—*МАРИЯ АДАСКИНА*. Now, I looked up at the fine-featured young woman in a plain frock, the intensity of her expression almost unbearable, as though she was witnessing every horror the world could conjure. Her long skirt and hair were blown back by the wind, and one leg was striding in front of the other, her woven shoes planted in the earth, and her hands raised, the left holding a hammer and the right a sickle, which led me to conclude that she was a tribute to the proletariat laboring in the factories and fields of Mother Russia.

Getting off the bench, Der pointed to the statue and said to me, "Her name was Maria Adaskina," and just as I recalled the afternoon at Eddie's house when Taft Mifflin had told me that Adaskina was Emma's maiden name, Der added, "She was your grandmother's sister."

I was astounded and wondered why he'd put off telling me. "You knew my grandmother?"

"I didn't know her well, nor do I know why anyone would harm her. Her father had been a grain dealer in Rostov-on-Don. So was my father, and they were friendly competitors."

"Wasn't Emma from a shtetl in the Ukraine?"

"Born there, moved to Rostov with her father after her mother died. Emma was eight or nine years older than Maria and raised her."

"Do you know the name of the shtetl?"

Der laughed, but it wasn't a happy sound. "From back then? No. Today? Dust or Ashes. You choose."

"And Emma's father?"

Der had a weary sadness in his eyes. "Like Maria, like my parents and brothers and sisters, like my aunts and uncles and cousins—the Nazis killed them."

I remembered finding Emma on the floor, and I thought about how it must have felt losing so many loved ones at once—the incalculable heartbreak, the helplessness, the outrage.

Der kissed his fingertips and pressed them to the hem of the statue's skirt. "'My little Communist,' I called her. In Rostov-on-Don, she was a leader of the Komsomol. She could quote Lenin and Marx the way a child sings songs, and I used to tease her, 'Masha, we will have none of that on our wedding night.' That made her laugh. But the young Communists did not love Masha for her quotes—it was because she was so kind. And everyone in Otvali loves the statue I commissioned for her. Am I right, Yuli?"

She rubbed a hand across his back. "*Da.*"

Der turned toward me. His beard needed trimming, and his face was contorted as if it hurt him to move. "Of course, almost everyone loves dead Jews. Jesus was a Jew, no? It is the live Jews who seem to bother people."

I thought he was going to cry, but the tears didn't come. All of them shed already, I guessed. "Where did Emma live? In Rostov."

His mood shifting abruptly, Der chuckled. "Ulitsa Yevreyev."

"The Street of Jews?"

"The street had another name, but no one used it."

I asked Yuli, "Can you take me there?"

She looked at Der. He nodded. "Your first right off Portovaya Street. The street looks like it did after the Nazis got done with it. Ask anyone you see for the Adaskin house. They will know it."

Before leaving, I glanced at my great-aunt, Maria Adaskina. She had the same round face and intriguing slant to her eyes as Emma, and I was surprised to discover that it was possible to miss someone you had never met.

22

Yuli was driving the Volga, and we rode uphill past snowy fields toward Rostov-on-Don.

"You're quiet, Michael."

Not wanting my jealousy to show, I'd promised myself that I wouldn't ask Yuli where she'd gone. But a minute later, as if reading my mind, she volunteered the information.

"I was skiing at Mount Elbrus."

That news didn't make me feel any better. "How nice for you."

"Not nice. It was a three-day drive each way. And I went for work."

"Are you ever going to tell me exactly what you do?"

Her sparkle of laughter was equal parts amusement and evasion. "Never."

When the Don River, wide and flat and the color of slate, came into view, I said, "I'm leaving."

"What—you're?"

I turned to study her face, the lovely angles, the dusk-blue eyes, the mouth perpetually on the verge of a smile. "Leaving. Going home."

Yuli didn't change my mind when she said, "I wish you would not," but it was flattering to hear.

Portovaya Street was snowed in, so we had to leave the Volga by the Don. It was a slippery hike up from the riverbank. Ruts of wagon wheels and hoofprints of horses marked the snow, and lamps shone in the windows of the three-story brick houses. The Street of Jews was a cul-de-sac on the top of a hill from where you could see white steamboats moored along the Don embankment and the barges in the harbor and the bridge being built across the river and the city with the gold onion domes of churches. Most of the houses on the circle were fire-blackened shells courtesy of the Luftwaffe and German artillery. It felt odd knowing that my grandparents and my father had once resided here, because it was so distant from the Shangri-la where I'd grown up, as if this ravaged street occupied another galaxy where suffering arrived as reliably as the Good Humor man ringing his bell on summer evenings as he drove down Montague Place.

Yuli and I walked to the far end of the cul-de-sac, where an old woman, wearing a black babushka and wrapped in a mousy-brown blanket, sat on an upturned crate outside a house drinking from a bottle of red wine.

"*Dobriy den',*" I said—good afternoon.

Her eyes, dark slits in her withered face, gazed up at us as if we'd come to deliver bad news. "*Chto ty khochesh'?*" she asked—what do you want?

Yuli said, "Excuse us, but do you know where the Adaskin family lived?"

The woman gave her a toothless smile and cackled. "Are you stupid, girl? The Fritzes took the Jews out to the Ravine of Snakes and shot them in two days. That's where the Jews live now."

"Not all," I said. "Not Emma Adaskina."

She took a pull from the bottle. "The pretty one. Her husband, Dainov, was as crazy as a drunk cockroach. Always babbling about his big dreams. He stole his father-in-law's money, left Emma, and ran off to America with their son."

"He divorced her?"

"Who bothers with divorce when they run away? And what did Emma Adaskina care? That man, Gak, he came for her."

"Gak?"

The old woman rose unsteadily to her feet. "The great Alexander Alexandrovich Gak. The artist. A Jew so rich no one treated him like a Jew. They say Gak came to paint pictures of the ships in the harbor, met Emma, and whisked her off to see the world."

I could understand why my parents had told me that my grandparents were divorced, a more socially acceptable explanation for their living apart. But I'd never heard of this other man, and that puzzled me. "Where did Gak and Emma go?" I asked.

Setting her bottle on the crate, the woman peered suspiciously at me. "Why do you question me? I have done no wrong. Not even Stalin would accuse me of doing wrong. I am too old and poor and alone to disobey the party."

"Emma was my grandmother."

She stood there, her eyes welling up. At last she said, "Come," and went into the house.

Inside, it was drafty and smelled of fish and fried onions. The old woman led us into a dining room with peeling wallpaper, a table and chairs caked with dust, and a china cabinet with glass doors. The woman pointed at the shelves. On the top shelf were four dinner plates painted with images of roosters. On the shelf below the china was a row of picture postcards of Paris—the Eiffel Tower, Cleopatra's Needle, Notre-Dame, and a bridge over the Seine.

"That is all that was left of the Adaskins," she said. "I did not steal them. I would not steal. Not even from Jews."

"May I look at them?" I asked.

She replied with a half-dozen quick nods. I removed the postcards, which were brittle and singed along the edges, and when I turned them over and saw the Russian words in washed-out black ink, I caught my breath. At the candy store, Emma used to scribble notes to herself in Russian, and I was sure that this was her handwriting. I handed the cards to Yuli.

Flipping them over, she said, "They are from Emma to Maria."

"Read one to me."

" 'My Dear Masha: Paris is gorgeous. We are living in the Marais section. There are many Jews here, so I speak Yiddish while I try to learn French. The apartment is across from a park with chestnut and lime trees and fountains. Everything is wonderful except my heart aches to see Lev.' "

"Lev?" Yuli asked.

"My father. He was eleven when his father took him to the States."

Yuli looked back at the postcard. " 'I love and miss you, dearest sister, and please write me at the address I gave you, 22 Place des Vosges.' "

The old woman, who had crossed herself as Yuli was reading, touched my arm. "This is from your grandmother?"

"Yes."

"I am sorry what happened to the Adaskins. I am sorry what happened to my whole country. Take the postcards. This is as God wants. You see now I did not steal them. I was keeping them safe because God knew you would come for them."

I took a hundred-ruble note from my pocket and held it toward her. She shook her head as if she were trying to get water out of her ears, but I pressed the money into her hand.

It was snowing as Yuli drove to Otvali. Her voice laced with a hesitancy I hadn't heard before, she asked, "Do—do you still want to go home?"

"To Paris."

"Papka won't like it."

"I'm going to try and find out why my grandmother was murdered."

Gently Yuli said, "Sometimes there is no reason."

I knew she was trying to be kind, but the facts, I believed, were on my side. "Someone shot Emma, someone tried to shoot me—there is a reason."

Der was sitting at the kitchen table drinking tea, and Yuli was right about his reaction. When I told him that I was going to Paris, he shook his head. "Too dangerous."

"If it was some KGB agent who tried to kill me, I'll be safer in Paris than here. And I'm not asking your permission. I can leave the Soviet Union whenever I want."

He gave me a hard look. "Maybe not. Taft—"

I felt my anger rising. "All Taft did for me was get me shot at and a friend of mine killed. I am going."

"Then you will take Yuli with you. It will be safer. It could be a week before I can make your travel arrangements."

I looked at Yuli. Her face was blank.

Der said to her, "You can travel on the American passport I brought you from Munich."

"Yes, Papka," she said.

Part VI

23

Paris, France
January 26, 1965

A late-afternoon drizzle dimpled the gray water of the Seine as the taxi exited onto Quai de Bercy. Yuli sat next to Michael in the back, trying to read *A Moveable Feast* in English while Michael chatted in French with the driver. Yuli was an ardent fan of Hemingway, starting when she had read *For Whom the Bell Tolls* in school, and after landing at Orly and exchanging a hundred dollars for francs, she had bought a copy of his Paris memoir and a map of the city because she wanted to go sightseeing. The memoir had recently been published, and Yuli was excited to read it, but she was having trouble concentrating because she was exhausted from the flights—Rostov-on-Don to Moscow and Moscow direct to Paris—and the anxiety of traveling under a false identity. Yuli relished having a family story in lieu of her eerie blankness—even if her biography had been concocted. Nonetheless, recalling the particulars that Papka had received from Taft Mifflin was difficult in her state of exhaustion. That her first name had remained Yulianna made it easier for her and Michael. Her surname, however, was Ukrainian, Timko, since her fictional self had been born in Odessa. Her father had been a garrulous steelworker, her mother a demure seamstress. In May 1941, a month before the Nazis invaded, the Timkos emigrated with their new baby to Parma, Ohio, a suburb of Cleveland. After graduating from Parma Senior High in 1959, Yulianna Timko earned an economics degree from Ohio University, and by the time she began her job at the Commerce Department in Washington, D.C., her parents were conveniently nestled beside each other in St. Andrew's Cemetery in Parma.

Michael tapped her on the arm. "The driver says the address on Emma's postcard is for a café."

"Maybe she uses it only for mail?"

"I hope not," Michael replied, then said to the driver, "*Y a-t-il des appartements au-dessus du café?*"

Yuli didn't speak French, so she couldn't understand the conversation, but she turned toward Michael as if she were listening because she liked looking at him. More than liked. That sandy hair falling across his forehead and curling up at his collar. And those shoulders. Where did they build shoulders that broad in America? In Chicago, according to the Carl Sandburg poem that she and Pyotr had translated together in school. Except Chicago had big shoulders in the poem, Yuli recalled. Big, broad, who cared? She liked looking at them. And his face, which was both wise and boyish. And his eyes. Papka had called them "poet's eyes," and though Yuli did see a bohemian gleam in them and a touch of sadness, there was nothing dreamy about them. Quite the opposite. His eyes didn't miss much, which unnerved her, and when Michael studied her, Yuli became angry at him, for it was as if his eyes were tempting her to tell him things that she preferred not to share. Lake Bereza, for instance. Yuli hadn't planned to take Michael there, but he was looking at her across the table in Café Victory, and she felt compelled to do it, only managing to catch herself before telling him everything.

And Yuli certainly had no plan to kiss Michael by the lake, but Michael was different from boys in Otvali. Grabby boys, unromantic boys in a hurry. As if they were on fire and it was her duty to douse the flames. So she did, without receiving any relief from her loneliness or the pain at the center of her, as though a spring were coiling there, tighter and tighter.

Why did she do it, then? Guilt, for starters. Yuli felt guilty disappointing anyone. Guilt had been gnawing at her ever since she had escaped the Germans and her mother had not. That was the beginning. Then those children had been killed. And Dovid, right in front of her. Yet Yuli didn't believe that guilt was the whole story. There was her loneliness, too. And maybe, she thought, the explanation was simply that she had been born a wild girl. Bashe had called her that, and beginning when Yuli was a teenager and started going out with boys, Papka appeared to hold the same opinion, sinking into an irritated silence when she left and scowling at her when she came home.

Lately Yuli wondered if Papka considered her no better than a prostitute. In all her years acquiring goods by bribing longshoremen and the apparatchiks who paced the docks with their clipboards and whose greed would have shamed the tsars, Papka had never suggested that she give herself to a man in the interest of a deal. That had seemed to change last month when he instructed her to go skiing at Mount Elbrus. Somehow Papka had learned that the teenage physicist Kazimir Zolnerowich, the missile designer Yuli had photographed in Dnipropetrovsk, would be taking a holiday at an inn near the mountain. Yuli was to stay at the inn and befriend him.

"And the purpose of this friendship?" she had asked.

"To find out if Kazimir would like a change of scene. In the United States, for example."

The assignment sounded ridiculous to Yuli. "Why don't I just ask him if he would like to defect?"

"Do not be silly, girl. Ask him in private. On a walk or in his room."

"His room?"

"He will invite you to his room. Surely you know you are difficult to resist. You have seen how Michael looks at you. And you at him. Try looking at Kazimir that way."

Yuli was dumbstruck by the suggestion and fumed at Papka while packing for her trip. At the inn, she encountered Kazimir in the salon, where he sat on a sofa reading the Russian translation of *The War of the Worlds* by H. G. Wells. Yuli had read the British writer's novel *The Time Machine,* and after sitting at the other end of the sofa, attempted to start a conversation with Kazimir, who glanced up, said that he was enjoying the book, and went back to reading. At the inn, several of Kazimir's colleagues flirted with her, but as far as Kazimir was concerned, Yuli was invisible. Upon returning to Otvali she reported to Papka that the missile designer was more interested in science fiction than women. Papka let out a sigh of relief, and Yuli concluded she had misunderstood his suggestion.

All the same, that Papka had noticed her interest in Michael made her uncomfortable. Yuli found her feelings for Michael unsettling, and on the drive to Mount Elbrus, she had told herself that he would be gone when she got back to Otvali, and because she had maintained a safe distance from him, she wouldn't miss him so badly. Yet Michael was there when Yuli returned. And while her spirits rose upon seeing him, Yuli realized, with a sudden disconcerting clarity, how much she resented Michael for filling her with hope that her dearest dream was true, that life had more to offer her than its current dreariness, that tomorrow could be different from today. Perhaps that was the real explanation, concealed behind the gibberish of ideology, for why Soviet leaders were so hostile to America; it was easier to govern citizens who didn't dream. They were more inclined to obey, to be satisfied living like draft horses: eating, working, procreating, sleeping, and dying without ever considering what might have been.

Then Papka had ordered her to go to Paris with Michael, later privately explaining to her what she must try to accomplish. Yuli barely listened to him. She thought coming to this city would lessen her resentment, but that wasn't the case. Sitting in the back seat and looking out the window at the cozy yellow lights in the cafés and the limestone buildings with their colorfully painted doors and shutters, Yuli felt as if all this beauty, and the happiness that must go with it, would forever be beyond her reach.

The taxi stopped outside a stone arcade on Place des Vosges with a grassy square, bordered by a pointy-tipped black iron fence and neat rows of trees on the other side. Michael said something to the driver, who pointed at the arcade and replied, "Café Hugo *est très excellent*."

"Are you hungry?" Michael asked Yuli.

"Starved," she said.

24

It was a lovely old café lit by an apricot glow from the glass globes suspended from the ceiling, and because of the stone walls and the arcade blocking the daylight from the windows, I had the feeling we were in a cave. We were sitting at a small table with our suitcases around us eating cheese omelets, salad with a mustard vinaigrette, crisp fried potatoes, and baguettes with fig jam, all of it washed down with the house Chardonnay.

I said, "Did you see the apartments above the café?"

"I did, but those postcards were from thirty years ago. Why do you think your grandmother has an apartment here?"

"Because she came to Europe every summer. Always to Paris. And I had to start somewhere." I took out my passport wallet and removed a color photo, laminated in plastic, which I'd taken of Emma with my Instamatic. She was standing behind the soda fountain and raising a finger to scold me because she disliked my taking her picture. I handed it to Yuli.

"You look like her. She is so pretty."

"No prettier than you."

Her face flushed, though I couldn't say whether it was from embarrassment or the wine. "If her apartment is here, how do we get in?"

Our waiter was coming toward us. "I have a plan."

A half-squint and half-frown indicated that Yuli wasn't overly confident in my skills as a detective. I scooped up the snapshot and showed it to the waiter. "*Reconnaissez-vous cette femme? Elle a un appartement ici.*"

Ever since eighth grade, when we began taking foreign language in school, my French teachers had complimented my accent, but I didn't impress the waiter, who answered in English.

"I do not know her. I work here one month. Mademoiselle Blum, the owner of the building, comes for *le goûter* soon. I will say to her your question."

While we waited for the landlady to show up for the Parisian version of teatime, Yuli and I drank café crèmes. We were done with our coffee when a stick-thin young woman, with her hair cut short and wearing a minidress with the swirly pattern of a finger painting, came to our table.

"*Bonjour*, I am Hélène Blum."

Standing up, I held out the photo, and before I could say anything, Hélène smiled. "This is Emma!"

"My grandmother."

"You are Michael, *oui*? Emma speaks of you."

"*Oui*. And this is my friend, Yulianna Timko."

Hélène nodded hello to Yuli. "Since I am little, Emma brings Mother and I the fireball candy from America. She—" Hélène must've noticed my expression because she paused.

I didn't think mentioning the shooting was necessary. "Emma passed away."

"Oh, Michael. *Je suis désolée.* Mother, too. *En novembre.*"

I told her that I was sorry for her loss, and that I had come to Paris to clean out Emma's apartment, but I hadn't been able to locate the key. Hélène waved her hand as if to brush away my concerns. "No hurry. Every summer Emma pays a year's rent with a bank check."

That explained why I hadn't seen any of the canceled checks when I went through her filing cabinet. What it didn't explain was why she kept the apartment and was so intent on hiding it that she didn't pay the rent with a personal check. Was she worried that my father, who did her taxes, would spot it on her checking statements? And if that was it, why didn't she mention the apartment to me after my father died?

"Let me take you upstairs," Hélène said. "And I will give you a key."

I felt as if I were on the verge of a breakthrough, yet my optimism evaporated after we climbed a flight of stairs and inspected the apartment.

Two bedrooms were off a hallway—the bigger one with a double bed and an empty armoire and closet, and the smaller one with twin beds and no armoire or closet at all. I told Yuli to take the larger room, hoping that she would invite me to join her, but she went in and closed the door, so I tossed my suitcases on one of the twins, located the thermostat in the hall, and cranked up the heat. The kitchen was tiny, with the refrigerator, unplugged and wiped clean, under the counter, but in a cabinet above the stove I saw evidence that Emma had been here: a red-and-gold can of Martinson Coffee, the brand that Emma drank. I popped off the lid, saw that the can was three fourths full, and inhaled a memory of my grandmother until sadness replaced the pleasure of remembering.

More evidence was in the bathroom: bottles of her favorites, Breck shampoo and Jean Naté after-bath splash. Oddly enough, because the old woman in Rostov-on-Don had claimed that Emma had lived in Paris with a painter, Alexander Gak, the walls were bare, but when I went into the salon and switched on the crystal sconces, I noticed nail holes and clean white rectangular spaces of various sizes on the walls. Gak's paintings, I imagined, had hung here. Where were they now? Not in New Jersey. Emma had never brought back any art from Europe.

"Find anything?" Yuli asked.

I held up a paperback of *Webster's New Pocket Dictionary* and a hardbound oversize book of Picasso's work that had been on a wing chair, which was upholstered in the same wine-dark silk with sky-blue stripes as the settee, the only furniture in the salon.

"Did your grandmother like art?"

"She checked out library books about Picasso, Chagall, and Matisse, and liked to watch me sketch. But she never talked about art or a painter named Gak."

Yuli came over. "I'm going to have a bath and go to sleep. You should rest, and we can make a plan tomorrow."

"I'm going to read for a while."

Yuli kissed my lips. I held the kiss, but she stood back and said good night to me in Russian.

I watched her disappear into the hall, then put the dictionary on the chair and stretched out on the settee, my feet dangling over one end. I stood the Picasso book up on my chest, reading about his life and perusing the color plates of his paintings. I heard Yuli running her bath and pictured her in the tub, her skin rosy from the steam, an image that, when added to my exhaustion, interfered with my reading.

I closed my eyes, intending to rest for a second, and when I woke up, I discovered that Yuli had turned off the lights, covered me with a knitted blanket, removed my Weejuns, and set them on the herringbone floor next to the Picasso book. Dawn was scratching at the windows, and I checked my watch: it was five after six; I'd slept for eleven hours. Glancing at Emma's Rolex, I wanted to talk to her about Yuli. After telling her that I'd never met anyone so resilient and brave and beautiful, I continued my silent recitation as I shaved and showered in the tub with the handheld nozzle, dried off and put on clean clothes, and then riffled through the pages again. I startled myself by asking aloud, "Emma, why were you reading this book?"

Part of that answer, or clues to it, I believed, had been listed on the back flyleaf. I carefully tore out the page and waited for Yuli to wake up.

25

The morning was clear and cold as Yuli and I crossed the Pont au Double and saw barges cutting foamy trails in the Seine.

"We don't know what your grandmother meant by that list," Yuli said.

"That's the plan. To find out."

"And how do we find out?"

"We start with breakfast."

"Brilliant," she replied.

Yuli wanted to eat at the Closerie des Lilas, a café recommended by Hemingway in *A Moveable Feast*, and she had consulted her map to plot our route. It was a long walk from Place des Vosges, and I thought it would give me a chance to figure out why Emma had written in the back of that book. No luck. Just as disappointing, Yuli and I had run into Hélène Blum as we left the apartment, and when I asked her if she'd ever heard of Alexander Gak, she said no.

On the Boulevard Saint-Michel, traffic was already heavy, and people were lined up at the kiosks for the newspapers. Students were streaming into the Place de la Sorbonne, and the tables on the terraces of the cafés were busy as orange-blue flames flickered in the mesh boxes of the tall steel gas heaters. We cut through the Luxembourg Gardens, walking along the gravel paths past the white statues and the pool and fountains. All around us the windows of the apartment buildings reflected the wintry light, and the bare branches of the elms and sycamores were black silhouettes in the silver sky.

Her voice wistful, Yuli said, "Paris is supposed to be the loveliest city."

"It gets my vote."

"Being here, I understand how little I see at home, how tiny my world is."

"It's no different in America."

Her wistful tone developed an edge. "Except you can go wherever you want on a real passport."

"There's the Closerie des Lilas," I said, changing the subject.

The café was on the corner of Boulevard Montparnasse and Avenue de l'Observatoire, but Yuli stopped to stare at a bronze statue of a soldier in a plumed hat, coat with epaulets, high boots, and a sword raised in his right hand.

Yuli said, "Marshal Ney. Hemingway writes about the statue in *A Moveable Feast* and *The Sun Also Rises*. Ney helped Napoleon invade Russia. He got the same welcome as the Nazis—winter and Russians that did not give up. The French came with half a million soldiers. They go home with twenty thousand. What do countries want with Russia? Most of the people have nothing."

I felt bad that even here, in this golden city, her history was with her. I took her arm, and we went to the café and sat at a table by a window with the sunlight warming us. Yuli asked me to order for her and gazed glumly out toward Marshal Ney. Her mood improved when we finished a basket of pain aux raisins and pain au chocolat.

As we sipped our second cafés au lait, Yuli said, "How are the French not fat?"

"Because they don't eat whole baskets of croissants."

"Their loss."

From an inner pocket of my denim jacket, I took out the page torn from the Picasso book and reread the list Emma had written in the center of the paper.

Art dealer Charleston?
Gak?

Ask Picasso?

Joost Ter Horst?

Why does God write our stories in vanishing ink?

Yuli shifted the paper toward her. "You never hear of these people?"

"Picasso."

Yuli grinned. "No joking. Did your grandmother know him?"

"If she did, she never mentioned it. Charleston could be an art dealer, but it's also an American city."

"In South Carolina. Your Civil War started there."

"It did?"

"They do teach in your schools?"

"You have to pay attention."

Yuli laughed.

"Emma wasn't a great speller in English, but every word on the list is correct, so she must have used the dictionary in her apartment. Thing is, she usually wrote notes to herself in Russian."

"The notes could be for someone else."

"Gak? Gak would read Russian. And his name's on the list."

Her forehead furrowed, and I felt as if I could see the wheels spinning in her head. "Michael, your grandmother knew you couldn't read Russian?"

"She did. You're saying the notes were for me?"

"Perhaps she worried something would happen to her and wanted to write it down for you. Or they were notes to remind herself to tell you later. And this God and vanishing ink. Is this words she says. An American—how you say, 'proverbial'?"

"Proverb. No, I haven't heard it before from my grandmother. Or anybody. And I never heard about Gak or this Joost Ter Horst. Where would Emma meet a Dutch guy?"

Yuli was studying the page and drawing an index finger back and forth over *Joost Ter Horst*. When at last she looked at me, her expression was serious, hesitant, regretful. Spreading her map on the table, she said, "I want to see Notre-Dame. There is a bookstore near it, Shakespeare and Company, on Rue de la Bûcherie. We could look up Gak and Joost in art books. Good plan?"

"Excellent," I said, though I already had put together a plan of my own. When Yuli got up to use the WC, I told her I'd wait outside, went to a telephone booth on Boulevard Montparnasse, and made a call.

————

Books make the prettiest wallpaper, I decided, because with the high wood shelving crammed with volumes the walls were every shade of the color wheel. At midmorning, the store was quiet, with the sweet, cozy mustiness of a library, and what I remember most about our two hours there was Yuli, in a red beret and a well-worn leather flight jacket—which she said Der Schmuggler had bought for her on one of his trips to Munich—lovingly opening up the books to read the indexes.

"Maybe Gak and Joost weren't famous enough to write about," I said.

We were crossing the Pont au Double again, and the wind was blowing off the Seine.

Yuli said, "You read French. There is a national library in Paris. We could try there."

"Or go in there and pray."

Notre-Dame was up ahead, its towers and spires etched into the soft gray light.

"You pray. I want to see the gargoyles."

We were in the square in front of the cathedral when I said, "I'm going to ask Picasso."

"Ask Picasso? How do you ask Picasso?" The incredulousness in her voice suggested that I'd misplaced my mind.

"Four Freedoms Radio has an office in Paris, and I called the news director. They did a story on Picasso we ran in Munich. The news director had his address and told me that Picasso, if he's in the mood, is approachable—even friendly. He talks to people at the beach and in cafés. Sometimes he'll sign autographs, and supposedly he once painted a journalist's car and signed it. He lives on the Riviera, in the village of Mougins. We can fly to Nice, take a taxi to the village, and I'll ask him about my grandmother's list."

"You do not just go see Picasso."

"Why? He speaks French, I speak French. You know something about him the news director didn't know?"

Yuli snickered. It wasn't a nice sound. "He is a member of the Communist Party and won the Stalin Prize."

"What'd he get for winning? Ten years in Siberia?"

I was trying to lighten up the discussion, but Yuli ignored my joke. "He is the most famous artist in the world. He will be busy."

"So what's the worst that'll happen? He'll hit me with his easel?"

"You Americans—you have everything and respect nothing."

I took one of her hands. She tried to pull away, and I held on. "Why are you angry?"

She answered by gazing down at the rough cobbles of the square.

"I'm tired of your secrets, Yuli. Tell me."

"Papka did not give me money to ride around Europe."

I didn't buy her explanation and speculated that her anger was a brick in the wall that she'd built between us. Yet because that was all she was giving me, I replied as if I believed her problem was economic. "I have the money to do this—my grandmother left it to me—so I'm going. You can come along or wait in Paris."

Yuli looked up at me. I couldn't read her face, but she didn't let go of my hand.

26

Getting out of the cab at Emma's, I asked Yuli if she wanted to accompany me to Mougins. She nodded, and I gave her the key to the apartment and went down Rue de Turenne to the Air France office. I bought tickets to Nice on my American Express card and cashed traveler's checks at a bank. When I got back to the Place des Vosges, Yuli was sitting under a heater on the terrace of Café Hugo, her smaller suitcase at her feet, and had ordered another glass of Beaujolais. She gave me the key, and upstairs I stuffed some things into my canvas rucksack, forming a loop with the shoulder strap and tugging the top through until the bag was closed tight.

We rode the Métro to Orly, where Yuli downed a petit rouge before we boarded. I had to help her up the stairway to the plane, and before takeoff she was asleep. Halfway through the flight I noticed Yuli looking at me.

She whispered, "I'm scared."

"Of?"

Yuli shook her head as if she had no explanation for her fear, and I put my arm around her, and she drifted off again. After we landed, she was quiet in the taxi as the blue of the Mediterranean flashed by, and then the old churches in the town squares and, outside the towns, the winter-brown vineyards and gray stone hills with patches of greenery and stucco houses up on the hillsides painted the color of walnuts and lemons with orange clay-tile roofs.

In under an hour, the taxi was bouncing along the cobbled streets of Mougins, past the art galleries and artists' studios, and we got out at a bistro. Yuli had recovered enough to tease me. She grinned, swiveling her head side to side. "I don't see Picasso. Now what?"

"Eat."

The weather was better here than in Paris, like a sunny autumn day, and we ate outside. I had never seen a waxed mustache until I met our waiter, who with robotic precision served us duck with red currant jam. I ordered both of us Evian water instead of wine.

My rucksack was on the chair next to Yuli, and she glanced at the olive-green bag. "Where did you get this?"

"We used it at the candy store to bring cash and coins to the bank."

" The Red Army carried them."

"The Red Army? This was Emma's."

Yuli smiled. "More mystery. How do we find Picasso?"

"We consult the waiter."

There was more than a hint of skepticism in her laughter. "Perfect. Waiters know everything."

When he brought the bill, I said, *"Pardon, monsieur. Savez-vous où réside Picasso?"*

"Oui."

The waiter glared at me with the hostility of a palace guard confronting a commoner, and clearly he had no intention of providing me with any further information until I recalled Emma saying, in Yiddish, that if you grease the wheels, you'll ride. I paid the bill and added a hundred francs, approximately twenty dollars, double the cost of the meal.

"Picasso *n'est pas à la maison,*" he said.

I told Yuli that Picasso wasn't home, then asked the waiter, *"Où est-il?"*

He folded his arms across his chest. I ponied up another hundred francs, and the waiter replied that Picasso was in Saint-Tropez. Every afternoon, by four o'clock, he would be eating and drinking at Sénéquier.

I checked my watch—it was already past two—and the waiter flicked his hand at us as though shooing flies. "Go! It is not a short ride."

Once we were in the cab, Yuli asked, "Do you believe Picasso is there?"

"Why would the waiter lie?"

"For money."

"An evil capitalist? I doubt it."

Yuli patted my knee. "My optimistic American."

27

Yuli saw him first. We were walking up through the port of Saint-Tropez, past the sailboats and yachts tied up along the quay, and Yuli pulled off the trick of both keeping her voice low and exclaiming, "There he is!"

Picasso was seated with a group of men and women under the red awning of Sénéquier, and all of them seemed to be talking at once. I felt my pulse quicken and it hit me that my optimism hadn't included a plan.

"Let's wait till they're done," was the best I could do, and we took a table on the terrace from where we could see him.

Yuli ordered each of us a café crème. To calm my nerves I removed my sketch pad from my rucksack and began to draw Picasso—the silver horseshoe of hair circling his bald tanned head and his face deeply lined, as if carved from a grainy block of teak. I was rehearsing my approach to him and studying my sketch when I heard Yuli say, "Michael, Michael. . . ."

I glanced up, and Picasso, short and stocky and wearing a white-and-blue-striped collarless shirt under a black sport coat, was standing at our table.

"You drew me," he said in French, rocking back and forth on the balls of his feet like a schoolboy incapable of standing still. "Now I will draw you."

Picasso held out his hands, and I gave him my pencil and pad. He studied us and suddenly looked away, drawing with swift deft strokes, his arm moving up, down, to the left and right, as if he was doing nothing more than covering the paper with scribbles. In a couple of minutes, he was done and, after returning my pad, set the pencil across the ashtray on the table and resumed his rocking.

It didn't seem possible, but in maybe fifty lines he had captured the essence of Yuli and me, our eyes narrowed against the afternoon light and the stunned expressions on our faces.

I looked up from the bottom right corner of the drawing, where he had written *Picasso*. "*C'est merveilleux, monsieur. Merci beaucoup. Vous êtes très généreux.*"

He grinned, nodding at Yuli, then at me, and as he turned to go back to the other side of the terrace, I said, "*Excusez-moi, Monsieur* Picasso. I hope you do not think I am being presumptuous, but I hoped you could tell us about the artist Alexander Gak."

His face hardened, the lines deepening. "And you are?"

I introduced myself and Yuli, and told him that Gak had been a friend of my grandmother—Emma Dainov."

"Emma Dainov? *Je l'ai pas rencontrée.*"

I was disappointed that he'd never met my grandmother, but figured anything I could learn about Gak would help, so I asked, "Did you know Gak well?"

Picasso studied me as though preparing to do another sketch. "You have never seen his work?"

"*Regrettablement, non.*"

He sighed. "*C'est dommage.*"

"I was told that my grandmother was in love with him. She wrote his name in the back of a book of your paintings."

A sad smile tugged at the corners of his mouth. "*Oui*, that makes sense."

"*Pourquoi?*"

Picasso sat across from us, planting his elbows on the table, then took the pencil off the ashtray and leaned back. "Because I used Gak's face for my painting *The Old Jew*."

"It was in my grandmother's book. The old man and the boy sitting together."

I wasn't sure Picasso had heard me. He was silent, rolling the pencil between his thumb and forefinger. Then: "I have not spoken about Gak in a long time. I can still see him; he might as well be sitting here. His beard was the reddish-brown of Van Gogh's, but not so neatly clipped, and he had a pious mouth. It was his eyes, though, his eyes . . ."

Picasso put the pencil on the table and signaled a waiter for a bottle of wine by holding up his hand and making a pouring motion.

Staring past us, he spoke slowly, as if each word weighed more than it should and refused to roll so easily off his tongue: "I could never paint precisely what I saw in Gak's eyes. Not on my first try, not on my tenth. My perception always disagreed with the image my brush left on the canvas. I did notice a shadow of his expression had made its way into a self-portrait of mine from—what is it now, fifty-eight years ago? But the expression wasn't the same, never the same. Gak had the eyes of an old man and a child. How do you paint that? The compassion and fury all at once? Like he ached for anyone who suffered and would never forgive the world its cruelty."

Picasso picked up the pencil again, tapping it on the table until the waiter arrived with a rosé and three glasses. After pouring some for Picasso to sample and approve, he filled glasses for Yuli and me.

"To Gak," Picasso said, raising his glass.

Yuli and I followed his lead. Picasso finished his wine, and he looked at us now, and his voice was more animated when he said, "I met Gak not long after coming to Paris. In 1901 or 1902. Gak had money when none of us did. Family money, I think, because he wasn't selling his paintings. Someone said that he was the bastard child of a cousin of the tsar and a Jewish girl. From the Gak family. Wealthy liquor merchants who lived in St. Petersburg."

"Leningrad," Yuli said. The name of the city had been changed to memorialize Lenin, but I had no idea why Yuli was correcting Picasso. Maybe to give him the impression that she understood French and shared his Communist sympathies.

"*Oui*, Leningrad," Picasso replied, opening his luminous eyes wide to gaze at Yuli. She returned his gaze, and he gave her a small smile before busying himself taking a cigarette from a powder-blue pack of Gauloises and sticking it in a short, lacquered wooden holder. "Gak used to travel between Paris and St. Petersburg. He sometimes taught at an art school there, which is how he met Chagall. But it was much better for the artists in Montmartre when Gak was in town. We would have frozen to death if he hadn't bought coal for us, and he saw to it that we ate and drank at Spielman's and Au Coucou by promising to pay our bills. And Modigliani—Modigliani would hardly have had the stone to sculpt if Gak hadn't taken care of the supplier."

The waiter appeared, flicked a lighter and refilled our glasses. Picasso puffed on the cigarette. "Gak had a lovely apartment and studio."

"*Sur la* Place des Vosges?" I hadn't planned to interrupt him, but I was anxious to know how Emma had wound up with an apartment in Paris.

"*Exactement.* Above the Café Hugo. I would visit him, and we would walk in the park or go to the café."

Picasso stared out toward the harbor, and I couldn't tell whether I heard nostalgia or a deeper sadness in his voice. "You wouldn't know the meaning of stubborn until you argued with Gak. We agreed with Cézanne that our job was to deconstruct the things around us. Gak applied that to the soul. His one subject. 'A delusional Expressionist,' I called him. When he painted, he sawed open every hideous chamber of the heart. His images were Russian, and whether he painted the steppes in spring or the tsar carving up children on a platter and eating them, his pictures were as blurry and terrifying as a nightmare that still haunts you in the morning."

At home and in Paris, I hadn't understood Emma's interest in art books. Talking to Picasso had solved that mystery. Yet I struggled to imagine her, a woman who was the opposite of flighty, as the companion of an artist. Maybe that was why she had fallen in love with him. Or maybe I just had trouble imagining her as young, full of joy and, even harder for me, lust.

Picasso dragged on the Gauloises, the sharp smell of the smoke cutting through the aromas of coffee and the sea breeze. "Gak hated bold colors. His paintings were done in black and white and gray. I told him, 'Gak, you see the world through an eternal snowstorm,' and he'd reply, 'Picasso, you blind me with your palette, make me dizzy with your shapes, but you teach nothing about the inner and outer hideousness that people ignore.' I thought about Gak often while I painted *Guernica* and *The Charnel House*. He would have applauded them."

"He never saw those paintings?"

"*Je ne sais pas*. We were no longer in touch. The last time we met was at La Rotonde. The café was crowded. It was a cold fall evening, the braziers were lit, but I don't recall the year. After 1933, because Hitler was in power. Gak and I were arguing about my *Seated Bather*. An argument we had whenever we drank absinthe together. He asked me how good a painting of a naked young woman on a beach could be if when you saw it, you had no desire to make love to her. I said, 'Who says no one wants to make love to her?' and Gak replied, 'She has arms and legs like cobras, Picasso. She is not welcome in my bed.' We were laughing when Chagall rushed over to us with a fierce expression that one never saw in his paintings. He shouted at Gak in Russian, and they almost came to blows. You see, Chagall was in the midst of painting his Bible stories, and Gak had painted his response: *The Tower of Babel*. A canvas four meters high and three meters wide, filled with fire-blackened towers of the dead—men, women, and children that were as mutilated as any that Bosch ever conceived. At the opening, Gak told the critics that he was dedicating the painting to Herr Hitler, who would soon be supplying the corpses, and to Monsieur Chagall, who believed in fairy tales."

"Did Gak sell that painting?"

Picasso removed his cigarette from the holder and stubbed it out in the ashtray. "His early paintings were handled by a Russian dealer. A few were sold, but most of them were stored in the dealer's mansion in St. Petersburg, and they were seized by the Soviets after the Revolution. His later work was shown in a gallery in Paris owned by a Jew who fled when the Nazis marched in, and the Gestapo burned the gallery to the ground along with the paintings."

"Did Gak survive the war?"

"He moved to Nice soon after that evening at La Rotonde. There were a lot of Russians in Nice then. They had been wintering on the Côte d'Azur since the nineteenth century. And Matisse—Matisse had been living in Nice for years. Conducting his love affair with the Mediterranean light. He occasionally saw Gak. Matisse told me that Gak had a Russian woman with him. A blonde with the greenest eyes Matisse had ever seen. Was this your grandmother?"

I twirled my wineglass in a circle. Taft Mifflin had asked me why

Emma had visited Nice on her annual European jaunts. Now, it seemed, I had the answer. "Sounds like her. My grandmother came to America in the late forties, but I never heard about Gak."

Picasso shook his head—sadly, I thought. "I'm glad she survived, and I can't explain her not mentioning him. But no one hears of Gak anymore. He was a wonderful painter, but so many who knew him and his art are gone, and his work has vanished. I was in Paris during the war, and for a while I believed Gak was safe. The South of France was controlled by the Italians, who left the Jews alone. Actually, Jews from around Europe went there to live. Then at the end of 1943 the Germans came, and they started putting Jews on trains. Most were taken to Auschwitz."

Picasso slid a Gauloises from the pack. He placed it in the holder and looked at me, his brown-black eyes shining. "There is a village, Haut-de-Cagnes, thirteen or fourteen kilometers from Nice. Matisse told me that a priest there had hidden Jews in his church, but I don't know if Gak was among them. Three years after the war I visited Auschwitz. I remember standing inside the gates hoping that Gak, his wife, and his two daughters had not died in those gas chambers."

I was so stunned I reverted to English. "Gak and my grandmother had two daughters?"

Picasso seemed puzzled. Yuli nudged me with her elbow to alert me to my mistake, and I switched to French, "Gak *et ma grand-mère avaient deux filles?*"

"That is what Matisse told me, but last I heard, ten, eleven, years ago, no one had seen Gak or his daughters. Will you try to find Gak?"

"*Oui.*"

"*Bon, bon.* If you do, tell him his old friend Picasso wishes to argue with him again."

"I will. By the way, do you know an art dealer named Charleston or one who lives in Charleston in America?"

"*Non.*"

"Was there another artist, friendly with Gak—Joost Ter Horst?"

"If there was, I never heard of him."

Picasso stood, and the waiter hurried over. Picasso gave him some franc notes.

I said, "Thank you for the wine and the drawing."

Picasso smiled, mostly at Yuli. "*De rien.*"

When he'd gone back to his table, Yuli said, "He knew Gak well?"

"They were friends," I said, and told her about the church in Haut-de-Cagnes where Gak might have waited out the war.

"And he and Emma had two daughters?"

"Had or have."

I gazed at the shadows falling across the port.

"Michael?"

"Let's go look for Alexander Gak," I said.

28

It was a two-hour ride back to Nice, and as the setting sun lacquered the hills of the Riviera with crimson and gold, I sat with Yuli in the taxi trying to understand why Emma had hidden the most important details of her life from me. I could understand why she didn't talk about her younger sister Maria being hanged by the Nazis. She must have preferred to lock that memory in its own box so it couldn't hurt her anymore, and she had always been protective toward me. Yet I was angry that she hadn't told me about Gak and their daughters. Even if my aunts had been murdered by the Germans, I wanted to know about them, feeling that my conception of myself was incomplete—bogus, even—without that information.

Before coming to France, I hadn't devoted much thought to the fact that I had no family, but now I was aware that it set me apart from everyone I knew growing up, and the strangeness of it was as awful to me as the loneliness. Yuli was the only other young person I knew in that situation, and at least she had Der Schmuggler. If Emma's daughters were alive, then I had two aunts and perhaps uncles and cousins. I wanted to meet them, and I was suddenly angry that Emma had saddled me with the mysteries of her secret life—mysteries that could have been responsible for her murder and the murder of Dmitry in Munich.

And what, I asked myself, had my father known? He probably knew

156

about Maria Adaskina—he had been in Rostov-on-Don when she was alive. So he had kept that from me, possibly because Emma had insisted on it. Had his mother told him about Gak? That was trickier. Maybe Emma didn't want my father to know that she had more children. That was possible, but couldn't she have told me after my parents died?

"Damn it, Emma," I said, and when Yuli tapped my arm, I realized that I had spoken out loud.

"You are all right, Michael?"

I nodded and asked the driver to recommend a hotel on the main street in Nice. When he dropped us off at the Hôtel Ruhl, a domed limestone relic of the belle époque, I could see the streetlights and the neon signs of the other hotels on the Promenade des Anglais reflecting on the tops of the palm trees and footprints of moonlight marching across the Bay of Angels.

Yuli and I were exhausted, both of us yawning as I gave the desk clerk my American Express card, and to dodge any discomfort about sleeping arrangements I requested a suite.

"Take the bedroom," I said.

Too tired to bother with the pullout bed, I lay on the couch, replaying everything Picasso had told me and wondering if I was kidding myself that I'd learn more about Gak or the others on Emma's list, the art dealer and Joost Ter Horst, or what had led my grandmother to ask God why our stories are written in vanishing ink.

My mind was racing, and I rotated from my side to my stomach to my back, despairing of ever falling asleep.

"Misha," Yuli said, and I opened my eyes.

The balcony doors were open, and the cool, breezy sunstruck morning air filled the suite. Yuli, in her black cashmere sweater and Levi's, was sitting in a chair that she had moved close to the couch. Her hair, as lustrous as honey, was swept up behind her head in a loose twist.

"Been sitting there long?"

She smiled. "I like watching you sleep."

There was something in her smile that I couldn't identify—not happiness, to be sure, or wistfulness. It was an impenetrable smile, a smile to hide behind.

"You okay?"

"You are asking if I am still scared?"

"I wasn't, but that's a good question. You have seemed preoccupied."

She showed me that smile again. "It is nine thirty. I went out to buy you a double espresso and croissant. The man at the desk tells me where to get the bus and gives me a map."

I washed up, put on fresh khakis, a polo, and my corduroy sport coat, and went out to the balcony with my breakfast. People were strolling and riding bicycles on the wide promenade, and the Baie des Anges was a translucent green near the pebbled beach and then a luminous turquoise all the way out to the horizon. So this was the Côte d'Azur, the Blue Coast. Aptly named. The sun and sea and sky seemed to infuse the air with a scintillating blue, and it was comforting knowing that on her visits to Nice, Emma had seen it, too.

Haut-de-Cagnes was a medieval walled village, and we stepped off the bus at the bottom of a long steep road. At the top were pale amber stone houses and a castle with the French flag flying from the turret.

"Do we walk up?" Yuli asked.

"No, we fly."

Yuli wasn't amused, and we hiked up, the sun on our faces. The one-lane road cut left and right with a low fieldstone wall on the outside so no one would drive off the road, and I wished that I wasn't wearing penny loafers. Yuli stopped to take off her flight jacket, and we rested by siting on the wall. Below were green hills and sun-faded tile rooftops and the bright blue sea. At the edge of the village, before the main cobblestone square, a jitney was parked at a bus stop in a turnaround, and it was a relief that we wouldn't have to hike down.

We drank Cokes at a café, and I asked the waiter for directions. Eglise Saint-Pierre was across from the castle, and the church was cool inside and dark except for the sunlight filtering through the stained glass and forming rainbows on the stone floor. The nave was several steps underground, and no one was there until, on our right, the door of a confessional opened and an old woman in a black dress with a black scarf over her head shuffled out.

Yuli whispered, "How wonderful that a woman can still be sinful at this age."

A young priest with a reddish-blond beard and bowl-cut hair longer than that of any of the Beatles emerged from the confessional and came past the altar to us. I introduced myself and Yuli in French and told him I'd heard the church had offered sanctuary to Jews from the Nazis.

"I am Father Paul-Louis," he replied in English, and I was too anxious to hear what he had to say to be offended by his implied criticism of my French accent. "Father Philippe would have been here then. He dies three years ago."

I had a terrible sinking feeling.

Yuli said, "Could the painter, Alexander Gak, have been protected by the church?"

Father Paul-Louis responded with a noncommittal shrug. "Sister Bernadette was alive in these years of the war."

Yuli asked, "Is she here?"

"Sister Bernadette takes care of Monsieur Gak."

"Gak is alive?"

"*Bien sûr*, he is alive. I tell you he is alive. I have been to visit Monsieur Gak."

As I pondered what quirky Gallic turn of mind had prevented him from telling me this when I first mentioned Gak, Yuli asked, "And where does Monsieur Gak live?"

"In Vieux Nice—the Old City above the market. At 2 Rue Honoré Ugo. On the top floor."

"Thank you, Father," Yuli said.

My head was pounding, and outside, I sat on a bench.

Yuli stood, looking down at me. "You want to know, and you don't want to know."

"That's about right."

In Russian, she said, "Better the unhappy truth than a happy lie."

"Who says?"

"Papka. He used to tell me that when I was a little girl, when I asked him what happened to my mother."

Taking my hands in hers, she pulled me to my feet. "And I will be with you, Misha."

29

Beyond the open-air market of Old Nice, we walked through a tangle of streets no wider than alleyways and perfumed by fresh-baked bread from the boulangeries and frying potatoes from the cafés. We went up flights of stone stairs toward Rue Honoré Ugo, the stairways hemmed in by old houses with facades of saffron or rose or cream and pistachio-colored shutters. Gak's building was five stories high with a creaky metal cage for an elevator, and his door was as weathered as driftwood with *M. GAK* engraved on a hammered-tin nameplate.

I knocked, and an elderly diminutive nun in a black dress and white wimple appeared, her face a pale, chubby-cheeked oval and remarkably unlined, a reward for decades of praying indoors.

"*Bonjour,*" she said, pleasant and businesslike, as if she thought I was seeking a donation to a worthy cause.

Good manners required me to say hello and explain myself, but I was staring over her at a room where, except for two tall windows, the walls were chock-full of ebony-framed paintings in black and white and gray—the eternal snowstorm through which, Picasso claimed, Alexander Gak saw the world.

Yuli also noticed the paintings. "They're all of one woman."

"My grandmother."

Some paintings were impressionistic renderings, presumably of Emma—her image obscured by dense layers of oils and swirling brush-strokes. Most were done with an obsessive attention to detail. Emma, young, sitting in a café with bubbles rising in the champagne flute she holds; Emma pregnant in a floppy hat and floral shift strolling the Promenade des Anglais; a series of Emma running on a beach, stepping from the sea, and astride a faceless man, making love. Embarrassed, I looked away. And felt sad. The hyperrealism of the paintings magnified Emma into an Olympian distortion, a goddess rendered in fine lines and somber shadings, as though Gak had labored to prove that the woman animating his sun-blessed walls was immortal.

"You are Misha," the nun said in English. "I am Sister Bernadette. Emma tells me of you and always has your new school photographs. And you are the girlfriend I hear of. *Pardonne-moi*, I am too old to remember names well."

Apparently Emma had told her about Beryl, and Yuli glanced at me, with a wry lift to her eyebrows, then smiled sweetly at Sister Bernadette. "Yulianna."

"This is a beautiful name," she said, using a fingertip to give herself a self-deprecating tap to the head. "Only an old woman forgets that beautiful a name. Please, you both come in."

The room was furnished with a sofa and tufted armchairs covered in burgundy brocade, glass-topped end tables with candelabra lamps girded by bronze grapevines, and a russet-and-green Persian rug that, after years of baking in sunlight, was as drab as a desert.

"*Alors*," Sister Bernadette said, sitting in a chair and waving at us to sit on the sofa. "Tell me how is your grandmother, and then we have café and tarte tatin."

Her serene expression was shot through with such kindness that the news got stuck in my throat. Yuli, her voice subdued, said, "It hurts me to say, but Emma was murdered."

Sister Bernadette trembled, her body tilting from one side to the other. "*Je suis vraiment désolée*, Misha. *Je suis très désolée.*"

I didn't know if Emma had told her that I spoke French or if she had unintentionally slipped into her native language. "*Merci.*"

A tear trickled down her cheek. Sister Bernadette didn't bother to wipe it away. "And you have come to me with questions?"

"To you and Monsieur Gak. Because the police have found nothing."

"Gak is very old and no longer speaks. The doctor says he suffers from dementia. Emma says he suffers from suffering."

"Is he home?"

"He goes out alone once a day for one hour, and I bring him back home."

"Where does he go?"

"We will walk there together, but it's not yet time."

"You met Emma through Monsieur Gak?"

"First, I hear about her. When Gak hides from the Nazis in the church. He talks about a woman. They are not married, but have two daughters. The woman was visiting her family in Russia with the girls when the Germans came, and she cannot return here. I meet her when the war finishes. After Emma comes, Gak becomes silent and remains silent."

"And their daughters?"

Sister Bernadette gazed at me with such compassion I guessed that the news about the girls would be bad. "You will see, but let me continue. Emma was married before Gak, and she misses her son in America."

"My father."

"*D'accord. Votre père*. And Emma could not live with Gak in Nice. He sleeps for days, he does not speak, and none of the doctors Emma brings can help, and they advise her to take Gak to an asylum. Emma refuses. I have retired a year after the war, and Emma arranges for me to care for Gak and goes off to America and comes in the summer. Gak even begins to paint again when she is here. Your grandmother is—how does *astucieux* go in English?"

"Astute."

"Astute, *d'accord*. Emma is very astute. In the beginning, she uses money from her candy store to support Gak, but then she sells some of his work."

My pulse quickened as Yuli asked, "To an art dealer in Charleston, South Carolina?"

"Yes, Emma calls him Monsieur Thaddeus, but I have his name and address in a drawer. And with the money from him, Emma buys this building. She rents the other apartments, and the rents go into a bank account in Nice I use to pay the bills."

I was impressed by Emma's financial acumen, and once again angry and bewildered by her hiding so much from me. "Sister Bernadette, why would Emma rent an apartment in Paris?"

"*Je ne sais pas.*"

"Did she mention a Joost Ter Horst?"

"*Non.*"

Failing to prevent my frustration from leaking into my voice, I asked, "Why didn't Emma tell me any of this?"

The kindness in her bittersweet smile was soothing, verifying that I wasn't the sole person mystified by my secretive grandmother. "Who can say, Misha? Emma, I always feel, is *une voyageuse avec trop de bagages.*"

"A voyager with too much baggage? I don't understand."

"Her life, I used to think, her past and present, was too heavy for her, and she wants no one to see her burdens. That would worry Emma, and the worry would make her burdens unbearable and her traveling impossible. But this is my guessing."

I pulled my sketch pad from my rucksack, wrote Eddie's address and phone number on a page, tore it out, and gave it to Sister Bernadette. "If you or Monsieur Gak ever need anything, contact this man. He will help."

"*Merci, Misha. Merci bien.* Now it is time to bring Gak home. And I will get you the name of the art dealer Emma wrote."

"And you will tell me about her daughters?"

Nodding, Sister Bernadette stood by pressing her palms against the chair cushion for leverage and pushing herself up, then headed, with a cautious gait, to the rear of the apartment.

Yuli inspected the paintings. Her back was to me, so I couldn't see her reaction as she moved along, pausing to study a canvas of Emma tilting a watering can over a planter spilling flowers like scarves from a magician's hat, the water missing its mark because Emma eyes the artist with a glimmer of amusement and suspicion.

Turning, with an expression as if she had been looking in a mirror, Yuli said, "I wish I'd met Emma."

"Me too."

30

Le Cimetière du Château was graced by grief sculpted in stone—great-winged angels, weeping mothers, children with bowed heads, Jesus trudging with the Cross to Golgotha. The Jewish cemetery next to it had no sculpture. We entered through a willow-green gate, the iron bars tipped with gold fleurs-de-lis, and passed a shed-sized peaked-roofed building. We followed Sister Bernadette past gravestones toward a rough-hewn log bench, where an old man with long white hair flowing out from under a black beret, a white Vandyke, and a black suit sat with his hands on the knobs of two ebony walking sticks.

"Monsieur Gak," she said as we came up behind him. He was staring down at a polished blue-pearl slab of granite with a raised Star of David and an inscription in silver:

À LA MÉMOIRE DE NOS FILLES

ALEXANDRA GAK   DARYA GAK
NÉE 12 AVRIL 1935   NÉE 24 JUIN 1938

ASSASSÎNÉES PAR LES NAZIS EN 1943

I was numb, and like a murky Polaroid sharpening into a distinct photograph, my mind filled with a memory of that wispy-haired old man saying Kaddish over the trench in Dachau. Had Emma's daughters—my aunts—been shot in the neck like that man's son while Emma watched? Or had they died in oxygen-starved agony in the same type of gas chamber I'd toured in the Dachau museum? I saw that old man crying for his son—tears like raindrops on his paste-white face—and Yuli walking around the bench. She needed no translation for the inscription, and she was already tearing up as she spoke in Russian to Gak: "I have my own sorrow from the same monsters who caused yours. It kills you inside to think about. And speaking of these things—that is even worse. But this man behind me is Emma's grandson, and he has traveled from the United States to talk to you."

Gak turned. His face was ridged, tanned the color of a peanut shell, and he bore a strong resemblance to an impudent hawk—without the predatory gleam in his eyes. Looking into those eyes was like peeking into an empty room.

Yuli tried again. *"Pozhaluysta."*—Please.

Gak glanced at her, at me, then began shuffling from the cemetery. I couldn't see myself informing him about Emma, but I was desperate to speak with him, this man who had loved my grandmother, who had endeavored to bless her, through his art, with life everlasting, and I called out to him in Russian, "Picasso says he wants to argue with you again." Gak pushed on, using the walking sticks like cross-country ski poles, and I shouted, "Who is Joost Ter Horst?" and Gak, with astonishing agility, spun around and glared at me.

"Joost Ter Horst?" I repeated, and Gak flung a stick at me, which fell five or six feet short, and then he resumed his shuffle and went out the gate.

I retrieved the stick and gave it to Sister Bernadette.

"I am sorry for you, Misha. Forgive him. He is sick."

"I know. Did he and Emma ever mention Joost?"

She said, "They spoke Russian together. I didn't understand. But he became silent soon after the war when Emma returned to Nice. She had to tell him about their daughters then. The gravestone is done before Emma goes to America to be with her son."

I knew more about my grandmother than I had before I'd come to

France, but my numbness hadn't receded, and trying to organize my new facts into a coherent account felt like reading a story in which every fourth word was Sanskrit.

Yuli asked Sister Bernadette, "Will you tell Gak about Emma?"

"*Non*. And he will not ask. Time means nothing to him. He only waits to go into this dirt with his girls."

"Thank you for helping," Yuli said.

Sister Bernadette flicked her wrist at us. "*De rien*. I wish I can do more. I must go. Gak has no key. You both come when you like. *À la prochaine*."

After she was gone, I stood there, hypnotized by the sunlight striking the slab.

"Misha?" Yuli said.

It felt as though a long time had passed before I replied, "Aren't you supposed to call me Michael?"

Yuli finger-combed my hair off my forehead. "Between us, you can be Misha."

I stared at the pearly blue granite. "My aunt Alexandra and aunt Darya."

"Yes."

"They were eight and five."

Yuli dropped her hand to hold one of mine.

"Did Joost Ter Horst kill them? Or have them killed?"

"Maybe. Gak was very angry when you asked about him."

"Gak was here, Emma was in Russia. When she came back to Nice, she had to be the one to tell Gak about Joost. Did my grandmother see her daughters die?"

Yuli didn't answer. Perhaps my tone unnerved her. To me, it sounded as if my numbness had attacked my vocal cords.

Yuli squeezed my fingers. I didn't have the energy to squeeze back.

"We should find Joost and ask him," I said, as though this was easily done, a matter of consulting a phone book.

"Let's go to the hotel or to a café."

I wanted to stay. I wanted to meet my aunts.

"Misha, come with me."

I picked up two pebbles from the ground and placed them on the slab, a Jewish custom to mark your visit with the dead.

Holding hands, we went by the marble facade of the building inside the gate, and I noticed the words embedded above the door stating that the structure had been erected by the Jewish community of Nice as a memorial to the local Jews killed by the Nazis. On the left side of the door was a marble urn that, according to the inscription, contained the ashes of Jews gassed and cremated at Auschwitz. It was the other urn, the one on the right, that froze me in place as I read the inscription: *CETTE URNE RENFERME DU SAVON À LA GRAISSE HUMAINE FABRIQUÉ PAR LES ALLE-MANDS DU III REICH AVEC LES CORPS DE NOS FRÈRES DÉPORTÉS.*

When we were in seventh grade, Birdman Cohen told me that the Nazis made soap from the fat of dead Jews, but Birdman was gaga about science fiction, so I'd told him he was nuts. And now here was an urn that proved he was right.

"What does it say, Misha?"

Dizzy, I was barely able to reply, "Soap . . . Jewish corpses," before letting go of her hand and sitting on the pebbly ground, waiting for my dizziness to pass and thinking about Emma losing Gak to his grief-stricken silence, Alexandra and Darya to genocide, and my father to the inopportune dovetailing of a marital squabble and an asthma attack. A soulmate, two daughters, and a son—all three of her children—enough to destroy anyone. Yet Emma survived. My head stopped spinning, but my numbness had been replaced by a searing pain behind my eyes, and I began to cry with a gasping rhythm and remembered how Emma relished handing out free candy to children and her chasing Miss Doyle from Sweets with a broom because she punched Rollie. All of that made sense now, but what eluded me was why my grandmother had borne her brokenhearted days and nights without mentioning her past. To protect me? *Don't ask*, she used to say, but was she waiting for me to ask again? I loved her, so why didn't I see her suffering? Because I was too interested in rock 'n' roll and girls and buying a convertible and going down the Shore, and it was my guilt at failing Emma that was most responsible for my weeping on this sunny afternoon.

As my sobs subsided, I became aware that Yuli had knelt down and put her arms around me. There was the violet-scent of the Hôtel Ruhl soap on her skin, and her breath was warm against my ear when she whispered in Russian, "Without sorrow, there is no joy," and while I was wondering if the phrase was a proverb or another of Der Schmuggler's maxims, she covered my face with feathery kisses, and I held on to her like a buoy while she worked around to my mouth. This kiss was different from the one on the shore of Lake Bereza, deeper, more forceful. Her fingers went past my sport jacket and under my polo to trace circles on my chest, and my hand crept under the rough cotton of her Breton-striped shirt to cup the heaviness of her breasts through her bra, and it was then that we reached a similar conclusion.

Yuli laughed. "The French are romantics. But—"

"It might annoy the mourners."

"There are no mourners at the hotel."

Inside our suite we didn't make it to the bedroom, shedding our clothes as if they had caught fire and falling onto the couch. Her hair was pinned up, and I brushed away the fine wayward strands to kiss her neck. She touched me everywhere, murmuring words in Russian that I'd never heard before but suspected were unsuitable for polite conversation. There was a brief pause when Yuli whispered that her best girlfriends Sofia and Viktoriya supplied her with birth control pills from the hospital pharmacy, and I gasped as she scissored her limbs around me. Her strength was ferocious, and turning to get more comfortable, I tumbled off the couch, which drew a burst of laughter from both of us. Then, like a supplicant, I got on my knees before Yuli, and our laughter became an up-tempo riff of my breathing and her garbled cries of protest and pleasure. She clutched at me, but I dodged her hands, keeping at it until she grabbed two fistfuls of my hair, a persuasive invitation to join her on the couch, and then we were together, each of us with our own history—our own darkness that couldn't be lit, our own fears that were never quiet—and so, for the moment, we lost these things in each other.

31

At dawn, I woke up in bed spooned around Yuli. She was looking away from me with her body against mine so that I could feel the rise and fall of her breathing. Careful not to wake her, I got up and went into the bathroom, then put on khakis and a sweatshirt and sat in an easy chair with my sketch pad. Ordinarily, my sketches were done in black, but I'd bought a box of color pencils in Munich, and I used them now to draw Yuli, the indigo light slanting in on her through the window, her hair a brown and gold cascade of satin across the white pillows, the enchanting bend of her spine and rounded globes of her bottom outlined under the plum-colored piqué quilt.

Yesterday, when we had finished and were curled together on the couch, Yuli, with more indignation than curiosity in her voice, had asked, "Where did you learn this?"

So she was jealous. Or wondering if her performance had measured up to my past. I understood it. I also had a fleeting bout of insecurity. Why not? At the party in the Malt Shop, Pyotr Ananko, displeased that Yuli had downgraded his romantic status, said that she had no shortage of "dance partners," a claim confirmed by Yuli herself right there on the couch. All the same, I wouldn't ask her for a comparative opinion: what would I do if I didn't like her answer? And honestly, just then, it wasn't the erotic that preoccupied me. I was busy noticing that the fear and sadness I hauled around like a pail of rocks were gone, and I was adjusting—warily and happily—to my new lightness. Since Yuli was responsible for this change, I wanted to tell her about it. But from her question, it was evident that her interest lay elsewhere, and because I had no sensible answer for her, I played for time. "This?"

Yuli cast a momentary glance toward where I had knelt on the carpet. "That."

"This and that?"

"Yes, where did you learn this, that, and some other things I don't want to say. "

"In the circus," a more politic response than the truth—a lonesome divorcée.

"Liar," Yuli said, and gave my arm a playful slap. "You make me feel shy."

"Just shy?"

"No, not just shy."

"I won't do it again."

"No, I want you to do it again."

And so I did, in the bedroom this time, and then we had fallen asleep without any further discussion of my romantic past.

Now I looked up from my pad and saw that Yuli was awake, squinting against the blaze of morning light in the window and sitting with the quilt covering her lap.

"I hope I'm prettier in your sketch than I am in this bed."

"That would be impossible," I said.

Her smile came and went like the sun playing peekaboo with the clouds. Then she disappeared into the bathroom. I heard water running, and she came out in one of the hotel's baby-blue terry-cloth robes and sat on the arm of the chair, inspecting my drawing.

"That's good. Yesterday, when I saw Gak's paintings, I was remembering you said that Emma used to like to watch you draw. Now I know why."

"I was thinking the same thing." I closed my sketch pad. "I have to make a phone call. To Eddie in the States. The family friend I told you about."

Yuli kissed me, and I tasted the minty flavor of Pepsodent. "Call him. I'll go shower."

Five minutes after I gave the hotel operator the number, the phone rang.

"Boyo," Eddie said. "Everything is good?"

"Fine."

"I spoke to Taft night before last. He's got nothing about Emma or that lousy business with you in Krautville, and me and the cops ain't doing no better here. But Taft says you gone off with a girl. That's progress. Where are you?"

"South of France."

Eddie laughed. "Like Cary Grant and Grace Kelly in *To Catch a Thief*?"

"Just like."

I told him about Gak and Emma and Sister Bernadette, and he said, "Jesus, your grandmother was a crafty dame. Bought an apartment house for him and paid his bills."

"And she never talked about her daughters with you?"

Through a crackle of static I heard Eddie sigh. "Not a peep. But I got the impression Emma didn't like being sad in public."

"I wrote down your number and address for Sister Bernadette and told her to be in touch if she or Gak need anything."

"Emma would've liked that. I'll take care of it. Maybe Taft will give you the all clear to come home now. And you could bring the girl."

"I'm trying to track down another guy who knew Emma." I figured it best to skip how Gak had reacted when I asked him about Joost Ter Horst. Eddie was a bigger worrier than my grandmother.

"Just because Taft and me have crapped out so far don't mean you gotta play Sherlock Holmes. And you're running up the charges on your American Express."

"You said I had plenty of money."

"You do, but you ain't Rockefeller."

My finances weren't the problem—even with my paying Yuli's end, I had more than enough. "Eddie, I'm being careful."

"Emma wouldn't like it, boyo. I promised her I'd look after you."

"I got it under control. I'll talk to you soon."

———

The Cours Saleya was an outdoor mall flanked by cafés and shops, and in the center, under striped canopies, peddlers standing behind tables bright with bottles of olive oil, fruit, cheeses, vegetables, herbs, and flowers. Yuli and I hadn't eaten in almost twenty-four hours, so our conversation was reduced to the bare minimum as we breakfasted on fried eggs, thick slices of ham, brioche with homemade strawberry jam, and, accompanying our second cups of café au lait, a specialty of Nice, a torte with a flaky crust stuffed with Swiss chard, raisins, and toasted pine nuts, and dusted with powdered sugar.

"I need to have a walk," Yuli said, licking the last of the sugar from her spoon.

We went out to the Promenade des Anglais and joined the crowd ambling along the sea.

"Could Joost Ter Horst be German?" I asked.

"Sounds more Dutch than German."

"Except Gak flipped out hearing his name, and if he was involved in murdering Darya and Alexandra, then I believe Joost has to be German. How do we find out?"

Yuli took my hand. "If Horst was in charge of a camp or an officer in the Einsatzgruppen—you know Einsatzgruppen?"

"SS death squads."

"Yes, then maybe Taft Mifflin. The Americans captured these shits and put some on trial. Taft might know who to ask."

"The Red Army also caught them. Could Der help?"

"Papka is in Otvali until next week. I cannot ask him on the phone at home."

"I'll call Taft."

We crossed the promenade to the Hôtel Ruhl. To the right of the entranceway, along a side street where taxis parked and the drivers gathered at a kiosk to talk and down shots of espresso, I spotted a baby-faced guy in a straw fedora and sunglasses standing by the kiosk and reading a newspaper. When he glanced up from the paper to stare at Yuli and me, I thought it was Pyotr Ananko. A wounded heart could lead an ex-flame to tail his former girlfriend to France, but that would be a mile past crazy, and Pyotr hadn't seemed unbalanced at the party. Besides, how would he know where we were?

"Something wrong?" Yuli asked.

I looked at her, then at the kiosk, and the guy was gone. I didn't want Yuli to think I was seeing her old boyfriends under the bed, so to speak, and I replied, "No, nothing."

———

In the suite, a stocky gray-haired chambermaid was changing the sheets, so I used the phone next to the couch in the sitting room and placed a call to Four Freedoms in Munich. Taft wasn't there. He was at the news bureau in Paris. I wrote down the number, then gave it to the operator and waited for her to connect me. Every day I left a tip for the maids on the desk, and the chambermaid came out of the bedroom and picked up the ten-franc note. Yuli, sitting at the other end of the couch reading *A Moveable Feast*, spoke to her in a language that sounded like Ukrainian, and with a slight bow, the chambermaid answered her and departed.

Taft came on the line, and he was angrier than I'd ever heard him. "You were supposed to stay put until we caught the bastards."

"How's that's coming?"

"No change."

"Then it doesn't matter where I am."

Taft snapped, "Stow the whimsy. This is more complicated than you know."

"Who's Joost Ter Horst?"

Taft didn't answer.

"Joost Ter Horst. Who is he?"

Taft said, "Not on the phone."

"Where?"

"Can you get to Paris?"

"Have you moved it?"

"Enough jokes, Michael. Lunch tomorrow. One o'clock. Come alone. Go to the desk at the Hôtel Régina and ask for my room. And goddamn it—watch yourself till then."

When he had hung up, Yuli said, "I could hear him. Does Taft always shout at you?"

"Only when he's being paranoid."

"Is that a lot?"

"He's CIA. That's the worst-kept secret in Munich. Paranoia is in his job description."

After giving Yuli the CliffsNotes version of my conversation with Taft, I dialed the hotel operator and asked her to connect me to Air France. I booked two seats on a nine A.M. flight to Orly and said I'd pick up the tickets at the airport counter. I'd told Eddie that I had things under control, and despite Taft's spy nonsense, for the first time since flying to Germany, I believed it.

Yuli slid down the couch to sit beside me, and I asked her if there were any sights she wanted to see when we returned to Paris.

She said, "We'll play by ears."

I chuckled.

"I have spoken wrong?"

"Play *it* by *ear*."

Yuli pressed her palms against my chest until I was on my back, and she leaned across me, her mouth circling my ear.

"Misha, is this playing by ear?"

"It'll do."

Part VII

32

Paris, France
January 29, 1965

Taft Mifflin was drunk. He wasn't swing-on-the-chandelier drunk or smack-your-wife drunk, though this latter category was hypothetical because two wives had already divorced him with the same complaint—*He doesn't talk to me.* Taft Mifflin was sitting-in-a-hotel-suite-alone drunk, a magnificent suite at the venerable Hôtel Régina with its own dining room and a view across the Jardin des Tuileries to the Eiffel Tower, the thousand feet of latticed iron giving off a coppery glow in the lilac twilight.

Taft refilled his tumbler with Glenlivet and told himself, once again, that he should've been a Congregational minister like his father, and lived on Cape Cod with his family and tended the flock at a whitewashed church in Barnstable. And Taft would've become a minister except the United States entered the war five months before his graduation from Yale, and the Office of Strategic Services deemed his Ivy League diploma and ability to read Blaise Pascal and Friedrich Nietzsche in the original to be superb qualifications for supervising arms drops to the French Resistance, sabotaging German supply trains, and playing hit-and-run with the Wehrmacht. After his discharge, Taft spent a listless semester at Union Theological Seminary before dropping out. How could he serve a God he'd quit believing in when, attached to the 45th Infantry Division to interrogate any captured SS or Nazi Party honchos, he entered Dachau and his definition of evil changed forever? In fact, after what Taft had done at the camp, he couldn't envision much of a future for himself until discovering that ex-OSS captains were prized by the fledgling Central Intelligence Agency, where past sins enhanced your résumé.

His present round of drinking had started when Taft got off the phone with Michael. So he had heard about Joost Ter Horst. Resourceful kid, and he had that Yulianna Kosoy with him, and that girl was no slouch. Taft felt a twinge of guilt that he had set the whole thing in motion. He wouldn't be the first agent to run an operation off-book and to use a civilian without his knowing it. He justified his plan by telling himself that in a career potholed with disappointments and moral compromises, he wanted, before he retired, to create one tangible moment of justice in a world of tragic unfairness, to compel the Lord to abide by His own rules, to reward the virtuous and punish the wicked. This goal, Taft knew, was unrealistic and grandiose, and he had no explanation for it beyond the fact that he was the son of a minister who had considered himself God's earthly representative.

Funny, Taft thought, how the past shapes your future without you knowing it until that future becomes your present. He had met Julian Rose in the OSS and fought alongside him in the Ardennes during the winter bloodletting of 1944. After mustering out, the two men had stayed in touch—over twenty years of occasional phone calls, lunches, and dinners. Taft was in a meeting at the Four Freedoms office in Manhattan when a secretary gave him the message that Julian had to cancel their get-together at '21' because his wife and daughter had been killed in a car accident. The funeral had been three days earlier, but the period of mourning was still being observed, and Taft rode out to New Jersey. The house was packed, and after offering his condolences to Julian, Taft went to the den with a beer and a corned beef sandwich and picked up a *Star-Ledger* that was in the wicker basket next to the Barcalounger.

The photograph and story were on the front page, below the fold. A woman smiling behind a soda fountain, the beloved owner of a popular candy store in South Orange, shot to death in an apparent robbery. Her name was Emma Dainov. Taft stared at the photo. Could it be her? The woman from Dachau, the one who had survived a mass shooting by hiding under the dead? He saw a resemblance around her eyes and mouth. Or was his mind welcoming him to middle age, when everyone began reminding you of someone else? He had often wondered about her. Taft glanced away from the photo, then stared at it again. It was her, he was sure of it, and checked her obituary for details. Emma was Jewish, born in the Ukraine, and emigrated to the United States in 1948. That fit, and though there was no mention of her having been in a camp, that also fit, because it wasn't a background that people advertised. He saw one other detail, a stunning coincidence. Emma was survived by her grandson Michael Daniels, whose name Taft recognized as the deejay who did the music show in Russian and English that Four Freedoms was rebroadcasting in the Soviet Union.

Later that week, when Taft was down at Langley for meetings, he asked research to dig up the travel records of Emma Dainov. He was already familiar with the files on Joost Ter Horst and his wife, Hildegard. When he saw that every summer Emma had traveled to Europe—Munich, Geneva, Paris, and Nice—he became convinced that she was searching for someone, an intuition that was reinforced when he noticed that Emma had submitted a visa application to the Soviet embassy.

Who was it, Emma? Your daughters? Joost? Hildegard, who, according to her file, was dead?

His desire to answer these questions was why Taft had decided to bring Michael to Munich. When he met him at Eddie O'Rourke's house and heard that no money had been stolen from the candy store and that Emma's Rolex had been left on her wrist, Taft's faith in his hypothesis increased exponentially, convincing him that somebody had murdered Emma, and her murder was connected to her summer travels in Europe. The shooting in Munich supported this theory. Taft had to keep Michael safe, so he put his plan on ice and had Der Schmuggler take him to Otvali. Once Michael took off for France and heard about Joost Ter Horst, Taft resolved to see his operation through to the end.

Until now, all of this had seemed logical to Taft. However, he hadn't factored in the impact of finishing a fifth of eighteen-year-old single-malt Scotch. It gave his thinking an intolerable clarity, and as he drank the last of the Glenlivet, Taft grew despondent and believed that he was deluded about Emma.

Fortunately, he had the cure for this doubt. Taft kicked off his wing tips and went to sleep.

33

The next afternoon Taft Mifflin had lunch sent up, and the beef bourguignon was served by a tuxedoed waiter on a cloth-covered table. Michael ate with gusto and talked about Gak, Emma, and their daughters, while Taft, hung-over, chain-smoked.

Michael said, "And when Gak heard me say, 'Joost Ter Horst,' he flipped out."

Taft waited until the waiter wheeled the cart out of the suite. Then he said, "We have a file on Joost. His father was Dutch—born in Rotterdam—but he married a German woman and moved to Schwanstetten, a village outside Nuremberg, when Joost was a kid. Before the war, Joost was a chef who owned one of the most famous restaurants in Bavaria."

"How do you—"

"I was in the Office of Strategic Services and attached to an infantry division that liberated Dachau. Joost was captured in the area, and I interrogated him. Joost told me he was no fan of Hitler. I heard that a lot during interrogations. It was mostly bullshit."

"Was there any connection between him and Emma?"

"Joost didn't mention one. He was a bitter guy who bitched about his wife, Hildegard. Her father was a Nazi Party bigwig, and when Germany began to draft soldiers, Hildegard's father got Joost into the SS, where he was given the rank of Obersturmbannführer—lieutenant colonel. She was ambitious for her husband, and after talking to Joost, I'd say he was ambitious for himself, so when an opening for a Reichskommissar came up—"

"A what?"

"When the Nazis invaded the Soviet Union, they set up administrative areas—Reichskommissariats—and each one had a man in charge, a Reichskommissar. Joost was supposed to oversee an area around the Don Basin, but it never got set up, and Joost became an assistant to the Reich Commissar of the Ukraine. The Poles put him on trial and threw him in prison. According to Joost, even the Reich Commissar loathed Hildegard and stuck them both in a Ukrainian hunting palace. Joost was around in the summer of 1942 when the Einsatzgruppen came through. The Ter Horsts assisted the killing squads that went to Rostov-on-Don and executed twenty-seven thousand Russians—the majority of them Jews."

"At the Ravine of Snakes. I heard about it from Emma's former neighbor in Rostov."

Taft said, "The way Joost told it, his wife hated Jews and Russians, and she was more helpful than he was to the Einsatzgruppen. But when he brought up the executions—I'll never forget this—he says that so many died because he did such a thorough job supervising the roundup. The prick was bragging and acting like he had no idea why the Einsatzgruppen wanted him to go get all those people."

"What happened to Hildegard?"

"When the Red Army launched their counterattack, Joost sent her back to Germany. She went to live with her parents in Nuremberg, and she was killed when the Brits bombed the city in January of 'forty-five. Joost was wounded in the Ukraine, and he was lucky to get out on a plane before the Russians grabbed him."

"Gak spent the war in France, so the only way he could've known Joost's name was through Emma. Did Joost have something to do with their daughters dying?"

Taft couldn't decide how to answer Michael, because he was positive that no remains were in the graves of Alexandra and Darya Gak. In Europe and the United States, it wasn't uncommon for survivors to erect headstones over empty graves for the loved ones they had lost. Yet with Emma running around Europe every summer, Taft speculated that she didn't accept that both of her daughters were dead. Let Michael meet Joost, and maybe they would learn more about the Gak girls.

Taft said, "Joost was in Russia, so who can say?"

"Could he have been involved in Emma's murder? Or with the shooting in Munich?"

"Not a chance."

"If you're so sure, you must know where he is."

"I do. And he's been there since 1946."

"Why wasn't he tried for war crimes?"

"Lots of people worse than Joost won't stand trial."

"That's a fact. Not a reason."

Taft popped a Lucky from a cigarette pack, tamping down the tobacco by tapping one end on the table. Michael felt as if Taft were stalling. He was correct. Taft was tailoring his reply to help push along his plan. "Remember, in Munich, I told you that the policy of the American government was to leave ex-Nazis alone?"

"Because West Germany is an important ally against the Soviet Union."

"Right. We also hired some of these guys."

"Like Wernher von Braun?"

Taft fired up the cigarette with his Zippo. "Right again. But we also hired guys who weren't rocket scientists. To bring us information."

"Spies?"

Taft chuckled. "It's not usually that dramatic. They keep their eyes open and our people talk to them or they write us reports. Joost is one of those. Of course, the Soviets would like to arrest Joost. They love trying Nazis. Revenge for the war, and who can blame them? But the KGB also likes to dig up war criminals and threaten them with trials unless they spy for the Soviets. West Germany wants everybody to forget Hitler, but another reason the Bundestag is leaning toward allowing the statute of limitations on war crimes to expire is to stop the Soviets from recruiting ex-Nazis. And most of the world, except the Russians and Israelis, is rooting for the Bundestag to do it."

As Taft sat behind a hazy rampart of tobacco smoke, it occurred to Michael that Taft probably had a boss at the CIA who wouldn't want him discussing these things.

"Why are you telling me this?" Michael asked.

Taft had an elaborate answer, but not only did he not want to tell Michael, he didn't want to think about it—that cold spring morning he entered Dachau. Corpses everywhere, sprawled on the ground, stuffed into boxcars on a side track, heaped outside a crematorium. Breathing through his mouth to avoid the putrid odor of death, Taft watched soldiers lining up thirty or forty SS guards against a wall until he heard a muffled cry to his left, where bodies, riddled with bullet holes, were tangled up like after a gang tackle on a football field. A woman had crawled out from under the pile, and she stood up a foot from Taft. She was naked, and Taft noticed that she'd been beautiful once, but her face was speckled with lice bites, her dark gold hair matted with dried mud, and starvation had flattened every curve of her body. A rifle shot rang out, and Taft and the woman turned as an SS guard fell and a soldier lowered his Garand. The woman nodded toward the submachine gun in his hands—a request, he realized, and asked himself why a concentration-camp inmate whose bones were so etched into her skin that she resembled a human fossil shouldn't be invited to the party. He flicked off the safety of the Thompson, retracted the bolt, and handed her the weapon. Taft saw her shoot three SS men in their chests before she returned the Thompson. He had just slung it over his shoulder when the woman grabbed the lapels of his field jacket and said in a scratchy, parched voice, "*Bitte hilf mir. Hildegard Ter Horst stoul meyn tokhter.*" It was Yiddish, but the words were almost identical to German: *Please, help me. Hildegard Ter Horst stole my daughter.* Letting go of his lapels, she collapsed. He caught her before she hit the ground, shouting for a medic, and when one came with a blanket, Taft wrapped her in it, then wandered off, discovering that the eyes become more accustomed to horror than to beauty. In a stand of birch trees, he saw a husky crew-cut guard swapping his black SS uniform for the striped pajamas of a prisoner. He was pulling on the pants as Taft approached, leveling his Thompson at him. The guard greeted Taft with a sheepish grin, as if he'd been caught playing hooky. In German, Taft asked him what had happened here. The guard shrugged: "*Die Juden sind unser Unglück.*" Taft repeated the phrase in English: "The Jews are our misfortune." When the guard responded with a big smile, saying, "I speak *Amerikaner.* I vant to learn more." Taft answered, "No need to," and the Thompson kicked and the guard flew back against the birches.

Taft waited for the memory to dissolve before putting out his cigarette and saying, "I'm telling you because somebody should pay for murdering your grandmother. And for Dmitry."

"Where's Joost?"

"You have to be careful, buddy boy."

"Why're you trying to scare me?"

"I'm trying to warn you. You might not be the only one looking for him. Remember, there's the KGB. Joost is in Amsterdam."

"We gave him a new identity?"

"We did." Taft handed Michael a hotel pad and pen. "And a name that's as common in the Netherlands as John Smith in the States—Johannes De Jong. Let me spell it for you."

When Michael was done writing, Taft said, "Johannes De Jong owns a coffee shop, the Magic Dragon."

"As in Puff the Magic?"

"Exactly. When I interviewed him, Joost was proud of his English. Claimed he should've been an American. The address of his place is 225 Prinsengracht."

Taft laughed, and the disgust in his laughter unnerved Michael as he wrote out the address.

"Did I miss the joke?"

Taft said, "Not yet, you didn't. But here it is. The coffee shop is a few doors down from the Anne Frank House."

"That's not funny."

"No, it isn't. And, Michael?"

"Yeah?"

"Try not to get yourself killed. Julian and Eddie wouldn't like that."

"Me either. Thanks for lunch."

Taft was standing at the window when Michael exited the hotel. Watching him pass the gilded statue of Joan of Arc on horseback and blending into the shoppers on Rue de Rivoli, he wondered if he had told Michael too much or too little. No matter. Both of them would find out soon enough.

34

Yuli and I went shopping at the Galeries Lafayette after lunch because it was cold in Paris, and the weather report in *Le Monde* predicted that it would be colder in Amsterdam, so we needed warmer clothes. In Otvali, I'd wanted to pack the quilted jacket that Yuli had lent me, but she said that with her traveling under a false American identity and speaking with an unmistakable Eastern European accent, it would be safer if we didn't bring any Soviet goods.

The department store was a brilliantly lit palace of haute couture with a stained-glass cupola above the main hall and gold ceilings with intricate carvings. Yuli had already selected a camel-hair coat, and now, as I settled into a chair, she was trying on silk and wool sheaths that accentuated her curves, examining herself in the tri-mirrors, twirling with a languorous grace. The saleswoman was draping scarves around Yuli's shoulders to demonstrate how they would complement the dress, while a fast-talking quartet of women surrounded her, offering their opinions in French, and Yuli nodded politely as if she understood their suggestions. A refined gray-haired woman standing by my chair, an obvious fan of Jackie Kennedy in a pillbox hat and leopard-print jacket, said, "*Pardon, monsieur. Quel est le titre de son dernier film?*"

She was asking me the name of Yuli's last movie, and for fun, I said,

"*King Kong*," raising my hand and wriggling my fingers to emulate the giant ape holding Fay Wray.

"*Non*," the woman replied. "She too young for *Le Roi Kong*. I see her in *Vogue Paris*."

Yuli selected three scarves, a simple black wool dress, and another in silk—by Emilio Pucci, a famous designer according to Yuli—with a tumultuous geometric pattern the color of plums, mulberries, tangerines, and lavender.

I would've been happy to buy the clothes for her, but she paid, and I carried bags.

"I told Papka if I was going to Paris I might go shopping. He gave me dollars and I exchanged them when you were at lunch. I want to buy for you."

"No—"

Yuli grinned. "It is not polite to let me dress well alone."

I stopped by the sparkly cityscape of atomizers on the perfume counter, the air smelling like a flower shop. "Okay, if you tell me."

"Tell you what?"

"That you know how beautiful you are?"

Yuli laughed, short and sharp. "Only a man could believe this is a serious question."

"Which qualifies me to ask it."

A moment passed, then another, until Yuli started talking in a matter-of-fact tone: "Boys at school try to touch me, but they touch any girls who let them, so does this mean I'm beautiful? The girls in school, they say to me, 'I wish I have your eyes, I wish I have your hair,' and I learn this means they are too jealous to be my friends, so I am alone." In a different voice, a confessional voice, reluctant and tender, she added, "But when you—like that—when you look at me, I feel beautiful. But if you weren't here to look at me—if you weren't, well. Let's go buy your clothes."

I came away from the Galeries Lafayette with a black-and-burgundy tweed topcoat, a flannel charcoal-gray suit with fine azure stripes, two black turtlenecks, and russet suede lace-up shoes. Yuli said that there was a sewing kit in Emma's bedroom closet, so she could hem the pants, and when I asked how she had learned tailoring, she giggled. "I probably altered half the Levi's in the Soviet Union."

At the apartment, we decided to test our new coats in the cold by walking to the Louvre. I had been anxious to see the Picassos, but at the museum I had trouble concentrating on them and wandered aimlessly from painting to painting.

"What's wrong, Michael?"

"Joost. I can't stop thinking about Joost."

"Be calm. We ride the train to Amsterdam in the morning, and we will go see him."

"If he hurt Emma—how do I not strangle him?"

"I will not let you."

We meandered back to the Place des Vosges. Yuli didn't have her map, but Notre-Dame was across the river, our lodestar in the failing winter light. Down past the cathedral, we crossed another bridge to the Île Saint-Louis. On the Quai de Bourbon, I spotted a Renault up ahead of us, one of those boxy economy models. As the driver opened the door and got behind the wheel, I saw her in profile, not quite believing my eyes as I dashed toward the oatmeal-colored car, waving and yelling, "*Attendez!* Wait! *Attendez!*" while people on the quay watched me run by, and Yuli shouted, "Michael!" I was sprinting, thankful that I was wearing my sneakers instead of my new shoes, and feeling the sweat break out on my forehead and the burning in my lungs, and I didn't stop until the Renault pulled away from the curb and disappeared around the corner.

Bending over, I rested my hands on my knees, panting.

When Yuli caught up with me, she said, "What—"

"Emma. It was Emma. Driving the Renault."

"Michael—"

"Same face, same hair. Emma. But younger."

Yuli put an arm around me, and I glanced up at her. From the furrowing of her forehead and the pursing of her lips, it was plain that my taking off after a woman I claimed to be a newer version of my grandmother distressed her. A reasonable reaction. It distressed me, too.

"I'm hungry," Yuli said. "Let's go eat. And we'll have some wine."

My breathing was back to normal. "Wine. Let's get some wine."

35

The tall skinny brick houses on Prinsengracht stood out against the sky in shades of autumn—chestnut-brown, dove-gray, oak-tree red, and sugar-maple orange. The houses had quirky gables and leaded windows, some of them lit by pale yellow lights that reflected on the wooden houseboats lining both sides of the canal, the dark water flecked with ice and running under the stone bridges, where bicyclists pedaled across and rang the bells on their handlebars to warn pedestrians, the jangling livening up the raw afternoon like music.

Our train had arrived at Central Station an hour ago, and we had hopped on a tram to the Hotel Americain. Yuli had selected it from the guidebook she'd bought at the Gare du Nord before we boarded in Paris, because the hotel was home to the famous Café Americain, among the oldest cafés in the city, and just a little over a mile from Joost's coffee shop. Both of us had dozed on the early-morning train, and the best thing about the trip was that we didn't discuss my alleged sighting of the young Emma.

Tired from the eight-hour ride, we perked ourselves up at a stall on Prinsengracht with cups of hot chocolate and a bag of poffertjes, bite-size pancakes sprinkled with powdered sugar. Farther up the canal we went by a picture window, where a bottle blonde, bathed in a ruby glow, posed in a black bra, panties, garter belt, and stockings, her arms raised like a belly dancer.

Yuli noticed me glancing in the window, and kidding around—I think—asked, "Are you interested to stop?"

"More interested in you borrowing her garter belt and stockings."

Playfully she nudged me in the side with her elbow, and we laughed until, a moment later, we went by the line of shivering people waiting for a tour of the Anne Frank House.

Yuli asked me if I had read Anne Frank's diary.

"In school," I told her.

"I used to wonder if it would have been worth dying in a camp if I could have died with some memories of my mother and father."

"What did you decide?"

"On bad days, I still wonder."

"Today?"

She threaded her arm through mine. "Today is a good day."

We smelled the Magic Dragon before we got there, the swirls of marijuana and hash smoke wafting toward us whenever someone opened the basement door to go in or out. Inside, it was dark except for the flicker of the candle chandeliers dangling from the low ceiling, and a blue-gray haze hung over the mahogany bar. On the jukebox, Peter and Gordon were singing their doleful ballad, "A World Without Love," and I felt as if the beatniks had fled Greenwich Village and reconvened at these wooden tables in Amsterdam, gabbing in English, passing joints and pipes, and wolfing down waffles and ice cream.

A stocky young woman was behind the bar, and I asked her if Johannes De Jong were around. She pointed toward a man at a table at the rear of the coffee shop. He was bald on top, with long grizzled hair down past the shawl collar of his sweater, and he was sitting in a wheelchair, with an afghan on his lap. Behind him, built into the wall, was one of those cages that passed for elevators in Europe.

"You speak," Yuli said. "My accent will scare him."

She stood behind my chair as I sat across from Joost. He had sunken cheeks, and his eyes were red and bleary, the result of the blackened nubs of joints in the white-and-blue saucer that doubled as an ashtray. Next to the wheelchair was a gray schnauzer who appeared as stoned as his master, lying on the plank floor with his front paws locked over his bearded snout.

I said, "Joost Ter Horst."

He stared through me. "I do not know him."

"Anymore. You don't know Joost anymore. But he used to be you, didn't he?"

There was no mirth in his smile, only scorn, and his teeth were crooked and stained.

"And Joost knew Emma Dainov."

On his right hand, Joost had two long brownish-yellow fingernails, one on his thumb, the other on his index finger, and he used them like tweezers, plucking a roach from the saucer, lighting it with a matchstick he struck against the table, inhaling, holding his breath, then exhaling the pungent smoke.

I said, "You figure the Bundestag will extend the statute of limitations on war crimes?"

"Why do I care?"

"Emma Dainov."

"Why do you continue saying this name?"

"She's my grandmother."

"Ask her, she tell you. Joost Ter Horst save her. Without Joost, she have died with the other Jews."

I was already sick of Joost referring to himself in the third person and calculated how satisfying it would be to break his jaw.

Joost dropped the burnt matchstick in the saucer. "Emma and Joost cook together. He teaches her the trick to Schmarrn mit karamelisierten Äpfeln."

I had no idea what that was, nor did I give a damn. "And while you were cooking, where were her daughters, Alexandra and Darya?"

"That is Hildegard. *Diese dreckige Hure.*"

I'd learned a handful of curses in Munich, and I was relatively certain that Joost had just referred to his wife as a "dirty whore."

Joost removed a matchstick from behind his ear, fired up another roach, took a hit, and let the smoke drift out of his mouth. "Joost should have married Hildegard's cousin or one of her friends. All are angels, but none want to marry a cook. Not even a cook with his own restaurant." He got rid of the roach and match by scraping his fingernails against the rim of the saucer. "Joost counts corpses in Russia. He not responsible for making them."

"And Alexandra? Darya?"

A pilot light appeared to flick on behind his red-veined eyes. "Hildegard doesn't like Alexandra with her curly black Jew hair, dark eyes, and a nose like a beak."

As I clenched and unclenched my hands, I heard Yuli catch her breath. "And Darya?"

"A beauty. Like Emma. She could be the Norse goddess Freyja. Blond with the green eyes. That is how Hildegard calls the girl, 'Freyja.'"

Rage boiled up in me, not just at the story, but that Joost was reciting it as if he were recalling a picnic. "Darya—her name was Darya. What happened to her?"

"I sent Hildegard away and then Bashe—"

"Bashe?"

"Diese *russische Fotze*."

Bashe was a Russian something, but I didn't recognize the word *Fotze*. "Who is Bashe?"

"Bashe—a girlfriend of Emma—and she put Joost in his wheelchair. After Hildegard leaves, Bashe arrives like a monster in a nightmare and shoots Joost."

"Alexandra and Darya—what happened to them?"

"Hildegard happens to them." Reaching down with both hands, Joost gently picked up the schnauzer, who let out a yip as Joost placed the dog on his lap. "Now Joost lives upstairs in this house and sits every day in his chair and watches children smoke and dream."

Joost spun the wheels so his chair went backward toward the elevator. "Let the Bundestag kiss the ass of the Nazi hunters. Joost do nothing wrong. Hildegard do it all, and she gets a bomb on her."

After backing his wheelchair into the cage and shutting the gate, Joost pressed a button, and as the elevator ascended, he said, "Joost does not care if the Jews arrest him. He is already dead."

I wanted to scream. Yuli looked dazed.

"Did you understand *Fotze*?" I asked.

Yuli replied with an almost imperceptible nod.

I waited for her answer, but she didn't offer one. "Is it a secret?"

"In English, I can't say. In Russian, *pizda*. You know this?"

Dmitry had taught it to me. "In English, it's *cunt*."

Yuli shut her eyes for a moment. Then she looked at me. "Did Emma ever mention a Bashe?"

"No, but if they were friends in Rostov, Der might know. Can you call him yet?"

"Soon," she said, and began walking out of the coffee shop.

36

By ten o'clock that night, neither Michael nor Yuli could sleep. They had eaten dinner at Café Americain and strolled through the Leidseplein, the square busy and bright with restaurants, bars, nightclubs, young merry-makers, and staid couples in black tie and gowns going to the Stadsschouw-burg for opera. Back in their room, they had made love, expecting to drift off in each other's arms, but now they were lying on their backs, with the nightstand lamps on, and gazing at the pink satin canopy of the four-poster.

Michael said, "I'm glad we dug up some of Emma's past, but after hearing Joost, I don't know if there's any way to tell if her killer came from there."

"Do you want to quit?"

"I want to know how Alexandra and Darya died."

"Joost didn't say they died."

"Joost did say Hildegard took care of the girls. And we saw the grave-stone Emma and Gak put up for them. Maybe this Bashe knows the story."

Yuli wondered if Bashe were the same woman who collected informa-tion from her in the bathhouse—the woman who taunted her by saying she was too wild for any boy to marry. Michael was right—if she were from Rostov, Papka would know. But Yuli couldn't tell Michael about Bashe, not until she spoke to Papka. There were so many things that Yuli couldn't tell

Michael. Or was afraid to tell him. Like the first time she had heard *russische Fotze*. Yuli was unsure of how Michael, this loving innocent American with the surfer hair and sparkly green eyes, would react to what she had done when the man called her that—this boy who studied her when she spoke as if he were curious about every thought in her head, this clever patient scheming boy who touched her in ways that frightened and thrilled her, the only boy who had made her feel loved. And yet—yet despite all of this—Yuli felt that her caring about his reaction was a character flaw, a weakness to be conquered.

Michael propped up his head on his hand. "If I can track down Bashe and talk to the art dealer in Charleston, that will probably fill in some blanks. Will you help me?"

"I will, but—"

"You have to get back to Otvali?"

"Sooner or later."

"I don't want you to go."

The apprehension in his voice set off a wave of loss in Yuli, and she almost confessed that she couldn't imagine going back to Otvali alone.

Yuli kissed him. "Let's sleep. We will think tomorrow."

He chuckled. "I hope so."

The lamps went off. They tossed and turned. Michael switched on the lamp on his side of the bed. "I can't sleep."

Yuli went to the bathroom. Her makeup bag, a small, stiffened cardboard suitcase covered in pigskin, was on a stool, and she opened it and removed four orange Seconal capsules from a tin pill box and returned to bed with the Seconals and a glass of water.

"Papka gave me these for travel. You take two and you sleep."

Yuli put the capsules in her mouth and sipped from the glass. Michael did the same, then turned off the lamp, and Yuli curled up behind him.

When his breathing was slow and regular, Yuli kissed the nape of his neck. He didn't stir, and she went to the bathroom, closing the door, turning on the light. After taking the capsules out of her mouth, drying them with a tissue and dropping them in the tin, she dressed in Levi's, a sweater, and Keds. Then she loosened four bolts on the right side of her makeup bag, revealing a false compartment and retrieving a black knit hat, a map she had drawn, a syringe with a needle, her horn-handled switchblade, and a yellow armband with a blue Star of David—the type of cloth armband the Nazis had made Jews wear. Her coat hung on the back of the door, and she put it on, then tied her hair in a ponytail, tucking it under her collar and pulling on the hat, and loaded up her pockets, hit the light, and checked again that Michael was out by kissing his forehead. He didn't move, and Yuli decided it was safe to tell him.

"I love you," she said.

37

Across from the hotel, an ash-gray Mercedes-Benz idled under one of the old-fashioned lantern streetlights. A flame flashed in the sedan as the driver, a bearded man in a cap, lit a cigarette. Out of habit, Yuli memorized the license plate—GZ-89-91—then started walking, going left on Marnixstraat and glancing back to see if the car or the driver had followed her.

Russische Fotze. . . . Yuli was shocked when Joost had uttered those words. She hadn't thought about them in years. Now they were stuck in her head along with the memory of the day she first heard them. Dovid emerging from the woods with Yuli behind him. The German soldier firing. Dovid falling. The German dipping into an ammo pouch on his belt. Yuli struggling to raise the *papasha*, the heavy Russian submachine gun. The soldier pressing bullets into his rifle. Yuli squeezing the trigger. Her ears still ringing as she stands over the horse-faced German, a mean horse, big yellow-brown teeth. Blood leaking from the holes in his greatcoat.

"*Russische Fotze,*" he says, and Yuli fires at him until his face is gone.

On Leidsegracht, the wind was rippling the black water of the canal, and Yuli admired the moonlight silvering the ripples. She had almost told Michael about the German when they had hiked to Lake Bereza, but he kissed her, and Yuli told herself that his kiss had distracted her. That was a lie, and she knew it. Yuli said nothing because that story was only one of another eight or nine stories—she resisted a strict accounting—about men Papka had sent her to kill in the service of governments. For America, a North Korean microbiologist in Lviv, who specialized in weaponizing viruses; for Israel, a Syrian arms merchant in Moscow who peddled his wares to radicals in the Middle East and the Chechen-Ingush Republic; for the Kremlin, a Cuban official, a personal friend of the Communist hero Fidel Castro, who tried to bribe a manager to acquire AK-47s directly from the factory in Izhevsk for resale to South American criminals—an average of one a year, give or take, and when Yuli envisaged telling Michael about any of them, she couldn't bear picturing the horror on his face.

Papka had practiced this trade, and after Yuli's formal education was done, he had introduced her to the art of stalking prey and escaping pursuers. He had hired Red Army veterans to help guard the compound and warehouses, and these men had tutored Yuli in hand-to-hand combat, knife fighting, marksmanship, booby-trapping doors and windows with plastique, and wiring a bomb to a car's ignition. It was Papka, though, who had taught her the one indispensable lesson, which permitted Yuli to justify the killing to herself. *Your targets are evil men,* he said. *Like the men who murdered Dovid and the children at the lake. Like the men who murdered your mother. Never forget that.* And Yuli never did. Nor did she question why she was expected to do as Papka ordered. He had rescued her from the forest, and Yuli loved him. Then Michael arrived in Otvali, and Yuli started wondering if her debt to Papka would ever be paid. Had Yuli been his daughter—the daughter that Papka, drinking his way to the bottom of an ArArAt brandy bottle, often said that he wished he'd had with his beloved Maria Adaskina—would Yuli's life have been her own? Wouldn't she be allowed to marry and move away to raise a family? Sometimes, Yuli thought Papka acted as though the Nazis slaughtering his parents, siblings, and Maria entitled him to hold on to her forever, to never sustain another loss, even one as inevitable as a child growing up and leaving home. Well, Yuli didn't share his perspective, and traveling to Paris, Nice, and Amsterdam with Michael had brightened her daydreams with the irresistible hues of overlapping rainbows, and she neither wanted to let go of them nor of Michael.

"Yuli, this is you?" a man's voice called out to her in English.

Her reflex, honed by training and experience, was to grip the switchblade in her coat pocket, but Yuli relaxed as she turned to the blond-haired man in a trench coat, realizing that the voice belonged to Pyotr Ananko. He was sitting on the terrace of a café decorated with cords of white lights entwined around the awning poles.

"Petya!" Yuli said, sounding as if she were pleasantly surprised—instead of being suspicious about his presence.

Despite the wintry evening, the tables were full, the terrace warmed by a big perforated metal brazier. Yuli entered the terrace as Pyotr stood and bent to kiss her lips. Yuli had dodged his lip kiss at the party in the Malt Shop and offered him her cheek, but hoping to determine why he was in Amsterdam, she accepted the kiss and sat at his table.

"Would you like a beer?" Pyotr asked, then took a drink from his mug.

"No, thank you, Petya. I'm out for a walk."

"You are on a vacation?"

He knew that she wouldn't be vacationing in the Netherlands, but Yuli had to calibrate her response to inform Pyotr and to mislead him. Soviet foreign correspondents were debriefed by the KGB. The Committee for State Security was obsessed with information about the West, mainly how Europeans and Americans felt about their governments, and whether certain individuals, with access to sensitive materials or with the ability to influence public opinion, might be willing to work for the Soviets. All the correspondents answered their KGB questioners. Otherwise, their credentials would be revoked, and they would trade the comfy perquisites of life in the West for public transportation instead of a car; a decrepit apartment with a communal kitchen; and quoting tiresome party functionaries at home. All the same, some of the correspondents were more dedicated to spycraft than to journalism, and Yuli was unsure which her childhood friend preferred.

"Papka has me doing errands for him." This was a safe reply. Pyotr knew that Der Schmuggler had connections among the state-security apparatus and in the Kremlin. The men in power tolerated his smuggling because he bribed them, and while a few of them may have suspected that he took on assignments for the CIA and the Mossad, no one had any proof. In addition, as Yuli came to understand, Der Schmuggler was clever enough to work in the little-known corners of the Cold War, where the interests of all his clients were aligned. For instance, the United States had reason to target that North Korean microbiologist, yet Soviet leaders had been distressed by his contacts with Ukrainian nationalists. Israel dispatched Arab arms dealers like picnickers swatting flies, but the Syrian was greedy and had arranged a delivery of rocket-propelled grenades to Chechens hostile to the Kremlin. And the Cuban official was a thief, which annoyed the bigshot party thieves. In these cases, the targets were from countries allied with the Soviet Union. Thus, the KGB couldn't leave its fingerprints on the corpses, so Papka was protected by his powerful friends in Moscow—for the time being.

Pyotr took out a flip-top box of Marlboros, and when Yuli eyed the pack, he said, "They sell these here."

She gave him a droll smile. "You are in Amsterdam for the cigarettes?"

"For an article on Ben Webster."

"That is the saxophone player you like? The man who played with Duke Ellington?"

"And Oscar Peterson and Coleman Hawkins and Art Tatum. Ben is disgusted with how he—and all Negroes—are treated in the United States, and he has come to live here."

Pyotr might be lying, but his explanation was plausible. To dig for the truth, her best course was to confront him head-on, a reasonable tactic given that she knew things about Pyotr that he would prefer the KGB not to know—that he used to sell German shortwave radios and Beatles albums in Dnipropetrovsk and that he had identified the missile designer Kazimir Zolnerowich for Yuli, so she could photograph him and pass the pictures, through Bashe, to the Americans, who were eager to persuade the young genius to defect.

With an accusatory edge in her voice, Yuli said, "I saw you in Nice, hiding behind the newspaper at the kiosk."

Pyotr smoked his Marlboro, his expression placid, as if Yuli was making chitchat. "That was you and the Mad Russian going into the Hôtel Ruhl? I thought so."

"And you would not come to say hello?"

"You were . . . engaged."

"It was odd seeing you in Nice."

"I was there for Ben Webster. He had a performance at La Caravelle in Marseille the night before, and one in Nice that night—at the Hôtel Le Negresco."

This was credible, primarily because Yuli couldn't figure out how Pyotr could have tracked them to Nice unless the KGB had been watching them when they first landed in Paris—unlikely given that Yuli had seen nothing suspicious. Yuli had more success figuring out how Pyotr could have tailed them to Amsterdam: that chambermaid at the Hôtel Ruhl. The KGB had more chambermaids on its payroll than Conrad Hilton, and the maid struck Yuli as Eastern European. As soon as Yuli spoke to her in Ukrainian and the maid answered, Yuli kicked herself for not checking the phone and the suite for bugs. But that would have alarmed Michael. Yuli wanted to protect him from that part of herself, but now she worried that her reluctance had exposed them to more danger, because in all likelihood the KGB had picked them up on their return to Paris, then shadowed Michael to his lunch with Taft Mifflin and to the train at the Gare du Nord.

"Petya, what does the KGB want with me?"

"With you?"

"Or does the KGB have a special department to assist jealous former boyfriends?"

Pyotr appeared wounded, frowning and poking out his Marlboro in the ashtray. "We are friends our whole lives. I am telling the truth—I am here to write about Ben Webster."

Yuli had hurt Pyotr by rejecting him, and she didn't want to rub salt in the wound, but she didn't believe him. His story contained too many coincidences, and Papka was fond of saying that every coincidence was a mirage, the result of adding stupidity to ignorance.

She stood. "Good night, Petya."

"It is late. Let me walk you."

She rolled her eyes at him. "To keep me safe?"

"Yuli, wait," he said, but she had already left the terrace.

38

She had intended to go straight up Prinsengracht, but after bumping into Pyotr, Yuli checked her map and altered her route, veering away from the canal onto Passeerdersstraat, quickening her pace and abruptly slowing down, her head swiveling to check for a tail, and cutting back to Prinsengracht, the streetlights buffing up the night with an amber sheen that fell like flames on the ebony surface of the canal.

That afternoon, when she and Michael had arrived to speak to Joost Ter Horst, Yuli had seen the ramp outside the front door of the house above the basement entrance of the Magic Dragon, and the ramp had inspired her plan. The window of the coffee shop was dark, and Yuli sat on a bench kitty-corner from the house. Several people passed by, hurrying through the cold, and across the canal, the lights of a houseboat were on, and Yuli heard the Beatles' "Can't Buy Me Love" coming from the boat. It wasn't the plan that made her anxious. Yuli was worried about Michael alone in the hotel. If Pyotr hadn't followed her in a fit of jealousy, she couldn't understand why the KGB would be shadowing them: whatever she was doing was being done for Papka, and the KGB didn't harass him. That left Michael. If KGB agents were watching them, they knew that Michael had met with Taft Mifflin, so maybe this was nothing but intrigue between American and Soviet spies. That would be good news. The bad news would be that Michael, in searching for his grandmother's killer, was poking around in business that interested the KGB. If that was true, then he and Yuli had a problem, which was why she was in a rush to leave Amsterdam.

Yuli was shivering when Joost, wearing the same ratty cardigan, rolled down the ramp in his wheelchair. He was holding a leash, and the schnauzer scurried beside him. The houseboat was dark and quiet. Joost wheeled over to the leafless trees along the canal. Yuli walked behind Joost and the dog, who had lifted a hind leg to relieve himself against a tree trunk. Seeing that the street was empty, Yuli dashed behind Joost, locking the crook of her left arm around his throat. He fought, rocking in his wheelchair, but because his legs didn't work, he couldn't push up to free himself. Removing the syringe from her coat pocket with her right hand, Yuli flipped off the cap with her thumb and, aiming at the jugular, jabbed the needle into Joost and injected him with phenol, the drug used by the Nazis to cleanse the world of *Lebensunwertes Leben*—life unworthy of life.

Joost stopped rocking. Yuli withdrew the needle from his neck and tossed the syringe into the canal. Keeping her eyes on the street and spotting no one, she knotted the yellow armband with the blue Star of David around his throat and shoved Joost and his wheelchair into the water. The schnauzer was barking and gazing up at her. She recalled a quote from *The Count of Monte Cristo*, one of the most popular novels at school: *Providence has punished him.* Then Yuli was overwhelmed with revulsion because she had felt nothing about killing Joost yet was concerned about his dog. Joost, she decided, got the fate he deserved, but the schnauzer was innocent. Yuli picked up his leash, intending to tie him to the front door of the house, but when she tried the handle and the door opened, she put the dog inside, a modest gesture that proved to Yuli that her vocation had not fully extinguished her humanity.

———

The car was parked thirty meters past the Anne Frank House. Through the rear window, in the faint wash of the streetlights, Yuli saw the outline of a driver in a cap. The shape of the car resembled the Mercedes she had seen outside the hotel, but there wasn't enough light to say for sure. The difference between paranoia and caution was the ending; if the driver blew her brains out, no one would accuse her of being paranoid. Not much of a prize, was it? Yuli changed her route, heading toward a bridge to cross the canal, and as she did, the car started, the taillights winked on, and she glimpsed the license plate—GZ-89-91—the same plate as the Mercedes sedan. She walked faster, going down a street too narrow for the Mercedes, and then another. Yuli had to call Papka before Joost was fished out of the water. She couldn't use a phone at the Hotel Americain, not the public ones in the lobby and not the one in the room, because the call would have to be placed through the hotel switchboard, and the KGB paid off switchboard operators as zealously as chambermaids. And Yuli avoided phone booths. She felt too vulnerable, frightened that somebody would attack her from behind.

Within minutes, Yuli was lost, but there was no shortage of Mercedes sedans in Amsterdam, and she didn't dare stop to check her map. Her salvation, she hoped, lay up ahead, where pinkish-red lights shone over windows on both sides of a canal, and people were ogling the prostitutes in negligees behind the glass. Yuli blended into the clusters of tourists, many of them couples holding hands, satisfying their curiosity, and single men appraising the wares. Off the main drag, Yuli darted down an alleyway lined with red-lit windows and serious shoppers, and as she reached the end, a hand clamped on her shoulder, pulling her backward.

A man in a sheepskin jacket with a shearling collar loomed over her and, breathing beer in her face, asked, "How much, honey?"

Yuli smiled helplessly, as if she didn't comprehend his request, and attempted to move out from under his grip. He held on to her, grabbing a lapel of her coat with his other hand, tugging her toward him. "You speak English, don'tcha?"

Yuli encouraged him to let her go with a knee to his groin, which doubled him over, and striking him under his chin with the heel of her right hand, and then she bolted out of the alley and down another street until she came to a corner with a weathered brick two-story house that had a red neon sign above the door that said *OPEN*, and at the bottom of the front window, decals of credit-card logos, American Express and Diners Club.

Stuffing her knit hat in a coat pocket, Yuli rang the buzzer. A tidy woman with short silver-blue hair, impeccable eyeliner and lipstick, and a black ruffle dress answered the door.

"You looking for the job?" she asked.

"No."

"We are for men here."

"What does a half hour cost?"

"This varies. Thirty dollars American will make a man grin."

"I'll give you sixty if you let me use your phone."

The woman eyed Yuli with more than a little suspicion.

"Please. Someone is chasing me, and I have to get off the street."

The woman let her in. Straight ahead, Yuli saw men and women sitting on couches and heard the simmer of conversation. An office with a metal desk was off to the right, and on the desk was a Tensor lamp, an adding machine, a ledger, and a telephone. Yuli gave the woman three twenties, and she went out, shutting the door.

In Otvali, Yuli had written Papka's schedule and contact numbers on the back of her map in her private code, a jumble of English and Cyrillic letters. He was in Bucharest, Romania, in an apartment building next to the Israeli embassy, and she got the international operator on the line, gave her the number and one of the phony Polish names she used when calling Papka and, in English, requested that the operator reverse the charges.

"*Allo*," Der Schmuggler said after telling the operator he would accept the call.

"*Allo*, Papka. How are you?"

"Fine, fine. When are you coming home?"

Yuli knew that discussion would be unpleasant, so, for the moment, she stuck to business. "The letter should be mailed. The subject is Joost Ter Horst."

Yuli had drafted the letter in English before leaving Otvali. It was short and to the point: *If the Bundestag votes to let the statute of limitations expire, then war criminals like —— will receive justice from those of us who have not lost our minds or our memories.*

Yuli had omitted the name, because neither she nor Papka knew if she would find anyone. Papka had translated the letter into German, and Yuli assumed that linguists at the Israeli embassy would translate it into Dutch, French, Spanish, and Portuguese, and the letter would be sent to newspapers throughout Germany, the Netherlands, France, and South America. They would skip the United States. With the reliance of Israel on America, the Mossad wouldn't embarrass the White House by assassinating war criminals there.

"Papka, I need an address."

"Yes, dear girl, which address?"

"Bashe."

Yuli heard the sharp disapproval in his voice. "No. Too risky. You should come home."

"Misha will keep looking until he finds her."

"Let him look. He will find nothing."

"Do not be so sure, Papka. Misha does not know our world, but he learns fast. And I . . ."

"And you?"

"And I will help him."

Papka was silent.

"I promise you, Papka. I will stay with Misha until he finds her."

They both knew it would take a long time to locate Bashe unless Papka provided the address; Bashe was a courier for intelligence agencies, and you couldn't run those errands without a flair for covering your tracks. Therefore, Yuli's promising that she wouldn't return until Bashe was located was a threat to be away from Otvali for maybe a year or more. Yuli felt sick to her stomach threatening Papka, but she wouldn't change her mind. She had a right to a life of her own.

Papka chuckled. "You are a wicked girl."

"Who has a wicked Papka."

"I taught you too well, yes?"

"You did, Papka. Bashe was friends with Emma, wasn't she? And you?"

"Bashe is from Rostov—from the Street of Jews. Emma and I meet her there."

"Where is Bashe now?"

"Hold yourself a minute."

Yuli heard him set down the phone on a desk or table, and what sounded like a door opening and closing. Then Papka came on again. "Bashe is traveling for a month, maybe more."

"And when she isn't traveling?"

"Atlanta. In the state of Georgia. Her husband owns Jack's Watch and Clock Repair. The address I don't have. But in America you can look it up in a phone book."

"Bashe lives in America and she never sees Emma after the war?"

"I never knew Bashe well. We rarely speak. But Emma disappeared during the war. Millions did, and we believed they died. The next time I heard of Emma, right before Michael came to us, she was dead."

"Thank you for helping, Papka. And I have something else to tell. When we were in Nice, and now in Amsterdam, I saw Pyotr Ananko."

"This is not good, Yulianna."

"I agree, Papka."

"I will get you two plane tickets for tomorrow—New York or New Jersey, wherever they land—and I will have a friend from The Hague take you to the airport."

The Israelis had an embassy in The Hague, and this friend, Yuli knew, would be a member of the security detail assigned to the embassy.

"We are at the Hotel Americain," she said, and read him the address and phone number from the matchbook she'd taken from the room.

"You get a call in the morning with the arrangements. But be careful. Remember, I always tell you: The worst thing that can ever happen to me is if something happens to you. "

Her voice breaking, Yuli said, "I will be careful. I love you, Papka."

Yuli took a cab to the hotel, getting out a block away, and, seeing that the Mercedes wasn't outside, went in and rode the elevator upstairs. Michael was still sleeping on his side, and Yuli undressed in the bathroom and crawled into bed. It seemed as if she had just drifted off when the phone rang, but as Yuli picked up, she saw daylight filtering through the blinds.

A man said, "I am Moshe. Two hours for ze plane. I vill be in lobby."

Before Yuli could reply, he hung up.

Michael sat up, his face fogged with his drugged sleep. "Who was that?"

"I spoke to Papka. And found Bashe."

"Where?"

"I'll tell you if you will buy me a pizza burger."

"Really? In America?"

"In America."

39

What is expected of you? How much of your soul belongs to others? And perhaps the trickiest dilemma—when do you know if you have done enough?

Der Schmuggler had been asking himself these questions since the conclusion of the Great Patriotic War, and speaking to Yuli in Amsterdam had brought them back with a vengeance. Yet, in the quiet of this ice-clear evening in downtown Otvali, as he sat on a bench next to his empty bottle of Armenian brandy and under the statue of his late fiancée Maria Adaskina, with the earmuffs of a ushanka pulled tight and bundled up in a surplus Red Army wool coat, the answers still eluded him. He had created this town from nothing. Even so, as he looked out at Adaskina Boulevard, which he himself had paved with Belgian block, and the shuttered shops and synagogue and church and school, and the glow in the misted windows of Café Victory, none of which would have existed without him, the fruits of his labor felt inadequate to discharge his obligation to humanity.

Why should this be? His parents, to start. His mother, with the energy of three women, tended to the less fortunate and never failed to invite them to share the Sabbath meal. And his father, a grain dealer forever studying the Talmud, instilled in his children that while no one must complete the task of perfecting the world, they were not free to refrain from it. And

207

those children . . . Der Schmuggler was the oldest of his seven brothers and sisters. He was off with the partisans that hot, muggy August day in 1942 when the Nazis herded the Jews out of Rostov to the Ravine of Snakes, shooting the men and killing the women and children in gas vans. His whole family had died, and Der Schmuggler had been unable to forgive himself for not dying with them.

The doors of Café Victory swung outward, and Der Schmuggler heard laughter and saw a young couple stroll out, their arms around each other. Stepping over a snowbank, they came across the deserted boulevard, the woman's long hair a shimmering black in the aura of the bell-shaped street-lights, and when they disappeared into a side street, Der Schmuggler gazed at the statue of Maria, her lovely face eternalized in bronze, and whispered out loud, "This is not the life I planned."

Man plans and God laughs. A mildewed scrap of Yiddish wisdom: *Der mentsh tracht un Got lacht*. Jews quoted the proverb as though it was the opening verse of the Torah: *In the beginning, man planned and God laughed*. Oh, the wit! Stalin and Hitler planned to perfect the world, and each of them only had to slaughter tens of millions of innocents on their roads to perfection. Did God laugh then?

And Taft Mifflin had a plan. To seek justice for the dead. A deluded man, thought Der Schmuggler, who with a bellyful of cognac was inclined to agree with that insect-worshiping scribbler Franz Kafka that the sole meaning of life was that it ends. Regrettably, Der Schmuggler had had to assist the CIA agent. Taft guaranteed his access to American goods, and without those goods he would lose his usefulness to the party bosses and his contacts in the KGB and the Kremlin. Once his usefulness was gone, they would get rid of him as surely as Stalin had sent that Spanish Communist to plant an ice ax in Trotsky's skull. Taft's plan had the potential to cause him trouble—not nearly as much as his two latest undertakings, but enough, and the worst part was that to help Taft, Der Schmuggler had to send Yulianna off with the American boy, and his wounded heart told him that she would never again live in Otvali.

Well, Der Schmuggler thought, watching two men in parkas with fur-trimmed hoods on their heads exiting from Café Victory, life was unpredictable. Maybe he too would one day land in America.

The men walked toward him across the boulevard, and as they passed, Der Schmuggler noticed that one of them was holding something against his side, and just as he realized that it was a truncheon, a cord dropped over his neck and the hard rubber club landed against his hat. Instinctively, Der Schmuggler tried to slip his fingers underneath the cord to pull it off his throat, but the truncheon hit him again while the cord tightened, and he couldn't breathe and felt as if his brain were about to explode. Glancing up at the statue of Maria, Der Schmuggler reassured her that he had never loved another woman, certainly not the ones he visited in the brothels on his travels, and as the cord cut into his neck and the truncheon kept striking his head, he stopped struggling, dropping his arms and closing his eyes. A great calmness spread through him, and he was happy that he would be seeing Maria again, a reunion that had filled his dreams ever since the Nazis had hanged her.

A Buchanka, a van that looked as if four wheels had been glued to the bottom of a steel crate, rolled up toward the bench. A man jumped out of the passenger side and helped the two men in the hooded parkas stretch out Der Schmuggler across the rear seat, and then the men got in, and the van drove away.

Part VIII

40

Snow was settling on the houses along Montague Place and up the hill of Radel Terrace. The silvery flakes spun through the light of the gas lamps and seemed to drift to evenings gone by, when I would sit on these steps and harbor no grander wish than that school would be canceled in the morning. Now it was as if this staircase ran through my present and past. Upstairs, I heard Yuli taking a shower. Downstairs was the doorway to the kitchen, and I remembered chopping carrots with my grandmother to prepare plov—one of her classic winter meals, a chicken and rice dish seasoned with cumin, garlic, and peppercorns.

Yuli and I had been here for three weeks. The morning after we flew in from Amsterdam, I had phoned Information in Atlanta, got the number for Jack's Watch and Clock Repair, and called. A man with a heavy European accent answered, and when I asked for Bashe, he replied, "Not here. She come in March," and hung up.

I delayed contacting the art dealer in Charleston; we would see him on our drive to Georgia. So for the next several weeks, Yuli and I had the rapturous illusion of living outside of time. Our lovemaking seemed to be without beginning or end, and as the wind blew snow against the bedroom windows, the air around us felt saturated with sunlight—a summery air, sweet as baby oil and briny as the sea. And we were always hungry. We went to Alex Eng for Chinese; Ann's Clam Bar for steamers; Town Hall Deli for Sloppy Joes; and Gruning's for hot fudge sundaes. More often than not, Yuli wanted to eat at Don's Drive-In, where she discovered that pizza burgers do exist and, in celebration of her discovery, devoured two of them.

A noisy, crowded hangout perfumed by the charcoal grills in the kitchen, Don's was popular with families, couples on a date, gangs of high schoolers on Friday and Saturday nights, and college kids home on break, so I shouldn't have been surprised when Birdman and Beryl showed up. It was evident, from their holding hands and the discomfort on Birdman's face when he saw me, that they were a couple. I'd grown up with the rule that best friends don't date each other's exes, but compared to Dmitry's death, Yuli's childhood, and the tragedy of Emma, Gak, and their daughters, the rule struck me as less serious than a nursery rhyme. I shook hands with Birdman, and Beryl kissed me on the cheek. I introduced them to Yuli, and they sat at the table next to us. Birdman, a senior at Yale, still resembled a gangly bar mitzvah boy and Beryl could still pass for Barbie—if the doll had renounced her teen queenliness to become a beatnik. Her long blond hair was parted in the center, and she wore a black leotard and black jeans.

"Where you been?" Birdman asked.

"Traveling in Europe," I said.

Beryl had graduated early from the University of Chicago and was now at the Yale Drama School studying to be an actress, which was how she got together with Birdman, and she dominated the conversation, giving us chapter and verse on how Yale was going to found a repertory theater.

"In school," Yuli said. "We had to perform Chekhov's *Cherry Orchard*."

"Where are you from?" Beryl asked.

"Ukraine."

"Your English is very good."

"So is yours," Yuli quipped.

Birdman and I laughed. Beryl smiled as though unsure whether it was a joke or a put-down. From what I knew of Yuli, it was both, but all she said once we were in the car was "Your friends are nice."

The next afternoon, wearing our Paris clothes, Yuli and I went to see *Fiddler on the Roof* at the Imperial Theatre, another of the Shuberts' Broadway palaces, with lavishly paneled walls and crimson seats. I think Yuli enjoyed being in the Imperial more than the show, because as the cast took their bows and the audience stood and applauded, she said, "I did not know Jews sang so often in the Ukraine."

"Between pogroms."

Yuli smiled, shaking her head, and out we went for an evening in New York. Yuli was enthralled by the city. We visited a dozen times, beginning with the typical tourist spots—the Empire State Building, the Statue of Liberty, Central Park, and the Museum of Modern Art. Usually, though, Yuli wanted to go to Greenwich Village. As a teenager, she had translated the poems of Allen Ginsberg into Russian and read several Kerouac novels, so we strolled through Washington Square Park holding hands, went to the White Horse Tavern for drinks, the Minetta Tavern for dinner, and Caffe Reggio for dessert. Yuli said little during these jaunts, but her eyes darted everywhere, and one night, stuck in traffic at the Lincoln Tunnel, she said, "America is—"

"Is?"

We were driving out the Jersey side of the tunnel when she answered, "So much."

Interestingly, the place that attracted her beyond all others was Sweets. Almost every day we stopped at the candy store. The Abruzzi thugs were operating the phones in back, Eddie was on his stool at the soda fountain, and his wife, Fiona, was running things. In her plain frock, with her ginger-colored hair pinned up, Fiona appeared to be a nice middle-aged churchgoing Irish lady, but there was a maniacal bluish-green fire in her eyes, and she barked out orders to the two women from her church she hired to help her.

The first time Eddie met Yuli was on a Saturday, with children jamming the store, and he gave her an appreciative look. "Jesus, you gotta be the biggest movie star in Russia."

Fiona was mixing an egg cream and winked at Yuli. "That's right, Edward. And Yulianna, say hello to my husband, the biggest idiot in New Jersey."

"Why am I an idiot?"

"Because you charged Billy Everts the nickel for his Snickers, and his mother's alone with five mouths to feed and don't have nickels for candy."

"I set up a charge account for Billy. For lots of the kids."

"And they're going to pay?"

"Hell no, they're not gonna pay. I am. But they'll learn about charge accounts."

Yuli was grinning, and she saw a little girl with a pink beret and pigtails at the row of penny-candy jars. Her arm was raised toward a jar, but she couldn't reach it. Yuli went over and whispered to her. The girl beamed, and Yuli picked her up until she had a handful of Hershey Kisses, and put her down. Then she said to Fiona, "If you tell me what to do, I'd like to help."

I led Yuli behind the fountain and taught her the quickest way to make sodas and milkshakes. From then on, she asked to go to the store in the afternoons and on weekends to work an hour or two. At Sweets, Yuli was as happy as I'd ever seen her, and one Sunday, when we were walking home, I asked her why she liked the store so much.

She stopped. "I always wondered what a happy childhood would look like. And watching those children, I know."

Being so wrapped up in my present with Yuli, I'd forgotten her past, and again I was aware of the gulf between her experience and mine. There were so many things I wanted to tell her—for instance, how I admired her courage—but I just looked at her behind the lacy curtain of falling snow, her face lit by a gas lamp, and folded everything I had to say to her into one simple sentence.

"I love you."

It was then that her hand reached through the curtain to touch my cheek, her eyes the slate blue of the late-afternoon sky, and in that moment before she spoke, I felt as though I was watching both of us from the tops of the trees, an improbable portrait done in the softer shades of winter, two lonely people, each with their own losses, who had, through a chain of coincidences, become bound together and now stood on this nondescript street of Colonials with one-car garages and two-family houses, in a small New Jersey town.

Yuli said, "I love you, too."

And I leaned through the icy lace and kissed her.

41

The first of March fell on a Monday, but I waited until Wednesday to try Bashe again, and as I got ready to dial, Yuli said, "Let me. I met her. She does errands for Papka."

Annoyed that she hadn't mentioned this before, I listened to her speak briefly to Bashe in Yiddish.

"She will be in Atlanta until April," Yuli said after hanging up.

A blizzard had blanketed the Northeast, so it would be a couple of days before we could get on the road. I went out to shovel the sidewalk and driveway, and later we did laundry and walked down to Sweets. In the evening, we hunkered down on the couch in the den, our shoulders touching, our legs tangled, and watched a movie on television, which was less interesting to me than the moonlight seeping between the slats of the jalousie windows and glittering on the mica-speckled gray linoleum. Then I heard music, breathy strings, and Debbie Reynolds, her voice full of longing, confessing that her character, Tammy, had fallen in love. The song brimmed with sentiment, yet that was its power—its defenseless, childlike yearning, the same feeling I had sitting with Yuli. I looked at her, she looked back, and the longing sharpened, then dissolved into a tranquil warmth.

The song ended, and I sifted through the backlog of mail I'd dumped in a wood crate next to the couch, picking up a copy of *Time*. Emma could've read her magazines at Sweets—a stack was delivered weekly—but she used to say the store was for working, not reading, and it made me sad thinking about canceling her subscription. On the cover was a painting of General William Westmoreland, with soldiers sloshing through a rice paddy behind him. Being out of the country and because my draft board had classified me 4-F due to a heart murmur, I hadn't followed the fighting in South Vietnam. Now, bored by the movie and intrigued by the chipper expression on Westmoreland's face—reminiscent of Norman Rockwell's boys in the swimming hole—*C'mon in, the water's fine!*—I skimmed the cover story. With Communist guerrillas attacking our bases and killing our soldiers, I didn't understand why the general was so chipper. I kept flipping through *Time* until I saw a page headlined *Netherlands: A Nazi in the Canal.*

I was fuming as I finished reading that story, my feeling of betrayal ratcheting up with every word. Yuli was coming back to the couch from turning off the TV.

"Misha, what's wrong?"

Standing, I gave her the magazine. She lowered her eyes to the article, which detailed the killing of Joost Ter Horst on the night of February 1—when Yuli and I were in Amsterdam. The former SS officer had been injected with phenol, a method of execution used at Auschwitz, and thrown into the canal near the Anne Frank House. Two days later, a letter arrived at publications in Europe and South America stating that if West Germany let the statute of limitations expire, Ter Horst would not be the last war criminal to die—a sentence, according to the article, that had probably been carried out by the Mossad.

I spoke slowly, barely able to control my anger. "You don't have to read it. You did it."

Yuli glanced up. "I did this?"

"Don't fucking lie to me. I woke up that night, you weren't there. In the morning, I'd figured you being gone was a dream or a hangover from those pills you gave me."

I tried to read her face, but it was like reading a block of heart-shaped marble—beautiful, flawless, blank. And the blankness infuriated me. "What is it with you Russians? You and Emma, with your secret lives. You don't trust anyone?"

"Don't shout."

I shouted louder. "Be straight with me!"

"Straight? This is to tell you what you think already. That I am only pretending to help you find your grandmother's murderer so no one will know I do work for the Mossad?"

"Damn right that's what I think."

"Then you are *durak*."

"A fool? Why am I a fool?"

The marble was briefly animated, with hurt. "Because these things I do with you, how I give myself to you, all of myself, and love you from my heart to my toes—this is a plot?"

"You were a virgin when we met? I didn't notice."

Yuli snapped, "People who live in glass houses shouldn't throw up."

I laughed, a harsh sound, and I loathed the harshness of it and the rage I felt at Yuli for deceiving me. "You mean 'people who live in glass houses shouldn't throw stones'?"

"I mean you shouldn't talk—you have secrets. Beryl, the way you looked at each other. You loved her. Was she your teacher? Or were other girls? I know it wasn't me. I'm your hunting dog."

I was disgusted with myself for letting her sidetrack me with an absurd fight about our pasts when I should have been persuading her to come clean.

"You don't want to tell me—fine. It's your business."

"Yes, it is."

"Then pack your stuff and go back to Otvali—back to your business."

"Go?"

"Go—go back to the life you won't tell me about."

As I left the den, Yuli flung the magazine at me. It landed on the linoleum.

Upstairs, in my old bedroom, we had pushed the twin beds together. Without bothering to undress, I got into the bed, lying on my side and staring at the ice-fogged window above me. The ice was glowing blue-gray from the light of the streetlamps, and I tugged down the shade, but I still wasn't sleeping when Yuli crawled across her bed onto mine, spooning herself around me.

"I killed Joost Ter Horst."

I was silent.

She whispered, "There were others."

I wondered if Catholics spoke this quietly to priests in the confessional, as if keeping your voice low mitigated your sins.

"They were bad men. Killers, arms dealers, a germ-warfare scientist."

I felt capable of killing the murderers of Emma and Dmitry, but that was a measure of my outrage and, more important, a choice I didn't have to make. This was bloodless, professional, and though it didn't change the way I felt about Yuli, it gave me the creeps.

Reaching over my shoulder, Yuli pulled on me so I would face her. "I don't want to be this anymore. I didn't tell you to protect you from what I am. And so you will not stop loving me."

I turned.

"Taft Mifflin told you KGB could also be searching for Joost, and I believe he is right. I saw Pyotr Ananko in Amsterdam, and a man following me. Now we go talk to Bashe, and KGB could know about her. I am scared for you and for me. This is dangerous. I will go if—"

"Don't go. Just tell me the truth."

"I have, Misha."

We held each other, eventually falling asleep in our clothes. In the middle of the night, we woke up and shed our clothing and, after a long, fierce, exhausting time, slept again.

Late the next morning we were eating pancakes when the doorbell rang. I answered it, and surprisingly, Taft Mifflin was on the stoop.

"I have more batter," I said, stowing his tweed walking hat and trench coat in the closet. "You hungry?"

"I should hold off. I'm meeting Julian for an early lunch."

I led him into the kitchen and introduced him to Yuli. He sat in the chair across from her, taking out a pack of Lucky Strikes. My mother's black plastic ashtray from the Copacabana was on the top shelf of a cabinet, and I retrieved it, setting it on the table as I sat.

Taft lit a cigarette. "You saw Joost Ter Horst?" It sounded like a question, but he glanced toward Yuli, so obviously he knew the answer.

I replied, "Joost said Hildegard took my grandmother's daughter,

Darya, back to Germany, and they died when Nuremberg was bombed. He also told us a woman, Bashe, shot him. She was a friend of Emma, and we located her in Atlanta. We'll talk to her this week."

"Good, good." Taft twirled the ash of his Lucky on the lip of the ashtray. "I have some bad news." He looked at Yuli. "Der Schmuggler. He's dead."

Yuli didn't flinch, and this, I realized, was the professional, the murderous technician who filled me with moral queasiness. "How?"

"Allegedly got drunk, passed out in front of his compound, and froze to death. But my information comes from a source who didn't see the body. He did say there's a rumor around Otvali that he was strangled and beaten by the KGB."

I put my hand on one of hers. I'm not sure Yuli knew it was there.

"This could be because of Joost?" she asked.

I felt sick with guilt, thinking my enlisting Yuli to help me had cost her the man who had raised her, and relief flooded through me when Taft said, "No, from the information I have, Der Schmuggler was involved in some other things—dangerous things. Where was he the last time you spoke?"

"Bucharest."

"Israel has an embassy there, and Der Schmuggler, I'm told, was arranging with the Israelis to bring in Russian and Yiddish translations of the novel *Exodus*."

I'd seen the movie, a historical romance about the founding of Israel with Paul Newman and Eva Marie Saint. "And the KGB would kill Der for that?"

Taft said, "The book's illegal in the Soviet Union. Get caught with a copy, they'll send you to prison. The Kremlin is threatened by Jewish nationalism. There are probably a million Jews who want to leave, and if they go, half the Soviets will apply for exit visas. It's an old story. Khrushchev put up the Berlin Wall because he knew if East Germans could get out, they'd go live in the West."

Yuli was studying Taft, her forehead wrinkled in concentration. "Papka did favors for KGB since I was little. Things they could not do, and he paid off their agents—American cigarettes, German radios, French perfume for their wives. Translations of *Exodus* are all around at home. KGB would not kill Papka only because of that book. Is there something else?"

Taft stubbed out his Lucky. "You ever hear of Kazimir Zolnerowich?"

Yuli had appeared encased in an eerie serenity, but now she sat back and exhaled sharply. "A Soviet physicist. Very smart, very young. Designs missiles."

"Right. I wasn't involved, but I've heard that we and the Israelis tried to get him to defect. Nothing came of it. Then, a month ago, Der Schmuggler comes to Germany. He doesn't call me, which was unusual, and he goes to Bonn, not Munich. West German intelligence spotted him meeting a man from the British embassy at the Beethoven Monument. They took a walk, and then Der Schmuggler left Germany. The Brits aren't saying much—failure doesn't encourage conversation—but word is that Kazimir got it into his head that he wanted to teach at Cambridge, and somehow— no one knows how—reached out to Der Schmuggler to help."

"Kazimir would know people who knew about Papka. And if someone wanted help, Papka would help."

Taft slipped his Luckies into his shirt pocket. "And if he was a missile designer, the Kremlin wouldn't like that."

"No, the Kremlin would not."

"And the KGB would put an end to it."

"Yes."

Taft stood. "Yulianna, I'm very sorry. Der Schmuggler was a good man."

"Thank you," she replied, perfectly calm.

"And one more thing. Odds are the KGB is trying to track you down, so you can't go back. We'll have to talk about that."

Yuli nodded, and I accompanied Taft to the door.

"Be in touch, Michael. And watch your step. If you can't get ahold of me, try Julian. He'll find me."

After shrugging into his coat and putting on his hat, he was gone.

In the kitchen, Yuli was at the sink, facing away from me and drying off a plate. I touched her shoulders. She put the dish in the drainer and turned, resting her head on my chest.

"I met Kazimir Zolnerowich once. He was reading an H. G. Wells novel."

I put my arms around her, and she began to sob, soft and shallow at first, then louder and deeper, and finally her arms came up and we held each other while she wept.

42

Charleston, South Carolina
March 5, 1965

There was a jangling beauty to Paris. Whether you crossed one of the bridges or passed statues and spuming fountains, the city seemed confident that she had set your eyes on fire. Of course, Charleston lacked the artistic pedigree of the French capital and the tidy grandness. That was apparent as Yuli and I left our hotel on King Street and walked along the seawall of the Battery. Yet Charleston possessed a wilder beauty than Paris, less self-conscious, subtly erotic. Part of it was the warmth—the temperature had to be over eighty degrees. But it was also the Ashley and Cooper Rivers, which made you feel encircled by water, and how the sun slanting through the live oaks, Spanish moss, and the palmettos dyed the light gold-green. The grand houses were done up in tropical yellows, pinks, and blues and, despite the obvious care, the side-yard gardens appeared to have flourished in untouched soil, a tangle of jasmine, azaleas, and a bonfire of other blossoms I couldn't name, all of them scenting the air so that I might have been walking among a crowd of perfumed women.

Yuli asked, "When do we have to see Mr. Benjamin?"

"He said any time today." When I had called Thaddeus Benjamin from New Jersey to tell him about Emma and ask if we could visit, he had expressed his condolences and given me directions to his house. The strangest aspect of the conversation was that he didn't sound the least bit surprised to hear from me.

My car was a block from the hotel, and we drove up Meeting Street through a shopping district. Yuli had said little on the ride from South Orange, and not a word about Der Schmuggler. We had stopped overnight at a hotel off I-95 in Virginia, and in the dining room she ate a few spoonfuls of soup for dinner and had no interest in breakfast. It had been easier to console her when she was crying. From my own losses, I knew that all I could do was wait for her sadness to fade, a conclusion composed of equal parts disappointment and helplessness, because there was nothing I could offer her other than my presence.

"The white people disappeared," Yuli said.

In less than fifteen minutes, we had passed some invisible line separating white from black Charleston. It reminded me of crossing from Newark into South Orange.

Yuli stared out the passenger-side window. "Segregation is illegal now, yes?"

"Yep. Just like Stalin denouncing anti-Semitism. It sounds better than it is."

The streets were mostly lined with cottages, many of them with sagging roofs and peeling wood siding, until we reached an enormous pale yellow Queen Anne, with a porch on the ground floor and another on the second. I turned into a driveway and headed up along a bright velvety garden, stopping in front of a garage. To our right was a lawn with a flagstone patio and a figure-eight swimming pool.

A smiling man came toward us from the flagstones. His face was the color of polished oak, and even in his orange cabana set with a terry-cloth collar he looked as debonair as Duke Ellington, with the same slicked-back hair and pencil mustache.

"Y'all must be Michael and Yulianna."

I shook his hand. He waved at the rear windows of the house, and by the time we were seated on the deck chairs by the pool, a uniformed Negro maid was placing a tray, with three glasses of lemonade, on a tile-topped table.

Thaddeus and I sipped the drinks, but Yuli didn't touch her glass.

I asked, "Mr. Benjamin, can you tell how you met my grandmother?"

"It was one of the luckiest days of my life. I stayed in Paris after fighting in the war—the First World War. Way it was down south, a colored man could do better there, 'specially since I married a white woman. Jane Ellen had been a nurse with the Red Cross in the hospital at Bussy-le-Château. I had shrapnel in my back, and we was a pair of lonely Southerners. So we move to Paris, and I'm tending bar in cafés. My mama—God rest her soul—was Cajun, so I could get by in French. Always loved art. Couldn't paint a lick, though. Jane Ellen and me went to the Louvre a lot and the shows in the galleries. That's how I met Emma and Gak. Gak had a Jewish pal from Russia, Soutine, a fine painter, and another Jewish fella, Modigliani. Neither of them couldn't sell nothing, and I bought everything of theirs I could. I even picked up a Matisse. But I didn't have the money to buy all I wanted, and Emma, she helped figure that out."

"What'd she do?"

"A lot of artists used to go see Gak, but if he was painting, they'd leave a note. And Emma, she made the artists sign them, and gave the notes to me. I sold them. Notes from Matisse, Picasso, Chagall, Braque, and some others to American collectors. Then I start goin' round to studios and buy any sketch they threw out. Chagall was a real peach: he gave me two of his old palettes and signed them. And Salvador Dalí, man, that was like striking oil. Dalí used to pay for his dinners with a check—he'd scribble a picture on 'em—knowing the café owner wouldn't cash it. He used to eat at the Sélect when I worked there, and I'd pay his bill and hold on to the check. Made a fortune. Jane Ellen's daddy, he's a good man, retired military, couldn't care less if I was chartreuse long as I take care of his baby girl. He's a widower and got sick, so we came on home. Jane Ellen's up to his place at Folly Beach now."

I finished my lemonade. "How did Emma find you when you moved here?"

"Mademoiselle Blum, her landlady. After I start making money, Jane Ellen and me was also renting at 22 Place des Vosges. And Emma calls me up from Nice and sends me some of Gak's work. Easy for me to sell it now that I got me a list of serious collectors. And Emma gives me the name of a lawyer in Nice, and I spoke to him about selling all Gak's work when he's gone. Emma says there's lots of paintings."

"There are. Yuli and I saw them."

"The lawyer tells me your grandmother says the money should go to her daughter and you. Emma, she tell me about you, but never say nothing about a daughter."

"That was a best-case plan. Her daughter seems to have died during the war."

"Sorry about that. And Emma, too. I owe that lady."

"My grandmother never told me about you. Gak's caretaker did."

Thaddeus laughed. "I knew that. Emma told me you'd find me—her Michael was a lot smarter than he thinks."

"That's standard grandmother talk."

"Sometimes the old folks see what we don't see."

Yuli slipped her hand into mine. "And you found Mr. Benjamin, didn't you?"

I smiled at her, feeling both grateful to Emma for her confidence and angry at her for keeping another secret from me.

"Yeah, I did."

43

If the present is bleak, Taft Mifflin thought, and you don't give a shit about the future, then all you have is the past.

That was his situation on this chilly afternoon, which was why he had insisted that the meeting be held at Martin's Tavern in Georgetown, his old neighborhood hangout, and why Taft had arrived early to walk by the brick Federals and Victorians and row houses. He was cheered by the familiar window flower boxes, austere gates, coach lights, and courtyards, all of it seeming to belong to a more dignified hour in the history of the Republic, when perfecting the future was only a few big ideas away, and the men riding the merry-go-round of Georgetown soirees had believed, with an infrangible faith, that they were up to the task.

N Street, however, was not so cheerful. Turning up the floppy collar of his Burberry, Taft paused outside the redbrick townhouse where Jack Kennedy had lived with Jackie in 1957 or 1958—he couldn't recall. Taft had lived across the street with wife number two. Those were the good times: potluck suppers with just the four of them; Sunday afternoons with Jack swapping their memories of Cape Cod while they drank Heinekens and watched the Washington Redskins on TV; even those evenings Jackie and his wife dragged them off to hear chamber music at Dumbarton Oaks, and Taft and Jack kept glancing at each other and swallowing their laughter like schoolboys. Then Taft was posted to Munich, and Jack made it to the White House. Their last meeting was in June 1963. Jack was in Berlin to excoriate the Soviets for ordering their East German puppets to divide the city with a wall. Taft had driven up from Munich and chatted with the president before Jack pledged to the West Germans that he too was proud to be considered a citizen of Berlin. The president had asked Taft his opinion of Vietnam, and Taft said, *Korea with a warmer climate—get out*. To which Jack replied, *We have to stand up to the Communists somewhere*, and Taft quipped, *So invade Greenwich Village*, and they started laughing. Five months later Jack went to Dallas, and Taft never quite laughed the same way again.

Martin's Tavern was all dark wood, hanging Tiffany lamps, and hushed voices. In the front room the booths were marked with plaques for the tourists—the rumble seat where a callow Jack Kennedy breakfasted after Sunday mass; the booth where he proposed to Jackie; the booth where Harry Truman dined with his wife, Bess, and their daughter, Margaret; and the booth where Richard Nixon enjoyed his meat loaf when he was in Congress and while he was Ike's vice president.

From the waiting line, Taft concluded, nostalgia was good for business, though he was baffled by the American propensity for worshiping the future while grieving for the past. No reconciling it, Taft thought, going to the Dugout, a private back room. Here, as a congressman and senator, Lyndon Johnson had once done his wheeling and wheeler-dealing, and William "Wild Bill" Donovan, Taft's boss at the Office of Strategic Services, had assembled his underlings to evaluate wartime intelligence.

Now a CIA agent, the size of a linebacker and dressed like an investment banker, was leaning inside the doorway, and Taft went by him and slid into a booth across from the CIA director's top assistant for overseas operations. He was a gimlet-eyed, pouch-necked man who two generations of agents referred to as the Bookkeeper, due to his habit of chewing on No. 2 yellow-wood pencils and regarding friend and foe alike as nothing more than entries on history's balance sheet.

"We couldn't do this at Langley?" the Bookkeeper asked.

"Does the cafeteria serve bread pudding with hot bourbon-caramel sauce?"

The Bookkeeper called out to the guard, "Tell the waitress I'll have tea with skim milk and a fruit cup, and to bring a coffee and bread pudding."

"You on a diet?"

The Bookkeeper said, "Thanks to our buddy Julian Rose. A few weeks ago I had to be in New York and met up with him in Jersey twice to eat. At this diner in some town—Verona? Jesus, the cheesecake. We're reminiscing about dynamiting railroad tracks in Normandy with the French Resistance, and I ate two huge slices both times."

Taft asked, "You got me here from Munich to talk cheesecake?"

Reaching into his navy chalk-stripe suit coat, the Bookkeeper took out a shortened No. 2 pencil. "Let's start with how the director wasn't pleased that Joost Ter Horst wound up floating in a canal."

"I bet Joost wasn't pleased, either."

"His information was solid."

"What information? That American, West German, and Italian teenagers with a crush on Che Guevara go to Amsterdam to smoke hashish and stuff their mouths with stroopwafels?"

The Bookkeeper clamped the eraser end of the pencil in the side of his mouth like a cigar. "They can set off bombs like any Commie revolutionaries, and East Germany's funneling them money and advice. There's going to be trouble."

"No trouble that Joost Ter Horst could've helped with. Or any of those other Nazi clowns we hired."

"Clowns, Taft?"

"Sadistic clowns, for Christ's sake. One of them was Einsatzgruppen, another used to execute POWs for laughs, and we had to get their sentences commuted to hire them. When I ran the Soviet spy section in Munich, most of the jackboot boys still thought Hitler was on the right track, and they were more devoted to bedding call girls than spying."

The Bookkeeper removed the pencil from his mouth. "Did the Mossad go after Joost?"

"The CIA still monitors foreign newspapers, doesn't it? You read the letter that was sent—it's a safe bet the Israelis haven't lost their minds or their memories."

"The Mossad hasn't chased any Nazis since Eichmann. And he was a special case."

Taft said, "If West Germany doesn't extend the statute of limitations for war criminals, the Mossad's going to open a whole new division. And there's no shortage of targets. Lots of them in the U.S. Chemists who made Zyklon B for the gas chambers; doctors who experimented on babies; scientists who used slaves to build rockets."

"Didn't you help put together the project to bring them here?"

Taft recalled those interminable planning sessions with the erstwhile director of central intelligence, Allen Dulles, a bow-tied, pipe-smoking product of Princeton in love with listening to himself talk about realpolitik, a term that Taft had come to regard as a pretentious euphemism for forgetting every lesson he'd learned in Sunday school. "I did my share on Operation Paperclip. Doesn't mean I'm happy about it."

The Bookkeeper asked, "Would you and the Israelis rather have them working for the Kremlin?"

"Can't speak for Israel, but I'd rather they were shoveling coal in hell."

The Bookkeeper had a sour, pained expression on his face, as if suddenly afflicted with hemorrhoids. "Hitler's been gone twenty years. I thought the Israelis would get over it."

"What the heck. Only six million."

"Lots of enemies let bygones be bygones. And your sympathies are well known. You caught a break not getting court-martialed for that crap you pulled at Dachau."

"Nobody saw me shoot anyone," Taft said, and heard the defensiveness in his tone. That was because even though those SS guards had been repaid in kind, Taft felt guilty for his part in it, a guilt that had crawled inside him ever since, spiny and venomous, like the lime-green io-moth caterpillars he'd caught as a child until he stuck himself on the spines, and his skin swelled and blistered.

As Taft pulled a Lucky Strike from a pack, the Bookkeeper took another shortened pencil from his suit coat. "Try this. It won't give you cancer."

Taft lit the cigarette. "That's because you can't smoke it."

Frowning, the Bookkeeper put away the pencil. "Bottom line: do we want the Mossad running around assassinating people?"

"What do you expect? Joost supervised the slaughter of twenty-seven thousand civilians, most of them Jews. The biggest massacre in Russia. And his wife, Hildegard, was a butcher."

"Hildegard is dead. Along with her mother and father. Died the second of January, 1945, when the Brits bombed Nuremberg. Seven witnesses said she was in the house, and the house was obliterated. I read her file, and you did, too."

Taft blew a smoke ring, deciding that if he shared his theory that Hildegard was alive, the Bookkeeper would order him to get a psych evaluation.

The Bookkeeper had his pencil back in the corner of his mouth. "The director wants to know how we can prevent any future incidents like Ter Horst. The president requested it, and you're the man to write it up."

"I'm supposed to give the director and LBJ the news we know they—and the West Germans—don't want to hear? That if the Bundestag extends the statute of limitations, the Mossad will stand down?"

"Write that. But present options. Presidents love options."

"How about LBJ invites Simon Wiesenthal and the press to his ranch for a barbecue, and Wiesenthal can show off his lists of Nazis he's tracked down? Or get West Germany to arrest Ilse Schmitz. Her métier was murdering children. Ilse got a kick out of teaching kids songs as she led them into gas vans, and now she works in a kindergarten in Cologne. If that irony doesn't light a fire under LBJ's ass, he can start a war and then Americans won't give a damn about the Mossad."

The Bookkeeper shook his head with disgust. "The president's already doing that in Vietnam. And the bigger the screw-up, the busier I get—I'm going to Saigon again in a couple of weeks. So write this for me, will you?"

The waitress brought their order. Taft looked down at a doughnut-shaped pudding under a syrupy brown glaze. "Dessert of the gods," he said, and picked up a spoon.

Taft should have caught a cab back to the Hays-Adams and started his report, but it was less than two miles to his hotel and he wanted to clear his head, so he walked down Wisconsin Avenue, calculating, on a scale from one to a hundred, how insane it was for him to believe that Hildegard Ter

Horst was alive. Ninety-five percent nuts—because Taft had no hard evidence. He had a theory based on a comment by Emma Dainov, when she was a half-dead inmate at Dachau, that Hildegard had stolen her daughter; Emma traveling to Europe in the summers and applying for a visa to the Soviet Union, Taft assumed, to search for the girl; and Emma being shot to death in a candy store that wasn't robbed.

Nonetheless, if Hildegard was alive, then where was she? On his last trip to New York, Taft had searched immigration records for a woman with the surname of Ter Horst or Kreit—Hildegard's maiden name—who had emigrated to America with a young girl between 1945 and 1955. He drew a blank and checked her file at Langley again to see if any recent sightings had been reported, but there was nothing beyond the statements of the witnesses who claimed that Hildegard had died in Nuremberg. That was why Taft had told Michael Joost was in Amsterdam. He knew that Der Schmuggler also freelanced for the Mossad if the job wouldn't irk the Kremlin, and he guessed that Yulianna did the heavy lifting, so when Taft gave Michael the address of the Magic Dragon, he was confident that Joost would die, because the Bundestag was scheduled to vote on the statute of limitations at the end of March, and it would be a timely chance for Israel to demonstrate its future response if West Germany chose to give Nazi killers a pass. Joost's assassination could scare Hildegard enough for her to make a mistake that would reveal her whereabouts or to seek a deal with the West German government to save herself. Luckily for Taft, the Bookkeeper hadn't questioned how the Mossad had located Joost, because if anyone at the Agency uncovered that Taft had made it possible for a CIA source to be terminated, he was finished as an agent and might well spend his golden years in prison.

A young goateed man in a Greek fisherman's hat, crewneck sweater, and jeans was standing on the corner of Wisconsin and M Street, playing the guitar and singing "Blowin' in the Wind." He had a rich, poignant voice perfect for that song, and maybe twenty men and women, probably students at Georgetown, had circled him, joining in on the chorus and tossing coins into an open guitar case.

Nice world they live in, Taft thought, detouring into the street to skirt the gathering and going down M toward Pennsylvania Avenue.

A moment later, there were footsteps behind him, moving quickly, and Taft stepped closer to the plate-glass windows of the stores to let the person pass. A man said, "Excuse me," and Taft watched him go by. He was wearing a trench coat and dark blue Washington Senators baseball cap and carrying a rolled-up newspaper, none of which appeared out of the ordinary to Taft until the man spun around, pointing the newspaper at him, and Taft heard a dull pop, as if someone had pinpricked a partially deflated balloon. The cyanide spray hit his face, and he collapsed on the sidewalk. Unable to move his limbs or cry out, Taft knew that his life was beginning its final ninety seconds, and as the blood slowed to his brain, his biggest disappointment was that he had believed that in his closing moments the purpose behind his earthly strife would be revealed. A fantasy, perhaps, but an understandable one for a boy growing up in a parsonage with a father who regularly spoke about everlasting life in God's embrace, yet now, staring up at the gray sky and hearing the traffic on M Street, Taft realized that his valedictory revelation was that we depart this world as ignorant of the great mysteries as the day we are born.

And far more than the end of his days, this was his greatest regret.

44

"Let's get going," I said. "Bashe should be there by now."

We had been killing time at the Golden Horn, a dimly lit coffeehouse, where onstage a reed-thin girl in a checkerboard pinafore was reading a poem so unintelligible it could have been composed in Sumerian. Before driving down from Charleston, Yuli had phoned Jack's Watch and Clock Repair, and Jack had told her Bashe would be in at three. It was almost four now, and Yuli was still dawdling over her tea.

"You will miss the end of the poem," she said quietly.

I knew Yuli was joking, but it didn't show on her face. "I'll live."

We walked through a hushed leafy neighborhood, with many of the stately old homes divided up into apartments, and the noise of the city didn't hit us until we reached Peachtree Street.

"Bashe makes fun of me," Yuli said, which explained why she had been dragging her heels about going.

"What does she say?"

"Nothing I like to hear."

I put my arm around her. "We'll hear her story and leave."

As we entered the store, the cuckoo clocks on the knotty pine walls were crying out as though someone had taken a match to their tails. Behind a long glass case of watches, a woman in a shapeless black dress with her hair tucked up under a brown scarf was perched on a stool, peering at us over her bifocals. She had a high-spirited lewdness in her expression, and the frankness of it was appealing, the unabashed pleasure of an older woman seeing a young couple and recalling her youth. Yet the longer I looked at the woman, the less appealing her expression became. There was something both troubled and troubling in her hooded eyes, a shiny hardness buffed up by sorrow and outrage.

"Well, butter my butt and call me a biscuit," the woman said to Yuli, her voice rough, as if her throat were coated with ground glass. "The wild girl does Bashe a favor and pays a visit."

I assumed Bashe was referring to her past, and I guessed Yuli was worried about my reaction. It was irrelevant to me, and all I wanted was to hear what Bashe had to say about Emma.

"Wild girl," Bashe said. "Does the cat got your tongue?"

"Don't call her that," I snapped.

Bashe smirked, her eyes gleaming like waxed ebony. "You are her defender?"

I said, "Bashe, you deaf or stupid?"

She seemed tickled by the insults. "And you, who are you?"

I answered in Russian, "Misha Daniels. Emma Dainov was my grandmother."

The smirk disappeared, the sorrow and outrage stuck around. "Your father was Lev. The little boy Emma's thief of a husband took to America."

"Why didn't she go after him?"

"Because her bastard husband stole her and her father's money, and he had connections with the Communists and paid off a son of a bitch to alter her records saying she was a criminal, and she couldn't get into the States. Then she fell in love with Gak and got pregnant. She was something, your grandmother. It's a shame you didn't meet her."

She had been speaking English, and for one awful moment, I wondered if Emma was really my grandmother. That, at least, would be a reason for her secrecy.

Yuli was also mystified. "Bashe, what are you saying?"

"That he couldn't have been no more than a baby when Emma was executed at Dachau."

"Is this Emma?" I placed a color photo of my grandmother on the display case, the one I'd taken of her behind the soda fountain.

Bashe stared at the snapshot, her right hand fluttering up like a hummingbird to her heart. "But the guards shot her. I saw her die."

"Emma survived and came to New Jersey and owned a candy store. She was murdered there, in September, and it might be connected to her past. That's why I'm here."

Bashe sighed so deeply I thought she'd fall off the stool. "How did you find me? Der Schmuggler? I ain't talked to him in a while."

I started to give her the news about Der, but Yuli stepped on my foot, signaling me to be quiet. "Papka told us you are here, but we heard about you and Emma from Joost Ter Horst."

"I left that wild animal alive—thank God the Mossad drowned him. I wanted to shoot him again, but Joost's wife, Hildegard, was taking Emma's daughter. Did Joost tell you his whore of a wife was in the SS?"

"He didn't tell us much," I said. "Can you start at the beginning?"

Bashe slid off the stool. "Come."

She pushed aside the purple doorway curtain behind the display case, and before we followed her, Yuli whispered, "Bashe gossips, so nothing about Papka."

The room had filing cabinets on both walls and a workbench, where a man in a skullcap with long white side curls, a beard, and a loupe in his left eye was probing the guts of a watch with a tweezer.

"Yankel," Bashe said, "if we get a customer, maybe you could go see what he wants?"

He waved at her, and Bashe said, "My husband, he works on watches and clocks all day and doesn't know what century it is."

Bashe opened an unvarnished plywood door and went into a small room with a barred window. From a pea-green refrigerator, she removed three bottles of Coke, popping off the caps with a magnetized church key stuck to the fridge, then sat at the metal table with us, taking out a pack of Winstons and a matchbook. Her hand trembled as she tried to light the cigarette, and she burned her finger.

"*Blyat!*" she said, using the all-purpose Russian curse and tossing the match into the tin ashtray.

Yuli got up and sat in the chair next to her, striking a match and holding it for Bashe while she put a reassuring hand on her shoulder.

Bashe blew smoke at the beadboard ceiling. "From the beginning?"

"Please," I said.

45

Bashe

You want beginnings? I got a beginning. June 22, 1941. That's the day we hear on the radio that Hitler sent his animals to invade the Soviet Union. Stalin, he vanishes, and his foreign minister, Molotov, tell us the fascists will be repulsed by our glorious army, navy, and air force.

I'm shitting hay bales. In 1939, when the Nazis march into Poland, my husband's in Lodz with our son, visiting his mother. They disappear. I'm frantic, make phone calls, send telegrams. Nothing for over a year. Then I get a letter from my mother-in-law's neighbor saying some drunk German soldiers shot them. The truth? After that, I don't want to live. So Emma, my closest friend, comes to Rostov-on-Don from Paris. To comfort me. To tell me to keep living. And to see her sister Maria. Emma was nine, ten years older than her sister. She raised her after their parents died. Maria still lives in the Adaskin home on the Street of Jews. My house is a few blocks over, and I'm there with Emma and her two daughters when we hear Molotov.

Your grandmother laughs. "I picked a nice time to visit."

The girls want vanilla ice cream in waffle cones. Alexandra's seven, a chatty girl with olive skin and dark hair, like Gak, and Darya's three, a quiet blond beauty like her mother. Walking by the river and watching them with their ice cream cheers us up, and Emma sends a telegram to Gak in Nice, saying she and the girls are safe, he shouldn't worry. The only way Gak ain't worrying is if he don't own a radio or read newspapers, because every day the news gets worse. In a couple weeks, half a million of our soldiers killed, a million captured, and rumors of the Nazis rounding up Jews. Maria's a ball of energy; she'll quote Marx till you and her go blue in the face; and she's out digging trenches around the city. The trenches don't stop the Germans. That fall, they take Rostov and hunt Jews. Don't catch many. Emma, the girls, and me hide in the attic of the Adaskins' house. I slip aside a loose brick in the wall and see Germans removing couches, bed frames, and crates of dishes and candlesticks from houses. A woman in a black uniform and jackboots directs them to the trucks, a pretty, young woman with long reddish-brown hair, and she's writing on a pad. The bunch of thieves steal a grandfather clock from the Adaskins' parlor, while me and Emma are in the attic with our hands over the girls' mouths.

The Red Army counterattacks, and a week later the Wehrmacht retreats. But we ain't seen Maria. From a steamer trunk, Emma takes out this pistol.

"That's a German Luger," I say.

"Swiss. My father imported them for a year and kept one for himself."

"Where you going with it?" I ask.

"To find Maria."

"Are you crazy? The Nazis might be—"

"Take care of my girls, Bashe."

That evening your grandmother returns a different woman. The Nazis hanged Maria, who shot a soldier with his own gun when he tried to rape her. The anger in Emma I can see—she had to cut her sister off a telegraph pole. But Emma was one of those kindhearted, soft-talking beauties people adore; being near her was like sitting by a fire on a snowy night. Now her warmth is gone. I don't begin to understand it till we bury Maria in the Old Jewish Cemetery. Maria's fiancé—Der Schmuggler, who ain't started his smuggling yet—is there, and tells me Emma saved him. He was searching for Maria and a retreating German soldier was about to shoot him when Emma shot the soldier.

Your grandmother don't say nothing about it. I'll tell you what, though. From then on, her Luger is nearby, and I'm feeling like she'd gladly use it again.

We wait out the war in Rostov. Alexandra goes to school, Darya plays with other children. Food can be scarce, but Emma and me got some money, and your grandmother's a wizard at the stove. On the radio, the news is bad and good and very bad by July of 1942. The Germans are heading back to Rostov. People flee, people hide. Emma and me think maybe we run into the Ukraine, but the Germans are there, and the Ukrainians been busy hating and killing Jews for eight hundred years, and Stalin starved millions of their peasants, so the Nazis got Cossacks fighting for them, and the Ukrainian Auxiliary Police hunting Jews.

Meantime, your grandmother comes up with a plan. Her father owned a cottage outside the city. On a wooded hill. An old farmer down the road looks after it, milks the cow, feeds the chickens. Maria and her young Communist friends would use the place to play peasant, take nature hikes, and recite Lenin. We go to the cottage, and in less than a week, Rostov is in flames. We hear the planes bombing and the shelling, and at night the fires in the sky are brighter than the moon. Emma and me tell ourselves we're safe. That don't last long.

One morning we hear trucks. Emma's father was a bird watcher, and we take his binoculars and go behind the trees on the hill. Less than a kilometer away, men in their shorts stand along the Ravine of Snakes. German soldiers start firing, and the men fall into the ravine. Other men—thousands of them—are lining up as if they're at a train station. They move to the edge of the ravine and are shot. Other soldiers open the back doors of the trucks— panel trucks, like big vans. They drag out women and children. As limp as rag dolls. Dead. I almost vomit and give your grandmother the binoculars.

Emma looks. "The gas-truck rumors are true. We have to go."

"Where?"

"Ukraine, Byelorussia, just not here."

There are two rucksacks and canteens at the cottage, probably left there by Maria's hiker comrades. We pack up and go, but we don't get far. Leaving a wheat field, we walk right into some Nazis having a picnic. One soldier aims a *Maschinenpistole* at us—one of those metal submachine guns you probably seen in the movies. But the other soldiers are smiling and waving at Alexandra and Darya. A tall, thin man in a jeep, obviously an officer, puts down his mess kit and bottle of wine and comes over.

And here's where we get a break. My grandparents on both sides were born in Germany before moving to Odessa and then Rostov. My parents spoke German. It was my first language, and I studied German and Yiddish literature at university in Moscow. I was a teacher before my marriage. So when the Nazi officer asks, in bad Russian, if we are Jews, I answer in perfect German, "Useful Jews. My name is Bashe, and I can translate from Russian and Ukrainian, and my friend, Emma, is a cook and a nurse."

Your grandmother ain't no nurse, but I guess the Nazis must need some. The officer asks, "Can you write in German?"

"Yes."

"What does your friend cook?"

"If you can eat it, Emma can cook it."

He grinned. His teeth were crooked, and his eyes slightly crossed. "I am Lieutenant Colonel Ter Horst. Before the war, I was a chef and owned a restaurant. You will eat with us and then we will go."

I explain everything to your grandmother. And pray she don't pull out her Luger. I seen her wrap it in a sweater and put it in the bottom of her rucksack. I have a few packs of Belomorkanal cigarettes and pass them out to the soldiers. After the picnic they take us to the trucks. No doors on back, so we ain't getting gassed. At sunset, the trucks pull over. The soldiers get out and let us sleep in the truck. By dawn, we're going again.

I don't forget that ride. Hours and hours in the heat and the dust, with Alexandra and Darya on our laps. We stroke their hair, kiss their heads. Anything so they're quiet—we don't want the soldiers hearing them speak Russian. The soldiers watch us. Teenage boys, a lot of them, nice boys you think. One boy, with a sweet face and shy smile, gives us tins of meat and crackers, and when we stop for the soldiers to piss, he nods for us to go behind bushes. A considerate boy. We shouldn't be scared. Except we're going west across the Ukraine, and the Nazis had been through. Boys the same as the ones in the truck. The farmhouses and barns are blackened skeletons, and women and children lie dead on the ground. They were lucky. Shot instead of burned alive. The boy who gives us food stands up with a movie camera. A film to show Mama and Papa when he gets home.

Then I seen it. A field of sunflowers like a sea of melted gold. On the other side of the sea, between fruit orchards and a woodland, a gray stone palace with a reddish-orange roof and more windows, turrets, and chimneys than I can count. Alexandra and Darya get excited and start pointing, "*Mamochka, Mamochka.*" Emma and me shush them because maybe even "Mommy" in Russian can anger the soldiers. Lucky us, the soldiers are distracted, talking about the *glückliche Haus*. I think the Happy House is how they call the palace, but after the trucks turn up a road, the soldiers jump out and hurry to a low log building with a line outside.

"What are they waiting for?" I ask your grandmother after we and the girls are out of the truck.

Emma snickers. "What men always wait for."

From the left Joost Ter Horst comes toward us; from the right, a woman, the same woman I seen in Rostov supervising the looting. Joost dresses in the same grayish-green as the soldiers. The woman and four men strutting behind her with their *Maschinenpistolen* wear black uniforms with SS on the collars, the men in those wedge caps and the woman in a billed hat with a death's-head above the bill. Like on a bottle of poison. She has auburn hair twisted in a long pigtail, a face as pale and flawless as a cameo, and dollars to doughnuts, her uniform had visited a tailor. It shows off what she got, and she got plenty. Emma and me, we're scared and trying not to laugh, because the soldiers behind the woman glue their eyes to her backside.

"This is Frau Ter Horst," Joost says when he and the woman reach us.

Later, I find out she don't have no official rank and the uniform is a costume to her. Nobody dares give her trouble about it; her husband's a lieutenant colonel; her father's friends with Himmler and Hitler; and she likes taking her clothes on and off—I'll get to that. So your grandmother and me are there with the girls, the four SS soldiers glaring in our direction like blue-eyed vipers, and Frau Ter Horst ignores us and asks Joost, "The map I made of the Jew neighborhoods in Rostov, it was helpful to you and the Einsatzkommandos?"

Those were the bastards who did the killing at the ravine, and Joost, he frowns when Hildegard asks him the question and says, "I told you we would not need your map. And I was correct. By my account, this was our most productive day yet in Russia. Over twenty thousand."

"Joost, I worked hard on that map."

She may have been a hot number, but her husband is looking at her like she's dried-up herring. Hildegard pouts, then glances at Alexandra. She's the dark one, Hildegard's got a sour expression on her face, disgusted, as if Alexandra is a mouse raiding the pantry. Then Hildegard eyes Darya, who is hugging Emma's skirt. Your grandmother's trying to be calm, but there's fear on her face as Hildegard touches Darya's braids and says to Joost with real tenderness, "This Jew could be the Norse goddess Freyja. What marvelous blond hair and green eyes. Freyja, I am going to call her Freyja. We should send our Freyja to school."

Joost says, "Her mother will assist me in the kitchen. The other one, Bashe, reads and writes German and can help with my present for the Führer in *Das Judenzimmer*."

The Jew Room? That don't sound too promising, and Hildegard says, "I moved my dolls in there."

I think, What the hell are they talking about? And Joost, when he hears about the dolls, stands up straight as a maypole and scowls at her. "You did not move out anything, did you?"

She shakes her head, but refuses to look him in the eye. And Joost is so angry his face is the color of a ripe apple, and I'm terrified for Alexandra. Darya will be in school, Emma in the kitchen, but where will Alexandra go? So I say to Joost, "Herr Obersturmbannführer, can Alexandra work in the kitchen with her mother?"

Joost shrugs, Hildegard don't object, and Emma seems relieved. Joost goes toward the palace, waving for Emma and the girls to come along.

Hildegard says to me, "Your German is good?"

"Very good."

She smiles like we're best friends. "Wonderful. Let me show you where you will work."

We start walking, the four vipers behind us. I see Joost, Emma, and her daughters go into the palace. Then I hear a shout, and Hildegard veers around a hedge. I follow. A crewcut man in a white, blood-smeared smock stands behind a chair next to a table with bottles on it. A wrinkle-faced woman in a babushka sits on the chair, and the man reaches over her and sticks something in her mouth. Twenty or so other men and women are sitting on the grass, spitting at the ground or pressing a hand to their jaws.

Hildegard snaps at the man in the smock, "I told you. You must give them vodka. This procedure is painful. You are not to hurt them."

The man stands up, holding a pair of pliers, and I see a saucepan on the table with a gooey layer of blood on the bottom and gold teeth in the goo.

"Frau Ter Horst, I—"

Hildegard don't wait for him to finish. She sends her vipers to bring bottles of vodka to the people on the grass. The woman in the chair grabs Hildegard's arm and shouts at her in Ukrainian.

Hildegard asks me, "What is she saying?"

"She wants to know why you do this to her."

"Tell her we need the gold and to let go of me."

I tell her, but the woman tugs on Hildegard and screams. From a leather holster on her belt, Hildegard takes out a pistol that could fit in your palm, and—*bam! bam!*—shoots the woman in the head. Blood spurts, and the woman falls off the chair. I freeze. A wrong step, maybe Hildegard shoots me. But she holsters her pistol, calls out to her vipers that when the people are done drinking, they should be taken to the woods.

The woods, I'm sure, will be their last stop. There's no time to worry about that because Hildegard, who is acting as if she ain't done no more than spank a disobedient puppy, says to me, "Let us get you settled."

Into the palace we go—the soldiers clicking their heels together as Hildegard passes. I never seen such a place—gleaming wood stairways, colorful tiled fireplaces, Oriental carpets, bear rugs, some of the windows stained glass, and stag heads mounted on the walls. We go down two dark hallways, and Hildegard opens a door.

"Joost calls this the Jew Room," she says.

I'm confused. Why the Jew Room? There are bare stone walls, a cluttered wooden desk with a chair on either side, and a bench under the window with a row of three Matryoshka dolls on it. You know Matryoshka? Russian nesting dolls. Carved from wood and painted beautiful bright colors. Hildegard goes over and lifts up a doll of a smiling, rosy-cheeked old woman in an orange and purple babushka.

"I find these in the houses," Hildegard says.

She talks like there's no difference between finding and stealing, but I don't see it helps me to explain it to her.

The doll is a foot tall, and Hildegard opens the old woman by pulling her apart. She takes out a younger woman and pulls off the top of her and keeps going, each doll smaller than the one before it, until five of them are lined up on the bench—from the old woman to a baby.

"It's a family," I say.

There is something sad about the way Hildegard stares at the dolls. As if they know a secret they won't tell her. "Not to me, Bashe. To me they are all the same woman, and the different people we are inside. Do you understand?"

I take a chance and make a joke, hoping she'll cheer up, because I'm still nervous not knowing why Joost calls this place the Jew Room. "I got enough trouble being one person."

I get lucky. Hildegard laughs and we go to the desk and sit across from each other. On the desk is a ceramic ashtray, green packs of Eckstein Cigaretten, a gold lighter with a swastika engraved in it, stacks of thick, cream-colored writing paper, an inkwell, fountain pens, and a copy of Hitler's book, *Mein Kampf,* next to a roll of tanned leather. I look closer at the roll and notice pores, like human skin. Now this being the Jew Room makes sense, I'm shocked, and Hildegard must've seen it, because she says, "That is for the binding. It is an old tradition, according to Joost. He wants you to copy *Mein Kampf* on that paper. Print it neatly and with no mistakes. The last Jew he had doing this made a mess, and Joost was very upset."

This is probably where the skin came from. "It will take some time."

"That is understood. It is a gift for the Führer, and Joost will not be with him for a while."

Hildegard catches me glancing at the cigarettes. "Bashe, help yourself."

I light a cigarette, and Hildegard says, "You people make no sense to me."

"A poet, Fyodor Tyutchev—he was also a diplomat in Munich—said you cannot understand Russia with your mind. And the same is true with Jews."

Hildegard chuckles. "Then what do you understand them with?"

"Your heart."

"I was not taught to use that organ. To my father, the heart—my heart—was of no consequence. I did not want to marry Joost and begged my mother to talk to Father. She tried, but he wouldn't listen. Father loved Joost's roast pork and sauerkraut and that he had his own table at his restaurant; it made him feel important when Himmler and the Führer visited Nuremberg, and

Father would take them there. So I did as my father ordered and married Joost."

Hildegard lights a cigarette, and we sit there, smoking, silent, until she says, "I was angry at Father; to tell the truth, I hated him. Bashe, why do we listen to people we hate? Do we think they will love us more if we listen? And then we can stop hating them?"

She is worked up, and I got no idea what to say. I never had the time to ask myself such foolish questions. I almost tell her to go ask the dolls, but I don't need no answers because she starts talking again.

"A month after my marriage, when I learn Joost has no interest in the bedroom, I tell Father, and he says, 'Be satisfied that you eat well.' But Father does not want to be embarrassed about his son-in-law, not in public, and maybe he believes it will help Joost act more like a husband, so Father gets him his rank in the SS. Still, Joost does not touch me, but he likes giving orders. Loves giving orders. I can't blame Father for that, and Father was right about some things—Germany should be the master of Europe, the Slavs, the Jews, all the Untermenschen, the inferior races who—"

I swear that Nazi bitch is embarrassed she offended me. For one instant, I'm human to her, and she can't meet my eyes.

"Father likes to say, 'God writes our stories in vanishing ink.' That is the way of the world, I suppose. It is an unfortunate business. Yet I ask myself: why should only men serve? Women can do their part, but people do not believe we are serious. Bashe, you believe I am terrible for shooting that Ukrainian woman?"

I tap out my cigarette in the ashtray, trying to figure out how to answer so Hildegard won't shoot me, and I thank God twice because she can't stop talking.

"Did that woman have the right to grab me?" she says. "To scream at me? Would she have done the same to a man? She did not attack the man pulling her teeth, did she? Because she thought a man would shoot her. Bashe, am I supposed to be different?"

I act like I agree with her, nodding, because I got no doubt she'd kill me quick as a cat kills a mouse and with less regret.

And bless her heart, Hildegard smiles, all friendly after our girl talk. "I should not keep you from your work. I will have Joost send coffee and cake. If there is a problem, ask the guard outside the door to find me."

For months, I copy Hitler's meshuggeneh ranting. Once in a while Joost stops in and stands over me, reading over my shoulder, checking that I got the words right.

"Can't you work faster?" he asks.

"Not without making mistakes."

He clamps his hand on my shoulder, squeezing until I want to scream. "This book is for the Führer. No mistakes."

"Frau Ter Horst has made that clear."

He laughs. "Then I guess she is good for something."

Usually it is Hildegard who comes, bringing coffee and strudel for us. We chat or she sits on the bench, taking apart the Matryoshka dolls and putting them together again. Sometimes, before she enters, I hear her and the guard go to the room next door. Where Emma, me, and the girls sleep on straw-stuffed mattresses. I hear them panting. Like thirsty dogs. Once, after the guard, Hildegard comes in and says, "In German law, sex between an Aryan and Jew is forbidden, Bashe, but if you are lonely I can order one of the young men . . ."

That's all I need. An SS viper between my legs. The Nazis murdered my husband, but Hildegard don't know that. "I can't, one day I'll go back to the man I married."

"You are fortunate."

"Blessed," I reply, and of course, Hildegard don't get the irony.

One day she says to me, "I might be pregnant."

I look at her, not knowing what to say.

And she says, "Won't you congratulate me?"

Then she starts giggling. "Joost will not care. He will have someone take a picture of me cooing at the baby on my lap, and Joost will frame it and put it on his desk. The perfect SS officer and father."

A week later, Hildegard tells me she don't think she's pregnant no more. All she says about this is "Too bad. I would have been a good mother."

I ain't in no position to disagree, and she don't got the time to brood about not having a baby. Her and Joost have a lot of parties—Nazi generals and officials passing through. They come for the cooking, which is why Joost wanted help in the kitchen, and to get under the uniform skirts of the young SS maidens who answer to Hildegard. I tell Emma about the guard and Hildegard, and Emma says she always selects a male guest to take on a tour upstairs and returns with her face flushed. Joost ignores it. Your grandmother says he don't try nothing with her. She's rubbed against him, hoping to get on his good side so he'll protect her daughters. Alexandra's in school with Darya now, the only student with dark hair. Nine Ukrainian and Russian kids in a palace room with an SS maiden teaching them German and organizing games for them.

I say to Emma, "We're safe here, and maybe Hildegard ain't that bad."

"Bashe, the Red Army has millions more soldiers than the Germans and eventually will win. As the Nazis go home, they'll kill every Jew and Slav they can. And we're both. What's that you told me Hildegard said? 'God writes our stories in vanishing ink.'"

"Her father said it."

"I don't care who said it. If you don't think Hildegard believes it, your brain's in your ass."

My brain is right where it's supposed to be. I want to help your grandmother relax. She's panicked about her daughters. I know the pain of losing a child—pain forever, pain you can't imagine till it's your pain. But I need Emma thinking clear. She's craftier than me; we will have to escape, and it'll be tougher than your grandmother knows. Hildegard allows me breaks from copying, and I walk outside and that's when I seen things too scary to tell your grandmother.

Truckloads of wounded German soldiers arriving. The SS maidens sit them by the sunflowers, and several nurses give them injections. The men fall back, dead. Hildegard counts the bodies, Joost writes the numbers in a notebook, and soldiers load the corpses onto the trucks and drive away. And Hildegard herding a group of girls—no more than thirteen or fourteen years old—to the Happy House. And other girls being taken out and Hildegard, with her quartet of vipers in tow, leading them to the woods. The worst was the children the soldiers caught taking apples from the orchard. A boy ran off, the soldiers fired at him and missed, and Hildegard, who was strolling by with Joost and some SS maiden, watched till the boy was fifty meters away and shot him with her pistol. Joost, he starts clapping, and Hildegard stands there, smiling up at him.

In February 1943, I finish copying the six hundred and eighty-seven pages of *Mein Kampf*. Hildegard's lost interest in the book. She's never shared no news with me, but now she rambles on about the war. The Germans surrendered at Stalingrad. Eight hundred thousand of their troops are killed, wounded, or captured. They lose at least half a million more at Kursk and Rostov. At the palace, the mood is somber. There are fewer dinner parties. Emma pilfers tinned meat and fish and biscuits from the kitchen, and hides them in our rucksacks.

"It's coming," she says.

In May, I'm almost done checking and correcting my written copy of *Mein Kampf*, and we can hear the artillery duels in the distance. The Red Army is getting closer. I'm in the Jew Room one morning with the window open. Trucks are outside the palace, and soldiers are yelling to each other to separate the furniture and carpets from the dishes and silverware. I go to the window. In the woods there is the crackle of gunfire. I'm scared, and it gets worse when I hear Hildegard outside the door talking quietly to the guard.

They stop talking. I wait. And wait. The soldier calls, "Bashe." I don't reply. The door swings in. I'm standing behind it. Your grandmother saved my life. She explained how to use the Luger and insisted I bring it with me every day, hiding the pistol by securing it to my calf with a belt. It's in my hand when the soldier fires a burst from his *Maschinenpistole* at my chair before realizing it's empty. I yank on the barrel of his gun. He stumbles forward. I press the Luger to his neck and fire. He staggers to the side. I stick the barrel against his ear and fire again. His blood splatters my face. I take his submachine gun and the three-magazine pouch from his belt. Nobody is in the hall. I go to the room where we sleep, slip my arms through the straps of my rucksack, jam the pouch and Luger into Emma's rucksack and sling it over my shoulder, then hurry down the hallway and out to the grand entryway, where Joost is standing with a soldier and the SS maiden who teaches the children.

"What is this?" Joost shouts.

I answer him with the *Maschinenpistole*. I don't know how to unfold the wire butt stock or aim the weapon, but it shoots so many bullets I just point it and squeeze the trigger, and Joost tumbles backward and the soldier and the teacher go down with him. I want to check if they're dead, except I hear Emma screaming. Shrieking and screaming from the other wing of the palace. I enter the hallway that leads to the children's classroom. The rucksacks are heavier with every step. Emma is silent. Did you know even if you got a broken heart, your heart can break some more? I didn't. Not till I looked in that room. Your grandmother sits on the floor, her apron bloody and Alexandra's head on her lap. Some children are slumped over their little desks. The rest are lying together.

"A soldier killed them," Emma says, her voice full of the cold fury you hear in the winter wind slashing across the steppes. "And Hildegard took Darya out the door at the end of the hall. Get Darya, Bashe. Get her."

"Your Luger's in here," I say, dropping a rucksack, then running outside.

A convoy of trucks and jeeps is a couple hundred meters past the sunflower field, and soldiers in coal-scuttle helmets run through the dust cloud churned up by the wheels.

I go to the classroom. Emma looks at me. I shake my head. She kisses Alexandra.

"I don't want to leave her, Bashe."

Her face looks like she's crying without tears. I help her stand and take off her apron. She removes the Luger from the rucksack and puts her arms through the shoulder straps.

Staring at Alexandra, your grandmother, as if stating a scientific fact, says, "We will find Darya."

I don't argue. Why bother? Emma says we have to stay off main roads—we don't want to bump into the Germans or the Red Army, who sometimes believe escaped prisoners are spies and shoot them. We tramp through forests, along fields, and around burned villages.

That night we slept under fir trees. Your grandmother is silent, and her silence continues until the following morning at the sugar-beet field. We smell the field before we see it, the stink of death so thick it seems to poison the sunlight.

Today, everybody hears about Auschwitz-Birkenau, Buchenwald, Dachau, the popular names. But there are other camps the Nazis set up because they need them at the moment, camps with no names, where the killing is so thorough no one survives to remember them.

That was the camp in the sugar-beet field. Posts with barbed wire enclose the field. There are four guard towers and shacks inside the wire, and bodies of men, women, and children in and out of the enclosure, like the black soil is growing corpses.

I ask your grandmother, "Is God going to destroy the world again?"

"It's not raining, so there can't be a flood."

"Maybe He's got another idea."

Two seared German armored cars and a tank, with black crosses painted on their sides, are across the field. Dead Soviet soldiers surround them, and dead German soldiers hang out of the cars, and another soldier is half in and half out of the tank turret.

I say, "Our army tried to free them."

The fury is gone from your grandmother's voice, but not the coldness, "We should see if there are weapons and some better clothing."

"Emma, the smell will kill us."

"Breathe through your mouth."

I feel like a grave robber, stepping over and around the dead, and I avoid their waxy faces. We come away with Red Army tunics and trousers held up by belts with a Communist star on the buckle; boots made of artificial leather that don't fit till we wrap several cloths around our feet; ponchos we stuff in two duffel-bag packs; a dozen more magazines for my *Maschinenpistole*; a holster and seven magazines for Emma's Luger; and a Soviet submachine gun with a big round drum underneath it for the bullets. Technically, I find out, its name is PPSh-41, but Soviet soldiers call it *papasha*—daddy.

I inspect us in our new outfits. "Now the Nazis will shoot us on sight."

"At least our toes won't be blistered."

I laugh, believing your grandmother has recovered enough to make jokes. As we leave, though, she pauses by a little red-haired girl on her back in the dirt, a stuffed bear held to her chest that don't fully cover her wounds. The girl is in an embroidered Ukrainian blouse and skirt, but her skirt is up, and she has no underwear. Emma pulls down the skirt, then gazes at the girl like she's intending to stand in that field till the Messiah shows up.

251

I tug her sleeve.

"I will find Darya," she murmurs, as if reciting a prayer.

And it was late one afternoon, with shadows darkening the steppes, that we smell stew cooking from behind a row of oak trees and become partisans.

Listen to me. It's important if you really drive all this way to understand your grandmother—if you can feel in your heart the woman the war made of my dear Emma. There was lots of brave partisans fighting, but after the war, when Soviets talk, you'd think every one of them witless braggers was partisans and rescued Mother Russia from the fascists. A dime gets y'all a dollar they did nothing except stand around burping like cows. If your grandmother was here, she wouldn't lie. We was partisans till the winter of 1944, and for many of them seven or eight months we hide in forests, in a hole in a hillside, in a barn or hut the Nazis don't remodel with their flame-throwers. But this is as true as you and Yulianna is sitting there. People lived because of us, and we made the German army a little smaller.

Here's how it starts. Your grandmother smells that stew and says, "These idiots are too close to the fields. They keep doing that, the Germans will get them."

"I'm hungry."

"Then let's meet some of the dumbest people in the Ukraine."

We go past the oaks, and there they are, a man and three teenage girls sitting around a cooking fire with a three-legged pot simmering over the flame.

The man, in a Red Army uniform, with a mustache like Stalin and a belly hanging over his belt, pops up to his feet. "I am Valentin Ivanovich Vedenin, commander of the Vedenin Partisans."

Me, I'm betting he's a deserter and his opinions is bigger than his balls, but I'm saying nothing. I want some stew. Then the oldest girl stands, kerchief on her head, a peasant skirt and blouse. She's maybe seventeen, with white-blond hair, milky skin, eyes the color of cornflowers—one of those virginal-looking dolls men can't wait to ruin.

"I am Katrya. And these are my twin sisters, Oxana and Olena."

The twins are younger—I guess, fifteen—with long thick brown hair. They ain't as pretty as Katrya, but got sweeter smiles and wide dark eyes. One of them ladles stew into a mess kit and says, "Please, eat with us."

"Hold it," Valentin says to Emma and me. "Do you want to join the Vedenin Partisans?"

Emma chuckles. "Can we have dinner first?"

"You do not believe we are serious?" Valentin says, and walks around a thicket.

We follow him, the three sisters follow us. Sitting on a log, their mouths gagged with cloths and their hands and feet tied with rope, are two Nazi soldiers.

Valentin says, "They were wandering near here, and we captured them. They don't speak Russian or Ukrainian, so I could not interrogate them."

I tell him I speak German, and he removes their gags. "Ask them where the unit is located."

I ask, and both give the same answer: if they knew where the unit was, they wouldn't have gotten lost. I tell Valentin, and then, what happens next, I won't never forget if I live to a hundred and twenty.

Your grandmother takes a snapshot out of her rucksack—the one she carries of her, Gak, and their daughters. It's bent and peeling on the edges, and she shows it to the two soldiers, and tells me to ask them if they've seen the girl on her lap. I ask. The soldiers shake their heads.

And your grandmother puts the photo in her rucksack, then raises her arms and shoots those two with her submachine gun. The papasha hurts my ears, and the soldiers fly off the log.

Valentin, the girls, and me gape at Emma, while she's acting like killing a pair of Nazis before dinner ain't nothing unusual.

"Is the stew ready?" she asks.

Your grandmother eats—it's a hare stew with potatoes—and reads a book Katrya lends her—*The Partisan's Companion*. It's put out by the government to teach partisans how to hurt the Nazis, something Katrya and her sisters want badly to do, because the fascists murdered their parents.

It's dark now, Emma and me wrap ourselves in our ponchos and try to sleep. Close by, Katrya says, "I don't want to. Not anymore."

Valentin replies, "If not you, then your sisters."

"No, no. They're too young."

"Then move over."

Emma says, "Go to sleep, Valentin. By yourself."

"Mind your business, woman."

"Sleeping is my business now, and you're disturbing me. Leave her alone."

"Perhaps you'd like to take her place."

"Sure. After the Nazis kill me, you're free to climb on."

Emma gets up, and in the dark I hear the click of her pulling back the bolt of her papasha. She sits by Katrya and again tells Valentin to go. He leaves, but to save face says he'll discuss this with Emma in the morning.

There's no talk when we wake up, but I don't have no more cigarettes, and Valentin's got packages of Makhorka—that's loose tobacco—and he's rolled himself a smoke.

"Comrade," I ask him. "May I have tobacco for a cigarette?"

He laughs. "Do you have five rubles?"

I do, but I'll be damned if I'll pay him that for one lousy smoke. I say no, and he replies, "Then maybe we can discuss an arrangement for this evening."

Emma, she's reading the handbook, and puts it down, stands up, and, just as I seen the Luger in her hand, your grandmother shoots Valentin in the forehead. This shocks me and the girls, but I'll tell you what—it's some kind of miracle. Maybe not like a cup of oil lasting eight days, but it's a sight to see. Valentin on his back with a hole in his head and the cigarette still in his mouth. Your grandmother takes the cigarette and gives it to me.

I say, "You're developing a bad habit."

"You should try it. It's more fun than smoking."

From then on, your grandmother leads us. The Nazis, they hunt partisans and kill the ones they catch. We hide and specialize in picking off their sentries at night or shooting those dumb enough to get lost. Fact is, we is lost most of the time. That's what happens when you ain't got a map. Katrya says we're south of Kiev, but that's as helpful as knowing we're south of the North Pole.

One adventure I remember. We seen seven Nazi soldiers riding toward a stretch of evergreens. We know this area, there's a trail that goes to a stream, and your grandmother tells me and the twins to hide behind the rocks across the stream and shoot the soldiers if they come. Start with the horses, she says. Then she goes up behind the stream with Katrya. The

Nazis ride down the trail like they're in the German countryside and don't got a care in the world. We fire at them. I feel terrible seeing the horses fall, but I don't got a chance to cry about it, because we don't hit all the soldiers and some is on the ground firing at us—till Emma and Katrya sneak up from behind and finish off the fascists.

That night, for dinner—God forgive me—we got grilled horse filets.

But like I says, your grandmother also tries to rescue people—any of the wounded in the ruined villages, but the Nazis don't leave many alive. The biggest thing we do is at a farm. We're on a rise, hidden by brush and trees, and seen three Nazi soldiers, fifty meters away, herding maybe a hundred people—women, children, and some elderly folks walking with canes, into a barn and shutting the doors. One soldier got the tanks of a flamethrower on his back, the other two got *Maschinenpistolen*. The soldier shrugs off the tanks, then drops his pants and crouches to take a shit. The other soldiers sling their submachine guns over their shoulders and light cigarettes.

"Let's go," Emma says, and we take off down the hill, shooting as we run. The soldiers are dead before we get to the barn.

Emma lets the sisters open the doors, and the people, the mothers in tears, come streaming out.

I'll tell you. Seeing those people alive—that's one of the best feelings in my life.

Okay, so it's the fall now, and in the woods, we discover a bunker in a hillside. It's empty except for crates of potatoes and sugar beets. Maybe the Nazis find the people hiding there. That's good for us, because they won't be back. And the autumn *rasputitsa* has arrived, the rain and mud, and it's difficult for the Germans to travel. We stay. Katrya, she could be a big-game hunter, I'm telling you. She shot two boars and two deer with her rifle, and we make sausage. Every day we patrol to make sure the area's safe. One afternoon, the weather suddenly turns warm, we go maybe two kilometers from our bunker, and the twins see a pond and want to swim. This is crazy, Emma tells them, but they don't listen.

Katrya says, "We will be fine. Go to our hill, and we will be there soon."

I remember seeing the twins undress and their young bodies, so white and slim, and wishing I never got old and that the war don't never come.

Emma and me is halfway back to the bunker when it starts to rain and we hear the hammering of machine guns. The firing echoes in the forest. Then there's an eerie quiet except for the rain slapping the last of the leaves off the trees. Behind us, dogs bark. Emma and me look at each other. Katrya, Oxana, and Olena, they're dead, they have to be. The dogs get closer, and we start moving through the hard steady rain. I ask Emma if she has a plan. Not to die, she says. Through the trees there is a muddy field, and beyond the field a road, where men are cursing in German. We crawl over wet leaves to the edge of the woods. A long line of canvas-top trucks is stalled on the road, their tires sinking in the mud. The wheel's fallen off the lead truck, and a soldier is rolling it back to a circle of soldiers smoking cigarettes and standing by the truck. Women, dozens of them, sit in the field, their heads lowered against the rain, their knees drawn up to their chests, their arms wrapped around them.

"Get rid of the army clothes," your grandmother says, digging a sweater and her old skirt out of her rucksack.

"Why?"

"We're crawling into that field."

"We don't know where those trucks are going."

"We know we can't outrun dogs."

Both of us change, take off our boots, leave our weapons and rucksacks. The rain is so heavy the women and trucks and soldiers are liquid shadows. On all fours, we crawl out into the field, our hands and knees pressing into the mud, till we get to the women. We sit balled up against the rain. No one notices. We're soaked and shivering when the soldiers order us to the trucks. Nobody looks at us. Your grandmother, I think, is a genius. My mind changes a couple hours later when the trucks stop and we're ordered onto cattle cars waiting on a railroad track.

That ride. All of us standing, packed together. And the smell. Like you're drowning in shit. There's one slop bucket and you can't get to it. The small window don't help. Light and dark flick on and off through it. I'm frightened, and Emma whispers, "If they wanted us dead, they'd have shot us in the field."

But your grandmother's as frightened as me. Her lips move, no sound comes out. And she's mouthing the same word over and over—Darya.

When the train gets to where it's going, the doors slide open. It's a Polish town—Oświęcim. You know what's there, don't you? Auschwitz-Birkenau.

Even then, we heard about those murder factories. We jump out of that cattle car, and before I can take a breath of fresh air, the SS guards are shouting at us, dividing up the passengers—you go left, you go right, meaning you live, you die—and children are crying, mothers and fathers screaming, and German shepherds, leaping forward on their leashes, snarl at us like they ain't been fed in a month and steak's dangling from our necks.

This is where me and your grandmother learn angels exist—one angel, that's for sure. Her name's Klara Fischer. She's the Lagerführerin—the Camp Leader—and she don't look like no angel in her uniform: no shape to her, her hair in a bun, and a face so prim and proper if she ever grinned her skin would've split like dry leather.

"I need farmers," she calls out to an SS officer, and grabs Emma and me by the sleeves.

"Who says those two are farmers?" the officer asks.

"Look at their hands, you'll see, they grew up on farms."

This is news to me and Emma, but we're not arguing, and the officer says, "Take them."

"I need more," she says.

"Two," the officer says. "We get the rest."

Not far is Jagoda, a camp where they got cows, pigs, chickens, and vegetable gardens. We get uniforms—light gray with purple stripes, a jacket with our number and a yellow Star of David, a skirt and kerchief. But Klara also gives us decent boots and wool coats—where the hell she finds them, God knows. The women prisoners—two hundred at most—live in an old shoe factory, sleep on wooden bunks with straw for mattresses. We feed chickens, slop hogs, collect eggs, muck out barns. But we eat good, and I ain't got much to say about Jagoda. The big news is me and your grandmother don't die. Because lots of people is dying at Auschwitz-Birkenau, and the Nazis are burning the bodies. The wind blows, you can smell burned flesh and hair, and sometimes the ashes go up in the sky like dark clouds. Other times they send us the ashes in barrels to use as fertilizer for the vegetables.

Klara keeps bringing in as many prisoners as she can. One day I ask her why. She says, "I was raised Catholic, in a small village outside Saarbrücken. Every Sunday, in our village, the church was always full, and the women wept as they prayed. And I ask my mother, 'Why do those women cry?' And

Mama answers, 'Because women know the horror men make of this world. The women suffer giving birth and men mock their suffering by sending their children to war.' The world should have less horror, no?"

And Klara ain't done helping your grandmother and me. We're at the camp maybe fourteen months—I remember two Christmases go by. Now it's January 1945. Klara says the Red Army is on the way, and prisoners are going to be evacuated to camps inside Germany. We'll have to march through the cold and the snow to the trains. Then she gives us four tablets each. Pervitin, she says. Soldiers use it for energy. Take two when you start walking and the other two a few hours later.

The march begins in the morning. Emma and me, we take the tablets, and we're in the middle of a line. I can't see the front or back. Even though it's freezing, we got energy, and I couldn't care less about eating. The hardest thing is not talking. I feel like I can talk for a week without stopping. I don't say nothing and swallow the other two pills and keep going—if you fall behind or squat to piss when you ain't allowed, the Germans shoot you. Eight, nine hours, I don't know how long it lasts before we get to the town of Wodzisław Śląski, and the Germans cram us into cattle cars.

I would've gone meshuggeh, but I know what to expect from the ride to Auschwitz. We wind up in Kaufering, a subcamp of Dachau. We live in huts barely above ground and dig trenches, carry bags of cement, nothing good, and many of the prisoners is sick and waiting outside death's door. We're there a few months, and in late April the guards march us to Dachau. American planes are bombing nearby. And we know their soldiers is coming. So did the SS. They're burning papers and shooting prisoners. Those SS bastards are convinced they was better than everyone, and when they found out they wasn't, they had one last party murdering the helpless—one final moment believing they're gods, pretending Hitler's lies are true. Your grandmother's been sick, she don't eat, she don't talk, not even about finding Darya. I get cups of water in her, but that's all. The last hundred meters of the march I'm holding her up. Then on a cold windy afternoon Emma's shuffling behind me and some other women crossing the Appellplatz, the open square in the middle of the camp. A group of SS men watch us, and one of them shoots at her and some others and orders the rest of us to keep going.

That's what happens to your grandmother.

I'm sad and scared and talk to Emma like she's with me. She says the SS plans to shoot us all, and I should escape. Other prisoners are thinking the same way. I go with them and live in a displaced-persons camp until a group of us get to Italy. That's another long story—how we got on that boat to Palestine. I meet Yankel in Tel Aviv, and we marry, but it's a hard life there. He's got a brother in Miami Beach, we move to Florida, Yankel fights with his brother, and we buy this business in Atlanta. Then a woman I met in Tel Aviv gets in touch. She knows I'm from Rostov and asks if I can travel to Russia and do errands for a group trying to save Jews. How can I say no? I got to try. For my first husband and my son. And because I couldn't save Emma.

That's what happens to me.

46

Bashe stood at the window, gazing through the bars. Seven blackened filters and a layer of ash overflowed the tin ashtray, and I imagined the filters as bones, and my grandmother breathing in the odor of smoldering corpses while ash from the fire pits of Auschwitz dusted her shoulders like snowflakes.

Outer space was infinite, but, I decided, so was hell.

"Anything about Hildegard?" I asked.

She shook her head.

"We heard she got to Nuremberg with Darya, and a British bomb hit her house."

"My heart breaks for Darya, but I hope that Nazi whore burned to death."

"Witnesses saw the house destroyed, but no one saw the bodies. Hildegard and Darya could've survived."

Bashe turned toward us. Her face was streaked with dried tears. "Maybe ask Nate Falk."

"Who's that?"

"Used to be one of our best customers—the man worships Patek Philippe. Nate is from Nuremberg and didn't get to America till after the war. He was an auto mechanic, so the Nazis put him to work and let him live. His wife died, and he just moved to Los Angeles to be by his daughter."

"You have a phone number?"

"A return address on an envelope, from the last check he sent. I'll get it for you. But I don't got the daughter's name, and a phone number won't do no good. Nate owned car dealerships, he sold them, and last time he was in, he says the best thing about retiring is he ain't never talking on the phone again."

Yuli and I stood. Bashe walked over. "I loved your grandmother."

I kissed her cheek, and Bashe gave Yuli a look, happy and sad with a touch of lewdness. "Yulianna, you got yourself a good one."

"Yes, I do."

———————

We sat in the Plymouth Fury with the sun flaming out.

Yuli said, "Now we know why Emma wrote that line about vanishing ink in the Picasso book."

I sat behind the wheel, my hand on the key, not moving.

"Should we find a hotel?" Yuli asked.

"Can we head home?"

"Are you okay, Misha?"

"I feel like driving."

We were an hour up I-85, with the sky a satiny indigo, when I said, "I wish Emma had told me."

"What would she say? 'Bubbeleh, let me tell you about the men I shot.'"

Picturing my grandmother mixing me an egg cream and giving me that information was so absurd it made me laugh. In fact, Bashe's story reeked of absurdity, as though Alfred Hitchcock and Rod Serling had come up with a movie so grotesque no one could believe it. Except it had happened. And to my grandmother, the smiling lady I always remembered handing out free candy to children.

I said, "She could've told me about the camps."

"Maybe she was ashamed."

I glanced at the speedometer. The needle was at eighty-five, and I tapped the brake. "How? How could she be ashamed?"

Yuli rested her head on the seat back. "Sometimes the worst feeling about losing my mother and my friends at Lake Bereza isn't the sadness. It's that I deserved it. That if I'd been a better person it wouldn't have happened, and I don't want anyone to know that about me."

"That's ridiculous."

"So?"

That gave me something to contemplate until we reached Greensboro. We were tired, and Yuli spotted a sign for a Howard Johnson's motor lodge, and we checked in and fell asleep without another word about Bashe or my grandmother.

Late the next morning, on the outskirts of Baltimore, we stopped at a diner. After the waitress brought us coffee and menus, Yuli went to the ladies' room. Someone had left a *Washington Post* on the next table, and I read the front-page story twice. When Yuli came back, I said, "The *Post* says Taft Mifflin, the general manager of Four Freedoms Radio, died yesterday from an apparent heart attack on M Street in Washington, D.C."

I passed her the paper, and she read the story. I felt bad that Taft had died, even though his bringing me to Munich had almost gotten me killed and cost Dmitry his life. On the other hand, he was also responsible for my meeting Yuli and learning about Emma's past. I wasn't shocked by his death, however, and that scared me, because if it was the KGB, we could be in danger. And Yuli thought so, too.

"Could be a gas gun," she said, putting down the *Post*.

Hoping she was wrong, I replied, "The reporter says no one saw anything but a man collapsing on the sidewalk."

"This is why KGB use cyanide gas. The police do not see blood, they do not treat it like a murder. And even if your FBI or CIA order an autopsy, by the time it is done the assassin can be eating caviar in Moscow."

"Could this be connected to Der?"

"Taft told us that was about *Exodus* and the missile designer. We are not involved."

"He also told us where Joost was and knew we were going to see

Bashe. And you thought the KGB was following you in Amsterdam. It could be connected to that."

"It could."

"I still want to go see Nate Falk."

Yuli glanced at the menu in its plastic sleeve, then pushed it aside. "And I still want to see the Hollywood sign."

Part IX

47

Los Angeles, California
March 11, 1965

During the flight across the country, Yuli sat in the window seat, occasionally fiddling with the bow at the neckline of her dress and reading a John le Carré novel, *The Spy Who Came In from the Cold.*

"Any good?" I asked, more from a desire to talk to her than out of curiosity.

Her eyes didn't move from the paperback. "Le Carré says spies are vain fools."

"You agree?"

"A person believing he has the answer for injustice, this is vanity. And vanity is foolish."

I was stung, thinking that she was referring to my fixation on tracking down Emma's murderer and who was behind the Munich shooting that killed Dmitry. "Are you saying—"

"I am saying I want to read."

Her voice was cold, and I swallowed my response, keenly aware that the death of a person you loved was infuriating—the insult of it, the feeling of how dare the universe or God or chance take away your loved one. Reaching into the canvas rucksack under my seat, I retrieved the *Guide to Metropolitan Los Angeles* that the travel agent at Vacations Unlimited in South Orange Village had given me when I'd booked our plane tickets.

After loosening my tie and sliding back my seat, I read through the guide and inspected the foldout maps, dozing on and off until the jet descended through the clouds and Yuli asked, "Is L.A. on fire?"

Leaning over the armrest between our seats, I looked out the window. A thick brown haze was shrouding the mountains and rolling across the city into the San Fernando Valley, where neon signs shone through the gloom, and lines of streets and houses and the irregular aqua dots of swimming pools seemed carved into the bottom of the brownish-green valley.

I held up the guide. "Smog. From the traffic, the chemical plants, and the oil refineries."

"I'm sorr—"

I shook my head, letting her know that no apology was necessary, and we were holding hands as the jet touched down on the runway.

We retrieved our suitcases, and I rented a burgundy Mustang convertible from Hertz. Even with the sun sinking toward the horizon, L.A. was a balmy Technicolor paradise compared to the slush-gray finale of the New Jersey winter, and after tossing our bags in the trunk and lowering the top, I perused the map, then drove out of the lot.

"Let's go talk to Nate Falk," I said.

"You really believe he might know where Hildegard is?"

I inched into the bumper-to-bumper traffic on the 405. "I'd settle for him knowing if she's dead or alive."

With a pronounced lack of confidence, Yuli replied, "This would be nice."

Aggravated by our slow progress and her pessimism, I said, "If you doubted Nate Falk could help, why'd you come?"

Yuli was gathering her hair into a ponytail and clipping it with a metal butterfly barrette. "Because I love you. Now watch the road."

The address was 450 North Rossmore Avenue, and according to the map, it was thirty or forty minutes from the airport. However, after an hour, we hadn't even reached the 10, which persuaded me, from then on, to avoid freeways. Yuli, I noticed, was studying the cars and trucks around us.

"What're you looking for?" I asked.

"A bearded man in a sedan. From that night in Amsterdam."

"Did you see him?"

"There was a bearded man in the car that just passed. Almost the same color as this car."

"That was a Chevrolet Impala." I preferred Yuli chatty and paranoid to silent and withdrawn, and despite her experience I doubted we were in danger. "C'mon, is it likely we were followed?"

"Misha, Americans love dopey Russians—like your Khrushchev routines on radio. And we have dopeys—"

"Dopes."

"Dopes. In Soviet Union, there are millions of dopes. But not in KGB."

"How could they know we're here?"

"You buy airline tickets with your American Express, KGB could be bribing contacts in that company. Bashe could have mentioned it to someone she thought was safe and is KGB. Same with Taft Mifflin. You think the KGB has no moles inside CIA? Think more. And who is to say KGB or an agent from the East German Stasi has not been in Nuremberg to search for Hildegard? If Nate Falk can know about her, why not KGB or Stasi? This makes sense, *da*?"

"*Da*."

The sky was dimming and streaked with crimson and gold when I turned into the driveway of the El Royale, a white high-rise grand enough for Paris, with carved gray stone archways over the doors. A valet with a wispy mustache and a crucifix on a chain dangling from his neck trotted over to the Mustang. I tipped him a dollar and gave him the key.

A prince and princess could have staged their wedding in the cavernous lobby, with its decoratively painted vaulted ceiling, old-fashioned iron chandeliers, and muted light glimmering on the inlaid-marble and parquet flooring.

"You capitalists know how to live," Yuli said, her heels clicking on the marble.

At the front desk, the concierge, a silver-haired gentleman dressed as formally as a butler, stood over a leather-bound sign-in ledger and a phone.

"May I help you?" he asked.

"I'm Michael Daniels, this is Yulianna Timko, and we are here to speak with Mr. Nathan Falk. Bashe, from the watch store in Atlanta, sent us."

"Mr. Falk is out. He lives with his daughter, and she and her husband are out as well."

"May I leave Mr. Falk a message?"

"You just did," the concierge replied. "I will tell him."

When we were in the Mustang, Yuli said, "Can we take a ride?"

"We have to. Our hotel's in Santa Monica."

"Not to our hotel."

"Don't tell me the bearded guy's around."

"Not that I saw. But could we go look at the Hollywood sign?"

I checked a map in the guide, then drove north, crossing Sunset Boulevard and going up, skirting the edge of the hills and all the houses, with windows overlooking the city, filling the hillsides like space-age pueblos, and there it was on the slope of Mount Lee. I stopped on the shoulder of the road, and Yuli stood on the seat, staring at the letters glowing in the twilight as if each one had been cut from a harvest moon.

"I've been seeing pictures of this sign since I was teenager. I feel like I'm on a religious pilgrimage."

"Do religious pilgrims get hungry?"

Yuli laughed. "This one does," and she sat in her seat, and I drove down into Burbank.

"Misha, what are we eating?"

"Classic American."

Bob's Big Boy was a long glass rectangle lit in glary shades of orange and red. Going inside, we walked by a hand-painted statue of the chubby grinning Big Boy himself, with his overalls and high pompadour, and holding up one of his original double-decker hamburgers, which we ordered once we were seated. Around us were the melodies of waitresses taking orders, the ringing cash register, the murmur of teenage couples in Hawaiian shirts at the counter sharing root-beer floats, and the chatter of families wedged into booths, the two children behind us debating, in tones of conviction and ecstasy, whether the best ride at Disneyland was the Monorail or Davy Crockett's Explorer Canoes.

Yuli's appetite had improved, and we all but inhaled our hamburgers, and as we waited for our dessert, she scanned the restaurant, her expression beatific and faintly confused, as though Bob's were swarmed by pixies and unicorns.

Yuli said, "This . . ."

"This?"

She tilted her head left, then right—her version of a shrug. "This is so different from Russia. The people. They aren't . . . they aren't waiting for something terrible to happen."

"Because nobody can lock them up for cursing the government, and the Nazis never invaded Burbank and slaughtered fifteen million civilians."

The waitress brought us two spoons and a plate with a scoop of vanilla ice cream between layers of devil's food cake covered with hot fudge, whipped cream, and a maraschino cherry.

"And," I added, scooping up a spoonful of the dessert and holding it toward her.

She cleaned off the spoon, then grinned. "And you get a cherry on top."

"Yes, you do."

48

We were staying at the Georgian, a charming old beaux arts hotel with a veranda across from the ocean, and in the morning I woke up with an arm around Yuli and a silken wave of her hair on my face and her legs enlaced with mine. I kissed her ear, her arms went around me, yet when I began kissing her neck, she responded with an exasperated sigh and stopped holding me. For the last couple of weeks, I had missed making love to her and began feeling as though I was a besotted hero in a Victorian novel discovering that his body could genuinely ache with desire—not lust, but an agonizing hunger to be joined to the only woman who could cure his agony. I felt a bit pathetic and, following a bout of self-pity, figured the best I could do for her was to keep quiet and order rolls and coffee from room service.

After we showered and dressed and ate, we walked in the shade of the palm trees along Ocean Avenue, where drunks were sleeping it off on the benches and elderly couples were out for a stroll, the men in straw fedoras and loud sport jackets and the women in floppy broad-brimmed hats and gaily printed dresses. The sidewalk was above a grassy slope that ran down to a broad sandy beach and the sun-sparkled sea, and Yuli paused to watch the surfers navigating the waves.

"I want to buy a bikini," she said.

"You won't get any argument from me."

It was good to see her smile. "I didn't think so."

She took my hand as we went by the pier with its Ferris wheel and the winding elevated tracks of the roller coaster.

"Do I have time to shop?" Yuli asked.

"Sure. Nate Falk is retired. He'll be home at some point during the day. We'll keep checking."

Beyond the pier, sailboats were cutting through the water, and we passed the white statue of Saint Monica in her habit, her eyes closed in prayer and her hands folded across on her chest.

"I'm sorry, Misha."

"For what?"

"For—for this morning—for—"

"You have nothing to be—"

"For being so—so sad. I remember a few years after going to live with Papka. I was in bed one night, thinking about those dead children at Lake Bereza and crying on and off until morning. I promised myself that I would not be that sad again. And here I am. Just as sad. And wondering if it will ever go away."

"It will." That was an attempt to comfort Yuli, not a faithful reporting of my experience. My sadness about Emma and Dmitry hadn't gone away. I just didn't notice it as much. And it helped to be angry. Sometimes I was so angry about the shootings I scared myself, unnerved by my rage and visions of strangling their faceless murderers.

Yuli bought a bikini at Henshey's, a department store that appeared to be constructed from beige Legos, and then we drove to the El Royale.

As we approached the front desk in the lobby, the concierge, the same courtly fellow from yesterday, asked, "Back again, are we?"

He dialed the phone and announced us. "I see," he said, then hung up. "Mr. Falk isn't in. Mrs. Cohen, his daughter, is home. Take the elevator to the penthouse."

Mrs. Cohen was a birdlike woman with a pointy nose, a helmet of dark, curly hair, and a pregnancy swelling her mauve chiffon maternity blouse as if she were carrying a basketball.

"Hello, I'm Irma. I got your message from yesterday. Come in."

She led us through rooms of Danish modern furniture, with artwork that looked as though an irate child had thrown buckets of paint against the walls, and out onto a roof deck with a champagne-colored awning and redwood couches arranged around a low glass-topped table.

Yuli and I sat next to each other across from Irma, who extracted a can of Fresca from a pail of ice. "Would you like a soda?"

Yuli shook her head, and I said, "Thanks, no. Bashe told us your father might be able to help us find a woman from Nuremberg."

"I was born in Nuremberg. In 1938." Irma stared past us, out toward the tree-studded hills. "My father isn't here. I haven't seen him in a week." She was silent, her eyes fixed on the magnificent view, and she trembled, fighting to hold off tears until she lost the battle and began sobbing, her swollen belly going up and down, so that I thought her child must feel as if he or she were on a pogo stick. Yuli went to sit beside her, took the Fresca from her, pulled the top off the can, and held it for Irma to sip.

I said, "We didn't mean to upset you. We can go and come back."

Regaining control of herself, Irma sat back, touching Yuli's arm to thank her. "No, no. I'm going crazy, the baby's due in a month, I'm trapped between my husband and my father. I have to tell someone."

Yuli gave her the soda. She sipped it. "The week I was born, the Nazis destroyed the Great Synagogue in Nuremberg. My mother's sister had moved to Atlanta—her husband got a job teaching at a college there—but she was visiting us and offered to take me till things got better. My mother had a rheumatic heart—my father says it was a miracle she survived my birth—and they had my three older brothers at home. So I went with my aunt to Atlanta. My brothers died in Sobibór, my mother died in Ravensbrück."

Irma drank some Fresca. "My father survived Buchenwald and found a new wife, Toiba, in a displaced-persons camp, and came to Georgia. My stepmother was the sweetest woman, and my father had just sold his car dealerships when she died. He was lost without her, and I asked him to live with us. He always liked my husband. Bert writes comedy for TV—*Leave It to Beaver*, *The Beverly Hillbillies*, *My Favorite Martian*—and then Bert's agent made a deal for Bert to help develop a new show, *Hogan's Heroes*. It'll be on in September."

Irma set the can on the table. "The show's about American, British, and French prisoners in a Nazi POW camp."

"And it is a comedy?" Yuli asked.

"The Nazis are supposed to be very stupid."

"The Nazis were stupid?"

Irma extended her hands, palms up. "In the show they are. And when Bert told my father about it—we were in Hollywood celebrating with a dinner at Musso and Frank—my father starts shouting, 'Why not Ozzie and Harriet go to Auschwitz? Or the Flintstones in the gas chamber?' Half the restaurant is gawking at us, the waiter told my father to put a lid on it or he'll call the cops, and my father leaves, comes here to pack a bag, and now he's gone."

I felt let down, imagining trying to locate a man I'd never met in a sprawling, traffic-clogged city that would've stumped Lewis and Clark. I asked, "No idea where he is?"

"He says Kaddish at eight in the morning for my stepmother at the Shul on the Beach. In Venice. Bert went to talk to him three days ago, and my father screamed at him."

"You have a recent picture of your dad?" I asked.

"In the den. I could show you."

Yuli said, "When we are done talking to your father, we will try and bring him home."

Irma put her hand on Yuli's arm. "Your accent—where are you from?"

Yuli patted her hand. "From a place where a lot of people feel just the way your father does."

49

As we waited for the valet to bring us the Mustang, Yuli said, "Will Americans watch this comedy?"

"Depends on their memories, I guess."

Yuli frowned. "Let's go to the beach."

The valet pulled up, I tipped him, and as we got in, Yuli asked, "Can you take a different route to Santa Monica?"

"Did you see the bearded guy on the way here?"

"I did not. But it doesn't hurt to be careful."

I removed the travel guide from the glove compartment, and from what I could see on the map, Sunset Boulevard could take us about anywhere we needed to go. I drove west into the sunny greenery and brilliant riot of flowers in Beverly Hills, past Mediterranean villas, French châteaux, English manors, Spanish ranches, and towering palms so impeccably barbered that I figured they were tended by gardeners levitating above the treetops with jet packs.

In the convertible, it was no sweat for Yuli to glance back to see if we were being tailed, and farther down Sunset, when I saw a sign for the Pacific Coast Highway and turned down a steep canyon road, she said, "I saw the car—what was it?"

"An Impala."

"I saw an Impala, but no beard."

Yuli let down her guard on the PCH, transfixed by the sight of the cream- and rose-colored buildings of Santa Monica rising up through the mist on the other side of the blue water. At Henshey's, Yuli had shopped for her bikini alone—to surprise me later, she said—so I didn't see the bathing suit until we were back in our room at the Georgian. And I was certainly surprised, because Yuli undressed and stood before me, one hand on her hip and the other holding the coral-pink bikini.

"Yes," she said.

I kissed her. "Is that *yes* like a question or *yes* like permission?"

"It's *yes* like I love you and want you to kiss me again."

We kissed, longer and slower, and backed up onto the bed. Ordinarily, this was an event for us to savor, a chance to explore, to tantalize. Not now, though. Perhaps it was our romantic drought or that Yuli had shaken off the worst of her grief, but we proceeded with a delirious single-mindedness, nudging each other toward that darkness where we relinquished ourselves, that stretch of frozen time, complete stillness, then an exquisite convulsion, a spate of whispers and cries, and stillness again.

On weekday afternoons, the beach beside the pier wasn't too crowded, and the sand was cold against my bare feet as Yuli and I passed the lifeguard tower and found a spot to spread our towels. Two children, a freckly red-headed brother and sister from the looks of it, were building a sand castle by the foaming edge of the water, down from where an elderly couple in sweaters had planted their web folding chairs and watched the children with smiles brightening their leathery faces. Sun-browned high school and college kids—lissome girls in colorful bathing suits strolling in threes and fours across the sand, their skin glistening with oil and their laughter like the ringing of glass bells, while sinewy shirtless boys in cutoffs and sunglasses sat in circles as if at a campfire, smoking cigarettes and pretending they weren't checking out the girls.

Yuli glanced at the revolving Ferris wheel to our left, then back at the beach. "I've never seen this many happy people in one place."

A breeze was blowing, carrying the odor of the sea and the coconut scent of suntan lotion. "You should see the Jersey Shore in the summer. Wall-to-wall happiness."

With sadness seeping into her face, Yuli gazed beyond the water to the Santa Monica Mountains, a jagged purple shadow with white shoestrings of clouds laced around its peaks. I knew that grief had a habit of playing peekaboo with your heart, and I wondered if Yuli was missing Der Schmuggler or if something else was bothering her. That line from a TV game show was going off in my head—*It's not what you say that counts, it's what you don't say*—and it occurred to me then that neither of us had spoken about her returning to Otvali since Taft had warned her that it would be dangerous for her to go home.

"Have you thought about what you'll do when we're done looking for Hildegard?"

Yuli poked her index finger into the sand. "Will we ever be done?"

"If Nate Falk can't help. Taft told us he'd gone through the German records. Where else is there? She could be dead."

"What about finding who shot your grandmother and Dmitry?"

"I've been getting used to the idea that I'm not going to—especially the guy who murdered Dmitry, now that Taft is dead. With Emma, it could've been an attempted robbery and the shooter got scared and ran off. I don't believe that, but maybe all I can hope for is the cops will arrest a guy for sticking up another store and ballistics will match his pistol to Emma. But I asked if you had a plan—for you."

Yuli scooped out a handful of sand. "I could keep digging, crawl into the hole, and live on this beach."

"Or you could live in South Orange. Go to school, get work as a translator, do anything you want. I'm thinking of selling the candy store and going back to deejaying."

Her face was expressionless, so I couldn't judge her reaction to my offer. What the hell, I thought. There was no way I'd know without asking. "And we could get married."

Yuli studied me. I watched her chest rise and fall. Then she grinned. "I can't."

I couldn't match her grin to her reply. "Why not?"

She giggled. "Because you didn't ask."

"I'm asking."

"Aren't American boys supposed to take you to dinner, get down on a knee, and give you a ring when they ask?"

I knelt on one knee. "Pick out a ring in town, I'll buy it, and we can walk over to the Galley on Main Street. The guide says it the oldest restaurant and bar in West L.A."

Yuli was giving me one of her more complicated smiles, meaning that I didn't have a clue about what was on her mind. Speaking so softly that I could barely hear her over the sea slapping and hissing on the shore, she said, "When we are together I feel happiness like I am exploding, and suddenly I am thinking about Papka, my mother, the children at Lake Bereza, all the things—the terrible things—I have done. I feel guilty and ask myself, 'Who am I to deserve this happiness?' And I answer, 'You don't deserve it.' Then you make me laugh or we go for a walk, and the happiness returns, and I wonder how I would live without you."

"And the bad thoughts start again?"

"Sometimes."

"Now?"

"Not now. Not at all."

"So we'll get married?"

With an earnest expression on her face, Yuli said, "Does dinner come with it?"

She laughed and put her arms around me, her body warm against mine, and I held on to her, recalling what my grandmother had told me a long time ago: *Mishka, whatever you do, remember this your whole life. You fix the past in the present, not in the past.*

50

Venice Beach was down the hill from the Georgian, and before eight in the morning we were watching for Nate Falk from a bench across from the shul, a modest building with two sky-blue faux windows shaped like the tablets of the Ten Commandments embedded in the white stucco facade. Out on the sand, volleyball games were under way, and surfers in wet suits were carrying their boards and wading out into the foam-tipped swells, and bicyclists veered among the dog walkers and roller skaters on the boardwalk, a cement strip bordering the beach with souvenir stands, tattoo parlors, restaurants, and bars. Just off the cement were makeshift tents fashioned from sticks and scarves knotted together, where winos, druggies, and certifiables had spent the night and were now greeting the cool sunlit breeze by babbling out loud to themselves.

As a bald compact man in a madras sport jacket entered the shul, I glanced at the snapshot of Nate that his daughter had lent us. "There he is."

Yuli sprang up, quick-stepping past the benches of old men and women in ill-fitting suits and shapeless floral dresses who appeared to be transplants from Eastern European shtetls, and disappeared into an alleyway to the right of the shul. I followed her, but when I got to the alley, she was on her way back.

I said, "The bearded guy again?"

"Maybe no. Behind the people on the benches—a stocky guy, bucket hat, sunglasses, stubble like he hadn't shaved in a week. He was staring at us, and I thought he went into the alley. But I was wrong."

We stood with our backs against the shul, Yuli watching the scene, and when Nate came out and stopped to brush sand off his suede horsebit loafers, I said, "Mr. Falk."

He squinted in our direction through his amber-tinted aviator shades, and I introduced us, saying that Bashe had suggested we look him up.

"Very smart lady, Bashe," Nate said, and with traces of a German accent, though evidently he had mastered his *w*'s. "So what can I do you for?"

"I had some questions about Nuremberg."

With his shrewd car-dealer eyes and a merry expression on his tanned, deeply lined face, Nate gave Yuli's tight cranberry polo and black capri pants an appreciative once-over. "You gotta talk, too."

"I will," Yuli said, summoning up a shy coquettish grin that I hadn't seen before. "If you let us buy you a coffee."

Not far from the shul, a restaurant was serving breakfast. We sat under an umbrella at an outdoor table, and a waitress brought us coffee and a basket of muffins.

"Irma didn't send you, did she?" Nate asked, sinking his teeth into a bran muffin as if it were an apple.

Yuli said, "She's a nice girl, your daughter. She told us where you say Kaddish and gave us your picture."

I handed Nate the photo, and he tucked it into the inner pocket of his madras jacket. "Irma and Bert belong to a highfalutin temple on Wilshire. It ain't for me." He dropped three lumps of sugar into his mug. "What'd you wanna know about Nuremberg?"

I bit into a corn muffin. "Have you ever heard of a woman from there—Hildegard Ter Horst?"

Nate sneered. "She was married to that murdering Nazi bastard the Mossad dumped in the canal in Amsterdam, and she died when the Brits blew up Nuremberg. At least that's what I read in the papers."

"You ever meet Hildegard?"

"Nah, but I seen her old man, Wilhelm Kreit. He was one of the biggest Jew haters in Nuremberg, which is saying something—the city was the biggest Nazi hellhole in Germany. Kreit was also a thief. If you were a rich Jew and wanted out of Nuremberg, all you had to do was give him your jewelry and your bank account. Rumor was that once a month he went to Switzerland to sell the jewels and stash the money. And when Kreit wasn't stealing, he was writing for *Der Stürmer*—a hate rag. Its motto on the front page was *Die Juden sind unser Unglück*—The Jews are our misfortune."

Nate sampled his coffee and added another sugar. "Funny thing is, Hildegard's mother's family was the opposite of the Kreits. Most of them was executed by the SS for aiding Jews. One survived—Ursula Becker. Ursula was a social worker, her husband owned properties in Nuremberg, and they hid Jews until the Gestapo shows up and shoots the husband. Ursula got away—I think she was hiding somewhere else. After the war, she winds up in the displaced-persons camp the American army set up in an old SS barracks, and Ursula meets a rabbi there and converts to Judaism. Some story, ain't it?"

"It is," I said, after swallowing the last of my muffin. "How do you know it?"

"From my buddies out here—survivors like me. Couple times a week we eat at Canter's, a deli over on Fairfax—you ever go, do yourself a favor and order the challah French toast. Me and my buddies are starting a Holocaust museum, for the stuff we save from Europe—pictures, menorahs, those goddamn armbands the Nazis made us wear. And I hear Ursula Becker's gonna raise us some money."

"How will she do that?"

"That's the best part of the story. Ursula moved to the States, and she gives some speeches and helps survivors with problems—they're sad, got nightmares, lots of problems. She lives in Los Angeles. I ain't met her, but the survivors say Ursula's a saint. A Jewish saint—only in California, yeah?"

I looked over at Yuli and assumed that we were thinking the same thing. I was anxious to leave, but Yuli said to Nate, "May we talk about Irma?"

Nate was done with his muffin and lit a cigar, puffing on it until his face was swathed in an acrid fog. "You're Russian, ain't you? I can hear it. I met Russians in Buchenwald."

"I am from the Ukraine. And the Germans murdered my mother and many of my friends."

"Then how come you get it and my daughter don't? Her three brothers and her mother died in the camps. Why don't Irma see I can't stick around her husband? That jerk thinks a Nazi prison camp is funny."

Yuli put her hands on one of Nate's. "Most Americans don't care about history. They can't. They're too optimistic. And history is tough on optimism."

Ursula Becker . . . Ursula Becker . . . The name reverberated in my head, and I was desperate to go and make a phone call. Yuli, however, asked the waitress to refill her mug, clearly inclined to stay until we convinced Nate to return to the El Royale.

"Mr. Falk," I said, "you want to get even with Hitler?"

Taking the cigar out of his mouth, he arched his bushy, grizzled eyebrows. "The bastard's dead. There's no getting even with him."

"Yes there is. You go be with your daughter and grandchild."

"How does that follow?"

"Because the Nazis with their Final Solution weren't planning on Jewish grandchildren."

Nate glanced at his mug and back at me.

"Jewish grandchildren—they make Hitler spin in his grave. *Fershtay?*"

Nate set the cigar in the glass ashtray. "*Ich fershtay*, boychik. I understand."

51

Nate Falk hadn't bought a car yet, and after the three of us had walked up to the Georgian, he asked the doorman to hail him a cab. Yuli volunteered to give Nate a ride, and he replied, "You think I won't go to the El Royale unless you take me?"

"Of course not. We were going out anyway. To look for a different hotel."

That was news to me, but I figured that the man Yuli had gone searching for in the alley was the reason we were going to move.

"I got myself a room. Ten minutes from Irma."

Nate sat in the passenger seat, reciting directions—Wilshire to Sunset to Hollywood to Franklin, an easy twenty-five-minute trip, proving that only long-haul truckers and masochists used the freeways. Except for the palm trees shading the glassed-in lobby, the Landmark Motor Hotel could have been transplanted from the Jersey Shore—a pair of stacked-up boxes with steel-railed balconies, sided with rough concrete, and spray-gunned the pale ice-cream colors of butter pecan and cherry vanilla.

"Thanks for the lift," Nate said, getting out.

"Is there a pay phone in the lobby?" I asked, and when he nodded, I said that we would wait for him because I had to make a call. As Nate went inside, I got a Bic pen and pad from my rucksack, and Yuli said, "You're not calling Ursula Becker?"

I shook my head, and at the check-in desk exchanged a five-dollar bill for dimes and quarters, and made my call. I was closing the phone book when Nate keeled into the lobby, clasping the handles of two big suitcases. I relieved him of his bags and loaded them in the trunk.

"Here," Nate said, holding up a key attached to a black plastic tag with the address of the Landmark and the room number printed on it in white. "I paid a month upfront, and instead of fighting to get my money, you take it."

I was about to decline when Yuli reached over the back seat for the key. "That's so kind, Mr. Falk. Thank you."

"Nate, I'm Nate."

Traffic was whizzing past on Franklin, and I peeled out into the right lane and drove to the El Royale. While the valet unloaded the luggage, Yuli climbed out and kissed Nate's cheek. He was beaming and flashed me a thumbs-up, and after he followed the valet into the lobby, Yuli asked, "Who did you call?"

"The office secretary at Beth El. My family's synagogue in South Orange. The cops had told me Emma was supposed to be there the evening she was shot—to hear a lecture about Holocaust survivors. I never knew the name of the lecturer. Now I do."

"Ursula Becker?"

I opened the travel guide to a map. "Ursula Becker. And I found her address in the phone book—1 Falcon Lane. It's out toward Pasadena. Fifteen, sixteen miles from here. Ready to go?"

"Not yet. First, we check out of the Georgian. Second, we go to LAX and rent a different car—a plain car, not a convertible. And tonight we sleep at the Landmark—it's perfect, we won't be registered in your name."

"But we haven't seen anyone. Why would—"

"*Tishe yedesh, dal'she budesh.*"

" 'The slower you go, the farther you get.' That's a Russian proverb?"

"*Da*, and a smart one. Not seeing somebody watching doesn't mean somebody is not. And if Ursula is Hildegard Ter Horst—"

The tiniest note of skepticism in her voice curdled my elation at finally locating Hildegard into anger at Yuli. "You doubt she is?"

"This is not a hundred percent, is this? I wonder why Hildegard would be helping survivors. It is possible, but strange, yes?"

"And also a smart way to hide."

"Even if that is true, we do not march into her house and say, 'Hi, you are arrested.' If Ursula is Hildegard, she has thought about this day and made plans. If the KGB or Stasi get her, maybe she plans doing as they ask, and they protect her. If the Americans catch her, she knows she can go to prison or be executed for murdering your grandmother. And if she is deported to West Germany, she can be tried for whatever her role was in Dmitry being shot, or worse, for war crimes."

"Unless the Bundestag votes against extending the statute of limitations for trying Nazis."

"And don't you believe Hildegard is waiting to hear? If the trials stop and she escapes the police for shooting your grandmother, her worries are over. We don't want Hildegard to escape. We want to end this, don't we?"

Her face was as beautiful as ever, but her expression was dark, cold, intent, and her question sounded as if she was committed to killing Hildegard. I started up the Mustang, choosing not to ask Yuli about her intentions because I didn't want to hear her answer.

———————

At the Georgian, we packed up, and Yuli accompanied the bellman to the car with our suitcases while I settled the bill. In a wing chair in the back of the lobby a man in a khaki windbreaker was reading the *Los Angeles Times*, and when he lowered the paper, I saw that he was in his thirties, with most of his hair gone and in need of a shave. He could've been the guy Yuli had spotted at Venice Beach, yet he didn't bother to glance at me, not the behavior of someone tailing us, and I concluded that Yuli's paranoia was as contagious as the flu.

The Hertz agent at the airport swapped the Mustang for a Country Squire station wagon—a light caramel color with a wood-grain trim. We bought two cans of Coke from a machine, and to get back to the city I had to break my streak of avoiding freeways and hopped on the 405.

"What do we do when we get to Hildegard's house?" I asked, taking a swig of Coke and giving the can to Yuli.

"It's too early to go. We should be there at four thirty. Before dinner. To see who comes home."

My temper flared. "We're going to sit and stare at her house?"

"Spies spy, Misha. Then they act."

"You're the expert."

"There is no expert. There is alive and not alive."

I breathed deeply, trying to relax.

She gave me the soda. "I promise. If this is Hildegard, she will pay."

Yuli switched on the radio, tuning it to KFWB. The Beach Boys were in the middle of "Surfin' Safari" when she said, "I used to read about Malibu in the movie magazines Papka bought me from the army base in Munich. Can we go see it?"

"Sure."

After Santa Monica, traffic was bumper to bumper on the Pacific Coast Highway, the sun glinting on the lanes of cars and trucks, and while Yuli looked out at the sand and sea, I drank the rest of the Coke, then glanced at Emma's Rolex and assured my grandmother that we would make things right.

Yuli rested her head on my shoulder. "Misha, your lips are moving. Am I marrying a man who talks to his watch?"

"That's the plan."

On the radio, Chad and Jeremy were singing "A Summer Song" and the gentle harmony of the guitars and the duo's voices seemed to lull Yuli to sleep. I couldn't see what was going on with the traffic because the Country Squire was sandwiched between a yellow school bus and a Calicut Farms milk truck, the exterior the same black and white as a Holstein. Sick of the stop-and-go, I exited the PCH, driving down a twisting bumpy road toward the ocean, past cottages behind walls of hedges. Below a bluff there was a small sandy lot with three cars in it, and I parked and gently shook Yuli awake.

She yawned, and I pointed at the bluff. "Great view from there, I bet."

We got out of the station wagon. Someone had marked off a trail up to the bluff by arranging rocks and bricks on either side of a path of sand and flattened grass. The climb wasn't too steep, and we sat in a patch of sunlight on an outcropping. Out on the impossibly blue water, a chorus line of surfers had caught the crest of a monstrous wave.

"Misha, do we still have other Coke?"

"We do. Want me to get it?"

"No, I'll be right back."

The entire chorus line wiped out, the surfers and their boards bobbing in the ocean like bath toys. I was sweltering in the sun, and my mouth was dry, and I walked over to the path, expecting to meet Yuli coming up with the soda. She wasn't there, and a Calicut Farms truck had pulled into the lot beside the Country Squire, so that I couldn't see her, and before it consciously registered on me that something was wrong, I was racing down the path, bending to pick up a brick without breaking stride and circling behind the truck. The passenger-side door of the station wagon was open, and a balding broad-backed man in a windbreaker was facing away from me—the same man, I thought, that I'd seen reading a newspaper in the Georgian. One of his arms was around Yuli's throat while the other one was around her waist, lifting her up so that her feet were off the ground. He must have come up behind her when she ducked into the car for the can of Coke, and she was attempting to free herself, wriggling her body, flailing her arms, and kicking her red sneakers back at him, all to no effect.

Had I thought about what I was going to do, I would have been too scared to do it, but I wasn't thinking—not about myself, but about Yuli, and especially Emma, how I hadn't been there to save her when her murderer arrived. Dashing toward the man and spreading my arms, I squeezed the brick in my right hand, careful not to drop it, and flung myself at him full speed, head-butting his spine and ramming my shoulders into his back. Grunting, the man flew forward, Yuli squirming from his grasp and spinning off against the Country Squire. I landed on top of the man, and he bucked like a beached whale, attempting to throw me aside by pushing up off the ground with one hand and reaching back to clutch my hair with the other. He was strong and skilled enough to do it, though it was unlikely that he had ever tried these moves while someone was bashing in his head with a brick.

More terrifying to me than my blinding rage or the harsh guttural grunts of the man when I struck him was the ease with which I surrendered my decency, shedding my morality like a snakeskin, this sugarcoated vision of myself that had been a cinch to maintain until I had to choose between protecting my precious moral superiority or someone I loved. I might as well have been born in a cave; I was no more civilized than a Neanderthal or the saber-toothed cats he hunted. I hit the man hard and fast, the blood splattering my face and greasing my fingers no more disturbing to me than rainwater, and when I heard Yuli frantically call, "Misha, enough," I rose up, gripping the brick in both my hands, and slammed it against his skull with such force that the brick split in half.

Shoving me so I'd get off the man, Yuli pressed the middle and index fingers of her right hand to the side of his windpipe. I stood as she rifled through his pockets, glancing at his passport, dropping it on the sand, and taking a thick envelope, then sliding her hand under his windbreaker, removing a pistol, and telling me to take off my shirt and wipe my face and get in the car and go, go, Misha, drive.

52

I sat on the bed in our room at the Landmark, blinking against the sunlight angling through the glass door to the balcony.

"I killed him," I said, and scraped at the dried blood under my fingernails with my Swiss Army knife.

Yuli ran her fingers up my neck and through my hair. "And saved my life."

"Why didn't he shoot you?"

"He would have—after taking me somewhere in his truck and interrogating me."

"He was in the lobby at the Georgian. I should have—"

"Don't blame yourself. If I hadn't fallen asleep in the car . . ."

I gave up on the dried blood and tossed the penknife on the night table. "Who sent him?"

The automatic pistol Yuli had taken from the man was on the desk. It was black, no more than six or seven inches long, and she brought it over, showing it to me in her outstretched palm.

"This is a Makarov."

"Soviet?"

She nodded. "Other Communist countries also manufacture it. The Soviet model has a brown grip. This grip is black and the pistol has a DF prefix with the serial number. It is East German."

"So he was from the Stasi?"

Yuli dropped the pistol in her leather shoulder bag and put the bag on the bed. "His passport was from West Germany. Probably forged or stolen and altered. To fly to U.S. a Stasi agent only has to cross from East to West Berlin. What is unusual is that he had three thousand dollars in crisp hundreds in that envelope."

"Why unusual?"

"If you are tracking someone, you should avoid attracting attention. And nothing attracts attention like paying with big new bills at a store or restaurant. Cashiers remember the crisp money and that they had to give you back a lot of cash, and this can also help them remember your face."

With the work she had done for Der Schmuggler, I wasn't surprised that Yuli knew such things. I just didn't like picturing her doing them. "Maybe the guy was a screwup."

"I say he got the bills from KGB agent he works with. Your government leaves alone many KGB agents because all they do is pass information you can discover by reading newspapers, magazines, reports from government agencies and businesses. In Soviet Union, real information is hidden, so Kremlin believes this American information is valuable, and the KGB here can get comfortable and lazy and forget about not attracting attention."

I went to look out the balcony door. The swimming pool and chaise lounges were empty. "But this KGB agent, he could be looking for Hildegard?"

"Probably, but he was not in Malibu or he would have helped the Stasi agent grab me."

"And what about me getting arrested by the L.A. cops? I kill—"

Yuli placed a finger over my lips. "When the police find him, they will check his passport, learn it is fake, and call federal investigators, who will learn he was Stasi. America has no diplomatic relations with East Germany. The federal investigators will not look hard because your government will be angry the Stasi was here and maybe they assume a freelance killed him—someone hired by CIA or Mossad."

"Someone like you?"

"Like I was."

I sat on the bed. "What about witnesses?"

"If our license plate was seen, the police would be chasing us already. It took two hours to drive here from Malibu, and on the way I saw seven police cars."

"Are we still going to Hildegard's?"

"Not today. To be safe we will stay in and watch the news on television and read the *Herald Examiner*. It comes later in the day, and there is a vending machine in the lobby."

I walked back to the balcony door. "And tomorrow?"

"Very early, we will go watch the house. To see who comes out."

I gazed down at the pool. "That man could've had a wife and kids."

"Yes."

"Did I really save your life? Or are you saying—"

"Once he got me in that truck, Misha, I was dead."

The sun shining through the door was hot on my face. "I still feel . . . not quite guilty but—strange? Strange to myself."

"Like you are living in a different place?"

"Yes."

Yuli put her arms around my waist. "You are. But that does not mean what you did to travel there was wrong. Take a shower, you will feel better, and I will order a pizza for delivery."

That evening, the East German was not mentioned in the newspaper or on the local TV news. We left a wake-up call for five A.M., and before getting in the Country Squire, we walked around the Landmark twice without spotting anyone staking out the hotel. In the *Herald Examiner* I had seen an ad for Canter's saying that it was open twenty-four hours, so we drove over for breakfast. At rush hour, Los Angeles was a cranky mess, and sometimes the smog was so hideous it seemed like nothing less than divine retribution for the sins of vanity and greed. Yet before dawn, with the orange fire of the sun heating the sky to a smoky sapphire and the streets quiet with the yellow, red, and green traffic signals flashing like fireworks celebrating the new day, and kitchen lights winking on inside the houses as paper boys pedaled under palm trees along the sidewalks, you feel, just before the Earth spins faster and the mundane rituals begin, that you are lucky to be here, a privileged wanderer in a pastel land.

Even at this early hour, Canter's drew a crowd, a line at the display cases in front waiting for pastries, rolls, and bagels to go, and sleepy-eyed men and women in the brownish-red leatherette booths, under ceiling panels of paint-drizzled glass, as if Jackson Pollock had seen to the lighting. The waitresses were zipping around like roadrunners, and Yuli and I opted for Nate's recommendation, the challah French toast. We were finishing up when the woman behind the register put out a stack of the *Los Angeles Times*. I went over and bought a copy.

"Anything?" Yuli asked when I came back flipping through the paper.

The three-sentence story was below the fold on the second page of the local section, and I read it with fear shaking me like the chills:

> A German tourist was bludgeoned to
> death near Point Dume in Malibu in
> an apparent robbery. The Los Angeles
> County Sheriff's Department is in-
> vestigating. Anyone with information
> please call (213) 555-9600.

I gave the section to Yuli. After scanning it, she said, "We talk outside. I'm going to the bathroom."

I paid the bill and bought a large bottle of seltzer at the register, then used the men's room upstairs. The station wagon was in Canter's lot, and as I pulled onto Fairfax, Yuli said, "The man had a passport. That means the police had his name. But they did not tell the newspaper."

"The sheriff could have been waiting until his next of kin was notified."

"The police would contact your State Department to do that, and the State Department would find the passport to be fake. That is why the reporter did not receive a name. Trust me, we won't be hearing about that dead man again."

I drove into the San Fernando Valley, past flat-roofed ranch houses aligned on fields like armadas of flying saucers. Below the San Rafael Hills was the neighborhood of Eagle Rock, which was more Norman Rockwell than George Jetson—the shopping district with a movie theater, pharmacy, hardware store, bowling alley, diner, and an adobe church that could have been left behind by Spanish missionaries. Our destination was above Colorado Boulevard, where roads zigged and zagged through hills far less built up than the Hollywood hillsides. Deer trotted over grasslands, pausing to peek into quirky houses inspired by Buddhist temples and imposing glass-walled cathedrals of that new American religion—the future.

Falcon Lane was hemmed in by bushes, firs, and rubber plants. At the end of the narrow graveled road, behind an iron gate on a square of lawn, was an A-frame sided with fluted straw-colored plywood and a carport outside the bright-red double front doors—the exact shade of red, I thought, as the Nazi flag. It was the only house on Falcon Lane, and about thirty yards from the gate was a clearing, and we parked there, partially hidden by the trees and with a view below to rooftops, hills bright with patches of yellow flowers, and, in the distance, through a brown haze, the office towers downtown.

"Now what?" I asked.

"We wait."

During the next fifty-three minutes I checked Emma's watch six times and listened to the Top Ten songs on the radio—moving up from Little Anthony and the Imperials' "Hurt So Bad" to the Beatles' "Eight Days a Week," and heard on the news that American planes had bombed a munitions depot in North Vietnam, and a white minister from Boston helping to register Negro voters in Selma, Alabama, had been beaten to death.

"Suppose someone sees us?" I said, switching off the radio.

"There are no neighbors."

"We should pretend to be doing something."

Yuli smirked, guessing what I had in mind, but as I put my arms around her, the gate swung inward and an MG drove onto Falcon Lane and stopped. The sports car was a milky toffee color and the ragtop was off, and a young woman in a stylish loose-fitting dress climbed out and flipped down the lid of the mailbox. I stared at her shoulder-length dark-gold hair and pale round face as she bent to look inside the box, then left the lid down and got behind the wheel.

"Holy shit," I said, hugging Yuli so she couldn't turn around as the MG kicked up gravel as it passed us.

"What? What is it?"

"The woman from Paris, the woman I ran after on Quai Bourbon."

"Who looked like your grandmother?"

"Exactly like. She could've come from one of the paintings on Gak's walls."

I let go of Yuli. We were silent, our eyes glued to the A-frame.

"That's Darya. My aunt Darya. Bashe told us Hildegard took Emma's daughter, so now we know Darya survived the bombing in Nuremberg. And I bet Hildegard also survived, and she's in that house."

"Misha, we sit here until we see her."

"We—"

"We wait."

Grabbing my canvas rucksack off the back seat, I removed a Bic and a pad, and wrote:

To the woman in the MG: Your real name is Darya Gak. You are the daughter of Emma Dainov and Alexander Gak, a painter who is still alive and lives in Nice, France. He believes you died in the Ukraine with your older sister Alexandra during the war. The woman who brought you to Germany is Hildegard Ter Horst, a Nazi guilty of war crimes. She probably murdered your mother, last September, in South Orange, New Jersey. My name is Michael Daniels. Emma was my grandmother, the mother of your late half brother. You are my aunt.

Yuli had been reading as I composed the note. "What is this?"

I tore off the page. "Insurance."

"This is reckless. Don't—"

I jogged down the road and stuck my note in the box, shutting the lid, hoping that Darya would notice and check inside.

Whatever happened, my aunt was going to know the truth.

53

Ten minutes later I was drinking seltzer out of the bottle when Yuli said, "Misha, look."

Ambling across the lawn was a man in a dark blue baseball hat and trench coat. He must have hiked up from the street below the hill. "Is that—"

"Pyotr Ananko."

A beefy blond thick-necked man in a T-shirt and baggy trousers lumbered over to meet Pyotr, clasping a trowel in his right hand. They spoke, the blond man gesturing with the trowel, thrusting it down toward the hill from where Pyotr had come. With his hands in his coat pockets, Pyotr turned, as if to go, then spun toward the man, pointing a short metal tube at him that jerked in his hand. The blond man lurched backward, wobbling, and fell over on the grass while Pyotr hurried toward the front door.

"Gas gun," Yuli said, taking the Makarov from her bag and getting out of the Country Squire.

I trailed her along the edge of Falcon Lane, and we kept out of sight by stepping between the trees. "You thought that's how Taft died. Did Pyotr—"

"Odds are, yes."

"Could Pyotr have—"

"Not Papka."

"Why not?"

When Yuli turned, there was something chilling in her eyes, as if ice could catch fire. "Pyotr knows if he hurt Papka, I will find him wherever he is. And kill him."

At the mailbox, as we left the cover of the trees, Yuli held up the Makarov. "I have the pistol. Stay behind me. Promise?"

"Let's go."

"Misha!"

"Okay. Go!"

Yuli skirted the lawn so that we were walking below the crest of a hill and not visible from the windows of the A-frame. In back, there was a cedar deck with sliding glass doors that led to a beamed, carpeted living room with a couch and sling chairs covered in tempestuous patterns of flaming sabers, lightning bolts, perched eagles, and serpent's tongues. The doors were moved aside to let in the morning air, but the screens were locked. I forearmed the mesh, separating it from the frame, and unlocked the sliders. We went down a wide hall with the murmur of voices up ahead, and to our left, as we were going by an iron spiral staircase, there was the *crack-crack-crack* of gunshots. Yuli tugged me into a den with shelves of bric-a-brac, crystal vases of silk flowers, and a TV built into a wall. Across the den, through partially open pocket doors, I saw a tall brunette in a blazer and skirt as pale as celery. She was standing, with her back to us, next to a rolltop desk, and in her right hand, which hung at her side, she held a small silver automatic.

In a voice no louder than a sigh, Yuli said in Russian, "Follow me," and darted across the oak floorboards, shoved at one of the pocket doors, and barged into a white room with the sun blazing in through a bank of triangular windows.

"Do not move," Yuli said to the woman, aiming the Makarov at her. "Or I will shoot you in the head."

Keeping about ten feet between herself and the woman, Yuli circled around to face her while I bent over Pyotr Ananko. He was on his back, his arms and legs splayed across a colorful woven rug, his cap off, his whitish-blond hair neatly combed, his eyes and mouth ajar, and three blackened, chest-high bullet holes leaving rivulets of blood on his trench coat.

I felt for a pulse in his neck. "He's gone."

"So I shoot a robber," the woman said.

I hadn't seen her face yet, but hearing her faint German accent, I discovered, to my horror, that I was unprepared for my fury—a fury so vast that I knew caving in her skull with a brick wouldn't satisfy me.

Nor was I prepared, as I stood and swiveled toward her, for the fact that I recognized the middle-aged woman standing by the desk, her lustrous brown hair with its au courant messiness, her big, dark penetrating eyes, upturned nose, and full lips red with lipstick—the kind of icy beauty that Walt Disney must have had in mind for the evil queen in *Snow White*.

"You were at Dachau," I said. "During the press conference. When I was asking the mayor a question."

"I do not recall you. But I was there with many other survivors when the convent was dedicated."

"And that ape dead on your lawn, he was with you at Dachau. Is he the one who shot at me in Munich and killed my friend?"

"You make no sense. I am Ursula Becker."

Leveling the Makarov at the woman, Yuli said, "Put that pistol on the desk."

"Why? I have rights to protect myself. First this burglar breaks in my home—"

I cut her off. "That burglar is KGB. What did he want? To sign you up as a spy? Doesn't matter now. His bosses will be unhappy with you. Do you think he'll be the last one they send?"

"I will shoot them as well."

"Why not? Hildegard Ter Horst is an accomplished murderer."

"And you believe I am this Hildegard?"

"I do."

She gave me a small, hesitant smile. "Prove it."

"We will when the police check your pistol and see the bullets match the slugs taken from my grandmother. And there's always Bashe."

Hildegard flinched when she heard the name.

"Remember Bashe? Who copied *Mein Kampf* in the Jew Room?"

"Bashe is dead."

"Then we must've been speaking to her ghost, and she'd be glad to identify you. To the Americans, who will deport you. To the West Germans, who may put you on trial. To the Israelis, who dumped your husband in a canal. And to Darya, who will never forgive you for murdering her mother."

"Darya? There is no Darya. You mean Freya."

"I saw your Freya in her MG. She looks just like Emma Dainov. There are photos and paintings to prove it—paintings done by Darya's father. Did I mention he's alive?"

She was muttering, as if debating with herself whether I was telling the truth. She must have decided that I was because she replied, "I am no longer Hildegard. She is dead. Ursula is a Jew who helps survivors. And is beloved for it."

"Ursula Becker was your cousin, and she died in Nuremberg. You became her and got yourself—and Emma's daughter—to America. What I don't understand is why you didn't hide. Why you ran around the country speaking when you could've been recognized. Is that what happened? My grandmother recognized you?"

Hildegard startled me with her laughter. "You Jews, you Jews and your memory. You believe people hate you for crucifying Christ or being rich and your spend, spend, spend. No, they hate you for your memory. Learn to forget, less people will hate you."

Hildegard glanced at Yuli, whose arms were trembling from holding up the Makarov. "Tiring, *ja*? Why don't you put down your pistol?"

Yuli cocked the hammer. "Because you'll shoot us. Michael, there's a phone on the table behind you. Call the police."

I hesitated, disgusted with myself for wanting Yuli to kill Hildegard.

In Russian, Yuli said, "Public shame is worse than death. Let her be alive to lose Darya and for a government to humiliate her with a trial and hang her."

She was right, I knew it, but before I started for the phone, Hildegard, perhaps frightened at hearing Russian and surmising that Yuli was also KGB, began talking about my grandmother, and though in all likelihood she was playing for time, I'd waited too long to hear the story to scare her silent by calling the cops.

"My plane was delayed," Hildegard said. "I was late for my talk at the temple. I get out of my rented car, there's hardly space to park. Everyone is inside at dinner. Except Emma. She comes up this walk. We see each other—only a moment—but she knows who I am, turns, and goes away. I was stunned, I thought she—"

Hildegard saw me eyeing her and didn't complete her sentence. That was when it hit me: I should've seen it the instant I knew Hildegard was alive. "You thought—you thought my grandmother and Bashe were dead. The guard was supposed to shoot Bashe, the soldier and the SS girl were supposed to shoot Emma. Which is why you didn't worry about being recognized. If Joost had survived, you knew he'd keep his mouth shut or the West Germans might arrest him, or the Russians or—"

"Stop your talking!" Hildegard snapped, and the hand holding the pistol against her side moved, and I thought she was going to shoot me.

Yuli stepped closer to the desk, keeping the Makarov on her, and in English said, "Misha, let her talk."

Hildegard looked at Yuli, then at me. "It is not so simple," she said, her voice shaking. "Why are Americans so simple? 'This is black, that is white.' You should listen, not judge. You were not in the East during the war."

She stared at me, and I stared at the automatic in her hand.

"Your grandmother leaves, and I meet the people in the temple, going table to table to say hello, and I see Emma's name card and empty chair, and two women, they talk about her, saying she must be tied up at Sweets, owning a candy store is tough work. That night I sleep at a hotel in Morristown—I have to be in Philadelphia next evening—but I can't sleep. I have to explain to Emma. I get the address for Sweets in a phone book and leave before dawn. She was in her store. I go in. She yells, 'Where is my daughter?' And I say, 'I will tell you everything if you do not yell.'

"She is quiet, and I tell her the truth. Hitler wants us to wage a war of annihilation, and Joost ordered the SS to kill every Russian and Ukrainian on the estate—man, woman, and child. I heard him give the order. 'Emma,' I say, 'both your daughters would have died if I didn't take Freya. This is why I take her. To save her. And I gave her everything. I sent her to boarding school in Switzerland. Would she have been better off with you in one of those horrid camps where they kept the Jews after the war?'

"Emma spit in my face. But I am not angry at her, I understand, and explain that the war is over, and I am different now, I am not Hildegard. I help the survivors. She screams at me, and I say, 'Emma, please, please listen. Doesn't the good I do cancel out the bad?' But all Emma do is scream. Screaming I am murderer, screaming I am kidnapper, screaming about contacting authorities, screaming and looking at scissors on the counter. This is what happen."

"So you had to shoot her?" I asked, and learned something new. It was possible to be boiling and numb all at once.

"Self-defense, this is an American right. And I, I alone—not a father, not a husband, no man—take care of myself."

"And the man who shot at me and killed my friend in Munich? Was that self-defense? Were you afraid my grandmother had told me who you were?"

Hildegard glared at me and didn't answer. I heard the throaty rumble of the MG and then silence, and I hoped Darya had stopped to get the mail.

I smiled. "It will be fun to hear you explain yourself to Darya. And in court."

As I turned toward the end table with the phone on it, Hildegard flicked up her wrist and fired the automatic. The bullet zipped past me, and I saw Yuli in her shooter's stance stagger back a step and puffs of smoke from the barrel of the Makarov. With my ears ringing, I looked for Hildegard, who was no longer standing. She was on the floor, and bloody fragments of her head, mixed in with strands of brown hair, were plastered on the white wall behind her.

"Misha." Blood was seeping from Yuli's left side as she wiped off the Makarov with the bottom of her turtleneck and, with a finger in the barrel, bent to place it in Pyotr's right hand.

Helping her onto a couch, I grabbed the phone, held it between my shoulder and ear, and dialed the operator while I flattened my palm against Yuli's wound.

"There's been a shooting. One Falcon Lane. In Eagle Rock. Send an ambulance. Please."

"Sir—"

"I can't talk. My friend's bleeding. Please, please hurry."

301

I dropped the phone in its cradle. Yuli was gasping for breath, and dread settled on me as I fought against the idea that I was losing her.

"Misha, listen. We met in—"

"Stop talking."

"Remember what I say. We met in Rostov when you were a student. We became boyfriend and girlfriend and have been traveling. We are here because you thought Ursula knew your grandmother."

Her chest was rising and falling faster and faster, and she wheezed, "Misha, we came in the back, we didn't see the dead man out front. The screen was broken, we were worried, we hurry into this room as Ursula shot Pyotr, then me, and before he died, Pyotr killed her."

Her blood was warm and running along my arm. "I love you."

"Remember, Misha, we were never in Malibu."

The front door opened, and a woman called out, "Mother, Mother," and entered the room. She looked at Yuli and me and the blood-splattered wall. I couldn't stop staring at her. Despite the shock on her face, as she bent over Hildegard, her resemblance to Emma was uncanny.

54

For ninety-six hours it was touch and go with Yuli due to blood loss and a postsurgical infection that set in while she was in the intensive care unit at St. Joseph's Hospital in Burbank. The bullet had gone through her, exiting above her hip, and her surgeon told me that this was fortunate, as less tissue was damaged and no arteries or her spine or vital organs had been hit. I was hard-pressed to appreciate how getting shot was indicative of fate smiling on you, but I told myself that a trauma surgeon, particularly one in a bolo tie, cowboy boots, and the equanimity of a sheriff from the Wild West, would have an altogether different take on what constitutes good and bad luck.

One major stroke of luck was that Darya was a fourth-year medical student at UCLA, and even after seeing that Hildegard was missing the top of her skull, she assumed a professional air, her face an unreadable mask, and tended to Yuli, bringing rolls of gauze from a bathroom and compressing Yuli's wound with both hands, assuring her that she would be fine, and directing me to a downstairs bedroom to grab a blanket and wrap Yuli in it. The ambulance arrived, the attendants lifted Yuli onto a stretcher and hooked her up to an IV, but when I accompanied them outside, the driver told me I couldn't ride to St. Joe's with them, and I should wait at the house for the cops—they would be along shortly.

Darya was standing in the doorway, as long and lean as my grandmother, her eyes with the same lovely slant and sparkling green color, but unlike Emma there was more gloom in them than amusement—fitting, given the circumstances.

"Thank you for helping," I said.

Turning her head to look outside, she nodded. My note was in her hand, but she had crumpled it into a ball.

"We should talk," I said.

She shook her head and kept looking at the lawn.

"Every word in that note is true."

"I don't want to talk," she replied, a symphony of European countries in her accent, though I couldn't pinpoint which one.

"I have to make a call. Can—"

"Go to the kitchen."

I phoned the candy store, person to person to Eddie, and reversed the charges. His wife answered and accepted the call.

"Michael, you and Yulianna are all right?"

Hearing the familiar lilt and the concern in Fiona's voice, I nearly burst into tears, and I had to swallow twice before saying, "Yuli's been shot," and adding, with no evidence to support my claim, "She'll be okay."

"Oh, darlin', Eddie and I can be on a plane today."

"No, no, I just need to talk to him."

Eddie came on, and I gave him the highlights, telling him that he was going to have to wire some real money to me to pay the hospital.

"Let me know how much."

"And I'm gonna have to talk to the cops."

"Keep it short, boyo—don't write 'em no novel. And I'll get the Essex County Prosecutor's Office to call L.A. Homicide. To check out the ballistics on that Nazi bitch's gat."

"Does Mr. Rose have any other pals who worked with Taft?"

"Julian knows a guy. A big wheel that loves cheesecake."

Darya came into the kitchen with a young, strapping uniformed cop behind her. I said good-bye to Eddie and hung up.

"I'm Officer Crolik. Can you tell me what happened?"

"Will it take long? I want to get to the hospital."

"I spoke to my lieutenant on the radio. The woman"—he flipped up the black cover of his pocket notebook—"Yulianna Timko is in surgery. The hospital says it'll be a while."

We sat the chrome-plated table, and Officer Crolik asked Darya if she lived in the house.

"I have an apartment in Westwood. I was visiting my mother."

"Ursula Becker?" he asked.

"Hildegard Ter Horst," I replied.

Darya winced, and guilt roared through me. While I was on my crusade to see that Hildegard was punished, it didn't occur to me that my success would compel Darya to confront the macabre reality that the woman who raised her, who presumably provided her with food and shelter and attention, all of which children interpret as love, was a murderer who had shot her mother. Unavoidable given the circumstances, I thought, another example of the moral perversity of the universe—punish the guilty, crush the innocent.

Officer Crolik said to me, "We got a difference of opinion here? Who are you?"

After telling him my name, I launched into the spiel that Yuli had given me before the ambulance showed up. The officer seemed to buy it, but he did ask, "And the dead guy on the floor who shot Miss Ter Horst. You say he's a KGB agent?"

"Hildegard was saying it before he killed her."

Officer Crolik had written my statement in his notebook, but he had seemed befuddled as he wrote, sighing and shaking his head. The doorbell rang, and Darya went to answer it.

"That's the crime-scene unit," Officer Crolik said. "And a detective."

Detective Gasquet was his name. He had a brush cut and hangdog eyes, and after he introduced himself and read my statement, he asked me to go over everything again.

Darya said, "Sir, do I have to be here for this?"

He shook his head, and both of us watched her leave the kitchen. Then I retold my story. Since all I was lying about was that Pyotr Ananko shot Hildegard and he most likely had that gas gun in his trench coat, I was only moderately concerned. When I was done, the detective said, "You can get over to the hospital now. And my boss heard from an Essex County detective about Mrs. Becker's pistol."

"Mrs. Ter Horst. Hildegard Ter Horst."

"Whatever her name is. We'll run the ballistics here and get the report to New Jersey. Also, we'll have a uniform at the hospital guarding Miss Timko. That's it. We're done."

Darya was sitting in a chair, watching the men and women in blue uniforms and rubber gloves in the study.

I gave her a slip of paper. "This is my phone number at the hotel and at home."

She stared up at me. Her eyes were red and swollen from crying.

"When you're ready, I have a lot to tell you."

She stood. "I'll see if the detective needs anything else," and headed for the kitchen.

55

When I got to St. Joe's, Yuli was still in surgery. Two hours later, she was wheeled into recovery. She spent an hour and a half there, and then they brought her to the intensive care unit. During that first day, I was permitted to visit her for ten minutes every hour. She was as wan as the bed linen, with so many tubes going in and out of her that she looked like a science experiment. I sat next to her bed while she slept and held her hand.

For the next four days, I was at the hospital from eight in the morning until eight at night, watching Yuli sleep, speaking to her and hoping that she heard me, my heart almost leaping out of my chest whenever she stirred, mumbling incoherently in Russian. She was connected to monitors, and I stared at the luminous numbers and lines as though God were sending me clues as to whether she would live or die. When I wasn't in the ICU, I was eating bad food and drinking worse coffee in the cafeteria or calling Fiona and Eddie to update them, and sitting silently beside the cop stationed outside intensive care.

Everyone loves a murder mystery and a spy thriller, which wasn't lost on the editors of the *L.A. Times* and *Herald Examiner*. The papers banged out daily stories about Hildegard Ter Horst, the Nazi war criminal masquerading as a Jew active in the survivor community, and Pyotr Ananko, a foreign correspondent for *Novosti* and a KGB officer, who brought the roughest brand of justice to Mrs. Ter Horst. The Soviet ambassador to Washington denied this claim, and neither the State Department, the FBI, nor the CIA had any comment. Holocaust survivors in Los Angeles were shocked, opining that the woman they knew as Ursula Becker was generous and compassionate. There were two stories about the late Joost Ter Horst, but there were no official comments on him, and a brief profile of Hildegard's daughter appeared, saying that Freya Becker would be graduating from UCLA Medical School in May and entering a residency program in psychiatry. Darya wasn't quoted, and there was nothing about her real identity, and I assumed that she was laying low and wondered if I would ever hear from her. Yuli and I were mentioned in the articles, but we were characterized as visitors to the home of Ursula Becker who were ignorant of her true history, and Yuli had regrettably been caught in the cross fire. When a reporter chasing that aspect of the story showed up at the hospital, the cop shooed him away.

By the fourth evening, Yuli's infection had receded, her fever broke, and on the morning that she was scheduled to be transferred from the ICU to a private room on a regular medical floor, my phone rang at seven, and I woke up terrified that she had suddenly gone downhill and died.

I grabbed the phone, and a man with a deep voice said, "I was a friend of Taft Mifflin. I'm in the lobby and would like to take you to breakfast."

"Give me five minutes."

If Taft Mifflin had resembled a high school chemistry teacher, this guy could have passed for a principal—wash-and-wear suit as dull as an oyster shell, a gray comb-over stiff with Vitalis Hair Tonic, and his neck flabby over the collar of his white button-down. When he folded his newspaper and pushed himself up off the couch, I noticed that he had the stub of a yellow-wood pencil sticking out from the corner of his mouth.

"I have a car," he said, and we went out and got into the plush leather back seat of a Lincoln Continental with a driver up front.

"What's your pleasure?" he asked. "It has to be close by. I have another plane to catch."

"Canter's has cheesecake."

He studied me—not happily—as if wondering how I'd dug up this information.

"Eddie mentioned it," I said.

"Oh," he replied.

I directed the driver to North Fairfax. He remained in the Lincoln when we went in and found a booth against the back wall. The man ordered cheesecake, and I asked for a cinnamon Danish. When the waitress had poured our coffee and gone to put in our order, he said, "You and Yulianna were Taft's project? The way he located Hildegard Ter Horst?"

"She murdered my grandmother."

"So I hear. And Joost Ter Horst?"

"I read about Joost. How supposedly the Mossad assassinated him in Amsterdam. To send a message to West Germany about extending the statute of limitations on war criminals."

"You and Yulianna were in Amsterdam when Joost went for a swim."

It was no surprise that he was aware of our itinerary, but it was unsettling, because I had to mislead him, and I couldn't tell what he knew and didn't know. My best bet was to stick to partial truths. "Taft suggested we talk to Joost. To see if he thought Hildegard was alive. Joost told us she'd died when Nuremberg was bombed, and he was sitting in his wheelchair in the Magic Dragon when we left."

He removed the pencil from his mouth and put it in the inner pocket of his suitcoat. "Taft had a bee in his bonnet about the Nazis and the Jews."

"You say that like it was a moral failing."

He didn't answer until the waitress brought our breakfast, and he tasted the cheesecake, nodding his approval as though he was sampling an exquisite wine. "People look at pictures of the SS guards at the camps and the gas chambers and the firing squads and the piles of corpses, and all of it scares them."

He sounded as though it was an overreaction. "Because it was horrible."

"That it was, but the faces of the killers are just as scary as the sight of the victims."

"The faces—"

"The ordinary faces of the killers. Decent people look at them and somewhere, deep inside, they say to themselves, 'That could be me. I've hated that much. I've felt that murderous.' Such thoughts frighten most of us, and we should be grateful that no Hitler has come along here to provide the permission to act. Taft, he was a good man, he expected more from people. I never have."

I thought about killing that East German with a brick, and then I didn't want to think about it anymore. Still, I couldn't imagine being Hildegard—forcing those young girls to have sex with the soldiers and shooting children. I sipped my coffee, but I was in no mood for the Danish. "Yuli can't go home."

"That business with what's-his-name?"

"The Smuggler."

"Did Taft have a theory about the Smuggler's demise?"

"Taft only had a theory. He said there are a million Soviet Jews who want to leave, and the Smuggler was stirring the pot by arranging to bring in Yiddish and Russian translations of *Exodus*. He was also helping a missile designer who wanted to defect to Britain. The Kremlin didn't like it."

He ate two forkfuls of the cheesecake. "And where does that dead fellow in Hildegard's yard fit in?"

"Working for her. She had him shoot at me in Munich, and he killed a friend of mine."

"The producer at Four Freedoms Radio?"

"Dmitry Lukin. But Pyotr Ananko evened things up. He shot the guy with a gas gun when he ordered him off the property. Yuli and I saw Ananko do it. Yuli thinks he did the same to Taft, because the KGB wanted to stop Taft running agents in Russia and wanted to use Hildegard to spy on American Jewish organizations who assist Soviet Jews."

"That checks out. The night before Taft was killed, Ananko was seen at the Bohemian Caverns in D.C. Allegedly to do a story on John Coltrane. But tell me something: Yulianna is here on a—creative passport?"

"She also has a real one. And we want to get married."

Most of his cheesecake was gone when he said, "The crime-scene unit from the LAPD can't say for certain that it was Ananko who shot Hildegard. You sure it was him?"

"Absolutely."

"Strange—a KGB agent using a Makarov manufactured in East Germany."

"The Makarov—that's the pistol?"

"That's the pistol."

He had to know I was playing stupid, and I thought he'd be angry about it, but his expression was only mildly curious, as if he were a long-lost cousin listening to me catch him up on the family. "I can contact a fellow at the FBI who can discourage the LAPD from proceeding with its investigation."

Obviously, he wasn't buying all of my answers, which made me nervous. Until he asked his next question. Then I was scared shitless.

"A German tourist was beaten to death in Malibu. Turns out, he wasn't a tourist. He was an agent for the Stasi. Know anything about that?"

"What I read in the *L.A. Times*. And Taft did tell us the East Germans might be working with the KGB on Hildegard."

He studied me with his watery eyes. "I am of the opinion that you and Yulianna should retire from the Nazi-hunting business."

"We are retired. Can Yuli stay in the States?"

He glanced at his watch. "I'd like to chat with her when I get back."

"Will you be gone long?"

His tone amused and indignant, he said, "Michael, we're not playing Twenty Questions." He smiled—not much of one, but a smile nonetheless. "We'll get the paperwork to classify Yulianna as a refugee started. But she'll have to be careful for a while. The KGB and the Stasi lost agents. The press has some of it, and we'll leak more to embarrass the Soviets and East Germans—they hate getting caught with their hands in the cookie jar. They'll blame someone for what happened, and the KGB knows who Yulianna is. I suspect she's aware of this, but mention it to her, and I'll have the LAPD keep the uniform outside her door until she's discharged. Anything else comes up, let Julian know. He'll get in touch with me."

I thanked him, and he replied, "Taft and I fought together in the war. He was one of my closest friends for over twenty years, and I'm helping you and Yulianna for him—because Taft would've done it. But I'll only do it once. So don't forget and tell your future bride. No more hunting Nazis."

56

Two weeks after surgery, Yuli was walking the halls of St. Joe's with me, moving with her normal graceful stride, but stopping to catch her breath and wincing occasionally from pain in her left side. She had asked me to pack her clothing and makeup bag and to bring her suitcase to her, so she could feel like herself again, trading her hospital gown and slippers for her Breton-striped shirt, Levi's, and red sneakers. Watching her brush her hair in front of the mirror in the bathroom, I was excited about leaving Los Angeles and beginning our life together. Taft's friend must have shut down the investigation, because while the LAPD kept an officer outside the hospital room, no one ever came to interview Yuli. I told her about my conversation with the CIA man, and his warning that the KGB and Stasi might chase her, but she dismissed it with a roll of her eyes. "They fry big fish, Misha. I'm a minnow."

On the day before Yuli was discharged, we strolled the grounds of St. Joe's, listening to the sizzle of traffic in Burbank, Yuli placing her hand in mine, toying with my fingers. A fleeting shadow of sadness fell across her face, but I ascribed it to the letdown of completing a task. With Hildegard dead and her Nazi past exposed, I was no less angry about the circumstances of how I lost Emma nor any less grief-stricken about losing her. So my vengeance wasn't free—is it ever? And I hadn't heard from Darya.

At lunchtime, the orderly delivered a tray for Yuli, but she was sleeping. I was reading an article in the *Herald Examiner* about Dodger spring training and the tenuous condition of Sandy Koufax's left elbow when the cop came in, pointed outside, and mouthed, "Visitor."

Darya was there dressed for doctoring, a short white lab coat over a dress, and her hair was in a loose bun. I was surprised and pleased to see her: I'd worried that the whole business was so painful to her that she wouldn't be in touch, and I'd never get to know my aunt.

"How is Yulianna?" she asked.

"Tired, but she's leaving in the morning."

"Good, good. I have to get back to work. Do you have a minute to talk?"

"I do."

We walked past the nurses' station toward the elevators.

Darya said, "Your note in the mailbox. That dead man I saw in the yard. I didn't know what to think."

"I just wanted you to have the truth—in case Yuli and I didn't make it out of the house."

She stopped outside the bank of elevators and turned to me. "I couldn't speak to you then. I should have, but—"

"Please, don't worry about it."

"I've been reading the papers, those terrible things that my moth—that Hildegard did. I feel like I wandered into the middle of a freakish play, and I can't get off the stage."

I wanted to comfort her, to touch her arm or put my hand on her shoulder, but she was standing so straight and still, it was as though there was a fence around her, borders that couldn't be crossed.

Darya said, "I would like to see my father. Can you help arrange this?"

"He doesn't speak, but I can call his caretaker or give you the phone number in Nice. You should know: he's done paintings that an art dealer in South Carolina says are worth a lot. And he lives in a building Emma bought. It will belong to you."

"It's not his estate I'm interested in."

"Emma would want the paintings to survive after he's gone. And she would want to leave you something."

She pressed the down button. "I have a break in mid-April—the week of Easter and Passover. Would you and Yulianna be interested in coming with me? I'll buy the tickets."

"I'll ask her, but if she's busy, I'll go. And pay my own airfare."

Darya smiled the saddest smile I'd ever seen. "I insist. And you must listen to me. I'm your aunt."

The elevator opened, and Darya got in, and the doors closed.

Bob's Big Boy was five minutes from the hospital, and I brought in takeout for dinner. As we ate, I told Yuli about Darya's offer and asked her if she'd like to see Nice again.

She looked away toward the window. "I would, but maybe it would be better for you to go by yourself with Darya."

"Yuli, I feel guilty, too. But Hildegard didn't give you a choice."

"What difference does that make to Darya? The woman she thought was her mother is gone, and it isn't Darya's fault that Hildegard was a monster. She must have so many questions about Emma. And you should answer them."

Yuli was quiet for the rest of the evening, and after we watched *Gunsmoke* on TV, I bent over the bed to kiss her.

She brushed the hair off my forehead. "I wish I was going back to the hotel with you tonight—even for an hour."

I chuckled. "An hour. That's all?"

She threw her arms around me and held on, pressing her lips to mine.

Yuli was scheduled to be discharged at nine the next morning. The police would be done guarding her door at eight, so I arrived at the hospital an hour early, stopping by the business office to make the arrangements to pay the rest of her bill. Upstairs, the charge nurse had her paperwork in order and told me that Yuli was ready to go. I walked into her room. She wasn't there, and her suitcase was gone. I panicked, thinking that something had happened to her. That wasn't it, though. No one would have been able to grab her without a fight, and there was no sign of a struggle in her room.

Yuli was fine. And Yuli was gone.

Part X

57

Nice, France
April 19, 1965

The Air France flight to Nice left JFK at five thirty in the evening, and we had been flying for an hour before Darya asked me if I had heard from Yuli. I shook my head.

"I'm sorry," she said. "This must be very hard for you."

It bordered on unbearable, yet I believed that Yuli had to have a good reason for vanishing—perhaps a clue that another KGB or Stasi operative was looking for her. I told myself that she would reappear any day now, because losing her was unthinkable, and I refused to count it as an option.

A steward brought us the glasses of Muscadet we ordered.

"*Merci, monsieur*," Darya said.

As he went about his business, I said, "*Je parle français*." Darya hadn't mentioned Hildegard or asked a question about Emma or Gak ever since I'd met her flight from L.A. at Kennedy. All she had talked about was that she would be doing her psychiatric residency in Boston, and when she came back east she wanted to get together in New Jersey. Since the passengers around us were speaking English—any French speakers must have been in the first-class cabin—I thought that Darya would be more comfortable discussing personal matters in a language that made eavesdropping a challenge.

Maybe I was right or maybe it was the Muscadet, but she asked, "The West Germans would have put Hildegard on trial?"

317

"They have extended the statute of limitations for prosecuting war criminals. So in theory, yes. First, she would've been tried in New Jersey. For Emma."

Darya stared at the seat in front of her. I couldn't say whether Yuli's killing Joost and the letters that followed had helped to persuade the Bundestag. But it probably didn't hurt.

Finally Darya said, "I am having trouble understanding how Hildegard worked with survivors and explained her past to herself."

"She said the good she does makes up for the bad she did. How did she explain your lives to you?"

"My childhood was a black space with flashes of light. I was told my father died in the war. That seemed true, I had no memory of him. I do recall holding a little girl's hand—that must be my older sister, Alexandra, you told me about. And speaking to a tall woman in a strange language."

"That's Emma. And you were speaking Russian."

"Hildegard said the woman was my *Kindermädchen*. I remember that when we arrived in Nuremberg, I was speaking German. But I do not recall learning it."

"Hildegard had you in a class to learn German."

"I have no memory of that."

"A soldier shot your sister in that classroom. And the other children. Whether Joost ordered it or Hildegard did, I don't know. They each blamed the other. But Hildegard took you with her. Emma had a friend from Rostov-on-Don—Bashe. She was also there and told me about it. You can meet her. She lives in Atlanta."

Darya held up her wineglass as the steward passed, and he gave her a refill. Darya drank half of it in two swallows. "I remember the bombing in Nuremberg. Being in a basement with other people. And being hungry. That I remember—the hunger."

"You were with Hildegard's parents. And her cousin Ursula Becker. Becker's husband was executed for hiding Jews, and she died in the bombing."

Darya drank the rest of the Muscadet. "When the bomb hit the house, Hildegard and I were in another basement. Why, I am not sure—I was six years old—but I recall going there and Hildegard stuffing documents in a suitcase. Later, I remember the American soldiers and another camp and Hildegard met an old man with a long white beard. She told me he converted her to Judaism, that we were now Jews, her first name was Ursula and our last name was Becker. From there, we went to Switzerland, and I was enrolled in boarding school, Institut Le Rosey."

"Her father was a Nazi big shot. He had money hidden in Switzerland."

"That would explain why she came to Zürich twice a year. I realized how odd my story was. My friends had families. I didn't, and my God, did I yearn for one. When my girlfriends' mothers came to visit, they were inseparable and chatting away. I felt so alone, unrooted, as if gravity didn't apply to me, and if I floated away, no one would notice. Every summer I went to L.A. for a month. Hildegard was busy, and even if we had dinner together, she had no interest in discussing the past. She was distant, strangely so. I knew that as a child, but then for a few days a year she was—I don't know—more alive?"

"How so?"

"A few days before I returned to school, she flew to New York City with me. We'd check into the St. Regis, and she'd take me shopping at Bonwit Teller, and to Pearl's for Peking duck and to Lutèce—she liked to hear me order in French. And she always wanted to go downtown—to this little store on Seventh Avenue—the Surma Book & Music Company. The books were in Ukrainian; there were Christian icons and ceramic eggs. None of these interested her. But in back was a display of wooden Russian dolls. You stack one inside the other, and she loved those. She bought dozens of them over the years. They are on shelves in her bedroom. The dolls have a name, but I don't—"

"Matryoshka. Hildegard discovered them during the war. She told Bashe the dolls nested inside each other represented different aspects of the same woman."

"I never knew any aspect of her, not really. And I believed she didn't want me to. I felt terrible about it for years. But after college I chose UCLA for medical school so I could get to know her. I'd already decided to become a psychiatrist, and since I needed to explore my own childhood, I had to learn more about my mother. After Le Rosey, I had gone to the Sorbonne."

"You lived in Paris? Were you there in January? On the Quai Bourbon?"

"Briefly. I was ending an unfortunate long-distance relationship."

"I saw you. And I bet Emma did, too. That's why she kept her apartment on the Place des Vosges. Every summer she came to see your father and to look around Europe for you. And she always started in Paris."

"I have a hazy memory of speaking French to a smiling man with a little beard."

"That's Gak. You had to be a baby when your parents relocated to Nice. I don't know where you lived then, but in early June 1941, Emma brought you and your sister with her when she went to visit Rostov-on-Don, and it was impossible for her to return to France when the Germans invaded."

Darya glanced at the overhead console, the reading light illuminating the gold of her hair and her face, Emma's face. I looked at her, and she peered back at me with a curious squint, as though puzzled by my presence.

I laughed.

"What is funny?"

"Emma used to look at me like that when I got caught cutting class or left the store without mopping behind the soda fountain." I removed my grandmother's Rolex from the pocket of my blazer. "Here. Try it on. I had some links taken out so it'll fit you."

"Michael, no. This is yours. And it is very expensive."

"It belonged to Emma. That red arrow pointing to numbers on the bezel is for keeping track of another time zone. Emma set it for Europe. She thought you were there, and I think she wanted to know the time where you were living. She checked this watch constantly."

"I can't—"

I held my left arm toward her, pulling back the sleeve of my blazer. "Emma bought me a different Rolex. An Explorer. Like Sir Edmund Hillary. So I'd learn to climb high."

Darya had a watch on her left wrist, so she fastened the oyster bracelet of the GMT on her right, then stared at the crystal. "*Merci, merci beaucoup.*"

Feeling as though I had closed some meaningful circle and made my grandmother, wherever she was, happy beyond measure, I replied, "*Pas de problème.*"

In the taxi from the airport, I was blindsided by a feeling of loss, remembering my trip to Nice with Yuli. It got worse when Darya and I stored our bags with the concierge at the Hôtel Ruhl, and the memories of that first afternoon Yuli and I had made love floated behind my eyes, as sharp and clear as the Mediterranean light.

"Coffee first?" Darya asked as we walked up the Promenade des Anglais.

"Sure. I have to call Sister Bernadette. Would you order me an espresso?"

She sat on a terrace of a café in the Cours Saleya while I went in to use the phone. When I came out, Darya was drinking a cappuccino and watching the shoppers in the open-air market.

I knocked back the espresso. "They'll be at the cemetery in fifteen minutes. Usually your father goes alone—he and Emma had a gravestone put in for you and Alexandra. But Sister Bernadette will be there. She was very fond of Emma and is anxious to meet you."

Darya set her cup in its saucer. "I am grateful to you."

"Hey, I want a family, too."

She smiled, and I paid the bill. As we climbed the narrow stone stairways up toward Castle Hill, Darya, who was in a sleeveless yellow jersey dress, paused to slip into the white cardigan she had tied around her waist. "Michael, you never say my name."

"I wasn't sure which one to use."

"My friends and some of the nurses and doctors I work with read about Hildegard in the papers, and they seemed embarrassed for me. Didn't mention it and could hardly look at me. And some writer already phoned the school. He's doing a book on Joost and Hildegard. If I spend my career as Dr. Freya Becker, I can imagine my colleagues and patients saying, 'I've heard that name. How do I know you?' So before starting my residency, I'm going to sell Hildegard's house, donate the proceeds to a survivors' group, and legally change my name. When I get to Boston, I'll be Darya Gak."

"Aunt Darya. I like it."

She laughed, but there was more weary resignation in her laughter than joy.

Sister Bernadette was standing outside the gate, and before I could make the introductions, she said, "*Bonjour*, Misha. And you, you are Darya."

The nun stared at my aunt, her chubby cheeks quivering, and I reckoned that it was only a lifetime of devotion and self-denial that prevented her from falling apart.

"You are the image of your mother. Go now, go see your father. But say nothing about Emma. He never asks about her, and there is no need to burden him with the truth."

I hadn't planned to join Darya, but she hesitated, looking at me, and I led her toward the bench where Gak was sitting with his hands on the knobs of his walking sticks. Darya stopped, gazing at the old man with white hair flowing out from under a black beret, white Vandyke, and black suit.

She knelt before him. "Papa, *c'est moi, ta fille*, Darya."

Gak had been focused on the pearly slab of granite that marked the graves of his daughters, and he shifted his gaze to the kneeling woman.

"Papa?"

Gak let go of his walking sticks. They clattered on the ground.

She held one of his hands. "*C'est moi*, Darya."

Something flickered in his eyes, like the sudden flare of a match that dies just as suddenly in the wind.

"*Alexandra est morte, mais Darya est vivante. Je suis* Darya."

"Darya?" His voice was as raspy as a plane shaving wood.

"*Oui*, Papa. *Je suis* Darya."

Sunlight was falling across Gak, and I saw tears, like rivulets of quicksilver, dribbling into the lines of his face.

With her thumbs, she brushed them away.

Gak pressed her hands to his face. "*Ma fille?*"

"*Ta fille.*"

Gingerly she put her arms around him. In the bright, relentless light, they might have been a faded snapshot. Gradually the photograph came alive. It was a movie, not a picture trapped in time. Gak slipped his arms around his daughter, and Darya let out a sob and another and finally a string of them, rapid, high-pitched, and then Gak was sobbing too, a deep, gasping sound, as though his lungs were unaccustomed to the air.

I left them to their private grief, walking past the memorial building with the urns of ashes and soap, and out the gate, past Sister Bernadette, and across the road. Down below, I saw palm fronds waving in the wind and the metallic gleam of cars and buses on the Promenade des Anglais and the emerald-sapphire sparkle of the Baie des Anges with the long curve of the beach, the pebbles dazzling white in the sun, and the apartment buildings and houses with orange tiled roofs, and above the sea beyond Nice, the hills as dark as shadows against the pale blue sky.

I stood there, waiting for Darya, and wondered if I would ever see Yuli again.

58

South Orange, New Jersey
April 24, 1965

At night, Yuli thought the gas lamp on the corner of Montague Place shone like moonlight in a jar. She was seated behind the wheel of her Rambler, farther down the street, watching Michael's house. Except for a light in the living room, the windows had been dark for five nights, and Yuli surmised that Michael had gone to Nice with Darya.

With her hair under a kerchief, she got out of the car and walked to the house, going in the walled backyard and letting herself into the den with the spare key Misha hid under the milk box. Flicking on a flashlight, Yuli went to the kitchen and unscrewed the receiver of the wall phone to make sure a mike and transmitter hadn't been planted, and she performed the same check on the phone in the bedroom. Yuli was tempted to leave Michael a smiley on a pillow, drawing the mouth with a Magic Marker and using her bra for the eyes. That she contemplated doing this, as she searched for bugs behind picture frames and in table lamps, was a symptom of her loneliness and how rotten she felt fleeing the hospital. Misha was bound to feel abandoned, and Yuli hoped he trusted her enough to realize that she had taken off to protect both of them.

The newspaper accounts had noted that Pyotr Ananko and Hildegard Ter Horst had shot each other and described Yulianna Timko and Michael Daniels as innocent bystanders, but that didn't mean they were safe. A KGB analyst at the Lubyanka headquarters in Moscow, who was acquainted with her past, might recognize the name Yulianna, then dig into the files for any reference to Michael and find that he had been in Otvali on a student visa, and put the story together. If the KGB or Stasi came looking for her, Misha would be watched, and if he exhibited the slightest sign that he knew her whereabouts, he would be snatched, interrogated, and killed.

Even before Michael told her the man from the CIA had said she could be in danger, Yuli planned to disappear. In the false compartment of her suitcase, she had the three thousand dollars from the East German, another four thousand she had brought from Otvali, and a forged driver's license for Natalia Adamik, who was born in Poland and emigrated to Chicago after her entire family had died in the war. On a cafeteria bulletin board, she had seen a flyer for efficiencies to rent a mile from the hospital, and in the gift shop she had bought a magazine about used cars and a newspaper. After slipping out the rear of St. Joseph's, she got into a taxi and had the cab wait while she went in to meet the landlord, an elderly gentleman with a hearing aid. He showed her the place, apologizing that it got no sunlight. Natalia Adamik replied that she didn't mind and gave him three hundred dollars for three months' rent and her most fetching smile when she asked him to hold her mail until she made her final move to L.A.

At a car lot on Hollywood Boulevard she paid eight hundred dollars for a black two-door 1959 Rambler American and fifty-six dollars for a year's insurance. Down the boulevard she bought an atlas at Pickwick Books and plotted a random course to see if she was being followed. First stop, Arizona, where in a roadside shop she purchased a flashlight, extra bulbs and batteries, a decade-old .38 snub-nosed revolver, and a box of ammunition. Then it was up to Utah, into Colorado, across Kansas and Missouri, south to Tennessee and north to Kentucky, West Virginia, and Maryland, north again to Ohio and Pennsylvania, across New York State, down through New England, over the Tappan Zee Bridge to Manhattan, and, after eighteen days of traveling, through the Lincoln Tunnel to the Garden State Parkway.

Since then, Yuli had gone past Michael's every day at irregular intervals from nine A.M. to nine P.M. The azaleas surrounding the house were in bloom, a pink fire that reminded her of the bikini she bought in Santa Monica and the look of wonder on Misha's face when she stood before him naked, the bathing suit in her hand. Yuli changed her motel every day, bouncing around the state, and she had not seen anyone tailing her.

At last, on this evening, she figured it would be wise to sweep for bugs. She worked quickly, pausing only to look at the drawing Picasso had done of her and Michael in Saint-Tropez. It was framed and hanging in the den, and Yuli felt wistful seeing it, and the wistfulness stayed with her even after she determined the house was clean and went back to the Rambler and tuned in Cousin Brucie on 77 WABC. Listening to the music, she decided to wait another month before returning to Michael, maybe two. Three months tops. If the KGB wasn't hunting her now, by July she could scale back her worrying. Papka was gone and Yuli was never going home, so she was scarcely worth the attention KGB agents in Western Europe and the United States would attract from the CIA and FBI and the drubbing the Kremlin would receive from leaders and the press in democratic capitals if Yuli were assassinated in America. As for the East Germans: even if a connection was made between her and the dead agent, the government of East Germany didn't fart without an okay from Moscow, and if the KGB chose to leave her alone, the Stasi would be forbidden from pursuing her.

Of course, eventually, Yuli could take another name. No big deal. *What's in a name?* Juliet asked Romeo. Natalia didn't feel right, but Juliet, that was a pretty one. Perhaps Yuli would become Juliet, and everyone would call her Julie. Yuli to Julie. Close enough.

And honestly, who remembers names? The names of the innocent who died at Stalin's depraved hands? Or the millions of souls who vanished, like clouds swept away by the wind, in the Great Patriotic War and the Holocaust? Men, women, and children who were laughing, weeping, running, crawling, yelling, whispering, praying, hiding, marching, fighting, until they were silenced and transformed into bone and ash. Hardly anybody remembered their names. Even memorializing the names in granite didn't help. Who bothered to read them? Unless the name belonged to someone you loved. And it wasn't the name you remembered, was it? No. It was the love. The name was a code, a cipher for the love you carried with you until you yourself were gone and your remembering was done.

On the radio, the Drifters were singing "Under the Boardwalk" and Yuli was imagining dancing with Misha when his Plymouth Fury came down Radel Terrace and turned into the driveway. In the dark, Yuli couldn't see him, but the garage opened, and with the interior light she caught a glimpse of Michael carrying a suitcase. The garage closed. Aching to be held by him, Yuli folded her arms across her chest and rubbed her shoulders, a poor substitute.

A minute later, the floodlight over the front doorway lit up, the door swung in, and Misha stepped onto the stoop. He was wearing his navy-blue Brooks Brothers blazer. Yuli liked him in that jacket; it widened his broad shoulders and narrowed his waist. He was looking straight up at the sky, with its silvery spray of stars, until miraculously he gazed in her direction. He seemed to stare at her through the windshield. She was almost convinced that he could see her in the starlit night, and any moment he was going to walk toward her.

Michael disappeared into the house, the door shut, the floodlight died, and it required every ounce of her discipline not to run to his yard and yell for him to come back.

Three months, Yuli told herself, throwing the car into gear. That was it—if everything went well. Then she would return to Michael. To Misha.

Three months.

And then her life would begin.

Acknowledgments

Nothing Is Forgotten is the most difficult book I've ever written. I began hearing about vanished members of my family as a child, and the stories told by my grandparents and great-grandparents have been with me ever since. I thought about these relatives as I wrote, but their presence was rarely comforting. Ghosts, it seems, have a well-deserved reputation for haunting us, and the memory of the Six Million, and the millions more who died in history's worst convulsion, will be with me, I discovered, for as long as I live.

Still, I'm grateful to have had the chance to tell this story. A number of people who assisted me were thanked in the Sources section, but there are many more whose help was invaluable.

My agent, Susan Golomb, was her usual wise and steady self, along with her assistant, Mariah Stovall; and the rights director and rights manager at Writers House, Maja Nikolic and Kathryn Stuart.

At Atria Books I was fortunate to benefit from the sound literary judgment of editor in chief Peter Borland, and editor Daniella Wexler, both of whom made this a far better novel.

Also at Atria Books, I'd like to thank publisher Judith Curr; associate publisher Suzanne Donahue; art director Albert Tang; cover designer Laura Levatino; assistant director of publicity Ariele Fredman; publicity manager Milena Brown; managing editor Kimberly Goldstein and assistants Paige Lytle and Luqman Hamaki; production editor Isolde Sauer; copyeditor Nancy Inglis, proofreader Andrew Goldwasser, and editorial assistant Sean Delone.

Comments by early readers of the manuscript were invaluable, beginning with the incisive suggestions of Marlene Adelstein and ending with the frequent phone calls from one of my oldest friends, Howard Dickson. Others have also been of immeasurable assistance: my sister and brother-in-law, Frann and Eric Francis; Susan Novotny, owner of the Book House of Stuyvesant Plaza and Market Block Books; Kathie Bennett and Susan Zurenda of Magic Time Literary Agency; my friends: Tracy Richard, Carol and Joe Siracusa, Ellen and Jeff Lewis, and David Saltzman; Paul Grondahl, director of the New York State Writers Institute; and the extraordinarily versatile author James Howard Kunstler, who guided me through the history of architecture and modern art.

I'd also like to send a heartfelt thanks to all of the owners and salespeople I met as I visited bookstores, and to Kathy L. Murphy and her Pulpwood Queens for their enduring love of books.

Once again, I found Facebook to be a rich source of photographs and scraps of history. For instance, one friend, Bob Masin, sent me a video clip of the Columbia High School Thanksgiving football game from November 28, 1963, which helped illuminate the darker corners of my memory. Another friend, Bob Moore, posted his candy-store memories from South Orange in the early 1960s, and I matched them against my own while I created the fictional Sweets.

These groups have been particularly helpful: Memories of Living in South Orange, NJ, or Maplewood, NJ; Columbia High School Alumni; Gruning's Ice Cream; I Miss Don's; Vintage New Jersey; Old Images of New York; Paris Photo; America in the '60's; Baby Boomers 1946–1964; Baby Boomer Lives; Baby Boomer Memories from New Jersey; Holocaust Studies; Holocaust Book Reviews Discussions; Echoes of the Holocaust; Holocaust Educators of America; The Holocaust Memorial Foundation; Free Voices of Children of Holocaust Survivors; US Holocaust Memorial Museum; and Study of the Holocaust.

As a wristwatch plays a role in this novel, I had some research to do, and I learned quite a bit from Tristano Geoffry–Michele Veneto, founder of the Urban Gentry YouTube channel, and the members of his Facebook group; and Jake Ehrlich and his website, Jake's Rolex World.

Finally, a tip of the hat to all of my Facebook friends who followed my posts during my research trips. Your comments and questions not only helped me clarify my thinking across a range of subjects, but were a relief from the lonely pursuit of writing this novel.

Sources

This work is a fictional treatment of the Holocaust and the Cold War. To re-create this history with the accuracy it deserves, dozens of sources were helpful, but the following most of all.

Russia

1 Brainerd, Elizabeth. "Marriage and Divorce in Revolutionary Russia: A Demographic Analysis." In *Russia's Home Front in War and Revolution 1914–22, Book 3: National Disintegration and Reintegration.* Christopher Read, Peter Waldron, and Adele Lindenmeyr, eds. Bloomington, IN: Slavica Publishers, 2017, 1–29.

2 Collins, Naomi F. *Through Dark Days and White Nights: Four Decades Observing a Changing Russia.* Washington, D.C.: SCARITH/New Academia Publishing, 2007. The itinerary of the train trip from Munich to Rostov-on-Don was informed by Dr. Collins's 1966 trip into the Soviet Union and can be found on pages 9–10.

3 Damm, Katherine. "Soviet Denim Smuggling: The History of Jeans Behind the Iron Curtain," September 14, 2014. www.heddels.com /2014/09/soviet-denim-smuggling-history-jeans-behind-iron-curtain. Retrieved November 17, 2015.

4 Eaton, Katherine B. *Daily Life in the Soviet Union.* Westport, CT: Greenwood Publishing Group, 2004.

5 Fainberg, Dina. *Notes from the Rotten West, Reports from the Backward East: Soviet and American Foreign Correspondents in the Cold War, 1945–1985* (unpublished, Rutgers University, 2012). This is a marvelous doctoral dissertation. Professor Fainberg also took the time to Skype with me from London and to discuss the experiences of Soviet journalists in the United States during the 1960s.

6 Hixson, Walter L. *Parting the Curtain: Propaganda, Culture, and the Cold War.* New York: Palgrave Macmillan, 1998.

7 Loscher, John D. *The Bolsheviks, Volume II: How the Soviets Seize Power.* Bloomington, IN: AuthorHouse, 2009. The characterization of *Govnyuk* as Lenin's favorite profane word is on page 455.

8 McDowell, Edwin. "*Exodus* in Samizdat: Still Popular and Still Subversive." *New York Times*, April 26, 1987.

9 Parker, Stephen Jan. "Hemingway's Revival in the Soviet Union: 1955–1962." *American Literature* 35, no. 4 (January 1964): 485–501.

10 Plokhy, Serhii. *The Man with the Poison Gun: A Cold War Spy Story.* New York: Basic Books, 2016. The gas gun used by my character Pyotr Ananko is a documented method of assassination used by the KGB; see pages 43–44, 48, 50–51, 63, 65.

11 Raleigh, Donald J. *Soviet Baby Boomers: An Oral History of Russia's Cold War Generation.* New York: Oxford University Press, reprint ed., 2013.

12 Von Bremzen, Anya. *Mastering the Art of Soviet Cooking: A Memoir of Food and Longing.* New York: Broadway Books, reprint ed., 2014. Stalin's reference to Sovetskoye Shampanskoye as "an important sign . . . of the good life" is on page 69.

13 Woodhead, Leslie. *How the Beatles Rocked the Kremlin: The Untold Story of a Noisy Revolution.* New York: Bloomsbury USA, 2013. Nikita Khrushchev declaring the Twist and other modern dances from the West as "unseemly, mad," and Soviet officials blaming rock and roll for "delinquency, alcoholism, vandalism, and rape" are quoted on page 63.

14 Zhuk, Sergei I. *Rock and Roll in the Rocket City: The West, Identity and Ideology in Soviet Dniepropetrovsk, 1960–1985.* Baltimore: Johns Hopkins University Press, reprint ed., 2017. Professor Zhuk generously spent an evening on the phone with me explaining some of the fine points of the underground rock culture in that city.

Cold War Radio

Four Freedoms Radio is the child of my imagination, but anyone familiar with the remarkable accomplishments of Radio Liberty, Radio Free Europe, and Voice of America will recognize the reality that inspired my creation. The following helped me to understand these stations:

1 Critchlow, James. *Radio Liberty: An Insider's Story of Cold War.* Charleston, SC: BookSurge Publishing, 2006. Mr. Critchlow, a former executive at Radio Liberty, was kind enough to answer my questions in an interview and via email; the experiences of the station's employees, the characterization of Munich by the Soviet government as the "Center of Subversion," and much of the response of local German politicos to the Dachau memorial are drawn from that interview and correspondence; the murder of émigrés by the Soviets is discussed on pages 55–57 of his memoir.

2 Cummings, Richard H. *Cold War Radio: The Dangerous History of American Broadcasting in Europe, 1950–1989.* Jefferson, NC: McFarland & Company, 2009.

3 Puddington, Arch. *Broadcasting Freedom: The Cold War Triumph of Radio Free Europe and Radio Liberty.* Lexington, KY: University Press of Kentucky, 2003. The reference to rock and roll by exiles from the Eastern Bloc as "'nigger' and Jewish music" is quoted on page 137.

4 Sosin, Gene. *Sparks of Liberty: An Insider's Memoir of Radio Liberty.* University Park, PA: Penn State University Press, 1999. The receivers recording shortwave broadcasts from across the Soviet Union is cited on page 9, along with the number of studios operating at Radio Liberty. On page 23 of *Sparks of Liberty*, Sosin describes the use of short on-air sentences so listeners could catch them through the jamming, a description I put in the mouth of my character Taft Mifflin.

German Attitudes Toward the Holocaust

1 Associated Press. "Convent Dedicated on Site of Death Camp at Dachau." *New York Times*, November 23, 1964. In my novel, the dedication of the Roman Catholic "Cloister of Atonement" occurs in October 1964; it was actually in November of that year, per this *Times* article. Details of the dedication are also drawn from the article.

2 Bach, Steven. *Leni: The Life and Work of Leni Riefenstahl*. New York: Vintage, reprint ed., 2008.

3 Breuer, William B. *Operation Dragoon: The Allied Invasion of the South of France*. Novato, CA: Presidio Press, 1987.

4 Cesarani, David. *After Eichmann: Collective Memory and the Holocaust since 1961*. New York: Routledge, 2014. For the Bundestag vote in 1965 on extending the statute of limitations for prosecuting war criminals, see page 44.

5 CIA Historical Review Program. "Soviet Use of Assassination and Kidnapping," released on September 22, 1993. cia.gov/library/center-for-the-study-of-intelligence/kent-csi/vol19no3/html/v19i3a01p_0001.htm. Retrieved 12/01/2015.

6 Diab, Khaled. "Taking Hitler off the Menu." *The Guardian*, October 29, 2008. Hitler's preference for trout in butter sauce can be found in this article.

7 Dulles, Allen W. *The Secret Surrender: The Classic Insider's Account of the Secret Plot to Surrender Northern Italy During WWII*. Guilford, CT: Lyons Press, 2006.

8 Gassert, Philippe, and Alan E. Steinweis, eds. *Coping with the Nazi Past: West German Debates on Nazism and Generational Conflict, 1955–1975*. New York: Berghahn Books, 2006. The vote on extending the statute of limitations and staff additions to prosecute war criminals are on page 58, in a chapter written by Marc von Miquel: "Explanation, Dissociation, Apologia: The Debate over the Criminal Prosecution of Nazis Crimes in the 1960s."

9 Grose, Peter. *Gentleman Spy: The Life of Allen Dulles*. Amherst, MA: University of Massachusetts Press, 1996.

10   Harvey, Elizabeth. *Women and the Nazi East: Agents and Witnesses of Germanization.* New Haven, CT: Yale University Press, 2003.

11   Lichtblau, Eric. *The Nazis Next Door: How America Became a Safe Haven for Hitler's Men.* New York: Mariner Books, reprint ed., 2015.

12   Lower, Wendy. *Hitler's Furies: German Women in the Nazi Killing Fields.* New York: Mariner Books, reprint ed., 2014. Tragically, women did murder children under the Nazis. Furthermore, women also had a role in the overall genocide and plunder and use of slave labor in the Ukraine. However, while my fictional portrait of Hildegard Ter Horst has been informed by Lower's work, Hildegard and her behavior, motives, and self-justification come from my imagination.

13   Marcuse, Harold. *Legacies of Dachau: The Uses and Abuses of a Concentration Camp, 1933–2001.* New York: Cambridge University Press, reissue ed., 2008.

14   Novick, Peter. *The Holocaust in American Life.* New York: Mariner Books, 2000.

15   Ohler, Norman. Translated by Shaun Whiteside. *Blitzed: Drugs in Nazi Germany.* New York: Mariner Books, reprint ed., 2018.

16   Pendas, Devin O. *The Frankfurt Auschwitz Trial, 1963–1965: Genocide, History, and the Limits of the Law.* New York: Cambridge University Press, 2010. In an interview, Professor Pendas reviewed the trial with me and discussed the debate in Germany on whether to extend the statute of limitations for Nazi crimes.

17   Pendas, Devin O. "'I didn't know what Auschwitz was': The Frankfurt Auschwitz Trial and the German Press, 1963–1965." *Yale Journal of Law & the Humanities* 12 (2000), issue 2, article 4, http://digitalcommons .law.yale.edu/yjlh/vol12/iss2/4. The survey that found 57 percent of Germans opposed any more Nazi trials was taken from this article by Professor Pendas.

18   P.J.C.F. "Concentration Camp Buildings There Can Be Viewed by Persistent Tourist." *New York Times*, August 6, 1961. In my novel, during the fall of 1964, Misha visits Dachau and walks through the museum; some of those details were culled from my own visit to the camp; others can be found in this article.

19 Riefenstahl, Leni. *Leni Riefenstahl: A Memoir*. New York: Picador, reprint ed., 1995.

20 Shane, Scott. "Documents Shed Light on C.I.A.'s Use of Ex-Nazis." *New York Times*, June 6, 2006.

21 Taylor, Frederick. *Exorcising Hitler: The Occupation and Denazification of Germany*. New York: Bloomsbury Press, reprint ed., 2013. When my fictional Taft Mifflin estimates the number of Nazi Party members in Germany after the war, his calculation is based on Taylor's estimate, which can be found on pages 254 and 255 of *Exorcising Hitler*.

22 von Halasz, Joachim. *Hitler's Munich: A Walking Guide*. London: Foxley Books Limited, 2007.

Death Marches and Forced Labor Camps

My account of Bashe and Emma as forced laborers, partisans, inmates of Nazi camps, and their participation in the Death Marches is fiction. However, it is fiction deeply rooted in real events and the places these events occurred, and these sources were especially helpful:

1 Arad, Yitzhak. *The Holocaust in the Soviet Union*. Lincoln, NE: University of Nebraska Press, 2009.

2 Berkhoff, Karel C. *Harvest of Despair: Life and Death in Ukraine Under Nazi Rule*. Cambridge, MA: Belknap Press, 2008.

3 Blatman, Daniel; translated by Chaya Galan. *The Death Marches: The Final Phase of Nazi Genocide*. Cambridge, MA: Belknap Press, 2010.

4 Clark, Alan. *Barbarossa: The Russian-German Conflict, 1941–1945*. New York: William Morrow, reissue ed., 1985.

5 Cooper, Matthew. *The Nazi War Against Soviet Partisans, 1941–1944: The History of the Greatest Guerrilla Struggle Ever Waged*. New York: Stein & Day, 1979.

6 Grau, Lester, and Michael Gress, eds. *The Partisan's Companion: The Red Army's Do-It-Yourself, Nazi-Bashing Guerrilla Warfare Manual*. Havertown, PA: Casemate Publishers, 2011.

7 Litvin, Nikolai; translated by Stuart Britton. *800 Days on the Eastern*

Front: A Russian Soldier Remembers World War II. Lawrence, KS: University Press of Kansas, annotated ed., 2007.

8 Roberts, Geoffrey. *Stalin's Wars: From World War to Cold War, 1939–1953.* New Haven, CT: Yale University Press, 2008.

9 United States Holocaust Memorial Museum. "Death Marches." ushmm.org/outreach/en/article.php?ModuleId=10007734. Retrieved March 28, 2017. I am especially grateful to Megan Lewis, a reference librarian at the United States Holocaust Memorial Museum, for pointing me in the right direction.

10 Veidlinger, Jeffrey. *In the Shadow of the Shtetl: Small-Town Jewish Life in Soviet Ukraine.* Bloomington, IN: Indiana University Press, reprint ed., 2016.

11 Wachsmann, Nikolaus. *KL: A History of the Nazi Concentration Camps.* New York: Farrar, Straus, reprint ed., 2016.

Death Camps

The Polish camp where Emma and Bashe are interred, Jagoda, did not exist, though it is based on two subcamps of Auschwitz-Birkenau that did—Harmense and Babitz. I used the following sources to create my fictional subcamp:

1 "Babitz" by Auschwitz-Birkenau State Museum, www.auschwitz.org /en/history/auschwitz-sub-camps/babitz. Retrieved March 30, 2017.

2 "Harmense" by Auschwitz-Birkenau State Museum, www.auschwitz.org /en/history/auschwitz-sub-camps/harmense. Retrieved March 30, 2017.

3 *Hitler's Henchmen: The Executioner, Heinrich Himmler*, part of a series produced by the Contemporary History team at ZDF; youtube .com/watch?v=yqQZBwxmTlM. Retrieved April 12, 2017. As grotesque as it sounds, a copy of *Mein Kampf* made of human skin appears to have existed, according to Martin Bormann Jr., a child during the war whose father was Hitler's personal secretary and among the most powerful men in the Third Reich. Bormann Jr. speaks of such a book in this video.

4 "The Unloading Ramps and Selections" by Auschwitz-Birkenau State Museum, www.auschwitz.org/en/history/auschwitz-and-shoah /the-unloading-ramps-and-selections. Retrieved March 30, 2017.

5 Williams, Amanda. "Museum Displays Skull of Pro-Nazi Officer Who Was Executed with His Own Gun After WW2 Atrocities as Part of Macabre Exhibition of Holocaust Relics Including Gold Teeth of Auschwitz Victims," *Daily Mail*, July 14, 2014. The extracting of gold teeth by the Nazis has been documented. A Google search on the subject on April 5, 2017, returned 136,000 results, but if one is interested in exhibits, see "Museum Displays."

Pablo Picasso

Indeed, as presented in this novel, Pablo Picasso could be magnanimous toward his admirers. For instance, Picasso's sketching my fictional Misha in a café was based on a report from the Associated Press, "Picasso 'Sits' for Artist, Then Does His Portrait," *New York Times*, July 24, 1962. The reference to Picasso's painting a car comes from Graham Keeley, "The Citroën That Picasso Painted," *The Telegraph*, August 27, 2005. Other sources that were helpful included:

1 Mailer, Norman. *Portrait of Picasso as a Young Man: An Interpretive Biography.* New York: Atlantic Monthly Press, 1995.

2 Roe, Sue. *In Montmartre: Picasso, Matisse and the Birth of Modernist Art.* New York: Penguin Books, 2016.

3 SalvadorDalí (1904–1989).www.artexpertswebsite.com/pages/artists /super_dali_mysteries.php. Retrieved March 24, 2017.

Cold War Washington

The information on Martin's Tavern is contained in a booklet available at the restaurant, though it's unclear whether the plaques were up in 1965 when my character Taft Mifflin stops by, but they certainly are there now.

If you do visit Martin's, you would be wise to sample the bread pudding with hot bourbon-caramel sauce.

1 Herken, Gregg. *The Georgetown Set: Friends and Rivals in Cold War Washington*. New York: Alfred A. Knopf, 2014.
2 Reeves, Richard. *President Kennedy: Profile of Power*. New York: Simon & Schuster, 1994.

Interviews

I owe a debt of gratitude to Peter J. Tauriello for his help with some of the fine points of deejaying; Professor Jonathan Steinberg for pointing me in the right direction regarding Nazi governance in the Soviet Union; and Professor Jeffrey Veidlinger, who explained that there were numerous sites in Russia and the Ukraine where "tens of thousands of people were killed [by the Germans] that still await full histories and investigations." In other words, as my character Taft Mifflin observes, Moscow and Kiev "won't be done counting their dead till the next century."

My interviews with Professor Hana Wexler, the daughter of survivors, and her husband, Rabbi Robert Wexler, president of the American Jewish University, were invaluable to my portrait of the survivor community and Jewish life in Los Angeles during the 1950s and 1960s.

Miriam Gershwin patiently answered my questions about surviving the Stutthof concentration camp, her years in Germany after the war, and her journey to the United States. She was also a stand-in storyteller for her late husband Nahum Gershwin, a survivor of Dachau. A number of years ago, I interviewed Rabbi David Hill and Morey Schapira, both of whom were exceedingly helpful regarding how American goods made their way into the Soviet Union.

Mary Ann Clayton, a former co-owner of the coffeehouse the Golden Horn in Atlanta, Georgia, spoke with me at length about that city's beatnik culture, and her son, Galen Chandler, emailed me photos of the coffeehouse and MP3s of music performed there. I was also fortunate to speak with the cook from those days, Martha Porter Hall, and her husband, Van Hall, who sang and played his guitar at the Golden Horn.